TROUBLED SEASON

A LOGAN FAMILY WESTERN - BOOK 5

DONALD L. ROBERTSON

CM Publishing

COPYRIGHT

Troubled Season

Copyright © 2022 Donald L. Robertson
CM Publishing

Books@DonaldLRobertson.com

❀ Created with Vellum

PROLOGUE

Liam MacGregor sat in the kitchen of the Double R ranch, going over the books. After last year's cattle drive, he and his partners, Hank Remington and Darcy Smith, had turned the Double R into a real ranch with money in the bank. The sound of horses riding into the ranch yard pulled him from his reverie.

He slid his chair back from the table, closing the books. Stepping from the warmth of the kitchen, he felt a chill run down his back. *Probably from the chill of this fine February morning,* he thought.

Riders sat their horses in front of the ranch house. He looked them over, most of them gun-wise and looking shady, except for the haughty man in the English riding outfit, sitting erect in the saddle.

"You'd be Liam MacGregor," the man said, more statement than question.

"Aye, what do you want?"

"I, my good sir," the man said, his shoulders rose more erect, and his chin lifted, "am Sir Wilford Pemberton Davies the Third. *You* are on my property. I am ordering you to leave immediately. If you do not see fit to vacate voluntarily, Mr. Langston and his men will use whatever force is necessary to persuade you." While he had been speaking, he reached to an inside pocket of his coat and pulled from it an envelope. From the envelope, he extracted two documents. Waving them, he continued, "This one is my proof of ownership as rightful owner of the Double R, and the second is the eviction notice to end your squatting on my land."

Liam was appalled at even the possibility this might not be their land, but Scotsman that he was, he was never at a loss for words. Stepping forward, he rested his hands on the heavy porch railing. "'Tis a sad day when a fine Scotsman like myself travels all these many miles from my homeplace to a new country. A country, it is, that allows me freedom from the bloodthirsty English. And what do I see riding big as life onto me own lovely ranch? A rotten Englishman."

Davies, face reddening, said, "You dirty Scotsman. Don't you dare speak to me in such a manner."

Mac's knuckles stood out large and white as he squeezed the railing. "I'll speak to you in whatever manner suits me. You're not in your British Isles, you see. Take your rowdy bunch of gunnies and ride yourself off this ranch, or it'll be you who'll be getting the persuading."

Davies glanced at the gunman to his right and said, "Langston."

Langston turned his horse just enough to clear his right side from the horseman next to him. His right arm moved, bringing his palm to rest on his side, just over the butt of the revolver on his hip. In a voice as cool as the February morning, he said, "Mister, I think it's time you stopped talking and started riding."

Mac knew he was in trouble. He was deadly with a rifle and could kill a snake with his revolver, but he was no fast gun. Langston would have at least three heavy chunks of lead in his body before he could ever get his gun from the holster. But he was no coward. He released the railing and stepped back far enough to allow himself room to draw. "'Tis your choosin', Langston."

Mac saw a smile drift across the gunfighter's face, and the man's hand moved from resting on his side to hover over the gun butt. *It is a good life I've had,* Mac thought, and smiled back at the gunfighter.

The silence in the ranch yard was punctuated by the metallic clicks of hammers being brought to full cock. "I'd be sitting calm and relaxed, was I you boys." The relaxed Texas drawl of Darcy Smith carried across the yard and yanked every head of the riders toward the barn.

Mac, never missing a beat, said, "Ah, 'tis my mistake. I failed to introduce you to another owner of the Double R, Darcy Smith." He raised his voice. "Darcy, me lad, would you believe this is none other than *Sir* Wilford Pemberton Davies the Third, here to invite us to *vacate* our ranch."

"Reckon I'll stay," Darcy said, "and so will the boys."

Several of the hands spoke up. "Yep." "Reckon." "Wouldn't think of leaving."

Mac watched Langston relax. His hand resting along his leg. He nodded to Mac, the smile still on his lips, and said, "Another day, then."

Davies' face was stiff with anger. "I'll see you thrown off of this ranch. You will find I am no one to trifle with." Stiffly he turned his horse, and the others followed. Langston tipped his hat to Darcy as they rode from the yard.

Darcy walked to the house with the cowhands following. "What was that all about, Mac?" Darcy asked.

"Laddie, I don't know, but I've a feeling we've some trouble ahead. That Davies claims he has documents showing he owns our ranch. I don't know what to make of it. We bought this place right and legal, but whatever it is, I wish Hank were here."

Mac had a thought and turned to Tom Strathen. "Tom, lad, is

it true what you've been saying? Are you planning on heading up Montana way?"

The slim dark-haired cowboy nodded his head. "Yes, sir. That's my plan. I appreciate this job you gave me, but I've always had a problem with itchy feet. I figured when it warmed a little more, I'd be moseying north. You know, see them tall mountains we've heard about."

"Tom, we might have a problem brewing. You've heard us talk of Hank Remington, the other partner in the ranch."

"Yes, sir, I sure have. From what I hear, he's a man with the bark on."

"Aye, that he is, and I'm afraid we'll be needing him here. I know it's still cold, but March is coming on. Would you consider riding out early? We'll give you an extra horse, stock you up with supplies and ammunition and whatever else you need, and pay you an extra three months' wages." He stopped and looked over at Darcy. "If that's all right with you."

"Sure, Mac, that's fine with me."

"That's mighty generous of you, Mr. MacGregor, but I've never met him, and one man? I ain't even gonna begin to try to guess what the odds are of finding him."

"Don't you be worrying yourself, Tom," Mac said. "When you get up in the Colorado Territory, you just start asking around. There aren't a lot of men like Hank. He's a couple of inches over six feet tall in his stocking feet. He's got an old bullet wound scar along the right side of his head where the hair has grown back in white, leaving a white streak in the brown hair. Like I said, a hard man to miss."

"When would you like for me to leave?"

"As soon as we can get you ready," Mac said. "You need to say any goodbyes?"

Tom grinned. "Naw, I'm thinking it's best for me to just mount up and ride."

1

From over six feet, William Wallace Logan gazed down into the soft brown eyes of his future bride, Deborah Coleman. Her full lips, now spread in an inviting smile, softened the firmness of her strong chin.

The two of them made a handsome couple as they stood facing each other. The morning sun slanting through the open church window settled on Deborah, giving her an angelic glow. Her soft, brown hair cascaded over her shoulders.

The thought of angels would be driven from any man's mind should his glance include Will Logan, unless it might be that of the archangel Michael or Gabriel. Though a smile now lit the groom's eyes, and humor tweaked the corners, there was hardness residing barely beneath their surface, waiting to be cast on anyone he deemed deserving.

Will tore his gaze from Deborah's face and looked out across the congregation gathered in the little church. Friends and family filled the building, some sitting on the hard benches, others, mostly men, standing against the walls. Tandy Jacobs, at six feet four inches tall, towered above all the men. Next to him stood

Bart Porter, the Texas gunman. Both of them had become good friends. Today, they, like all the others, were in their Sunday best.

He took a deep breath, and the black broadcloth suit pulled tight across his shoulders, doing little to hide the power resting beneath the cloth.

His ma and sister, Kate, sat in the front row of the church, next to his younger brothers, Colin and Bret, who were both grinning at him. Behind them sat his other brothers, Callum and Josh. Josh's wife, Fianna, leaned her head against her husband and said something to him, inaudible except for the two of them. She looked toward Will and rolled her eyes as she tried to retain a grip on Matt, their two-year-old son, who appeared to be committed to dashing to the window. Josh leaned over, extended a long arm and corralled his son, bringing him close and saying something in his ear. The boy settled down immediately.

Will moved his vision back to Deborah's face when the preacher said, "Shall we begin?" Without hesitation he continued, "Dearly beloved, we are gathered—"

He halted at a sudden noise from outside. The unmistakable clanking of military rigging, multiple hoofbeats ceasing, and commands given as a body of cavalry came to a halt.

Everyone turned to the front door of the church, waiting. They had a brief wait. The sounds of boots and spurs dinged and jingled as men marched up the front steps of the church. The door opened, and a skinny private pushed into the church, slightly ahead of an officer. The man stopped, pointed at Will, and shouted, "That's him, sir! He's the deserter I saw. Yessir, that's the yellow belly what deserted our regiment when we wuz under enemy fire. I saw him hightailing on that there big black horse of his'n."

"Quiet, Private," the captain snapped. He removed his hat and walked forward, obviously uncomfortable with the frowning preacher and the eyes of everyone following him but determined to do his duty.

Will's brother Josh, who had been a major in the Union Army, handed Matt to Fianna and stood as the uniformed captain approached.

Deborah was looking at Will. She saw the dark cloud of anger settle over her future husband at the private's statement, and laid a comforting hand on his arm. "Relax, darling, they don't know what happened. You can quickly straighten this out. I can vouch for your statement as being true."

Will nodded and smiled down at her. "Yes, you're right. This should only take a moment."

Josh stepped into the aisle as the captain approached, and extended his hand. "Good morning, Captain. I am Major Joshua Logan, late of the Sixth Michigan and now ranching west of here. What can we do for you?"

The captain held up his left hand, stopping the line of troopers following, dropped it, removed the gauntlet from his right, and grasped Josh's hand. "It is a pleasure to meet you, sir. I am Captain Grayson Smyth."

Will looked the man over as he spoke. He had a trustworthy look about him, gray eyes wrinkled at the corners from staring into the distance, searching for unseen enemies. His hair almost matched his eyes, mostly gray with a few dark remnants remaining. A man at least in his mid-forties. During the war, the captain's rank had likely reached colonel or above, but he was probably one of the unlucky ones caught in the reduction of force following the fighting. Likely he had been given the choice of captain or out.

Captain Smyth continued, "Unfortunately, I fear that I am about to disrupt this wedding. I am here to arrest First Sergeant William Wallace Logan for desertion in the face of the enemy." He nodded toward Will and continued, "I believe the groom is our man."

Will stepped forward, drawing near the captain and towering

over him. "Captain, I am William Wallace Logan, but I am no deserter."

"First Sergeant Logan," continued the captain, reaching into his tunic and taking out a folded piece of paper, "this document calls for your arrest, trial for desertion, and if found guilty, execution by hanging."

He turned to Josh. "I am sorry, Major, but I must follow orders." He then turned to the sergeant accompanying him and said, "Take that man."

"You heard the captain," said the sergeant as he waved four of the troopers forward. Looking up at Will, he said, "Come along peacefully. There are more men outside."

Will saw Colin slip the thongs from his two .36-caliber Navy Colts. He also knew that likely every man in the church, with the exception of him, was armed, but he also knew he wanted no bloodshed. Deborah, Ma, and Kate were here, along with many other wives and children. "There'll be no trouble from me, Captain."

"Yeah," the private who had pointed him out yelled, "he ain't got the guts to make trouble."

As the captain was spinning around to face the private, Callum, Will's brother, made a quick move. Stepping near the private, he grasped the man's shirt and neckerchief in his big hand. He lifted and twisted, jerking the man's face within inches of his. In a voice as cold as a December wind off the Rockies, he said, "Mister, you don't have the grit Will Logan has in his little finger."

Silence reigned in the small church. The windows were open, for the day was warming. A soft breeze wafted through, rustling the curtains alongside the windows. Outside, dogs were barking, and wagons could be heard rolling along the rough dusty streets of Pueblo. Bark scraped as squirrels raced through the limbs of the big cottonwood next to the church.

"Sir," the captain said sharply, "put my man down. I apologize for his behavior, but he is a representative of the United States government."

The private's face was turning blue as he vainly flailed at Callum's forearm in an attempt to suck air through a closed windpipe. Slowly, Callum turned a cold stare toward the captain and, with an exaggerated Tennessee drawl, said, "Reckon if he's goin' to represent the government, he oughta have better manners." He held the captain's gaze for a moment and turned his glare back to the private. He gave him one last shake and tossed him away with disgust. The private staggered on his feet, almost falling.

His glare as cold and hard as Callum's, Captain Smyth said, "Sergeant, escort the private to his horse, and place him under arrest." He then looked around at the faces, stopping on Callum's. "I apologize for his rudeness. The sergeant will see that he is properly instructed."

Will, drawing everyone's attention back to him, said, "Captain, at the ranch there are documents to verify I never deserted. Also, there's plenty of folks here who will vouch for me."

Deborah had been standing at Will's side. Now she pushed forward. "Captain, I am Deborah Barrett Coleman. I am a nurse and served at Douglas General Hospital in Washington during the war."

The captain nodded. "Thank you for your service, ma'am. I am familiar with it. I was sorry to hear of its closure. Many men were saved there."

Deborah nodded. "Yes, many lives were saved, but my point is that I attended to Hank, as he was known then. He had received multiple wounds, one of which caused amnesia, which only recently did he recover from. For his actions he was awarded the Congressional Medal of Honor. Now, I ask you, does that sound like a deserter?"

The captain stood taller as he took a moment to look at Will. Then he shook his head. "No, ma'am, it certainly does not, but unfortunately, I am detailed by Colonel Cracken to locate and return Mr. Logan to the fort for trial. I can do no less." At this point he looked at Will and then Josh. "I would recommend getting the documents necessary to prove your innocence, and bring them to Fort Lyon, along with any witnesses you may have. You are welcome to ride along with us. The trial will be held the day after our arrival. Colonel Cracken believes in swift justice." Though his voice did not change, the captain could not prevent his lips pursing, and the right side of his mouth turned down in a faint sign of disgust.

"Captain," Josh said, frustration showing through his outward calm, "our ranch is sixty miles west of here. Fort Lyon is close to a hundred miles east. We need the time to get to the ranch, get the documents, and make it to the fort. You're setting impossible goals for us."

"Captain, please," Deborah pleaded, "let us have more time."

He shook his head. "Ma'am, Major Logan, if it were up to me, I'd give you all the time you need, but when Colonel Cracken learned of a possible deserter in Pueblo, he could hardly contain himself. He wants the man captured, tried immediately, and I hate to say it, hanged. I'll try to stall an extra day out of him, but don't bet on it. Go as fast as you can. I promise I'll take a full two days to get back to the fort. But after that . . ."

"Then, Captain," Deborah said, "would you allow us to marry before you leave?"

Will spun back to her with an emphatic head shake. "No! No, Deborah. We don't know what might happen." He started to turn back to the captain, and she laid her hand on his arm.

"Will, we didn't know what the future held before these troopers arrived. Nothing has changed. No one knows the future. This will be straightened out in no time. Let's get married. Now. Everyone is here for a wedding. They've brought all this food. It'd be a shame to waste it, and you know how hard it is for many of these folks to be here. They've had to leave their farms and ranches. I think we should thank them by carrying on." Her smile lit her face. "Let's just do it. Let's celebrate optimism and life."

Will grinned down at her. "I've waited a long time. Reckon I'd prefer to wait no longer." He turned back to the officer. "Captain, there's plenty of food for your men. If you allow us to complete the service, I'm sure everyone will be pleased to have you and your troopers join us."

The captain, after glancing at Josh and Callum, who both nodded, said, "I'm sure we can spare a couple of hours, especially for a good meal, before heading back."

Immediately Josh looked at Callum.

Callum turned to Colin. "Colin, you think you and Virgil can keep up with me on Shoshone?"

Both boys said in unison, "Yes, sir!"

"Good," Callum said, turning back to Will. "Where do you keep those papers?"

"Look in the top drawer of my bedroom dresser. There should be a large envelope with three documents, the letter from Dr. James, my discharge papers, and the citation for the Medal of Honor. If you'll bring those to Fort Lyon, they should take care of this problem."

Will turned back to the captain, about to speak, when Deborah spoke up. "Also bring the medal. It has more weight than a letter."

Grinning at his future wife, Will said, "Thanks, honey, sometimes it does. You heard her, boys, add the medal to the list." Growing serious, he turned back to the captain. "Maybe then all of this can be put behind us."

"Yes," the captain replied, "I feel sure those documents will do the trick, First Sergeant."

Callum nodded his head toward the church doors. "Come on, boys, we're burnin' daylight." The three, their spurs jingling, hurried from the church.

Waiting for the sounds of their departure to fade, the minister finally said, "Now, shall we continue?" He led the couple back to their places. Once satisfied and with peace restored in his church, he began. "Dearly beloved. We are gathered . . ."

Will put the army captain out of his mind and concentrated on the lovely woman beaming up at him. *How could I, just a poor boy from Tennessee, have been so lucky?* His mind drifted back to his stay in the Washington hospital.

Deborah had been the first person he had seen when he opened his eyes after being in a coma for five months. At first, his confused mind took her for an angel, which she had truly been for him and many others. On awakening, he had no memory of the past, no idea how he had received his wounds, nor what his name was.

The new friends, who had brought him in, had given him a name. A name they thought was accurate and fitting, Henry Remington. When he had arrived, galloping in on Blacky, they were under extreme fire from the Rebs, short on ammunition, and almost overrun. He saved them with his Henry Repeating Rifle and his Remington revolvers, thus the name. He took multiple hits and a bayonet wound. Blacky had stood firm, giving him protection, but died in the hail of bullets. Thanks to their courage, the attack was stopped, and men's lives saved. Three, now his friends, had been assigned to take him and the written report of his heroism back to the hospital. Everyone, including the doctors, believed he would die, but the Logan tenacity brought him through and back to good health, though his memory didn't return for several years.

And now, he still could not believe his good fortune to not only have found her, but his family here in Pueblo. With the return of his memory, he had put aside Hank Remington, though it had stood him in good stead through several trying years.

"Will?"

Surprised, he looked at the minister. "What?"

"The ring? You do have a ring?"

His face edged to red, but under the sun-darkened skin, only his ma and Deborah could tell. "Yes."

Minister Blake grinned at him. "Put the ring on her finger."

He dug the ring from his coat pocket. When he looked back at Deborah, her face showed a combination of humor and concern. He had recovered his memory, but sometimes he had lapses. Over the past months, it was happening less frequently but was still occurring. Will took her hand in his. His big hands dwarfing hers, he gently slipped the ring on her slim finger.

"I now pronounce you man and wife. You may kiss your bride."

Even with the threat of the trial hanging over his head, he felt his heart fill with happiness. Throughout the last three years she had always been on his mind, and now they would have a life together.

Her face was turned up to his, cheeks flushed, dark brown eyes glowing, and full lips waiting. He bent and kissed her, the soft warmth of her lips causing his chest to grab and his heart to jump.

When they separated, she whispered to him, "I love you, my husband."

He grinned back and spoke in a low voice. "I've waited a long time for this. Many's the night I never thought it would happen."

Together they turned toward the door. Will looked a question at Captain Smyth, who nodded his consent. He held his arm for Deborah. She took it, pulling him close. He could feel the heat from her side. He smiled at his ma, who dabbed at her blue eyes while returning his smile. Together, they walked down the aisle, following most of their family and friends, who were hurrying outside. Stepping into bright sunlight and onto the porch of the church, they were greeted with cheers, whoops, and even a few gunshots.

Captain Smyth, from behind, stepped to Will's side, his face grim. "First Sergeant, you have two hours. After that, I will be forced to place you under arrest and escort you to Fort Lyon."

"Understood, Captain. I'll be ready." He nodded toward the tables under the cottonwood tree. They were loaded with food, and a young beef was roasting on the spit. "In the meantime, there is plenty of meat and trimmings for everyone, including your men. Enjoy it."

"Thank you for your kindness, First Sergeant. I know I'll enjoy a break from army food, and I'm sure my men will." He quickly made his way down the church steps.

Will looked across the crowd, a few still clapping, all watching expectantly.

"Will," Deborah said softly to him, "they expect you to say something."

His eyes were pulled to the diminishing dust cloud across the Arkansas River. He could still faintly make out the three individuals riding hard to the west, each leading two additional horses. *Be safe and successful, boys*, he thought. *It's all up to you.*

He sighed, then his face broke into a big grin as he looked across the many faces of the people who had welcomed him into their town and lives. Laying his hand over hers still gripping his arm, he said, "Thanks, folks. Deb and I sure appreciate you showing up for our wedding. It ain't many people who have this many friendly folks in their lives. I ain't much of a speechmaker, so I'll just say eat up and have fun."

With that, he and Deborah waved to everyone. Whoops broke out, and gunshots echoed across the plains. Will caught the emphatic nod from his ma toward the minister, acknowledged her look, and raised both hands.

The crowd, already starting toward the tables, turned back and quieted down again.

"Folks, my ma, standing right down front here, gave me one of those looks I'm sure you're all familiar with when you don't quite step up to the mark. Just like you do, I got the message. We'd best get a blessing on this food we're about to enjoy."

He looked at the minister coming back up the steps. "Parson, we'd appreciate you giving us a real good blessing on all this food." Then he grinned. "Course, we all know you're mighty fond of the spoken word."

At that, many eyes in the crowd rolled, and heads nodded in agreement, with some chuckling and comments traveling through the group.

Will continued, "If you could keep this one kinda short, there's a bunch of folks who'd be mighty grateful."

The preacher, who was a good friend to almost all those who were attending the wedding, grinned at Will and shook an index finger toward him. "It probably wouldn't hurt *you* to be a little more conversant with God, Will Logan."

The crowd roared again, and Will saw his ma nodding and smiling.

"You're probably right, Parson. Reckon it wouldn't hurt me at all."

The crowd quieted, and the preacher began. "Lord, we're mighty grateful for this bounty thou has set before us. We'd like to ask you to bless it to the nourishing and strengthening of our bodies, and we'd like to ask a blessing on these newlyweds. We know life ain't easy, especially in this country. If you could be with them and give them your strength to meet and overcome whatever challenges lie ahead for them, we'd be much obliged. I also ask a blessing on all these folks who are here partaking of thy goodness. Watch over them and keep them safe. In the name of Jesus Christ, amen." He looked at Will. "Wasn't my shortest, but it sure wasn't my longest."

Will extended his hand. "Thanks, Parson." Over the minister's head, he could see the soldier who had pointed him out. He was glaring at Will while talking to a hulking trooper.

2

The travel from Pueblo to Fort Lyon had been an enjoyable interlude for Will, since Deborah was there. After they had eaten, changed, and said their goodbyes to the well-wishers and family two days ago, they had mounted and departed to Fort Lyon. Before they left, several of the Pueblo businesses' owners advised Will they were planning on traveling to Fort Lyon and testify on his behalf. They would not be far behind the army patrol. Against Captain Smyth's objection, Deborah had insisted on accompanying her husband to the fort. Josh, familiar with the military, would also not wait or be prevented from riding along.

Will was torn. He loved and wanted to be near his new wife, but if something happened and he was, indeed, executed, he did not want her witnessing the execution. Reluctantly, but with relief, he had agreed. It was good to have her here, and Josh. Maybe Josh, having been a major, could at least keep him out of the stockade.

The land was dry, and dust boiled up from the horses' hooves, enveloping the riders. To insure she would be able to keep up, Deborah had elected to ride instead of bounce along in a wagon or buggy that might break down halfway to Fort Lyon. Now she rode next to her husband, troopers in front and behind in column.

Will looked across at his new bride. Her strong jaw and high cheekbones contributed to her regal appearance on the back of her horse. Her radiance shone through the trail dust that covered her.

He licked his lips, tasting the dust, smelling the sage, and feeling the intense afternoon sun. *Even with the dust of the trail on her face, she's beautiful,* he thought. *I'll be glad when this is done. Uncle Floyd has talked a great deal about the northern country. Perhaps we'll do like Josh and Callum have with Ma, and start our own place there.*

Repositioning herself on the sidesaddle, her head turned, catching him watching her. She smiled. "What are you looking at?"

"Why, the prettiest woman I know."

Angling closer, she reached across and slapped him on the arm. "You are a rascal, aren't you?"

He grinned at her and grabbed her hand. "If I am, I'm a happy one."

She gave him a haunted smile, worry pulling at the corners of her mouth. "This would have been a wonderful trip but for the army. I do hope Callum and the boys arrive soon."

"Don't worry, they will. When this is finished, we'll head back to Pueblo. I'd like to continue our discussion about heading north, if you're alright with that. I know you're helping your uncle in his practice . . ."

Her eyes widened. "Will, we're together. I'll be happy wherever you are. I'm sure my skills as a nurse will be put to good use no matter where we might be. A family, and a big one"—now the worry disappeared. The corners of her mouth lifted, showing even white teeth, and her eyes twinkled—"is all I've ever wanted."

A grin spread across his broad face. "That sounds fine with me. Why—"

The column had halted, and Captain Smyth and Josh, who had been riding at the head, rode back and pulled up on either side of the two with the captain alongside Will.

"Sorry to interrupt, folks," the captain said. "First Sergeant Logan, the fort is just over the next rise. We'll be in full view from the ramparts. You'll be wearing the manacles from here on in. Colonel Cracken is a stickler for regulations."

Will nodded and, seeing Deborah about to protest, spoke quickly to her. "Regulations. You remember those?"

She paused and nodded, saying nothing. Her horse stomped impatiently, then stood still.

Will turned back to the captain. "I understand."

The captain ordered a trooper, "Corporal, manacle the prisoner."

The corporal had dismounted and, with the manacles in hand, stepped next to Will. During the two-day trip, Will had gotten to know most of the men. They were all soldiers, some better, some worse, but all mostly friendly, except for the private who had pointed him out and his burly friend. The corporal didn't meet Will's eyes as he reached for an arm.

"That's all right, Frank. You're just following orders. I'll be shed of these things and this warrant in a couple of days."

Frank fastened the manacles around both wrists and looked up. "Thanks, Will. They too tight?"

Will shook his head. "Nope, can't feel a thing."

The captain continued, "When we get in, we'll be seeing Colonel Cracken. There's a chance we can persuade him the stockade won't be necessary. I suggest you be polite and do nothing to rile him."

Will gave a short nod. "Good advice."

With those words the captain moved back to the front of the

column, turned, and spoke to the sergeant. Moments later the sergeant shouted, "Move out."

The column started forward again, Josh remaining next to Will.

They rode to the crest of the rise in silence. Topping the hill, they saw the fort in full view. It wasn't impressive as forts go, other than being new. Up until a year ago, the army had been using Fort Wise and Bent's Fort, both about twenty miles down the Arkansas. The new fort, less prone to flooding, sat on a bluff well above the river. Except for jutting above the terrain, the buildings blended into the landscape, the same dusty color as the terrain.

"I've a feeling this won't be fun," Josh said.

"Yep."

Josh went on. "I've been talking to some of these boys, and they don't hold this Cracken in very high regard. The name's not familiar to me, so I can't comment on him for sure, but I second Smyth's recommendation. Keep it polite. This fella not only has your future in his hands, he's got your life."

"Reckon I've come to the same conclusion. I'll be nice and polite, do my yes sirs and no sirs, and hopefully the documents will get here soon, and that will be it." He glanced at Deborah. Her eyes were locked on the fort. She rocked slowly with her mount's motion as they moved closer and closer to the fort. The worry had returned. Though only twenty-eight, the strain of nursing during the war, the maiming, the death, had embedded tiny wrinkles at the corners of her mouth. Today, they were more prominent than usual.

"Don't worry, honey. This'll be over soon, and we'll be on our way to a new life."

He could see her mentally pull back from wherever she had been. Turning to him, a wan smile crossed her lips. "I know, but after all you've been through, you shouldn't have to endure this."

Attempting to make light of the situation, Will said,

"Remember what we talked about when I told you about my experiences in Cuba? If it doesn't kill you, it makes you stronger." Immediately he saw the pain in those dark pools of brown, but quickly her eyes changed back to the tough, resolute woman he had met in the hospital.

"Not funny, Will," she snapped. "This man could have you shot or hanged."

Will was not a man who apologized to anyone. If he said it, he meant it. Throughout his adult life, most of his dealings had been with men. But he was talking to the woman with whom he had chosen to spend the rest of his life. The woman he would do anything to keep from hurting. "Sorry, honey. That came out before I thought."

He watched a guilty smile slide across her face. "Me too. I just didn't like the death reference."

They rode the last hundred yards to the fort in silence.

Just before passing through the entrance, she turned to him and mouthed three words. "I love you."

"Me too," he said back, winked, and began giving the fort a closer examination. This was his first time at the new fort. It was not fully enclosed except for a portion on the river side that was a large high-walled, adobe corral and stable. The corral's walls rose higher than those of the buildings surrounding the open review grounds. East of the corral was a long, low, connected building that continued farther east. He stood in the saddle and surveyed the interior of the fort. He could see no guard posts at the entrance or any of the open corners. Buildings made up the remaining three sides.

Will's eyes were drawn to the only two-story building in the fort. It rose above the reviewing field on the opposite side from the corral and was the only building made of lumber, obviously the headquarters.

The column followed the street as it circled the perimeter of the wide field. Two men stood in front of the building. As they drew nearer, Will could see one was a lieutenant colonel. The other, much younger man, was a newly minted shavetail lieutenant. Both of the men's uniforms were spotless, brass and boots shining in the remaining sunlight.

Captain Smyth halted the column in front of the pair, dismounted, approached, stood at attention, and raised his right hand to his hat brim in salute. Before returning the salute, Colonel Cracken's eyes traveled along the column of dusty, tired men, stopping momentarily at Will, Deborah, and Josh. His lips pursed tighter at the sight of the three, then continued along the column, then up and down the captain standing at attention before him, finally tossing him a return salute. The captain snapped his arm down to his side.

"You took your time, Captain Smyth. Did you have Indian trouble?"

Still at attention, Captain Smyth replied, "No, sir, I felt, rather than tire the animals and men, we should take our time so we would be rested should we encounter Indians. Plus, sir, we do have a lady with us."

Will and Josh did not wait for the captain to dismount the men, but swung down from their horses. Will stepped around, reached up, and though the manacles were awkward, helped Deborah from her saddle. Her arm hit the brim of his hat, knocking it from his head. After placing her gently on the ground, he stooped, picked up his hat, and placed it firmly back on his head. He smiled at his wife while hearing the colonel's sharp reply to Smyth.

"I can see that, Captain. I can also see that you do not appear to be guarding your deserter very closely. I assume the man in the manacles is First Sergeant William Logan. And perhaps you would be so kind as to tell me who the woman and the other man might be?"

While the colonel was speaking, the three handed the reins of their horses to troopers and walked up to him.

"Colonel," Josh began, "I can explain. I am—"

The colonel turned a frosty stare toward Josh. "Sir, I am receiving the report of one of my officers and would thank you to be polite enough to wait until we are finished, but, since you are here." He turned to the lieutenant. "Lieutenant Parker, call the sergeant of the guard, have him place the prisoner in the stockade."

Will knew his brother Josh. He was cool under fire, but with little patience for fools, and it looked like that was what this colonel was shaping up to be.

"Colonel!" Josh said.

The lieutenant had opened his mouth to call for the sergeant of the guard when Josh snapped his reply.

Josh continued, "I am Major Joshua Logan, and First Sergeant William Logan is my brother. The lady with him is Deborah Logan, his wife. I can attest to his character, as can she. He is no deserter. In fact, he is a decorated hero. Having him in manacles or, even worse, in the guardhouse is a travesty of justice."

The colonel's face turned red at Josh's response. "*Major* Logan." He waved a piece of paper in Josh's face. "I have here an order for the arrest of one First Sergeant William Wallace Logan for desertion in the face of the enemy. This is an order from head-quarters in Washington." His tone full of sarcasm, he continued, "I do believe this takes priority over your word." Turning to the lieutenant, he said, "Follow my orders, Lieutenant Parker—now!"

The lieutenant shouted for the sergeant of the guard, who, with all the commotion, had moved to within arm's length of the lieutenant. Flustered, seeing the man so close, the lieutenant stammered, "Take him to the guardhouse," indicating Will.

The sergeant stepped forward as Deborah's grip tightened on Will's arm.

Will patted her hands. "Don't worry, honey, I'll be fine. Now let me go."

The sergeant waited a moment too long to allow Deborah to

release Will, and the colonel barked, "Sergeant, follow my orders!"

"Yessir," he snapped back, and reached for Will's arm.

The sergeant, shorter than Will, but wider, his blue blouse stretched tight around a barrel chest, thick neck, and arms, said gruffly, but in a respectful voice, "First Sergeant."

A slim cowboy, gun slung on his right hip and dusty from riding a long trail, stepped in front of Will and addressed the sergeant. "Mind if I have a word with this man?"

The sergeant stepped forward between Will and the cowhand. "No talking to the prisoner. You can check at the guardhouse during visiting hours."

Will had never seen the man before. He saw the hostility flash in the man's face, watched him stiffen and then relax before moving aside. He nodded to the stranger, gave Deborah a reassuring smile, and started off with the sergeant.

He heard Josh say, "Colonel, this is not necessary. We have witnesses that he is not a deserter. He came with Captain Smyth voluntarily and will remain for his trial."

"I will *ensure* he remains, Major," was the colonel's icy reply. "Now please step aside and allow Captain Smyth to carry on with his troop. If you have anything else to say, you may address me in my office."

Will was ushered across the parade ground to the stockade located in the long building next to the corral. He could faintly hear Deborah saying, "Please, Colonel, he doesn't need to be in the stockade. He didn't desert. He was injured," and then sound from outside was muffled by the closing door.

Leaving the bright sun, it took a few moments for Will's eyes to adjust to the gloomy interior. Sitting at the only desk in the room was a slovenly-looking corporal, blouse unbuttoned to his big belly, boots resting on the desktop, and a huge plug of tobacco in the corner of his mouth. At the sight of the sergeant, he casually rolled his head to the side and spit a long stream of tobacco juice toward a filthy bucket, half of which didn't make it in the bucket. "Got the deserter there, huh, Sarge?"

"Get your boots off the desk and your butt out of that chair, Locher. Find a broom and sweep out this place. It smells like a pigsty."

Locher slowly removed his boots from the desk, stood, and sauntered over to the broom standing in the corner. Half-heartedly, he started sweeping at the dust on the floor. "Reckon the colonel's gonna hang him? The colonel ain't got much care for deserters. Fact is, don't think the colonel's got much care for anything 'ceptin' that pretty wife of his'n."

"Shut it, Locher, and get that blouse buttoned."

Will, ignoring the corporal, for he had seen others like him, said to the sergeant, "What's your name, Sergeant?"

The sergeant guided Will to a narrow hallway with a heavy locked door. "Mitchell, First Sergeant." On the wall, to the left of the door and far enough away to be out of reach from anyone's outstretched arm reaching through the upper barred portion of the door, was a wooden peg with a ring of keys on it. The sergeant pulled the ring from the peg, selected a key, and unlocked the door. Once open, he motioned with his head for Will to enter, and said, "The cell at the end, First Sergeant."

In a falsetto tone, Locher said, *"First Sergeant,"* and spit again, the spittle echoing as it struck the inside wall of the metal bucket. "Why, he ain't no first sergeant, he's just a deserter who'll git his comeuppance here mighty soon."

Sergeant Mitchell turned his head and glared at Locher. "Locher, if you don't shut that whiney mouth of yours, as soon as I get this man locked up, I'll come back and sweep this floor with you. Now shut it!"

Will turned his head to look at Locher. The man was leaning on his broom, staring insolently at him. He opened his mouth to say something, thought better of it, and went back to sweeping, smearing the line of tobacco spittle across the floor. With the pressure of Sergeant Mitchell's hand on his arm, Will returned his gaze to the hallway and moved forward.

Beyond the doorway the hall ran between barred cells. They passed six smaller, empty cells, three on each side. The end cell, at which the hallway stopped, was the largest. It ran across the full width of the containment area and had four bunks where the smaller cells had only two. Four small twelve-inch-square windows let in light from the parade ground. "Why no windows on that side?" Will asked, indicating the opposite wall.

"That's an exterior wall. We don't want to make it easy for anyone to break a prisoner out of here."

"Makes sense," Will said. He bent his six-foot-two-inch frame to enter through the six-foot-high cell door and turned to Sergeant Mitchell, hands extended.

Without a question the burly sergeant pulled another key from his pocket and unlocked the manacles, then swung them over his shoulder.

"That's mighty trusting, Sergeant."

"First Sergeant, I've worked the guardhouse off and on for nigh on to fifteen years. I'm many things, but trusting ain't one of 'em. Happens I recognized Major Logan, and you being his brother, I know you ain't done what that paper is saying. Anyway, I suspect you're a smart enough man to know you'd be up against long odds, trying to make it off this fort."

Will nodded. "You're right about that. I'd also figure it long odds to make it past you, though it might be possible."

Sergeant Mitchell had a rough face to go along with his gravelly voice. His face, sun-burned and wind-worn along with his hands, bore the marks of many a scrap. He broke into a grin. "Yessir, it might be possible, maybe, for a big fellow like you. That's something I'd be cautious on betting either way."

Will chuckled. "Yes, Sergeant Mitchell, I think you're right. By the way, I'm no longer in the army. Call me Will or Logan. First sergeant's in the past."

Mitchell's grin disappeared. "Guess I'd better stick to first sergeant for now. The colonel is a stickler for formality. He also has a liking for punishment. I hope you've got some proof like the major's saying. Otherwise, he'll see you hanged, and enjoy it."

"I've got proof, Sergeant Mitchell, as long as the boys can get here in time. The ranch is a hard day's ride to the west from Pueblo. Even though Captain Smyth took his time coming back, they could be two days behind us if they had no trouble. Plus, respected citizens will be arriving from Pueblo as witnesses, businessmen and a doctor who knew me before my memory returned. They should be here tomorrow, and with them I don't see how the trial can go any other way than setting me free."

"Pshaw. He won't pay no never mind to witnesses, and I'll promise you, First Sergeant, he'll have your trial tomorrow come hell or high water. If you're found guilty, he'll have you hanged the next morning."

"It sounds to me like the colonel has already made up his mind. Thanks for letting me know."

"Don't mention it. By the way, Locher's going to be on duty tonight. Hopefully you'll be able to get some sleep. He's been busted several times, likes to torment prisoners, and be careful of him. He looks sloppy, but under that fat is some real strength, and he likes to hurt people."

"Sergeant, I've dealt with his kind many times in the past."

Sergeant Mitchell nodded. "Reckon you have." He stepped through the cell door and swung it shut. He inserted the key and rotated it, causing the bolt to go home with a cold finality.

Will sat on the hard bunk, watching the wide, friendly back disappear through the main door. The little additional light from the office was almost completely shut off when it closed. Through the barred window of the door, he could see Sergeant Mitchell as he disappeared from sight.

He slowly inspected the dreary interior of his prison and walked to the small barred window that faced the west. Except for a few troopers exercising horses on the parade ground, no one else was visible. Where had Deborah and Josh gone? Where was Deborah staying in this fort? Was she being taken care of? He knew his brothers would be coming with the papers to exonerate him, if they arrived in time. *They will,* he thought. Then his mind filled again with his sweet Deborah. What torment she must be going through. *I wish I could spare her this, but it will be over soon.* Then the grim thought filled his mind, *Either way.*

He stretched out on the bunk, and as he drifted off to sleep, a deep and ominous feeling enveloped him.

3

W ill jerked his eyes open, every sense alert. He lay still, listening. Darkness surrounded him. Through the small window, he could see stars set in a clear moonless sky. Suddenly, he heard the whish and squeak of booted feet attempting to be stealthy, slipping down the hallway.

An errant breeze, for there was little in the cells, brought the smell of rancid, unwashed bodies. He had been on his back when the first sound awakened him. He slowly turned his head to the left, providing a clearer picture of the entrance. In the minimal light from the windows, he could make out the forms of at least three people moving in his direction. From the past brawls he had been involved in, he felt confident he could handle three, but if there were more . . .

He lay still, waiting. They were coming for him. The thick walls of the stockade would drown out any cries, though he had no intention of crying for help. The commotion, which his assailants had not planned on, would eventually be heard, but he planned on being the one standing when others arrived. He had been here before and survived. Though he had no weapon, he had his big hands, elbows, and feet. Most of all he had his strength and determination.

Sergeant Mitchell had not taken any personal items, like his watch or money, but Josh had said, and Will agreed, it would be better for Josh to take his weapons than to let them be confiscated by the army.

He heard the rasp of a key carefully inserted into the cell door lock and slowly turned. The door emitted a long low squeak as it was pulled open, and the men entered the cell one at a time and started spreading out. Now he could see them clearly. Three, four, five filtered into the cell. Had Sergeant Mitchell been in on this? Was that why he had put him in the larger cell?

They were only a few steps away. He could see each man carrying a club. The big man in the center eased forward and raised his weapon. In a conversational tone Will said, "You boys think you might have bit off more than you can chew?"

For a moment they were frozen at his voice. A moment was all he needed. Will came out of his bunk like a coiled rattlesnake. His wide, hard fist drove with all the power he could muster. These men were here to kill or maim him, so he would offer them the same quarter they were prepared to offer him. He felt his fist lightly brush the big man's chin. It slid smoothly past the chin and smashed into the man's throat. The thud of struck meat and cracking cartilage filled the room. Will's assailant lost all interest in the attack. He dropped to his knees, the club rattling to the floor. Both of his hands whipped to his throat as if by being there they would help the air pass into his now starving lungs.

Will knew the doors were open to the outside, but he didn't dare race past and onto the parade ground. There would be sentries posted, and all they would see was the outline of an escaping prisoner. He'd be shot down like a dog. He had to survive here. This would be his stand.

When he struck the first assailant, one of the others yelled,

"Look out!" Momentarily the four men jumped back. Will charged the nearest one, realizing this move would allow one or more of them to get behind him, so he had to be fast. The man saw him coming and swung his club at his head. Fortunately he rushed his swing. Will ducked, allowing the club to sail over his unscathed head. He slammed a powerful uppercut into the man's belly and heard the rush of air blast from his lungs. Will grabbed two handfuls of hair as the man's head swung down and drove his head into a swift rising knee. Again, the sound of breaking bones and cartilage could be heard. The man crumpled, blood flowing all over the floor, and lay gasping alongside his partner.

Two down, Will thought and spun just as a club collided with his head. Like all Logans, he had a hard head, which was a good thing, for the club was swung with power by Corporal Locher. Will dropped to the floor.

"You got him, Locher, you got him."

He could barely hear the familiar voice, for he was fading fast with an intense ringing in his ears. Pyrotechnics were going off in his eyes, and he felt like vomiting. His dimming vision caught the blur of a cavalry boot descending toward his face. His head raged against moving, but the desire to survive and be with his Deborah overcame the sick pain that filled his head and the weakness filling his body. Summoning every ounce of strength he could muster from his fading body, he twisted toward his enemy. He felt the heel of the boot tear across the back of his head. Now in a position between the man's legs, still weak but his strength returning, he stood, grasped Locher's thighs and hips with his big arms, ripping the man from the floor. The man yelled as Will spun, swinging him like a club, and knocked the two remaining men into each other. With the built-up momentum, he threw Locher toward the cell's bars. The fat man hit the hard rock floor with a sickening thud, lay there for only a moment, and struggled to his feet, unsteady.

"Look out," the one who had yelled before shouted to his partner.

Will turned to the speaker. The cell had grown lighter. Will glanced toward the window to see the stars disappearing. The darkness was giving way to dawn. The fort would be awakening soon. All he had to do was hold out a little longer.

Locher pulled a revolver from his holster, but Will hoped he wouldn't fire for fear of waking up the garrison. "Get him, boys, we've got to get this done quick, or they'll catch us." He looked down at the blood on his blouse that he had picked up from the floor. "Go for his head. It's already banged up good."

The remaining two men, looking at the big man with blood streaming down his chest and back and fierce determination in his eyes, hesitated.

"Locher," Will said, "if you'd been in my army, I'd have thrown a pig like you out a long time ago."

The man's face reddened. "Get him, I said. If he moves, I'll shoot him. Now!" he shouted.

With raised clubs, the two men rushed Will. He went for the scrawny guy who had pointed him out in the church, as the other closed. The uncoordinated little man swung his club at Will's head. Will reached down and grasped the man's wrist. He spun, gripping the wrist in his big left hand, and twisted. The man screamed from both the pain and fear. A shot rang out in the jail, and everyone froze.

Josh was standing inside the jail cell, a big 1860 .44-caliber Colt Army smoking in his right hand. The muzzle waved toward the window. "Drop those clubs and move over by the window." He kicked the man on the floor, who was sitting up, holding his face, blood pouring from between his fingers. "You too. Get over there."

The man used one hand to push up from the floor while he kept the other protecting his nose and staggered to the other three, finally leaning against the wall.

"You all right, boy?" Josh said to Will as his eyes swept over his brother's bloody body.

"Been better. I'm mighty happy to see you."

"Reckon so," Josh said as footsteps could be heard.

Deborah, leading the pack, rushed in, saw Will covered in blood, and rushed to him. "Oh, Will, what have they done to you?"

"I'm guessin'," Josh said with a grin, "it's more like what he's done to them."

Deborah ignored Josh and, holding Will's head gently, blood coursing down her fingers, said, "Are you all right? Do you recognize me? Are you dizzy? You should sit down."

Will smiled at his new bride. "I'm fine. Yes, I recognize you, and I'm only a little dizzy." He let her push him back to his bunk, sat down, and nodded toward the man still on the floor. "I think you might take a look at that feller turning blue on the floor. I hit him in the throat."

Deborah turned her head and looked at the man now lying still, only little gasps coming from him. She looked back at Will and said, "I'll be right back."

As she knelt by the man, Captain Smyth, followed by Sergeant Mitchell, Lieutenant Parker, and several armed troopers, rushed into the guardhouse.

Captain Smyth slid to a halt, took in the scene, and said, "Please lower your weapon, Major Logan." He watched Josh lower the hammer of the .44 and slide it back into its holster. As he was about to speak again, Deborah interrupted.

"Captain, you'd better send for the doctor. This man will die if he isn't operated on soon."

Smyth immediately turned to one of the troopers and said, "Boren, get the doc. Make it quick."

The trooper spun and ran from the guardhouse.

Captain Smyth turned back to Locher. "Tell me what happened here."

Locher hesitated, obviously laboring to come up with a lie valid enough sounding to get him off the hook.

"Answer the captain, and make it quick, Locher," Sergeant Mitchell chimed in.

"Well," Locher said, paused for a moment, and continued, "it was like this. This here deserter raised a ruckus in his cell, and as big as he was, I needed some help to calm him down."

A voice shouted from behind the troopers who were blocking the hallway. "Get out of my way!"

The men jumped to clear a path, pressing their backs against the cells' bars.

Barefooted, blouse partially buttoned, and nonregulation red galluses hanging to his sides, the doctor pushed his way between the troopers and went straight for the man lying on the floor. He knelt, felt the man's throat, and opened his kit. From it he removed a scalpel.

Deborah, kneeling on the other side of the man, said, "I'm a nurse."

The doctor nodded and made an incision in his patient's throat. To Deborah, he said, "Hold that open," turned, and removed a metal tube from his bag. After examining the incision, he thrust the tube into the man's throat—nothing happened. He bent and blew a long breath into the tube. The man's chest first expanded, and then air flowed back out of the tube. He did this two more times, and finally the man gave a sharp gasp, coughed a couple of times, and started breathing. Immediately his eyes opened, and he stared first at Deborah and then at the doctor.

The doctor patted him on his shoulder. "You'll be fine. You may have to breathe with a contraption in your throat, but you're alive."

The man's eyes opened wide with fear, and the doctor added, "Maybe not. We'll have to see how well your throat heals." He looked at the troopers. "Go to my office and bring a stretcher." Then he looked down at the man. "Lie still, and hold this tube in place. Don't drop it, or you're liable to be in the same predicament you were in earlier."

The man's hand jerked up to the doc's. His fingers clinched around the tube. The doc stood, helped Deborah to her feet, and said, "Thank you for your quick thinking and assistance. Left untended, this man would have died soon. I'm Dr. Taylor, Charles Taylor."

"How do you do, Dr. Taylor. I am Deborah Col—Logan. Sorry, I'm recently married."

"Well, congratulations to the lucky man. Where might he be?"

"Right here, Dr. Taylor."

"Ah," the doctor said and moved toward Will to check his head.

Captain Smyth, about to continue, was again interrupted by a shout from a trooper in the office. "Atten-shun!"

Ignoring the men in the office and hallway, Colonel Cracken, in full uniform, boots and brass glistening in the lamplight, marched through the hallway and into the cell. His glance took in the injured, those lined against the wall, and he turned to Captain Smyth.

"Captain, can you tell me what is happening here, and who fired the shot? I assume the prisoner was caught trying to escape."

Sergeant Mitchell spoke up. "Sir, this is First Sergeant Logan's cell. I put him in it last evening. All these men are inside it. I doubt seriously he was trying to escape. It looks more like they came in here to do him harm."

The colonel turned an icy stare on his sergeant. "Sergeant Mitchell, I was not addressing you. I was addressing the officer present." He turned back to Smyth. "Captain Smyth?"

"I agree with Sergeant Mitchell, sir. Every one of these men is a troublemaker, and none of them, except Corporal Locher, have anything to do with stockade duty. However, when you entered, Locher was about to give us his version of what happened."

"I'll have no assumptions here," Colonel Cracken said. "Corporal Locher, please tell us what took place here, from the beginning."

"Well, sir, begging the colonel's pardon, I heard this here prisoner makin' a ruckus back here in his cell. Now, sir, you can rightly see how big he is. I sure didn't want to try to calm him back down all by my lonesome, so I looked outside, and these boys was apassin' the guardhouse. I just rightly called them in to give me a hand."

"Why didn't you call Sergeant Mitchell, Locher?" Captain Smyth asked.

"Well, sir, you see"—at this point Locher looked down at the rock floor—"Sergeant Mitchell ain't real fond of me, and I ain't hankerin' to pull him out of bed if I can take care of somethin' myself." He looked up. "I am a corporal."

"So," the captain continued, "these four men just happened to be walking by, and they just happened to have clubs with them. Is this what you're telling us?"

Now Locher's voice took on a whiney tone. "I'm just tellin' you what happened, Captain. I had to do something to git the prisoner to quiet down. If'n I didn't, I'd be gittin' in trouble with Sergeant Mitchell. And look what happened. I'm just glad you got here when you did. That there other Logan might have killed us, him with a gun trying to help his brother escape. When he fired, I just knew we was all dead."

"That's enough, Captain," the colonel snapped. "I can see clearly what happened here."

"Yes, sir," Captain Smyth replied. "It is quite evident. These five men slipped into First Sergeant Logan's cell with the intent of maiming or even killing him. Unfortunately for them, it was not as easy as they expected. It is a good thing Major Logan arrived when he did, and put a halt to this assault. Otherwise, we might have had more troopers on sick call."

While the conversation had been going on, Dr. Taylor had been working on Will. He had bandaged the two head wounds, and now, with white bandage wrapped around his head, and blood over the front and back of his shirt, he rose.

"May I say something, Colonel?"

The colonel turned to him and gave him a cold nod.

"Those men let themselves into my cell with the full intention of beating my brains out. Just before I hit him, the one who is on his way to the infirmary had his club raised to smash my head in while I was sleeping.

"I put up no fuss when Captain Smyth arrested me. In fact, I'm glad it happened. I'm only sorry that as soon as I was well I didn't ride over here and get this straightened out. But, Colonel, I did not try to escape, and my brother, Major Logan, showed up just in time. He stopped this from getting any worse."

The colonel thought for a moment. He looked from Locher to Will and back to Locher. "Captain Smyth, I think it might be necessary to disarm Major Logan and place him under arrest for attempting to break a deserter from our stockade."

Will heard Deborah gasp.

Captain Smyth turned, in disbelief, to the colonel. "Colonel, you can't be serious. It is perfectly clear what these men had in mind when they broke into this cell. It is also clear there would have been further bloodshed if Major Logan had not shown up when he did. There was no attempt to flee on First Sergeant Logan's part, nor is there any evidence the major was doing anything except stopping an intentional, brutal act by Corporal Locher and his cohorts."

The muscles around the colonel's jaws clinched and unclinched. "Captain, I am giving you a direct order. Arrest Major Logan for attempting to break his brother from our guardhouse and discharging a firearm in a military stockade."

Captain Smyth's eyes widened. "Sir, it is obvious Major Logan stopped this assault. He did not try to break—"

"Captain, I said arrest Major Logan. Do you intend to disobey a direct order? If you do not arrest him immediately, I shall relieve you of command."

4

R esigned, Captain Smyth said, "Yes, sir," and turned to
Josh. "I'll need your weapons."

"Colonel," Will said, "can't you see Locher is lying?
Josh doesn't belong in here." He pointed at Locher and the other
attackers, who had all but been forgotten. "Those are the ones
who need to be locked up."

"Captain," the colonel said, completely ignoring Will, "after
you've completed your duties, see me in my office. It's already
daylight. We need to make certain preparations are underway to
begin the trial this morning. It appears there will be more
charges against First Sergeant Logan. And we'll have Major
Logan's trial to consider. A busy day."

The colonel spun and marched down the hallway. He could
be heard muttering, "Yes, yes, a very busy day."

Josh stripped his gun belt. "Captain Smyth, how would you
feel if I gave this to Deborah. I know how the army is once
weapons fall into its possession."

"Go right ahead."

"Captain," Will said, "this is completely wrong. Josh should not be arrested, it should be that scum." He nodded toward Locher and his gang.

"I agree with you, but my hands are tied." He turned to Sergeant Mitchell. "Relieve Corporal Locher from his duty." To Locher he said, "Corporal, you're busted to private. My preference is to put you all behind these bars, but since I can't do that, you are assigned to permanent latrine duty. Now get out of here.

"Sergeant Mitchell, see these four are put to work on their new duty immediately."

Locher's whiney voice filled the cell. "But I've been up all night on guard duty."

"Shut up, Locher," Sergeant Mitchell said, "and get moving." He looked at the others. "Follow him."

Locher glared at the sergeant but held his tongue as he led the others from the guardhouse.

Captain Smyth also sent the other troopers from the guardhouse, leaving only Will, Josh, Deborah, Dr. Taylor, and himself.

"Captain, this is an injustice," Dr. Taylor said. "It was clear for anyone to see what happened. Those men slipped in here with evil intent." He turned to Will. "It's a good thing you were awake. They would have killed you."

Even in his grim situation, Will chuckled. "Those cavalry boots scraping on the stone floor would have woke the dead. I could tell they were *trying* to be quiet, but no one could have slept through that noise." His forehead wrinkled, pulling his thick eyebrows together in consternation. "I just don't understand why they were so set on killing me. As far as I know, I've never done harm to a one of those men. And the little guy I had by the wrist when Josh came in, he's the one who fingered me in the church. He seemed so pleased to be pointing me out, as if he has something against me, and I don't think I've ever seen him before."

Captain Smyth spoke up. "He knows you alright. The man's name is Dirksen. He joined the army during the war. In fact, a few weeks back, he was in a patrol led by Sergeant Mitchell. They passed through Pueblo, and you were there. Sergeant Mitchell says Dirksen recognized you instantly and started telling the troopers around him you were a deserter. The more he talked about it, the more agitated he became. He wanted to arrest you then and there."

Deborah moved closer to Will and slipped her arm through his. He could feel her warmth next to him.

Captain Smyth continued, "He'll be the main witness. He says your unit was in a fierce battle, and you were sent with a dispatch. The other dispatch riders had been killed, and your horse was fast. That's why the colonel sent you, but you never returned. Everyone figured you had been killed, for you were never seen again."

Will, his face a picture of bewilderment, nodded. "He's right, as far as he goes. Shortly after that, I was shot in the head and completely lost my memory." As he was speaking, Will's hand moved to the three-inch scar on the right side of his head. His hair, light brown sprinkled with gray, had a white streak through it. When he moved the long hair aside, the brutal scar could be clearly seen, a deep indention in his skull, with no hair growing in the crease. His hair naturally fell over it when he moved his hand, the white streak the only indication of an injury.

"I don't doubt you," Captain Smyth said. "However, I must be reporting to the colonel. I'll try to persuade him to postpone the trial until at least tomorrow, but please do not expect me to be successful." He gave Will a worried look. "I just hope your family can get here with those papers." He turned to Josh. "I'm sorry, Major Logan, but I must ask you to remain with your brother. I'll have some breakfast brought with the new guard."

"I understand, Captain," Josh said.

Deborah looked up at her husband and placed her hand against his cheek. "I'm so sorry this has happened to you."

Will pulled her close, ignoring the others in the cell, and whispered in her ear, "You are here. That's way more than I could ask. Don't worry. I'll be fine." He pushed her far enough away to see her face, smiled at her, lowered his head, and felt the warmth of her soft lips. She pulled him close for a moment. Someone cleared their throat, and the two parted.

"I'll bring you some clean clothes," Deborah said.

The captain stood by the door of the cell. "We must go."

Will gave her one last smile, seeing the sadness and concern for him in her eyes. She turned and led the way from the cell, followed by Dr. Taylor and then Captain Smyth. He closed the cell door, locked it, nodded to the two brothers, and followed the others out the main door. Will could hear Smyth giving instructions to the new men on duty, then the outer door opened. The last he heard were the determined footsteps of Deborah as she exited the guardhouse.

Will had a pounding headache. The blow to his head had also set his ears ringing. It sounded like a thousand crickets locked up inside his skull. He bowed his head for a moment, shook it, and looked up.

His brother's steel gray eyes were peering intently at him, brow wrinkled in concern. "You all right?"

"I imagine I'm gonna live, though that club sure rang my bell. You don't have anything for a headache, do you?"

"You think that blow could mess up your memory again?"

Will paused, looked at Josh intently, and asked, "Who did you say you are?"

Will could see his brother's concern deepen. He could keep a straight face no longer. He turned loose a belly laugh and shoved his younger brother good-naturedly on the shoulder. Immediately Josh's face turned from concern to relief and finally to anger.

"If you weren't such an old man, I'd give that hard head of yours something to ache about." Then his face broke into a grin. "Come on, let's sit. We've got to figure out what we're going to do if the boys don't get those papers here in time for the trial."

The two big men sat side by side on Will's bunk.

"Wish Uncle Floyd were here," Will said. "He's a comfort to have around."

Josh nodded. "He is. He has certainly been over the mountain. Come to think of it, I'd say we both have. We should be able to figure a way out of this."

"The best way," Will replied, "would have been for me to go to the closest army unit as soon as I was well. I kept putting off the travel to be around Deborah. I didn't want to lose her again. I always figured the papers would straighten out any problem that might arise. And they will if they get here soon enough."

"Don't beat yourself up, Will. That water's long passed under the bridge. Hopefully they'll be here in time. We've got to think about what we're going to do if they aren't. Normally, I'd say we have enough on our side, your scar, testimony, and witnesses, to swing whatever court is hearing this, but with Cracken . . . That man concerns me. I don't know if he's just a martinet or if he's unstable. Either way is not a good sign for us."

"Josh, all I can do is tell the truth. Deborah will testify, and Dr. James, her uncle from Pueblo. Then we can expect several of the townspeople to be able to testify of knowing me as Hank Remington before my memory returned. In any sane world that would be enough." Will rubbed the scar on his head. "Shoot, this scar alone should be enough. Anyone can see it's a bullet crease."

"You're right, the papers would just make it more official, but we've got more than enough to ensure your release without them. Any other officer than the colonel would take the information, clear your name, and it would all be over. There's really no need for a trial."

Will nodded his agreement. *That sniper had no idea how much trouble he was causing when he sent that slug for my head,* he thought. His headache continued to pound. "Josh, I think I'm going to stretch out for a while. That fight kinda wore me out."

"Sure, rest up. I'll wake you when breakfast comes." Josh moved to the barred window and gazed out at the fort.

Will leaned over, lifted his long legs, stretched them out on the bunk, and was asleep within minutes.

WILL HAD BEEN asleep for an hour when their food arrived. The private bringing it slid the two metal plates under the bars. There was a fork on each plate. "I'll be checking for those forks when I come back to pick up the plates," he said, turned and left. He returned quickly with a bucket of water and a dipper. He set it down just outside the door, where they could reach it, and left without a word. They each picked up a plate, moved back to their bunks, and sat.

Will looked at the beans and salt pork before he started eating. Then he held the plate to his nose. There was no rotten smell from the salt pork, and the whole thing smelled pretty good. He scooped up a forkful and thrust it into his mouth. *Not bad,* he thought. "I've tasted worse," he said to Josh.

Josh just grunted as he ladled his second fork load into his mouth. The two finished and stood together. If it weren't for Will's gray hair, from behind, they looked like twins. Both had the wide shoulders of a hardworking Logan and stood two inches above six feet, without their boots. They towered over the average man.

After sliding their plates under the bars, Will reached through and scooped a dipper full of water. Bringing it carefully back through the bars, he handed it to his brother. Josh took it and drank it down. "Thanks. I needed that after the salt pork."

"More?"

"No, that's plenty for now," Josh said, and walked back to his bunk.

Will got himself a drink and had just dropped the dipper back into the bucket when he heard Deborah arrive. The private brought her back, slid the plates aside with his boot toe, and moved the bucket so that it could still be reached but no longer blocked the cell door. Once the door was clear, he unlocked it and stepped aside, allowing Deborah to enter.

"Thank you, Private. You've been very kind."

The young man, with the wide scrawny shoulders of youth, blushed pink. "Why, it ain't nothin', ma'am. I'm powerful pleased to help. I heard you was a nurse during the war, and you helped a bunch of soldiers. That was mighty nice of you."

"Yes, I was a nurse, and it was my pleasure to help such brave men like you."

The private now turned a bright crimson and said, "Yes, ma'am," as he locked the door behind her. "Sorry I have to lock this door. Regulations, you know."

"It's quite all right." She smiled to him, turned, and stepped quickly to Will.

The private turned to go. "Private?" she said. "Would it be possible for the major and first sergeant to get a pitcher or two of water to freshen up some. My husband has quite a bit of blood on him he needs to wash off. A couple of towels would also be very nice."

A warm, tender feeling flushed through Will upon hearing Deborah say my husband.

"I'm right sorry, ma'am," the private said. "I ain't got any pitchers or washbowls, but I can bring another couple of buckets if that would help."

She smiled at him and said, "That would be wonderful."

He hurried off on his mission, and Deborah held out her loaded arms to Will. "I've brought clothing for you both." Turning to Josh, she said, "I hope you don't mind. I had to go into your bag, but I felt you might like to change before the trial."

"I appreciate you thinking of me," Josh said as Deborah handed him the trousers, shirt, and socks.

She grinned. "Us Logans have to stick together."

Josh and Will both laughed. Will picked her up and swung

her in a circle, all three of them laughing as if they didn't have a care in the world.

"Put me down, you animal," she said through her laughter.

He finally stopped, placing her gently on the floor, and moved his hands from her waist to her shoulders. Gazing into her uplifted brown eyes, he said, "Mrs. Logan, you are a joy to behold."

She stepped closer, went on her toes, and kissed him lightly on his lips. "Thank you, Mr. Logan. Now get that shirt off. I hear the private returning."

Sure enough, the young man returned with two buckets of water and two towels slung over his shoulder. "Sorry about the water, ma'am. It ain't heated, but it's the best I can do. I grabbed a couple of towels from the laundry. There ain't no washcloths."

"You did very well. Thank you so much."

The young man set the buckets by the door, took the key, opened the cell door, and swung it open.

"You must tell us your name," Deborah said.

The private grinned. "My name's John Frederick Grayson, ma'am, but everyone just calls me Johnny."

"May I call you Johnny?" she said.

Blushing again, he said, "Oh yes, ma'am. I'd be pleased."

"Good, and you can call me Deborah."

When the door swung open, Josh jumped up to give Private Grayson a hand. It startled the young man, and he quickly started to close the cell door.

"Oh, no, Private Grayson," Josh said, "I'm just coming over to help with the water. You needn't be concerned with any of us."

Relieved, Private Grayson said, "Yes, sir, I'm not used to having such fine folks in here as you. Most of 'em what gets tossed in here would stick you as soon as look at you. 'Ceptin' those who get tossed in for tying one on. They's mostly harmless."

Will watched the private's immediate response to Josh's quick movements. *He might be young, but he's alert, probably does a good job at anything he's told to do.* "Thank you, Private Grayson. It's a kind thing you're doing. I'd hate to go into a courtroom with blood all over me."

"You're welcome, First Sergeant. I'm glad to help. By the way, the doctor did mention he would be coming over before the trial to check and rebandage your head."

"That's good to know, thanks."

The private nodded, locked the cell, and retired to the front office.

Will had pulled his bloody shirt off. While Josh had done the same and was cleaning up across the cell, Deborah grasped one end of the towel, wet it in the bucket, and began to wash the dried blood from her husband's body. Her small hands worked expeditiously across his chest, shoulders, and back, cleaning and moving on, hesitating almost imperceptibly when they reached a scar from an old wound.

As she cleaned, she looked over at Josh. His thick chest, a pale white contrast, like his brother's, to the sun- and wind-darkened hands, face, and neck, bore similar scars. "You two are alike in more ways than size and temperament."

Will grinned and said, "That's why the girls like us."

Deborah drew back and punched him in the old bayonet scar on his right side. He bent over, groaning and feigning pain.

Unfazed, she said, "Don't try to kid me, mister, and there'd better not be any girls seeing these scars."

Josh winked at Deborah as he spoke to Will. "You'd better listen to her, kid. I get the feeling she is one nurse you can't put anything over on."

"You are so right, brother," Will replied. "And they don't come any tougher."

"Sit up straight now, and be still," she ordered. Deborah carefully unwrapped the bandages. She wet the bloody ones nearest the wounds and gently removed them from his head, then continued cleaning gently around the wounds. "Your poor head," she said. Then, almost to herself, "How many blows can one man take to his head? I wonder how it affects the brain."

"I'll be fine, honey. We didn't find each other again to have anything else crazy happen. We have a good life ahead of us. We'll take this one day at a time, and before we know it, all this will be behind us."

She sighed. "I know you're right, Will. I would just like for it to be sooner than later. Oh, I didn't tell you. Aunt and Uncle James came in earlier, along with your mother and most of your family. I was surprised to see your uncle Floyd riding in with two of his friends."

Will smiled at the mention of Floyd. Their uncle had been a mountain man with the likes of Bridger, Beckworth, Carson, and Jedediah Smith. "Were the friends his age, or thereabouts?"

"Yes, Morg and Shorty. And the two were arguing."

Both Will and Josh laughed at her response. "Honey," Will said, "those two have been arguing since they first met over thirty years ago. At least, Shorty has been arguing with Morg. Morg mostly just lets it run off him, like water off a slicker."

5

Will heard the guardhouse door slam open, and Floyd Logan's voice reverberated within the adobe walls. "What the blue blazes is this? What's my nephews doing locked up in here? This army doesn't have the sense God gave to a stump."

Shorty's deep voice joined in. "They ain't never had no sense, Floyd, and you know it. Now, boy, let us see them Logans."

Private Grayson's voice, though young and shocked, responded in a firm tone. "You gentlemen must calm down. You can see the major and first sergeant, but you can't take those weapons back there. You'll have to leave them here."

"Dad-blame it, boy," Shorty said, "I ain't leavin' these guns nowhere but where they are right now."

"Then, sir, you will immediately leave the guardhouse."

Will heard Shorty say, "We'll see about that." Then solid footsteps marched toward the door.

"Unlock this door, boy," Floyd said.

"No, sir," Grayson replied. "You will not go back there armed."

Will shook his head and yelled to the office, "Floyd, give your weapons to Private Grayson, and calm down. We're fine, but we'll be leaving for court anytime. If you want to see us, make it quick."

There was silence from the front, interrupted only by what must have been Shorty murmuring. Eventually, the door opened, and the three men marched down the hallway, led by Private Grayson. He gave Will a look of relief as he unlocked the cell door to allow the three to enter.

Floyd pushed through, going straight to Deborah. "Boy, what in Sam Hill are you doin' gettin' hitched to this pretty young thing while we're off guiding pilgrims? Don't you have any respect for your uncle?"

He grabbed Deborah, lifted her off the floor, and gave her a huge hug.

Her laughter fill the jail as he released her to Morg and then to Shorty. When Shorty released her, she slapped Floyd on the shoulder and said through her laughter, "We told you we were going to marry in May. You three are the ones who decided to disappear into those mountains." She stopped and looked around. "Where's Jeb? Isn't he with you?"

Shorty jumped in. "He shore is, but he's gettin' to be an old man. He headed for the ranch afore we met the folks headed over here. Though he might run into Callum and his bunch headed back with them papers Will needs."

Will watched his uncle. He didn't look his age, if you discounted the sun-scorched and wind-blasted hide of his face. He stood tall, not as tall as his nephews, but pushing six feet. The wide shoulders hadn't lost muscle as many old men did, but still filled out the buckskin shirt covering them. He looked the hard man that he was, tempered in the furnace of survival in his beloved mountains. The knife scar, from the left side of his chin to his jaw, the first of many, still showed plain in the dark skin. But the eyes were most striking, the color of the deep ocean that could pierce a person like an arrow.

Once the greetings were over, Floyd said, "Now tell me, boys, what's going on? I truly ain't never heard of such a thing. And I heard troopers talking about a hangin'? What's with that? Even if you were guilty, I can't say I can remember more than one or two men hanged for desertion. Maybe a short term in prison, cutting logs, or getting drummed out of the service, which has always seemed stupid to me, seeing that's what a deserter wants anyway, but not hangin'."

"You haven't met this colonel, Uncle. I'm not sure he isn't a little off-kilter. He's got some witness who says he knew me during the war, back in my unit, but I have no recollection of him."

Deborah joined in. "That could be from your head injury, Will. There is so little known about brain injuries and memory loss. It's possible to get some memories back and not others. We just don't know."

"Doesn't matter," Floyd said. "There will be no Logan hanged if I can do anything about it."

"Don't do anything rash, Floyd," Will said. "At least not yet. Hopefully the papers will get here in time, and this will all be settled."

The sound of the guardhouse door opening, followed by a chair scraping on the stone floor, reached them. Private Grayson could be heard greeting the doctor and Captain Smyth. Then Captain Smyth ordered men to wait in the office, and he, along with the doctor, entered the hallway with Private Grayson. At the sight of the three mountain men, he looked at Grayson but said nothing. The private continued to the cell and unlocked the door.

When they entered, the doctor headed straight for Will, and Josh said, "Captain, Doctor, this is our uncle, Floyd Logan, and friends Morg James and Shorty Zebulon."

The captain shook hands with all three men. "Yes, I have heard many good things of you all. I'm sorry we have to meet under these circumstances."

"You ain't the onliest one, Captain," Shorty said. "Sounds like this colonel of yours needs a little straightening out. His kind of justice don't float the boat out here in the west."

Before the captain could respond, Floyd jumped in. "We want justice for Will, Captain Smyth, as I'm sure you do."

"Yes, sir, I certainly do. Hopefully we will get it."

"Sit, Will," the doctor said after nodding to the other men. While their conversation continued, he asked, "Tell me, how do you feel? Are you having any dizziness, any headache, nausea?"

From when he had been in the hospital for his battle wounds, Will had learned to be straight with the doctors. If he told them the truth, they were better able to help him, rather than if he tried to tough it out. As Will spoke, the doctor began examining his head. "I haven't had any nausea. There was some dizziness right after the incident, but I haven't had any since. This morning I had a pretty bad headache, but I lay back down, slept for a short while, and when I woke, it was gone. Other than just a sore head and neck, I feel good."

"Excellent," the doctor said. "Your wounds look fine. I don't think I'll need to sew anything." While he worked with the bandage, he said to Deborah, "You did a fine job of cleaning him up. I wish I had you here to work with me. All I have are orderlies to assist."

Floyd smiled and said, "Too bad, Doc. She goes with me."

"Yes," he replied, finishing up the bandage. "I can certainly understand why. Hopefully the two of you will be on your way this evening."

"Thank you, Dr. Taylor," Deborah said.

Will heard Captain Smyth say, "We must be on our way. Court starts at precisely ten o'clock."

Standing, Will picked up his hat and tried it over his bandage. It was snug, but not too tight. "I'm ready when you are, Captain."

"Fine. I'll need to put the manacles back on."

Floyd bristled. "Captain Smyth, we're on an army post. You've got guards. Can you explain to me why you need to put those things on him?"

The captain stiffened. He turned to Private Grayson, who had fetched the irons. Before answering Floyd, he said to Grayson, "Latch them on him, but you can make them loose." Then he looked back at Floyd. "Mr. Logan, I understand you're concerned for your nephew, but you have been a scout for the army. You know that as a captain I follow orders, and as you are a civilian, I owe you no explanation."

Morg stood calmly watching the captain, but his eyes were pulling down tight, and the back of Shorty's neck was turning red. Will could see his uncle had locked the captain in a cold stare.

"However, I will tell you I do not believe your nephew should even be in here. The colonel has ordered he be transported with the shackles on. That is the end of it."

Will stepped forward and extended his wrists for Private Grayson. "Here you go, Private. Let's get it over with."

The young man muttered softly, "Sorry," and fastened the manacles around his wrists.

Will moved his wrists and was thankful they were loose. Tight, they would have the skin from his wrists in no time. He looked at Captain Smyth. "I'm ready."

The captain nodded and said, "Mrs. Logan, you and Dr. Taylor, along with the other visitors, may go ahead."

She gave the captain a tight little nod and, as if it took extreme effort to take her eyes from the manacles on her husband's wrists, stood tall and gave Will a kiss on the cheek. "I'll see you in court." She squeezed his arm, and back straight with chin up, she marched down the hallway, followed by the doctor.

Will felt pride well up within him and thought, *She is my wife.* He watched the others go ahead of him. Once Shorty had passed, Josh stepped up to follow, but the captain held up his hand.

"Sorry, you stay."

"What?" both Josh and Will said simultaneously.

Will shook his head. "Captain, you can't do this, I need my brother there. He deserves to be there."

"I know, First Sergeant, but those are the colonel's orders."

Will's mind raced. He needed Josh there. His brother had been a major and had dealt with these types of situations, these types of trials. He would be able to correct or even guide whoever might be his defense. Without him, he had no idea how this farcical trial would go. Then the idea hit him. Of course.

"Captain, my brother, Major Joshua Logan, retired, will be my counsel. He must be there."

Will saw the surprise in both the captain's and Josh's eyes, but the captain hardly lost a beat.

"Very well, I agree. You must have your counsel there." He waved Josh ahead of Will.

As Josh walked by, Will caught the questioning look. He had seen it before. Josh was six years younger. Growing up, he had tossed Will that look every time Will was about to try something crazy. But it wasn't crazy. It might have been several years since his brother was in the army, but he knew Josh had a quick mind. He had confidence he was in better hands with him than anyone else. This was his life, here and now, and he knew Josh would take care of him as best he could.

A guard escort awaited him at the guardhouse entrance. If the trial was being held in the two-story building where the colonel had been waiting, then Will would be marched across the parade ground. He estimated that would be at least one hundred and fifty yards. *Well,* he thought, *the spectators will certainly get an eyeful.*

He stopped at the door. A typical Colorado morning awaited him. He could hear the larks singing on the parade ground. His eyes adjusted quickly to the brilliant sun. The sky reminded him of his mother's deep blue eyes. He could make out four buzzards sailing slowly in a circle on the heat beginning to rise from the ground. He watched their effortless flight, feeling the same foreboding he had felt the night before. *Shake it off,* he told himself. *You're not a superstitious man, and there's no reason to start now.* He stepped through the door to the outside.

At the same moment, as if he had been waiting for Will's eyes to adjust, Captain Smyth, in a conversational tone, said, "Forward, march." His six armed guards, three on each side, moved briskly across the parade ground, headed straight for the two-story building. Unconsciously, Will fell into step with them. Movement in the fort stopped, and all eyes tracked them, like a coyote watching a mouse.

Thankfully, they were across the parade ground in short order. They approached the porch and steps, and Smyth ordered, "Ready, halt."

Will stopped to let everyone else go in before him. He waited until everyone was clear, then without Smyth giving an order, he walked up the steps, across the porch, and into the vestibule. A soldier was just inside the door, directing traffic. Deborah and Josh had waited inside, and Will followed them across the small room, turned left down the hallway, and entered a large room that had been preplanned for a courtroom. He saw his mother and the rest of the family, along with friends, sitting behind what he guessed must be the defendant's table.

His ma, in the first row, had saved a place for Deborah. She had turned and was watching him. He felt sorry for her having to watch her son brought to a courtroom in manacles. For the first time, he was angry. This was all uncalled for. It could have been easily explained without going through all of this pomp, but he felt sure this was what the colonel wanted. He just happened to be the unfortunate subject.

He smiled at her, and she returned his smile, though she did look worried. Thankfully Deborah was there, and though his ma was tough as boot leather, this was an unfamiliar environment.

She might not be frightened, but he knew for sure she would be apprehensive.

His sister, Kate, was sitting on the other side of Ma. He almost grinned at his sister. She usually had an exceptional poker face, but today he could see her anger flash every time her eyes crossed a soldier.

"Move to the table in front of your folks," Captain Smyth said to Will. He simply nodded and kept moving. He could see several friends in the audience. He knew the men here from the Pueblo area would stand with him should a problem occur, but that was the last thing he wanted to happen. These were good men, and they didn't need to get crossways with the government.

He walked down the center aisle and, upon reaching the last row of spectators, turned left and walked to the table in front of his ma. Between the front row and the two tables, the one to the right was occupied with the prosecution, a rope had been strung to separate the active participants from the audience. Upon reaching the table, he held out his hands. Captain Smyth removed the manacles and nodded at the chairs. Josh took the one nearest the prosecution's table. Will sat in the remaining chair, leaned forward, and looked past Josh at the men in his jury, seated against the wall to his right, nearest to the prosecution.

At least the jury seemed to be a fair split, eight men, four of them officers, the senior a major, and four senior noncoms headed by a sergeant major. He saw no one who appeared angry at him. Hopefully, none of them had already made his mind up. Glancing farther to his right, he examined the lieutenant at the prosecution's table. He looked old for a lieutenant, had probably lost his more senior brevet grade, awarded during the war, to stay in until retirement.

As he was examining the table, a more junior lieutenant entered the courtroom and walked up to the table, looking perplexed. The young man stopped, looked down at Josh, and said, "Sir, I am Lieutenant Nixon, and that chair is for the defendant's counsel."

Josh stood, towering over him, and extended his hand. As the two men shook hands, Josh said, "Nice to meet you, Lieutenant Nixon. I understand your confusion. I am Major Joshua Logan, and I will be acting as First Sergeant Logan's counsel."

Lieutenant Nixon looked first at Josh, then Will. "You are First Sergeant Logan?"

"Yes," Will replied.

"And this is your desire?"

"Yes, Lieutenant. I want my brother to represent me."

The young man looked back at Josh. "But I have been appointed by Colonel Cracken to represent the first sergeant."

Josh nodded. "Of course, but, as you have just heard, First Sergeant Logan has requested I defend him. Is that a problem, Lieutenant?"

At this point, the prosecuting officer rose and stepped to the lieutenant's side. "I am Lieutenant Hooper. Is there a problem?"

"No problem, Lieutenant Hooper. I was just telling this young man, I am Major Joshua Logan, and I will be defending the First Sergeant. Is that an issue?"

The older man shook his head. "As far as I'm concerned, I see no problem, Major. But I will tell you, the colonel will not be happy, and he is the presiding authority today."

Josh gave the man an icy smile and said, "I am sorry to hear that. On both counts. Thank you for the information."

"Glad to be of assistance." He turned to the younger man. "Give Major Logan your documents, references, and manuals. The colonel will be out shortly. Don't leave until he dismisses you."

"Yes, sir," the young man said, and stood, embarrassed, next to the desk. There was room at the table for three or four people, so Josh stood, slid his chair to Lieutenant Nixon, and motioned to a private near the back door to bring him another chair. "You can sit at the table if you like. I might be a little rusty, and you will certainly be a help."

"Yes, sir. Thank you, sir," the lieutenant said, and seated himself. Josh, still standing, turned to the audience, slipped past Will, and stopped when he reached his second-youngest brother. "Bret, we need your help."

"Sure," Bret said. "What can I do?"

"Get yourself a couple of horses, and hightail it back toward Pueblo. The boys are coming in with tired animals, so they'll be slowing down. If you could meet them with fresh ones, grab the papers, and head right back, could be those minutes might make a difference."

Floyd had been listening. "I'll go with you."

"Sure thing, Uncle Floyd," Bret said.

Will had been listening. He leaned back and said, "Floyd, you already have a lot of riding under your belt today. You sure you want to do this?"

"It isn't about what a man wants, boy, it's about what's needed. We'll be back with the papers."

Shorty and Morg started to rise. Floyd shook his head and gave the two a knowing look, his eyebrows slightly raised. "You two best stay. You might be needed, if you get my drift."

A glance passed between the two. Morg and Shorty nodded. "You can depend on us, Floyd. Luck," Shorty said.

Floyd gave a nod and said, "Let's go, boy."

Will watched his kin, one his uncle, the other his brother, hurry from the courtroom. *Godspeed,* he thought.

A door slammed at the side of the courtroom, and a sergeant called, "All rise."

_____

6

Will stood at the call. His muscles felt like they had been pulled taut with tension, and his senses were alive. Among the odors filling the room, some from unwashed bodies, others perfume, and still others the scent of shaving soap, he could pick out the faint bouquet of Deborah sitting just behind him. The perfume was that of soap. Clean and crisp, yet soft, like a rose in the morning.

The hustle and bustle of a busy fort was missing. There was no sound of horses neighing, hooves or boots on the parade ground, or commands. It was eerily quiet, as if the post knew something was about to happen and was holding its breath in anticipation.

Colonel Cracken, in full dress uniform, boots and brass glistening in the light from the open windows, marched to the desk located at the front of the room, pulled the chair farther out, sat, and slid back to the desk. "Be seated," he ordered.

Will, along with everyone else, sat. He heard the rustle of dresses, combined with that of boots scraping, and a general sigh from the gallery. He watched the colonel take out a small pair of glasses, hook the wire ends over his ears, adjust the small round lenses in their proper position on his sharp nose, and begin silently reading from a folder he had opened. The room was silent except for an occasional cough or sneeze while he read. Just before he spoke, a small mouse stuck its head out from a crack in the corner molding, tiny eyes surveying the room, nose twitching rapidly, and ducked back into his safe space. An almost imperceptible grin slipped across Will's face. *I don't blame you, little fellow. If I could slip through that crack, I'd be right there with you.*

It was that moment Colonel Cracken chose to look up, and the frown that had already been on his face deepened as he said, "First Sergeant Logan, I see nothing funny about your situation. Perhaps you could share with the court what gives you the reason to smile under your dire circumstances here today."

Before Will could stand, Josh leaned over and said softly, "Keep your head. This is not the time to say what you'd like to. This nut holds your life in his hands."

Will took a deep breath and stood. "Sorry, sir. I was just watching a mouse."

"A mouse?"

"Yes, Colonel. He stuck his head out from that crack in the corner." At this point Will pointed to the corner. The colonel turned to his side, looked, and Will could hear the people in the audience moving and shuffling to get a better view. "He came out, looked around, decided he didn't want to be here, and disappeared back in his hole. I was wishing I had a hole to disappear into. I wasn't trying to disrespect the court."

Colonel Cracken coughed, cleared his throat, and said, "While you're up, can you explain what your brother is doing here?"

Josh rose, along with Lieutenant Nixon. Josh said, "Colonel, my brother, First Sergeant Logan, asked that I be his counsel. I have checked with the prosecutor, and he is fine with it."

The colonel turned back to Will. "Is this a scheme to get your brother out of the guardhouse? He will still be tried for discharging a firearm with intent to harm inside a military building and his attempted rescue of you."

Will started to answer, but Josh laid his hand on his brother's arm and said, "Colonel, I discharged my revolver in the defense of the first sergeant. I was rescuing him from the attackers, but certainly not trying to break him out of the guardhouse."

The colonel picked up his gavel by the mallet head and pointed the handle at Josh. "I have witnesses who say different. They say you would have killed them if Captain Smyth had not arrived."

"Colonel, those are bald-faced lies, and those men are the dregs of the army. I'm here to defend an innocent man, and that's what I'm going to do."

Colonel Cracken's face turned bright red during Josh's defense. The gavel handle centered on Josh as the colonel shook it at him. "You are not going to defend him. He has a defense. I appointed Lieutenant Nixon. That is who will defend your brother—not you." Spittle flew from the colonel's lips with the last words, almost a shout.

Lieutenant Hooper was on his feet. "Sir, I beg your pardon, but I would be remiss, as counsel for the prosecution, if I did not remind you that First Sergeant Logan has the right to request anyone as counselor. Major Logan is more than qualified. I am afraid that higher command will look very dimly on this proceeding if the major is not allowed to retain his position as counsel for First Sergeant Logan's defense."

The colonel leaned forward in his chair, elbows on his desk, fists clinched, left forearm lying flat, and right guiding the gavel. His bloodshot eyes, wide and glaring, shifted from first Lieutenant Hooper, then to Lieutenant Nixon, and finally to Josh. He sat in that rigid position for several moments, as if considering the ramifications of the higher command that Lieutenant Hooper had mentioned. Then, abruptly, he relaxed, laid his gavel down, and fell back in his chair.

He tossed a regal wave of his left hand. "Yes, yes, of course. The guilty man should have the counsel he requests."

Josh immediately said, "Colonel, I object to you labeling the first sergeant as guilty. That has not been proven, and in fact he will be proven innocent of the charge."

The colonel again waved a hand and said, "Noted. Lieutenant Nixon, you will remain as assistant counsel, and let me know if anything untoward takes place."

"Yes, sir," Nixon said haltingly as he looked at Lieutenant Hooper, who shrugged and gave a slight shake of his head.

Colonel Cracken leaned forward again. "Shall we get on with this?" He looked around as if expecting someone to challenge him, then continued, "This is a hearing to determine the guilt or innocence of First Sergeant William Wallace Logan, of the charge of desertion under fire. He will be tried by eight good men and if found guilty will be hanged by the neck until dead."

There was a gasp in the room.

Lieutenant Hooper started to rise, paused, and sat down again.

Colonel Cracken surveyed the room, with obvious satisfaction, and said, "Lieutenant Hooper, please present your case."

The lieutenant rose. "Colonel." He turned to the eight men who would be hearing the case. "Members, I will provide evidence of First Sergeant Logan's desertion under fire, given by the testimony of a living witness." He turned back to the colonel. "I call Private Dirvish Dean Dirksen to the stand."

Hearing the full name of the private, Will's mind clicked. It was as if a light had turned on, illuminating every detail of the evil little man. He leaned over to Josh.

"I remember Dirksen."

Josh leaned over to him and whispered, "He was in your unit?"

"Oh yeah. I'm surprised someone didn't kill him years ago. When they attacked me in the jail, I'm glad I didn't remember who he was. If I had, I might've killed him. He is the lowest form of life you'll ever meet."

"You remember clearly enough to testify about him and his actions?"

"Yes."

Josh slid several sheets of paper and a pen to Will and said, "Write down as much as you can remember so I can cross-examine him with it."

Will began writing as Dirksen, his forearm heavily bandaged and in a sling, walked forward and was sworn in. He sat in a chair just to the left of Cracken's desk, directly in front of the prosecution and between the colonel and the jury members. He took his seat, grinned nervously at the colonel and then the members.

Lieutenant Hooper, still standing, addressed the witness. "Private Dirksen, how long have you been in the army?"

"Why, Lieutenant, we figgered that out together. You know."

"Yes, I know, but the members would like to also know. Would you please tell them."

Dirksen turned to the eight members. "It's been nine years. I joined in sixty-one, right after the war began."

"Thank you," Lieutenant Hooper continued. "Now tell me, in your own words, how you know First Sergeant Logan."

"Why, like we done talked about, he was in my unit. I took care of the horses. I done a right smart job, too. But that there Logan, he's a mean man." Dirksen held out his arm, pointing at Will. "For some reason he took a big dislike to me."

Lieutenant Hooper turned, and he too pointed at Will. "You're sure this is the man, First Sergeant Logan? The man you speak of?"

Dirksen's face twisted in confusion. "Why, hell, Lieutenant, ain't we done agreed that's him?"

Colonel Cracken had been sitting relaxed in his chair, leaned back, listening to Dirksen. Now he whipped forward and banged his gavel hard. The sound reverberated in the room, causing Dirksen to jerk, almost leaping from his chair. Leaning toward Dirksen, the colonel said, "Private, I will have no swearing in my courtroom. Do you understand me?"

Dirksen looked up at the colonel, then quickly diverted his eyes to the floor. "Yes, sir. I surely do. I'm mighty sorry."

"Good," the colonel said. "Lieutenant, you may continue."

"Yes, sir," Lieutenant Hooper said. He took a deep breath, for he too had jumped when the gavel was banged, and said, "In your own words, Private, tell me what happened."

"Well, sir, it's pretty simple. Nearing the end of the war, we was whipping them Rebs something fierce. I was taking care of the reserve horses when they sent word to send up the first sergeant's horse to the command tent. It was a big black horse, a real beauty. I get there in time to see the colonel hand a packet to First Sergeant Logan, and I heard him say it was important to get those dispatches to the general."

Lieutenant Hooper nodded as if he were hearing the information for the first time. He turned to face the jury and asked, "Was there a battle going on?"

"I'll say, one big"—he turned quickly to look at the colonel—"old battle, for sure. Guns of all kinds was goin' off. Cannons were blastin'. It was a sure enough big fight. Though we had 'em on the run, them Rebs, every now and then, would turn around and fight like regular catamounts."

"When did the first sergeant return?"

"That's just it, Lieutenant, he ain't never returned. Why even after the fighting ended, we ain't seen hide nor hair of him. All them officers and senior sergeants walked around all mopey like. They all figured he'd been kilt. That's what everybody figgered until I seen him in Pueblo. I'd know him anywhere. Why, he just rode off and never come back. Just like the yellowest slinkin' coward they is."

"All right, Dirksen, that's enough," Lieutenant Hooper said. He returned to his seat and before sitting said, "I'm through with this witness."

At his words, Dirksen stood and started back to his seat.

"Just a minute, Private," the colonel said. "Sit back down in the witness chair. You're not done yet."

Dirksen looked around, confused. "But I just testified. Ain't that all?"

Josh, with the notes Will had written, stood, blocking Dirksen's path to his chair in the gallery. "No, Private Dirksen, I get to question you now."

"Logan, it is not your place to tell the witness anything. I will take care of this." The sharp tone the colonel used to address Josh softened as he spoke to the private almost like a person would speak to a child. "Private Dirksen, the defense gets the opportunity to ask you a few questions. It shouldn't take long. Understand, you are still under oath. Now please take your seat."

Dirksen looked like a fox caught in a chicken coop. His eyes were wide, but they grew even wider when they looked up at Will and saw the grim expression on the big man's face. He returned to the witness chair and licked his lips several times, his head turning left and right as if looking for an escape route but finding none.

"Private Dirksen, it is private, isn't it?"

The skinny man's oversized Adam's apple bobbed up and down as he swallowed. He managed to get out, "Yeah, private."

"Let's see," Josh said as he walked toward the jury. "You've been in the army for nine years and have never attained a higher rank?"

Again he swallowed. "That's right."

"Never?"

"That's right."

"You never wanted or worked for a promotion?"

"Guess not."

Lieutenant Hooper stood. "Colonel, I don't see the need to badger the witness. The fact that he has never attained a higher rank has no bearing on this case."

Colonel Cracken looked at Josh. "Move along. Get off this rank subject."

Josh nodded. "Colonel, if you will bear with me, you will soon see the importance."

"Make it quick."

Josh walked back to the table, shuffled the papers, picked up one, and while examining it turned back to the witness. "I will give you one more chance to correct your testimony, Private. Have you ever held a higher rank than private?"

Dirksen turned to Colonel Cracken. "It ain't important, Colonel. It was a long time ago."

Scowling, the colonel said, "Answer the question, Private Dirksen."

The little man coughed, cleared his throat, and mumbled, "Yes."

"I'm sorry, Private. I couldn't hear you. Would you repeat that?"

This time he looked up, hate in his eyes, and loud enough for everyone to hear him, said, "Yes."

"What rank was that?"

"Corporal."

Lieutenant Hooper leaned back to a sergeant sitting behind him, and whispered something. The sergeant jumped up and rushed from the room.

Josh watched the man leave the room, held Lieutenant Hooper's gaze for a moment and turned back to Dirksen.

"*Private* Dirksen, would you please tell the court why you no longer hold the rank of corporal."

"I was busted."

Josh nodded. "In my experience, a man can be reduced in rank for many reasons, being away without leave, dereliction of duty, drunk and disorderly, just to name a few. Were any of the reasons I mentioned the reason you were, as you said, 'busted'?"

"No."

"Well, then, Private Dirksen, perhaps you could tell the court the reason for your demotion."

Dirksen squirmed in his chair. Sweat covered his forehead, and his blouse had darkened at his armpits.

"We are waiting, Private Dirksen."

Dirksen again muttered his answer so low it was barely audible. "Cruelty to animals."

Josh repeated the man's statement and added, "This, in an army that is used to having to run horses, mules, and oxen until they drop from exhaustion, starvation, or thirst. An army that understands, as unfortunate as this cruelty is, it is necessary." He paused and took the time to look each member of the jury in the eyes. "An army that at times must do this, *busted* you for cruelty to animals. Is that correct?"

The little man's eyes flashed. He sat up straight in the witness chair, stabbed a rigid arm at Will, and said, "'Cause of him! He always hated me and picked on me 'cause I was smaller than him. He gave me all the"—Dirksen caught himself, looked up at the colonel—"all the dirty details. It was all his fault."

Josh, standing in front of the jury, turned and looked at Will. He gazed silently toward his brother for several moments, then turned back to Dirksen. "Why didn't he like you, Private?"

At Josh's question, Lieutenant Hooper stood. "Colonel, why Private Dirksen thinks First Sergeant Logan either liked or disliked him has absolutely no bearing on this case."

Colonel Cracken nodded, turning to Josh. "Logan, how much longer do you plan on questioning this witness?"

"I'm about finished, Colonel."

"Good. Then drop Private Dirksen's feelings and move along."

"Yes, Colonel. I only have one more question." He turned back to Dirksen. "Private, what happened to your arm?"

"I was in an altercation."

"Where?"

"You know where. You was there."

"Yes, but would you tell the court, please?"

"I got it tryin' to keep your brother from escaping the guardhouse."

"So you work there?"

"No, I was just walking by when Corporal Locher called for help. So I went in to help him."

"I see," Josh said. He had moved back to the defense table and was studying the paper he had picked up previously. He laid it back down and looked up at Dirksen.

"By yourself?"

Here again Dirksen hesitated.

Finally, Josh said, "Private Dirksen, if you will answer the questions, this will go much faster for you."

"No, I wasn't by myself. Some friends was with me."

Josh nodded at the answer. "Some friends. Would you tell me what you were doing, just strolling within earshot of someone deep in the guardhouse, at five o'clock this morning?"

Dirksen, now covered with sweat, took a dirty handkerchief from a pocket and wiped his face. "I don't know. We was just there." He turned to the colonel, his voice, except for his outbursts, had become high and whiney. "Colonel Cracken, sir, how much longer do I need to do this? My arm is hurtin' something fierce."

The colonel looked at Josh.

"Truly, Colonel, I am just about finished."

Colonel Cracken looked back at the private. "Just a few more minutes, Private," and he gave Josh a warning look.

Josh nodded. "Private, you and four of your *friends* just

happened by the guardhouse this morning? You and those same friends just happened to be armed with clubs? I found all of you inside First Sergeant Logan's cell, attempting to kill him, though you seemed to be getting the short end of the stick. By the way, how is your friend who tried to smash the first sergeant's skull in while he was sleeping?"

A low rumble came from the gallery as everyone began speaking at once. Lieutenant Hooper leaped to his feet, and Colonel Cracken reached for his gavel.

Josh raised his voice to be heard over the crowd and said, "No more questions, Colonel. I'm finished with this witness."

Private Dirksen looked at the judge, who nodded, and surged up from the witness chair and hurried out of the courtroom.

"You have any more witnesses, Lieutenant Hooper?"

The lieutenant rose and said, "No, sir. Other than asking that the Order of Apprehension and Arrest for First Sergeant William Wallace Logan, from the Department of the Army, be read into the record, the prosecution rests."

Though the high temperature in Fort Lyon, in May, rarely reached eighty degrees, the heat from the packed crowd in the courtroom was approaching ninety with little airflow, though the windows were open. Will could feel the sweat trickling, in tiny rivulets, down his back. He could see the men in the jury were suffering in their dress uniforms and felt sure the women in the gallery must be suffering in their uncomfortable dresses. The swish of many fans could be heard as those who had them plied them diligently. He watched a note passed from the jury to the colonel. The man read it and nodded.

"Ladies and gentlemen, we will take a short break of no more than fifteen minutes. There will be no luncheon break. I want to finish this today. When we return, we will hear from the defense." He rose, and the jury and gallery did likewise. As soon as the colonel was out of the room, the jury and most of the spectators followed his example. Captain Smyth and the guards remained to keep watch on Will, but did not approach.

Will stood and said to Josh, who was still standing, "What do you think?"

"I think the jury is on our side, but I'm not so sure about the colonel."

Will nodded, unable to keep the signs of concern from his face.

7

F loyd and Bret raced from the fort, each leading an extra
horse. Floyd glanced at Bret dashing alongside him.
Though feeling the urgency, he felt proud to be riding
along with another of his nephews. Matthew, his brother, and
Rebecca, his sister-in-law, had done a fine job of raising their
brood. Bret had grown taller than him. He grinned into the wind
as he thought, *Guess I'm truly the runt in the family. All my brothers
and now all my nephews are taller than me.* He laughed out loud,
the buckskin under him eating up the plains in a long, fine stride.
*But Ma and Pa still didn't do bad by this old man. They got me over six
feet and gave me the strength and wit to last years in these here mountains.* He laughed again, this time receiving a strange look from
his nephew. He turned and flashed a toothy grin at the young
man and saw it returned. The boy's hat brim bent back in the
wind as he guided the big gray west.

Though they raced across the plains, Floyd continuously
scanned the prairie ahead, both near and far. He had survived
more than thirty years in this country and had learned the neces-
sity for being alert at all times. *It might be 1870,* he thought, *but
there's still hostiles around who can lift your hair as quick as a minute.*

But he also watched for other dangers. He wasn't worried about rattlesnakes. As fast as the horses were moving, a snake wouldn't have time to strike before they'd be gone, but a prairie dog hole could. He'd seen more than one horse dead and his rider killed or permanently injured from the racing animal shoving a foot into a prairie dog hole.

A herd of antelope dashed from a nearby buffalo wallow. He watched them glide across the plains for a short distance, wheel, stop, and stare. It was that curiosity that made the antelope susceptible to the hungry hunter. The riders continued their race west.

After a while, Floyd slowed his horse to a walk, Bret alongside.

Bret was grinning. "I know this is important for Will's sake, but I never get enough of galloping across these plains." He lifted an arm to point west. "Look at those blue mountains sticking up like God's own fingers. I still can't believe we live over there."

Floyd grinned back at his nephew, then grew serious. "Yep, boy, we're mighty lucky, and I dearly love them mountains. Howsomever, my old eyes are hankerin' for a sight of dust. The sooner we can spot those boys, the better."

Bret grew serious and, along with his uncle, strained his eyes for the first sight of dust that might indicate Callum and the boys arriving from the ranch.

THE JURY WAS BACK. Will, seated in the witness chair, relaxed as best he could and examined the gallery. All the women had fans going. At least that stirred the air, which was both a blessing and a curse. The sharp sweet smell of many unwashed bodies, cramped in a small hot area, filled his nose. But it wasn't distracting for him. He had smelled many things worse.

He had watched the jury from the defense table, but

somehow they looked different from this perspective. All eyes were turned toward him, waiting. It was as though he could see their minds weighing his appearance against Dirksen's description. He only hoped they had seen the little man's true character.

Then his eyes settled first on his ma, who was holding Deborah's hand and smiling reassuringly at him. He had admired her and Pa his entire life, except for the time of his amnesia. *I think I still felt her presence when times really got tough. She has always been an anchor, for all of us,* he thought. Then he looked into Deborah's eyes. He could read the concern in those deep brown eyes. She didn't look at all like his ma, but she was much like her. They both were strong women. Ma had had to be, with all the strong-willed boys she'd raised, not to mention Pa. He'd been quite a man. He had never made it out to see this western land because he'd given his life, back in Limerick, to save Callum and Bret.

Through the windows behind him, he could hear trace chains rattling and the squeak of a wagon as it slowly rolled by, accompanied by the laughter of two boys and a barking dog. There was a smell of dust in the light breeze that drifted through the window, battling with the smell of the crowded courtroom.

He was aware of the dampness under his arms and mentally examined himself. Was he scared at the possibility of a guilty verdict and a waiting rope? He didn't think so. He felt sure, even with the colonel's animosity, he would be acquitted. Those members of the jury were honest men, and once they heard his story, not one of them would convict him.

His mind returned to Deborah and the new life they would make. They'd go north, build a home of their own. He'd like to have a ranch much like Josh and Callum had built.

Josh's voice broke into his thoughts. Without rising from the defense table, he said, "Will, why don't you tell the members what happened and why you didn't return to your cavalry unit."

Will nodded, looked at the jury, cleared his throat, and began. "The battle was pretty much like what Dirksen said, up to my riding out." He then explained about his ride through the woods and the delivery of the dispatches. As he told the story, his mind traveled back to that horrendous day.

Blacky had been doing a supreme job, as he always did, cutting around the tall pines as he tore through the tall pine forest. The acrid smoke of burnt powder filled the air. The whine of deformed miniballs glancing off boulders, combined with the solid thunks of other slugs slamming into the trees around him, spurred them on.

He was low over Blacky's back as they raced through the trees. He knew how those Southern boys could shoot. He had grown up with their breed, had learned, like them, to shoot a long rifle as soon as he could lift it. If it weren't for the speed and dexterity of his big black horse, he'd have long ago been dead or wounded. He marveled that he and Blacky had made it all through the war without ever receiving a wound, neither from bullet nor saber.

Dashing in and out of the edge of the forest, he saw a Union detachment in the open field. They were cut off from their main force, and as hard as they were fighting, they were outnumbered and would soon be overrun and slaughtered. Pulling his Henry rifle from the scabbard, he turned Blacky straight for the carnage, rose up and started firing. He didn't wait to see the result of each round, but jacked the lever, throwing another .44-caliber round in the chamber, moved on to the next target, and pulled the trigger.

He pulled Blacky to a sliding halt in the midst of a hail of bullets. He bailed off and continued firing his Henry. It was aim, squeeze the trigger, move on to the next target, squeeze the trigger, target another, and another. He fired until the rifle was empty, then yanked out his first .44 Remington revolver, emptied it, and drew another from the holstered pair he had on the saddle. A Reb bullet found his left leg, and he fell against Blacky, but the big horse held steady, supporting his weight. He continued firing until that pistol was empty. He could feel bullets slamming into Blacky, but his horse didn't move. Another round hit him in the left arm as he was drawing his last Remington from the holster. He continued the draw with his right and kept firing. A Reb drove his long bayonet into his side, and he shot him. Then it was over. The attack had broken. Blacky was staggering, and he was stroking his horse's cheek, knowing both he and the great, black horse were about to fall.

"And then, gentlemen," Will said to the jury, "the lights went out. It was like a curtain had been dropped over me, and everything stopped."

Will took a deep breath. He was sitting on the edge of the chair, leaning slightly forward, facing the members of the jury. Each of them had been leaning toward him, and they all took a deep breath, as he had, and leaned back in their chairs. He turned and saw his ma, her back stiff, dabbing at her eyes with a hankie. Kate and Deborah gripped each other's arms, tears streaming down their faces.

He looked at Josh and then back at the jury and said, "Sorry, don't think I've ever talked about that time like this. I sure liked that horse."

Josh cleared his throat. "Will, what happened after that?"

Will leaned back, listened to a mockingbird singing just outside the window, and said, "I can't rightly tell you. Several months later, I woke up in the hospital in Washington." At the thought, he grinned. "First thing I saw was this angel hovering over me. Figured I was in Heaven, 'cause Hell couldn't have anyone who looked that fine. Turns out it was my nurse, and I married her."

At that, everyone roared, some in humor, many in relief, happy for an opportunity to erase their personal tension. Even Lieutenant Hooper and the jury were laughing until Colonel Cracken banged his gavel, reminding everyone he was in charge.

"I'll have quiet in this courtroom, or I *will* empty it." He looked at Josh. "Keep your witness under control, Logan. I will not have levity in my courtroom."

Josh cleared the grin from his face and said, "Yes, Colonel."

"So, Will, how long did you have amnesia?"

"About three years."

"By what name were you known during that time?"

"Henry, I went by Hank, Remington."

At the mention of his alias, a cowboy sitting in the back row of the courtroom looked up, shoved his fingers under the edge of his hat, scratched, and then shook his head. Will saw the dusty man.

"Could you tell the members how you came up with that name?"

Will shook his head. "I didn't. Three men in the detachment that had been under attack gave it to me. They were Sergeant Liam MacGregor, Wade Dillon, and Darcy Smith. They became good friends."

Josh, looking puzzled, said, "Any reason they would give you that name?"

"Well," Josh said, a small grin on his face, "MacGregor said that I showed up blasting away with my Henry rifle and Remington revolvers, so it was only fitting I be called Henry Remington."

Heads in the gallery and in the jury nodded, along with a low chuckle that ran through the room.

"That was it. I wore that name for three years until my memory returned just a few months ago. Dr. James, not the fine gentleman who is in the courtroom, but his son, he treated me in Washington and specializes in brain injuries. He said this type of amnesia could last forever or return at any time, quite often with another traumatic event. That's what happened a few months back."

He had been looking out at Dr. James and now turned back to the jury. "I don't want to bore you with the three years I lived with the amnesia, let me just say that, in Pueblo, I was attacked and knifed in the back. The blade nicked a lung, and I developed an infection and near died. Fortunately, some of my family was in town, recognized me, and took me back to the ranch, along with Deborah. They all nursed me back to good health. It was during that time my memory returned."

Josh asked, "Did the army accept your alias?"

"Yes. Due to the report Dr. James filed, I was paid and discharged from the army under the alias of Henry Remington. At that time, I was told it would simplify things. If my memory ever returned, I was to return to a military facility and correct the records. They mentioned there was the possibility of the records listing me as a deserter under my correct name, but with the papers they gave me, the discrepancy would be cleared."

Josh, still seated, leaned forward and said, using Will's title for the first time, "First Sergeant Logan, did the army give you anything else?"

"Yes, they did. For the action that caused my amnesia, they gave me the Medal of Honor."

Suddenly, it was so quiet in the room you could hear the dust settle. All eyes were on Will.

Into the silence, Josh said, "Do you have the citation or medal or even the papers with you here in the courtroom?"

"I do not."

Josh frowned, tilted his head, and asked in a puzzled tone, "Why not?"

Will explained the location of the ranch and the time it would take to ride from there to Fort Lyon, closing with, "Colonel Cracken would not put the trial off until my family arrived with the papers."

Cracken, stoic behind his desk, made no comment.

Josh let the silence permeate the courtroom and finally said, "No more questions."

"Good," Colonel Cracken said. "Lieutenant Hooper, your witness."

"Thank you, Colonel," the lieutenant responded, then turned his eyes to Will. "That was a spellbinding and touching story, First Sergeant, but all we have is your word. Do you have anything else here that will prove you were in fact shot in such a manner as to cause you to lose your memory?"

"Sure, Lieutenant." Will reached up and started unwinding the bandage from around his head.

"Here, what are you doing?" Hooper asked.

"I'm unwrapping these bandages so that you can see the scar."

Dr. Taylor and Deborah leaped up at the same time. When she saw the doctor stand, Deborah sat back down.

"Colonel," the doctor said, "I need to be unfastening that bandage." Without waiting for permission, he marched to Will's side, took the loose end of the bandage and slowly continued unwrapping. The wounds he had received just this morning were still seeping blood. Dr. Taylor unwound enough of the bandage for Will to get to his hair.

Will knew the crowd could see a little of the gray showed through the long hair that covered the gouge. He said, "This is where I was shot in the head." He reached up and lifted the hair from over the wound, leaned forward so that it could be seen clearly, and heard the crowd gasp. He knew what it looked like, and after all this time, it still wasn't pretty. He turned his head so the jury members could get a good look. Each of them had leaned forward. Will said, "I think they've seen enough, Dr. Taylor. Why don't you go ahead and wrap it up."

The doctor made short work of wrapping, tucked the loose tip under the bandage, and moved back to his chair.

Will could see Deborah mouth, "Thank you," to Dr. Taylor as he walked past her.

"First Sergeant, did you get those fresh wounds during your escape attempt?"

Will smiled at the lieutenant. "No, Lieutenant, I did not."

"I'm sorry," Lieutenant Hooper said, "I thought you received those last night or, more correctly, early this morning."

"You are correct about the time, Lieutenant, but not about the occurrence. Corporal Locher, along with Dirksen and three others, slipped into my cell to either kill or maim me. I prevented that from happening. In the process, three of the attackers received injuries. The only thing preventing others from being hurt was my brother Major Logan showing up and discharging his firearm.

"And your main witness, Private Dirvish Dean Dirksen, is a cruel little weasel who would never tell the truth if he could lie."

A murmur traveled through the gallery.

Again, Colonel Cracken grasped his gavel, leaned forward, resting his forearms on his desk, and glared at the gallery. Finally, he sat back up and addressed Will. "First Sergeant Logan, please refrain from speculation and name-calling."

"I'm not name-calling, Colonel. Nor am I speculating. Dirksen is right about being in a unit I served with. I was battalion first sergeant, and he was in one of the companies. I will give him credit, he was, and is probably still, good with horses. Unfortunately, that is the only animal he is kind to."

Will looked over at Josh, who nodded for him to continue.

"Earlier than the action I was wounded in, but late in the war, we had set up camp near a home with a burned-out barn. One afternoon, I heard a thin cry, cut off quickly, coming from the barn. Drawing my weapon, I advanced quietly, expecting a wounded Reb. I entered, being as quiet as possible, and saw a man bent over something squirming. I was curious and slipped closer. There was a tiny kitten, on its back, legs tied and staked in four different directions. It had a rag stuffed into its tiny mouth. I will not continue to describe what this man was doing to this defenseless little creature, but he was using his knife, and it was disgusting. The kitten was in great pain. I took two quick steps, and the man turned and looked up at me. Just before I kicked him across the barn, I recognized Corporal Dirksen."

All of the jury and gallery were staring with shocked amazement at Dirksen. He squirmed in his chair only for a moment, then hurried for the courtroom door and disappeared down the hallway.

Will took a long breath, letting it out slowly. "I grabbed him by the collar and dragged him to battalion, where he was summarily busted by the battalion commander. If he hadn't been needed for the horses, I believe the colonel would have whipped him within an inch of his life.

"I will tell you something else," Will continued. "If small animals, especially cats, have been disappearing from the fort, don't make the mistake of blaming coyotes, Indians, or trappers. My bet is on Dirksen. He did it then, and I don't believe for a minute he has changed. The man is sick."

Even Colonel Cracken sat quietly, his face a picture of amazement.

Lieutenant Hooper, his face whiter than Will would expect of an army officer, for all of these men had seen the cruelty of battle, said softly, "No more questions, Colonel."

"Very well," the colonel replied. He turned to Will. "You may step down."

Once Will had returned to his seat, Josh stood and said, "Colonel, I'd like to call Deborah Logan to the stand. Until three days ago, her last name was Coleman."

The colonel called Deborah. She was sworn in and took her seat in the witness chair, her dress rustling around her hips and legs as she sat and placed her hands in her lap.

"Mrs. Logan, you are testifying freely?"

"I am," Deborah said.

Josh walked to a position in front of the jury and turned to face his sister-in-law.

"What is your profession?"

"I am a nurse."

"Where did you work during the war?"

"At Douglas General Hospital in Washington, DC. I worked directly with Dr. Louis James Jr. He dealt primarily with brain injuries."

"Is that where you met First Sergeant Logan?"

She looked into Will's eyes as if she were seeing the shot, unconscious man who was brought into the hospital.

"Yes, Douglas was where I first saw him. I didn't speak to him for several months because he remained in a coma."

Josh walked closer to Deborah. "I know this is hard, Deb—"

"No," she interrupted, "this is not hard. What is hard is seeing my husband falsely accused of desertion, something he would never do, and to see an evil little man have the opportunity to desecrate our military court system by being allowed to testify. That's what's hard."

Before her statement was ended, Cracken was banging his gavel. When she stopped, he shot a stern look at her. "Mrs. Logan, I will have you removed from this court if you have another outburst. Mind your manners and keep your place." His livid face turned to Josh. "Continue."

"When did he regain his memory?"

Her face was flushed, and Will knew she was angry. Deborah was a strong person, who was kind with patients, but let no one abuse her, and now, for his sake, she sat in the witness chair and listened to Cracken.

She said quietly, "Three years later. Long after the war. He was at the Logan ranch, west of Pueblo, a few months back."

Josh nodded, returned to the table, and said, "No more questions."

Lieutenant Hooper stood. "Mrs. Logan, are you a doctor?"

"No, I am a nurse."

"Then you are not licensed to proclaim diagnoses. Am I correct?"

"I am not."

"Thank you," Lieutenant Hooper said and started to sit.

"I am not," Deborah continued, "but my uncle is. He has seen Will both during and after his amnesia, and he is in this courtroom."

"I said thank you, Mrs. Logan," the lieutenant said and quickly sat.

"Are there any more questions for Mrs. Logan?" Colonel Cracken asked.

Both acting attorneys shook their heads.

"You may step down, Mrs. Logan," the colonel said.

As Deborah walked past him, Josh stood and said, "Colonel, I'd like to call my next witness."

The colonel, his face still flushed, said, "No, you will call no more witnesses, Logan. This trial will now go to the members of the jury. It will not be prolonged any longer."

8

The light was growing dim in the room. Though time had passed slowly to Will, it had passed, and the sun was setting. It had been a long day in the courtroom, but almost every person who was there for the beginning of the trial remained, tense in their chairs. Many sat aghast at the colonel's words. A stunned silence filled the dusty courtroom.

Will tried to contain himself. He had always been slow to anger. Even as a boy, it had taken quite a bit of aggravation to get him mad. But since yesterday, his temper had been rising. Because of this colonel, and yes, he was willing to concede, his negligence for not taking care of this as soon as his body healed from the stabbing, he was here in this courtroom being accused of treason against the country he had given so much to defend. He was mad. He was boiling mad.

He jumped to his feet, alongside Josh. "Colonel, I was ripped from my wedding, thrown into a guardhouse, assaulted in that same guardhouse by your own troopers, and then dragged into this mock court to be tried on a groundless charge. You bring me to trial, and now you won't even hear from the people who can exonerate me."

Behind him, Will heard a sharp intake of breath from the spectators, then someone yelled "Yeah!" and the crowd broke into raucous clapping, yelling, and boot stomping.

The colonel, his face turning brilliant red, yanked up his gavel and began pounding on the desk. "You will not address this court in such a manner, First Sergeant Logan! You are out of order!"

"No, sir," Will said. "*You,* sir, are out of order. You did not have to rush to trial. You didn't even need to have this trial. The papers coming from our ranch are the proof of what I've been telling you. All you had to do was wait for their arrival. But you wouldn't. I don't know why you have made this personal, but you have. I, sir, am not a deserter."

Throughout Will's statement, the courtroom was filled with the crash of the gavel. Over and over it slammed against the colonel's desk while he shouted, "Order! Order!"

In a loud, shaking voice, his eyes bulging as if they might explode from his head, he pointed the gavel at Will. "You will address me with the respect I am due. I am a colonel in the United States Army! I am the commander of this post! I can order anyone to do anything. No enlisted man of any rank will . . . will . . ." He jerked back from his desk and struggled to his feet while still waving the gavel in the general direction of Will. Abruptly, the gavel crashed to the floor, and both hands seized his head, holding, pressing against his skull. He stood for a moment, swaying like a sapling in an erratic breeze, said something unintelligible, and crashed to the floor.

Dr. Taylor and Deborah started forward even before the colonel collapsed. Will stood watching the two in action as they attended the fallen man. The colonel's wife rushed forward and knelt beside him, cradling his head while Deborah quickly unfastened his jacket and the doctor began examining him.

"Hold his head still," the doctor said to Mrs. Cracken, for the colonel was rolling his head back and forth.

The fallen man was talking but saying nothing coherent. Dr.

Taylor reached into his open bag, pulled out a bottle, shook it, and removed the cork. "Mrs. Cracken, you must hold his head still. This is laudanum. It will calm him if I can just get him to swallow some."

Will had moved forward and, along with many others, was watching the drama play out. He saw the colonel's wife trying unsuccessfully to hold the man's head as it jerked back and forth. The doctor spilled the narcotic down Cracken's cheek. Will dropped to his knees next to the colonel's wife and said, "Please, ma'am, let me help."

She looked at him, tears in her eyes. "But he has done such harm to you."

He shook his head. "It doesn't matter right now. He's mighty sick. I can help."

She relinquished her grip on her husband's head and moved far enough to allow Will to slide in and grasp the man's head in the iron grip of his big hands. He was amazed at the power in the colonel's neck. It took a tremendous amount of effort for him to hold the colonel's head still long enough for Dr. Taylor to administer the laudanum.

As soon as Colonel Cracken's head was motionless, Dr. Taylor placed the bottle to the man's lips and tilted. He watched the liquid flow into the colonel's mouth, let it pour for a moment, and lifted it.

"Good," he said to Will. "Continue to hold his head. The laudanum will work quickly, and he should start relaxing soon." He looked around and called, "I need a stretcher, now!"

While Will hung on, waiting, Dr. Taylor, seeing the crowd, waved his arm. "My gosh, folks. Give the man room to breathe. Move back. There's nothing else to see here."

The major who had been in the jury stepped forward. "Doc, is he going to be all right?"

The doctor looked up to see the concerned face staring down at him. "Major Forest, at this point, I cannot be sure." He looked at the colonel's wife kneeling beside her husband, her hands holding tight in her lap. "Let me get him to bed. Once I further examine him, I will be able to give you a more informed answer."

Will had relaxed his grip on the colonel's head, glanced at the man's wife, and moved away. As he moved away, Mrs. Cracken, in the same motion, moved in, sliding back under the colonel's head and cradling it in her lap. "Thank you, Mr. Logan. Thank you so much."

"Glad to help, ma'am."

He stood and turned to Josh. "So what now? Do I go back to the guardhouse?"

Major Forest looked across the prone, now relaxed, body of Colonel Cracken. "Have a seat back at the table. As soon as the colonel is out of here, we'll continue with the trial." He turned to a private and said, "Light the lamps. It's getting dark."

The private jumped to attention, said, "Yes, sir," pulled some matches from his pocket, and began lighting the lamps along the walls.

Dr. Taylor waved the stretcher bearers to the colonel's side. "Gently," he said to the two men. "Take him to his quarters. He'll be more comfortable than in the infirmary." He turned to Deborah. "I again owe you my thanks." She extended her hand. He took it and said, "It is a pleasure working with you."

The major helped Mrs. Cracken to her feet, and holding her husband's hand, she accompanied the stretcher from the courtroom.

Will and Josh, along with everyone else in the still crowded courtroom, returned to their seats. Major Forest remained standing at the front of the room. "Folks, we're going to finish this trial today. You are free to leave or stay."

He walked to the colonel's desk and sat, looked across the many faces, and said, "This may be a little unorthodox today, but I will replace Colonel Cracken and remain a juror." He looked at Josh, as if waiting for an objection. When he received none, he said, "Major Logan, feel free to call your next witness and as many as is necessary."

Josh stood. "Major, you can look through the rows behind me. There are quite a few character witnesses, but I will only call one more witness, Dr. James."

"Very well. Doctor?"

Dr. James rose, walked to the witness chair, swore to tell the truth, and sat.

"Dr. James," Josh began, "you are a medical doctor?"

"Yes," he replied.

"And you met William Logan when he was still Hank Remington."

"Yes, Josh. In fact, I met him when he first came into town, and when I met him, he was introduced to me as Hank Remington. My son, also Dr. James, had written me, several years previous, about Hank or Will's amnesia case."

"Thank you, Doctor. And when did you learn of Will's memory return?"

"When I rode out to check on him at the Logan ranch a few weeks after the fight and his stabbing. His memory had returned, almost fully."

"Thank you, Doctor," Josh said, and then to the major, "I have no more questions."

Major Forest glanced at the prosecutor, and Lieutenant Hooper shook his head. "Major Logan, do you have any other witnesses you'd like to call?"

Josh stood again and said, "I do not, Major. I do have a summation."

At that moment, Dr. Taylor returned to the courtroom, walked between the two tables, stepping close to the major. He leaned over and said something softly into Major Forest's ear. The major shook his head as Dr. Taylor stepped back.

He rose and said, "Colonel Cracken died on the way to his quarters."

There was an initial gasp and then silence in the courtroom.

The doctor left, and the major stepped over to the jury. All the men rose as he approached. They huddled together for a few moments, heads nodding. Major Forest stepped back, the jury returned to their seats, and he to the desk, though he remained standing, facing Will and Josh.

"As I mentioned after the colonel left the courtroom, this is quite an unorthodox ending to this trial. Major Logan, your summation will not be required. I have consulted with the other members, and we have a unanimous verdict. We find in favor of First Sergeant William Wallace Logan."

His announcement was greeted momentarily by a stunned silence, then the room broke into a cheer. Will stood and turned just in time to catch Deborah as she threw herself against the rope, knocking the stanchions over, and into his arms. She clutched him to her, then stepped back, allowing his ma to give him a hug. "I knew they'd set you free, son. Even with that crazy colonel, God rest his soul."

Next was Kate, and then handshaking from everyone. At the very end was Shorty. He looked up at Will and said in a low voice, "We weren't gonna let 'em hang you, boy, army or no. I reckon you knew that."

Will nodded at the old mountain man. "Yeah, Shorty, I knew that for sure."

"See you later, Will," he said, winked, and joined Morg and the family.

When Will finally turned back, the major was standing on the other side of the table, patiently waiting. He extended his hand. "First Sergeant Logan, first I want to apologize for your having to go through this. I don't understand why the colonel wanted this trial to move on so quickly. Maybe his illness affected him. He has always been a tough but fair man, at least until recently. Three months or so ago, he started getting these headaches and became suspicious of everyone. I've served with him for eight years. I considered him a friend, but he started questioning everything I did."

The major caught himself. "Sorry, you don't need to hear all of that. When your people arrive with your documents, bring them to me. We'll get them recorded and notify Washington. You will probably have back pay coming." A sergeant entered the courtroom, and the man motioned toward the office.

"Gentlemen, if you'll excuse me." With that, Major Forest left the courtroom.

Josh said, "I wish no man ill, but I have to tell you, I didn't like the way this trial was shaping up. It sure appeared the colonel had you marked for hanging, and nothing was going to stop him."

Will shook his head. "I don't know what he had against me, or if it was just his sickness, but I agree with you. I think if it had been up to him, I would have been stretching hemp in the not too distant future."

Josh clapped Will on the back. "Ole son, I think the hemp stretching is over." He looked at Deborah, who was carrying on a conversation with her new mother-in-law. "Yep, it looks like your life is back on track. Are you still planning on heading north?"

"I am, Josh. I like what you and Callum have done with Uncle Floyd's valley. I've talked it over with Deborah, and she's excited about an adventure. I think we're going to do the same thing. I hear there's plenty of good grass up in the Montana Territory."

"Yeah," Josh said. "Plenty of Indian trouble, too. You might be a bit early. I know a lot of your scalp has already been shot away, but I'm betting one of those Blackfeet braves wouldn't mind it hanging from *his* lance."

"Nobody's getting any more shots at *his* scalp."

Josh and Will turned to see Deborah standing near. She looped her arm in Will's. "I think we will be just fine, especially with the fine guides I've employed."

"Guides?" Will said.

"Yes, guides." She turned and pointed at Morg and Shorty. Morg was smiling at Ma, and Shorty, as usual, was carrying on with one of his many stories, Kate listening with just a touch of skepticism on her face.

Will grinned. "I'm betting it didn't take much arm twisting to persuade them."

Deborah smiled back. "None at all. In fact, all I had to do was mention it, and Shorty volunteered the both of them."

The three enjoyed a chuckle among themselves. Josh was about to say something when the dusty stranger Will had seen take notice at the name Hank Remington sidled up.

"Excuse me, folks," the stranger said, and addressing Will, he continued, "Sorry to interrupt, but you've been known as Hank Remington?"

"You're the man who tried to stop me on the parade ground," Will said. "Yes, that used to be my name. What can I do for you?"

"You know Mac MacGregor and Darcy Smith?"

"I do. They own the Remington Ranch, down in Texas."

The cowboy nodded his head. "I'm Tom Strathen. I went to work for Mac and Darcy when they returned from their last cattle drive, worked for a while, and got itchy feet. Had a hankerin' to head up to the tall grass country in Montana. Heard there's some ranchin' going on up there. They asked me to keep an eye out for Hank Remington. I ain't believin' I was lucky enough to find you."

"You've found me," Will said. "What's going on?"

"They're in trouble. A big outfit has moved in. They're saying the Remington Ranch is on their land and have told Mac and Darcy to hit the road."

Will shook his head. "That's all wrong. Those boys purchased the land and the water rights fair and square. I saw the deed. That other outfit doesn't have a leg to stand on."

"They may not," Strathen said, "but they've got the money to buy people. When I left, they weren't bein' shy about spreadin' it around, and Darcy was ambushed. Whoever did it just winged him, but those boys are in big trouble."

Will thought for a minute, then said, "Are they asking for my help?"

Strathen shook his head. "They didn't say that. Mac just said to tell you what was happenin' if I ran into you. He ain't said nothin' about askin' you to come back and help him."

Will thought for a minute. Those boys had worked hard for the ranch they now owned. Wade, their other partner, had died there. Hard work and the willingness to take a chance had paid off for them. After two cattle drives, they had accumulated quite a bit of operating capital. In fact, when he had left them in Abilene, after the cattle drive, they had tried to pay him for a third of the ranch. He wouldn't accept that amount of money, so Mac had placed a third of the proceeds for the cattle in the Abilene Bank for him, thirty thousand dollars. It was still there. He hadn't touched it.

Will looked around. The family, a few close friends, and several of the officers and their wives were the only ones remaining in the courtroom. He looked at his wife, who had been watching him.

"Those are your friends, Will. We're going, aren't we?"

"Honey," Will said, "the last thing I want to do is drag you into a range war. It could get bloody. I know you're more gutsy than most men, and have seen the worst men can do to each other, but I'm asking you to stay here in this Colorado country. I'll be back, trust me."

She was silent as she stared into his brown eyes. He could see her eyes fill and her jaw set, and he knew she was battling within herself. He knew her strength. She would be a great asset both as a person and a nurse. He had seen her shoot. She was good with a gun, but she was a healer, a fearless healer, but nonetheless a healer. He didn't want to drag her into what he felt sure could happen.

"Let's go back to the ranch," she said, "and talk about it there. That way, you'll be able to get supplies, horses, and whatever else is needed." But he could see, even as she said it, she knew it couldn't happen.

"No," he said, shaking his head, "that'll add eight days or more to the trip. In that time, we could be almost a third of the way there. I'm thinking leaving from here in the morning will be the best thing."

In one step, she was in his arms. He felt her warmth as his long arms encircled her.

He stroked her hair. "You know I'm right, honey. I wouldn't be able to concentrate on what I was doing, knowing you were there in the thick of it.

"At least we'll have tonight," he said.

He felt her nod. "I know. If it was anything else, you couldn't tear me away, but I know you don't want to be distracted with the need to protect me. I don't like it, but I'll stay." She gave a singular sniff, pulled away, and said, "Yes, at least we'll have tonight."

Captain Smyth stepped forward, a brunette, about his age, with graying hair and soft eyes on his arm. He nodded to Will and spoke to Deborah. "Ma'am, I'd like you to meet my wife, Polly."

Polly extended her hand. "It is nice to meet you, but I am so sorry you had to go through all of this. Thank goodness it is over."

"Thank you," Deborah said.

Polly looked at her husband to Will and back to Deborah. "Grayson told me you are only *just* married?"

Deborah nodded.

"And . . . I'm sorry, I'm trying to be delicate, but I will just get to the point. You haven't had any sort of honeymoon?"

Deborah smiled at Polly. "Yes, you are certainly correct."

Polly cleared her throat. "From what I hear, Mr. Logan will be leaving in the morning, and you will be returning to Pueblo.

Since the accommodations at the fort are quite sparse, Grayson and I would like to offer you our home for the evening. We will stay with friends."

Will watched Deborah tear up again. She reached out and grasped Polly's hand. "Oh, Polly, that is so gracious of you. Are you sure it won't be too inconvenient for you?"

Captain Smyth spoke up. "Mrs. Logan, it will be our pleasure, a belated apology on my part for causing all of this disruption in your life."

Deborah ran her arm around Will's waist and gazed up into his eyes. "Isn't this wonderful, Will?"

He smiled down into her dark brown eyes now brimming with tears of happiness. "It truly is."

9

W ill pulled the slate gray horse to a halt and said, "Whoa, Smoky." He watched the black-tipped ears swing forward toward the approaching men. The horse had been a good choice. Unusual in his color, black legs and black-tipped ears, with a black stripe running the length of his dark gray back, he was a seldom-seen breed, a grulla, but his best qualities were intelligence, speed, and endurance. Will leaned forward and patted the animal on the neck while he waited for his four companions to draw up alongside. They sat on the north side of a narrow arroyo, watching five men trot their horses up the slope toward them. While they approached, Will scanned the familiar countryside. They were on the northern edge of the Remington Ranch.

The landscape was dotted with the contrasting dark and light green of oak and mesquite thickets. They had just passed a small herd of longhorns with the RR, Double R, brand on their hips.

Will glanced at Callum, his younger brother by two years, sitting his big roan appaloosa to his left. Callum tossed him a slow nod, his light blue eyes as cool as the Colorado mountain sky after a summer rain. Callum was quick with a handgun, but not quite as fast as young Colin. It was good to have his brother here.

To his right and nearest rode Tandy Jacobs, and Bart Porter. Bart was a Texas man who had been cornered into becoming a gunfighter. Thanks to Bart, Will had survived gun trouble in South Texas when he was looking for his old friends from the war. Tandy was altogether different. When Will met him, he had been headed for bad times on the wrong side of the law. With his massive size, he had the potential, and had used it when he was younger, to be a brutal bully. After he'd challenged Will and was soundly whipped, he latched on to Will like a calf to a mama cow and was growing into a huge but good man.

On the other side of Bart rode Will's uncle Floyd. He was one of the toughest men Will had ever known. *Getting a little long in the tooth*, he thought, *but tougher than most men half his age.*

Though having traveled, and traveled fast, from Fort Lyon, on the other side of the Arkansas, in Colorado, and all worn to a frazzle, other than dusty, they looked fresh as daisies.

Floyd looked back to Will and grinned. "Looks like we might get a chance to say howdy to your neighbors." As he said it, he reached down and pulled his seven-shot, .56 Spencer from the boot and laid it comfortably across his upper thighs.

As the riders closed the distance, Will examined them and their horses. They were astride some fine riding stock, much better than the average cowhand could afford. Bart must have noticed the same thing, for, without taking his eyes from the men, he said, "Mighty fine horses. I'd say those boys do more riding than the average hand, and probably not much of it workin' cattle."

"I agree," Will said. "You boys let them open the ball. I'm hoping they just want to put a scare into us, for now." Will glanced again at his younger brother. Callum's left hand was relaxed, gripping the reins lightly and resting on the pommel of his saddle. His right hand lay on his leg, comfortably resting near the butt of his .44 New Army Colt.

There was a light, southeast breeze stirring the tall grass and mitigating the hot, June sun. In the arroyo, Will watched a horny toad scurry to the top of a rock, stop, and stare back at him. He didn't know why, but he liked those little lizards. They always seemed friendly to him.

The riders halted before reaching the far edge of the arroyo, leaving themselves plenty of turning room should they need to leave the country fast. The man in the middle, at least six feet, wide of shoulder, with a hawklike face, wore a black hat, black neckerchief, and black vest over a dirty gray shirt. He sported several days' growth of beard.

Which is nothing unusual for most riders, Will thought. *Most don't worry about a shave unless they're headed for town.*

When the man spoke, he had a rough, gravelly voice. The kind that gave orders and expected them to be followed. "You're on Circle Double B range. Turn your horses and git off."

Will just stared at the man, then said to no one in particular, "He's mine. You boys divvy up the rest."

The next sound was Floyd's Spencer going to full cock. "Reckon this feller on the end will be my dance partner."

Will watched the four toughs look nervously at their leader, then back at them. It was obvious they had planned on riding in and buffaloing the strangers. Now they were being put on notice, and he could see they didn't care for it. They weren't ready. One of the riders had been eyeing Bart uneasily, as if he thought he knew him but wasn't sure.

Will said softly, just loud enough for the other riders to hear, "Bart, you know these fellows?"

"Can't say as I do, but we can see if there's anything on them when it's all over."

The uneasy rider's eyes got larger. He turned to the big man in the middle. "Langston, I thought I recognized that feller. He's Bart Porter. Story is he's slicker'n a greased pig with that six-gun."

Will chuckled and then said, "You guessed it, pardner. He's Bart Porter, and that is one story you can bank on. Now you boys can turn around and crawl back under the rock you came out from under, or start the music. We'd love to dance."

It was apparent the man called Langston didn't like it. He didn't like it even a little bit. His eyes shifted from Will to Bart and then Floyd. The old mountain man, after all his years, still wore buckskins and his old slouch hat.

Will watched the man's eyes. Pa had always said, "Watch the eyes. They'll be the tell of what a man will do." Langston's eyes were pulled tight. He wanted to make a move. But he just didn't like the odds.

Langston growled again, "You heard me. Get off this land, or the next time we meet, you won't be so lucky." He spat, said, "Come on, boys," and yanked his horse around.

The other four men followed suit, turning their horses after Langston and slapping the spurs to them. All five raced away, dust boiling, faster than they had come.

"Well, wasn't that a nice little welcome," Floyd said. "I always like it when folks extend such hospitality." He lowered the hammer on his Spencer, slid it back into the scabbard, and leaned on his saddle horn, facing Bart. "Young feller, looks like folks around here aren't real anxious to make your acquaintance."

"Floyd, you might say several citizens east of here felt they just couldn't breathe the same air as me. It proved out they were right. As far as I know, I'm not wanted by the law, maybe by some of their kin, though."

Floyd nodded. "Yep, some folks just can't leave well enough alone." He looked at Will. "What's your plan, nephew?"

Will watched the riders disappearing behind a patch of oaks, then said, "Well, I'm not liking the looks of what we just saw.

Those boys claiming this as Circle Double B land is not a good sign, but I don't see any reason to change our plans. We might as well ride to the house and see what Mac and Darcy have to say."

He paused for a moment as he scanned the countryside, then turned back to Floyd. "Uncle, I know those men. There isn't the slightest chance they'd sell out. I'm a mite concerned for Mac and Darcy."

The five men started their horses forward, crossed the arroyo, and continued in their original direction. They hadn't ridden far until they ran into another small herd of longhorns.

Callum pulled up when they were close enough to see the brands. The others followed suit. Callum untied his rope and shook out a loop, looked at Tandy, and said, "Give me a hand with that smaller cow?"

"Sure nuff," Tandy said and grabbed his rope.

In no time, they had the big longhorn cow on her side, Callum's rope around the wide horns, and Tandy's around both of the cow's rear feet. She was stretched tight with the brand side up.

"Will, take a look at that brand," Callum said.

Will rode close, stepped down from his horse, and knelt by the cow's hindquarters for a close look. He ran his hand around the fresh burns. Parts of the *B*s were blurred. He shook his head. "I swear, if we killed and skinned this cow, we'd see she's been rebranded, and the fellow doing the branding isn't very good." He stood. "I don't know what's going on here, but I don't like it."

Tandy said, "We could kill it, skin it, and take the hide. We'd have proof."

Will nodded. "That's a good idea, Tandy. But if someone came along while we were doing it, they'd swear we were rustling. Let's find out what's happening around here before we do anything. I'm betting there'll be plenty of cattle with the wrong brand when we need them."

He mounted and rode off a ways while first Callum and then

Tandy loosed their ropes. The cow lay still for a moment, then jumped to her feet and turned to face the riders.

"I'd say she'd like a little bit of Callum or Tandy, here," Bart said.

That brought laughter from all of the men. They rode away from the angry cow, everyone keeping an eye on her until well clear.

"Tandy," Callum said, "you reckon these longhorns ever get tame? They always seem to have a burr under their saddle."

Tandy laughed and said, "I have seen a tame one. When I was growin' up, a neighbor boy found a just-born calf, all to itself. Its mama must've been kilt or somethin', 'cause they ain't gonna leave their babies. But he raised that calf till it was full grow'd. That cow would follow him around like a dog. That was the durndest sight to see."

All the men were shaking their heads as they pictured the sight of a wild longhorn doing anything other than trying to stomp a man into the ground.

Floyd spoke up. "What happened to the pair, boy?"

Tandy shook his head. "War come along. Weren't hardly no food to be had anywhere. They had to kill that cow and eat it. Near broke that feller's heart. But it weren't for long. Shortly after, what with all the men gone, Comanches raided their place. Killed and scalped them all."

Floyd nodded. "Life can be hard sometimes."

The men continued south in silence.

THE SUN WAS low in the west when they topped the rise north of the ranch headquarters. There was still activity, but Will, through his field glasses, couldn't recognize anyone. He handed the glasses to Tandy. "You recognize anyone down there?"

Tandy looked, shook his head, and handed them to Bart. The

gunman was watching when a man walked out on the front porch of the house. Bart took a quick look and, while handing the glasses back to Tandy, said, "That's not good."

Tandy quickly passed the glasses, and Will brought them to his face, looked for a moment, and said, "Blast! It's Langston."

Floyd and Will had been watching through field glasses of their own. "That's definitely not a good sign, Will. Any ideas?"

Will nodded. "I'm going down there."

"Now just you wait a minute," Callum said. "You don't know what you might run into down there, and if you go inside, we can't keep watch on you. *And* it's gonna be dark shortly. There's no telling what they might do to you once they get you inside the house. I don't like that idea at all."

Will looked at his brother. "Look, there's four of you. You can keep that bunch under fire for a long time. They already know that Bart's with us. I saw Langston eyeing Floyd. They're going to be pretty cautious about doing anything to me, and I've got to find out what's going on."

Floyd spoke up. "He's right, Callum. I don't think those fellers will try anything yet. Who knows, maybe they just bought your friends out. I'm thinking this is a good time to find out what's happening around here."

"Well, I don't like it, but it's not my call. You'd best be on the alert down there."

Will grinned at his brother. "I'll for sure be at the ready." He turned to his uncle. "Floyd, if you'll unlimber that Sharps, should I need the help, I'd be much obliged."

"I'll do it, boy." He reached back and patted the smooth stock of the long-barreled Sharps protruding from his bedroll. "It'll be ready if'n you need it. Good luck to you."

Will slipped the thong from the hammer of his revolver and walked Smoky down the slope toward the ranch house. The men working at the corral soon spotted him, rose and watched his approach. A yell drifted up the hillside, and shortly, a second man came out of the house. They stood on the porch, keeping a close eye as the grulla meandered around tall cactus and large rocks.

Nearing the house, Will recognized Langston as one of the two men on the porch. The other man's clothing stood out from the Texas cowhands'.

He wore a stiff, straw sailor hat. It was short crowned and narrow brimmed. A bright blue silk flowered cravat encircled his neck over a pale blue shirt. His darker blue, short-cut waistcoat was covered by a dark gray frock coat. His trousers, a pale gray and blue check, topped a pair of short lace-up boots.

Will had recovered from his war wounds in Washington, and he was familiar with how the eastern city men dressed. But this gent, on a Texas ranch, stood out like a dance hall girl in a Baptist revival.

But Will noticed something else. No one was laughing, there were no snide looks or comments from the cowhands, and Langston treated him with respect. The man stood ramrod straight, and under the sailor hat, though dressed like a dandy, he demanded respect. *Must be pushing fifty,* Will thought, *and no pushover. I'd guess he was military, senior officer of some type. He's used to people jumping when he gives orders. Texas must have been a rude awakening for him.*

Several men came out of the barn and stood around, watching. Will continued to the hitching rail in front of the house, pulled up the grulla, and said, "Howdy, I'm Will Logan."

"He's the one headed up that bunch I was just tellin' you about, boss," Langston said.

The man turned a haughty stare on Will, his hard gray eyes drilling through him. "What, my dear sir, are you doing on my land?"

Will said, "Before I tell you anything, mister, I'd like to know your name."

The man's face turned red, and Will thought, *Oh, boy, I hope this guy doesn't keel over like the colonel.*

After continuing to stare at him, the man said, "I am Sir Wilford Pemberton Davies the Third. I am from Great Britain. You may call me Sir Wilford."

Will had been keeping an eye on the cowhands. The ones in and around the corral and those who came from the barn had started spreading behind him, forming a half-circle. He was thankful Floyd and the others were ready on the hillside. "How about I call you Davies, and you can call me Logan. My friends call me Will, but I don't think we're headin' down the friendship trail."

Davies started to speak, but Will interrupted. "You mind telling me why you are on this ranch? It belongs to Mac MacGregor and Darcy Smith."

"This is now my ranch. In fact, it has been for years. MacGregor and Smith, along with another ruffian by the name of Remington, who disappeared, squatted on it, and I have, lately, regained possession. Furthermore, I do not like your insubordinate attitude. Insolence in the British Army is rewarded with stripes. Would you care to have a taste of the British lash, my insolent man?"

"Reckon that wouldn't be too smart on your part," Will said.

Davis turned to Langston. "Have the men take him and give him, oh, let us see." He brought his left arm across his body, cupped his hand, placed his right elbow in the cup, and tapped on his cheek as he considered the number of lashes. Once decided, he said, "I do believe twenty stripes should be sufficient." He turned to Langston, who was scanning the hills surrounding the ranch. "Have the men tie him to a corral post and give him twenty solid stripes."

Langston, his brow wrinkled in concern, said, "Uh, that might not be a good idea, Sir Wilford. He rides with four other hombres who look to be mighty salty. I don't think he would have ridden down here without an ace in the hole."

"Nonsense," Davies said. "Do as I say."

Langston backed up until he was standing where, with one leap, he could be through the door and in the house. "Alright," he said, his gruff voice low, "just don't say I didn't warn you."

Four cowhands were less than ten feet behind Will. Langston said, "You four, pull that man off his horse and tie him to the gatepost."

The four men started forward.

Suddenly, dirt and small rocks erupted from the ground between the leading cowhand's feet, blasting into his legs and crotch, followed by the bellow of a .52-caliber Sharps. The cowhand reacted like a snake had struck him and leaped straight up into the air. The others scattered for cover. Davies dropped behind the waist-high porch banister and searched nervously through the space between the heavy balusters for the source of the blast. Langston had disappeared inside the house.

Will leaned forward, rested his left forearm across his saddle horn, and with his right forefinger pushed his black Stetson to the back of his head. Light brown hair tumbled down over his forehead, making him look younger than his thirty-six years. "Davies, you should've listened to Langston, seems he's the only smart one in the bunch. I've got more shooters up in those hills. You make another move at me, and the next shot will make a mess of that nice clean shirt you're wearing."

Will's voice had been soft and friendly, but now it turned harsh. "Stand up, Davies. If we wanted you dead, hiding behind a few little posts wouldn't save you."

Davies slowly stood, brushed the dirt from one sleeve, straightened his vest and jacket, and composed himself. When he spoke, his was also a threatening voice. "You have no right to ride in here and threaten me. I'll have the state police after you."

Will straightened his hat and sat erect. "I didn't ride in here to threaten you, Davies. I came in for an answer to my question, and I don't think your state police threat amounts to much. Where are Liam MacGregor and Darcy Smith?"

"They sold out to me."

"Really? I doubt that. But that wasn't my question. Where are they? Speak up and I'm gone."

"I do not know. The last time I saw them was in a courtroom in San Antonio. The court awarded me the right to this land and all the property on it, and evicted MacGregor and Smith. I have not seen them since."

Will looked around the ranch yard, remembering the last time he was here, in much happier times. He turned back to Davies. "I'll find them. Then I may be back."

"Stay off my land, Logan. You *and* your rowdy bunch. I will have you shot as rustlers the next time you come on my property. Do you hear me?"

Will backed his horse a few steps, turned him toward the hillside, clucked and started Smoky walking. He touched the brim of his hat and, in the fading light, rode back up the hill.

---

andy led the way. The quarter moon gave sufficient light for the men to make their way through and around the prickly pear and mesquite as they pushed their way west. Tandy had often spoken of the Mexican family he had boarded with before he started working for the Double R, and, if they were still there, he felt sure those good folks would feed them as well as their horses.

The sun had been set for a couple of hours when a faint light came into view in the distance.

"That's it," Tandy said.

Thirty minutes later they could make out the adobe structure. The house was larger than Will had expected. When he had been in Texas before, Tandy had talked about Armando and Ana Ruiz, but Will had never seen their home. From the outside, it looked to be two, maybe three rooms. There was a covered area outside with a firepit, a large oven, and a plank table. He could also make out two long benches and a couple of chairs at the table, all looked homemade.

In the moonlight, they could also make out the large barn. It looked inviting to the tired men, a place where, with a little straw or grass, a man, or five, could be comfortable and still have room for the animals. They rode within hailing distance. Tandy continued closer to the house, dropped to the ground, and called, "Armando, Ana, *buenos noches*. It is Tandy."

The front door burst open, and kids boiled out. Will counted five with ages ranging from around six to eleven or twelve. They all raced toward Tandy. When they saw the other horses and riders, they slowed, but Tandy opened his arms and said, "I need a hug." That did it. All five, even the boys, piled into his big arms. Will watched the excitement. This was a side of Tandy he had never seen. The big young man hugged them all, genuinely happy to see them again.

Behind the children, a Mexican man and woman stepped from the home, their smiles visible in the light of the house. The two were holding hands when they stepped through the door. They recognized Tandy, but upon seeing other rough-looking men in the darkness, they stopped, their smiles fading.

Tandy saw their looks of concern. Still holding little Marco, he stood, while the rest of the children hung on to a leg or wrapped their arms around his waist. "Don't worry, these are all friends. They are good people. They will not harm you or your family."

Armando and Ana walked forward, and both threw their arms around the big man.

"Tandy, you have grown so large, *mucho hombre*," Armando said.

Tandy grinned back at him. "It was all those tortillas, frijoles, and peppers Ana stuffed me with that did it."

"Oh," Ana said. "Where are my manners?" She turned to the men still mounted. "Please señors, step down. There is food for your horses in the barn, and I will have a little something in just a few moments." Turning to her oldest daughter, she said, "Isabela, come with me."

Will and the others stepped from their saddles. Before his

father could say anything, Felipe, who looked to be about eleven, took Tandy's reins from him and said, "Señors, Pablo and I will be glad to take care of your horses for you."

Bart spoke up. "Well, thank you. What's your name?"

"I am Felipe, señor."

"Well, I'm Bart, and this here fellow next to me is Callum. There's a bunch of horses here, why don't we give you a hand, and we'll all get done a mite faster?"

"Thank you, señor. That will be very fine."

Tandy completed the introductions of everyone. Callum and Bart, with the older boys, headed for the barn. Armando beside Tandy, with little Alexa holding the cowboy's big hand, led Will and Floyd to the table.

As they neared the outside table, Armando said, with a little pride, "Señors, we have a well at the corner of the house toward the barn. Señor Tandy and I dug it together." Then he smiled as he looked at his large friend. "Maybe Tandy dug a little more than me. But it has plenty of water, and Alexa will get you a clean towel if you would like to wash up first."

Alexa released Tandy's hand, said, "Yes, Papi," and dashed into the house.

"Mighty kind of you," Floyd said.

"Yes, thank you," Will joined in, and he and Floyd headed for the well.

Tandy let little Marco down, said, "*Gracias, amigo,*" and followed Will and Floyd just as Alexa came dashing from the house with the towel. She held the towel under one arm, stuck her hand back in Tandy's, and together they continued to the pump.

The men quickly drew water from the well and, using the dipper hanging by a nail on the upper frame, took turns drinking the sweet water from the bucket. Then each began to wash their faces and hands in the cool well water.

Trail dust washed off as best they could, Alexa, carrying the now dirt-laden towel, led the men back to the table. The family had been busy while the men were taking care of the horses and washing up. The table was laden with food. There was nothing fancy, but it was all of the stick-to-the-ribs variety and plenty of it.

Armando stood at one end of the table. At the other end Ana held a chair and said, "Please, Señor Floyd."

Floyd walked down to the end, looked at the chair and then at the plain, sweet woman holding it, and in perfect Spanish, said, "Thank you, ma'am, you are very kind to an old man, but I cannot take your place."

In Spanish, she replied, "It would be my honor to have you sit here, please."

He took her hand, gallantly bent and kissed it, and said simply, "*Gracias.*"

Armando was smiling at the exchange, and Ana beamed at him as she scurried by. He spread his arms and said, "Please, gentlemen, sit. I am sure you are hungry, eat."

Will sat on the bench next to Floyd and across from Callum. Tandy sat next to Armando and across from Bart. They wasted no time. They'd had an early breakfast of bacon, had eaten some jerky about dinnertime, and were ready for a hefty feed bag. There was a big bowl of frijoles along with a tall rounded platter of meat. Each man filled his plate with meat and beans, along with several steaming corn tortillas. While the eating took place, there was silence around the table. The children also sat quietly, having eaten earlier, and now the excitement was wearing off. It was past their bedtime, and eyes were growing heavy.

Marco, who had crawled into Tandy's lap as soon as he had sat down, was sound asleep. His head drooped at an odd angle against Tandy's chest. Ana came to the rescue, lifting Marco into her arms.

"Come, children, it is past time for bed." All of the kids rose, without complaint, gave Tandy a final hug, and followed their mother back into the house.

Having finished eating, Will said, "Armando, I thank you for your hospitality. If we might impose further, we'd sure appreciate bedding down in your barn."

"Señor Will, all of you are most welcome."

"Thanks," Will replied, "and that was a mighty fine meal. The venison tasted fresh."

Armando smiled. "It is very fresh, señor. I killed it this afternoon. The deer, they like our garden.

"Tandy," Armando said, turning back to his friend, "you have grown much since you were here last. We are glad to see you, but what brings you and your friends here? The last we knew of you, you took a herd of cattle north to Abilene."

"Yep, we did that. A lot has happened." Tandy looked over at Will, a question on his face.

Will gave an almost imperceptible nod of his head.

Tandy continued, "It's Mac and Darcy. We got a message they're in trouble."

"*Si*, they have lost the ranchero." The smile left Armando's face. "Do not go there. A man called Davies claims he owns it. He is *muy malo*, very bad. He is spreading out. He has run several of our friends from their homes. His man Langston has come by our place. They say we must leave. I was not here. He told my sweet Ana, right here in the yard, in front of *mi niños*, they didn't want any dirty Mexes around."

Listening, Will felt his anger bubbling up. He looked at Callum and Floyd. The only indication from his uncle was the narrowing of his eyes, but Callum, hands resting on the table, had clenched his fists, and his knuckles were white. *Langston had best walk a straight line,* he thought, *That kind of talk doesn't float with the Logan family.*

His family still talked about when Uncle Floyd had come back to Tennessee for a visit. It was around Christmastime. Will had been only six, but he could vividly remember his uncle telling about when the bear attacked him and gave him that scar on his head. It was also the time that Floyd cut his visit short so he could help a black couple escape through the Underground Railroad. As a boy, Will had been taught that a man is a man, doesn't make a bit of difference what his color is. Treat folks like you want to be treated. Yes, sir, Langston would get his come-uppance.

Will spoke up. "Sorry about Langston. If it would be alright with you, some of us can stay here while the others search for Mac and Darcy. How long ago did Langston make that threat?"

"It has been over a week ago. We have been concerned they will come back, but we have no place to go. This is our home. We have family in Nuevo Laredo, but we do not want to leave, and it is a long trip for the family.

"But Señor Will, you were saying you must search for Mac and Darcy. I know where they are. They are well hidden from the *bandido* Langston, on the Nueces, north of here."

Will and Bart looked at each other. They both knew the Nueces country. They'd choused tough old longhorns from among the pecan trees and mesquite thickets lining the river. There were places along the river where it was mighty rough for a rider.

"How long have they been there?" Will asked.

"Since they left the ranch. They did not want to go, but the sheriff brought a paper, and the two of them, along with maybe two or three hands, had to leave. It is my understanding Señor Darcy wanted to fight, but Señor Mac persuaded him not to. They wait for something from Austin, but that is all I know."

"We know that Nueces country pretty well, Armando. Do you think you could tell us how to find it?"

"I can do better than that, I can show you."

Will looked at Floyd, then Callum. They both shook their heads. When he looked back to Armando, he could see Tandy and Bart doing the same thing.

Will joined in with the head shake. "No, I don't think that's a good idea. Davies has already said the next time his men see us, they'll be shooting. We don't want you caught in that."

Armando leaned forward, forearms on the table and head thrust forward. "But, Will, this is my fight, too. They have threatened my wife and called her names. I am not afraid. I have fought before, and I would love to have a chance to fight them."

Floyd spoke up. "Armando, I've been fighting Langston's kind for over thirty years. I know what I'm doing, and so do these boys with me. You need to stay with your family and protect them in case Langston and his gang come back."

Will could see that Armando was firm in his decision to guide them. He leaned toward the man. "Armando, what Floyd says is true. These men are professional fighters and killers. I hate to be brutal, but how would you feel if you rode away with us and upon returning found your whole family murdered?"

In the candle and moonlight, Will could see Armando's expression turn from anger to horror as he contemplated the picture in his mind. His head dropped, and when he raised it, he said, "You are right. You are all right. It would be foolish for me to leave after what Langston has said to my Ana. I can tell you how to get there. You know this country. You will be able to find it."

Will gave a firm nod. "Good. I think it might be best if only two of us head out to find Mac and Darcy. The other three can stay and provide a little surprise for *Mr.* Langston should he decide to give you a return visit."

"Who do you have in mind stayin'?" Floyd asked.

"This is what I'm thinking. Callum and I will ride north. You, Tandy and Bart hang around here and make up a welcoming party. You can set it up any way you want, but I think if you and that Sharps could pick a little place that covers the approach to the house pretty well, that might help Bart and Tandy with the surprise."

"That'll work," Floyd said. Knowing how cowhands hated to do anything that couldn't be done from a saddle, he grinned down the table at the two men who would be staying with him. "I'll go find me a nice restin' spot, where I can look after these boys while they help around the house." Still grinning, he looked at Armando. "You have any work that needs to be done around here that's a mite much for one man?"

Catching on, Armando said, "Oh, *si*, Señor Floyd. I have *mucho trabajo*. There is fence fixing around the garden, inside the barn needs new framing and painting, and—"

Bart, a wry frown on his face, broke in. "Alright now, Tandy and I get the point. We don't mind working like dogs as long as Ana keeps fixing this fine food." Now he cast a sharp look at Floyd. "And as long as you don't decide to take a siesta in that nice warm sun. I'd hate to have you snoring when Langston's bunch rides up."

Floyd squinted one eye, turned his head sideways, and shot Bart a threatening look. "Boy, I've spent more days lying in the brush in them mountains, lookin' for Injuns, than you've been alive." Then he lightened up and, eyes twinkling in the candle-light, said, "But I have to admit, these days I do like my naps. You keep needlin' me, and you never know when I might see fit to take one."

Callum and Will broke out in soft laughter, not wanting to wake the kids.

"Best stay on his good side, Bart," Callum said. "He's getting crotchety in his old age, and you want that Sharps limbered up should you need it."

"You're right there," Bart said, and grinned at Floyd.

They all chuckled, and Will turned back to Armando. "Now for directions?"

"Yes, if they haven't moved, it will be simple for you to find them. It is an easy two-day or hard one-day ride. You remember where the Soldier Slough runs into the Nueces?"

"Yes," Will said as Bart and Tandy nodded their heads in agreement.

"Good. Just up the river from there, you will find where the Nueces makes a tight U, with a . . ." Here Armando paused as if searching for a word. Curling his fingers, he stood them on the table, arching his hand in such a way that it resembled a spider. "How do you say hump or small hill?"

Will said, "You mean a knoll?"

Armando gave a vigorous nod. "*Si,* yes, a knoll. Where the river makes this tight turn, a knoll stands inside the turn. It looks like a swollen thumb. For a short distance the river runs west, but just past the swollen thumb, it turns back north. At the next bend, on the west side, is their camp. It is hard to see until you are right on top of it, for it is in the thick pecan trees, and outside the pecan trees, on both sides of the river, are very thick mesquites mixed with many prickly pear. A man without chaps would be in trouble. For the same reason, you must find a trail, at least a deer or javelina trail, so you protect your horse. The prickly pear is very bad."

"If I remember correctly," Will said, "a rider is better off crossing at the slough and paralleling the Nueces until you're even with the thicket. From there, you can ride in fairly easily."

Tandy and Bart, along with Armando, nodded. "Yes," Armando said, "you are correct. That is the place."

Floyd slid his chair back. "There's been enough talking to last me for at least a year. I'm putting these old bones to bed. You boys be quiet when you come in."

Will stood at the same time. "That strikes me as a good idea. I'm mighty tired myself. Why don't we all hit the sack and plan on getting an early start in the morning."

Everyone stood, and after thanking Armando, Ana had already joined the children, they headed for the barn.

On the way, Callum drew Will to the side. Once they were out of earshot of everyone, he said, "I'm thinking you might be better off taking Bart with you tomorrow. He knows this part of the country a lot better than I do, and he's more familiar with the folks. He can watch your back better, since I don't know most of the people around here."

Will considered what his brother had said. As much as he'd like to have Callum on this run with him, he knew Bart would be handy in recognizing folks Will didn't know, and that could be important. "Not a bad idea. You don't mind staying?"

Callum grinned back at him and said, "Let's see, jerky or Ana's cooking. No, I think I'll be fine with staying."

11

Callum paused at the open door, his head up, listening. The sound of approaching horses carried above the laughter from the children playing behind the house. Looking toward the trees to the northeast, he scanned the tree-line but saw nothing. Exactly what he expected. Floyd had scouted and found several good hides over the past few days and even now was bedded down in one, waiting. Callum could picture the old mountain man stretched out with the Sharps extended, ready and waiting to burn powder.

He had just left Tandy and Armando inside the barn, working. He stuck his head into the house and said, "Ana, someone's coming. Gather up the children and find a safe spot in the house. There could be shooting."

Callum kept his eyes on the distant oaks, knowing the riders would have to circle around the north end. He started to call Tandy, but the hammering was so loud from the barn he knew no one would hear him. Walking to the barn, he saw Ana rush to the back of the house and gather the children, then, carrying little Marco, herd them inside their home.

"Tandy," Callum called, nearing the barn. The hammering

stopped, and moments later, the bulk of his young friend appeared in the doorway.

"Whatcha need, boss?" Tandy asked, blond hair wet and dripping over his forehead. He had removed his shirt, and the sleeves of his sweat-soaked red long johns were rolled to the elbows, exposing massive forearms.

"Riders coming." Callum knew that was all he need say. Both Tandy and Armando had their rifles in the barn, and Tandy wore his belted six-gun. Callum saw him flip the leather thong from the hammer, check to make sure the heavy, nine-shot LeMat revolver was free and clear in the holster, and then step back for his Winchester. Armando moved into sight, carrying his Henry rifle.

"Armando," Callum said, "why don't you go inside with your family and be ready."

The husband and father, brow wrinkled and lips pursed with concern, ran to the house.

Tandy grinned at Callum. "We gonna have some fun?"

Callum, his face serious, said, "Depends on what you call fun, but something's going to happen, so be ready."

"I'm ready, boss."

"Good, stay hidden in the barn for now. You'll know if you're needed. Just don't shoot me with that blasted LeMat."

Tandy's grin got bigger. "I'll try not to. You know how I am with guns when I get excited."

At that, Callum couldn't help but grin. The giant young man seldom missed his target. He shook his head and said, "Just hit what you shoot at. That's all I ask."

"Sure thing, boss." Grinning, Tandy stepped behind the barn wall.

Callum hurried back to the house and slipped inside just as the riders broke around the oaks. They were still about a hundred yards away, but riding fast. He glanced over at Armando, who had gathered his children and wife behind the thick adobe wall, and well below the windows. There wasn't a bullet in existence that could penetrate the thick adobe walls. Callum knew Armando's family was safe, for now, unless the riders made it inside the house, and he planned to ensure they never set foot inside.

As Tandy had done, he checked to make sure his .44-caliber Colt New Army was loose in its holster, and eyed his Spencer leaning against the door frame. He had placed it within easy reach from outside the door, should he need it. For now, he remained inside the darkened interior. He knew the riders, in the bright sunlight, could see nothing inside the house. He waited.

There were seven of them. They gave little concern to the chickens that flew or the pigs and tiny piglets who ran from under their horses' feet as they raced into the yard, sliding their animals to a stop. Langston was not with them. Leading was a young man of no more than twenty-five and probably younger. He wore two revolvers, both hung low on his hips. His were the first words spoken. "Hey, Mex, where's that pretty woman of yores? Send her out so's she can meet some real men."

At that, all the riders broke out in harsh laughter. When no one answered, the young man said again, "Send her out, Mex, now, or I'm coming in after her. I understand you've got a couple of hot-lookin' little girls. I bet they'd like to meet us, too."

Other of the riders could be heard commenting, "Yeah, send 'em out. We'll take good care of 'em." With those statements the riders roared with laughter.

Callum stepped through the door.

The laughter died like water over a fire, but without the sizzle. In its place could only be heard the chickens still fussing and the pigs grunting.

The men stared at the lone man, gun holstered low, calmly looking over the group.

"You boys best turn your horses around and go back where you came from." Callum paused, looking at each man and finally settling cold blue eyes on the young leader. "If you're dead set on something hot, I'm not a little girl, but I'll be glad to accommodate you."

The riders had formed an arc in front of Callum, and the far rider to Callum's left, closest to the barn, spoke up. "Feller, you don't know who you're a-talkin' too. That young feller there is Quick Jim McNabb."

At the mention of his name, the young man's chest expanded like a little banty rooster ready for a fight, and he squinted his eyes down at Callum.

"Last chance," Callum said. "Turn your horses around and get outta here. You can take Snappy Jimmy with you."

Callum saw the fingers of McNabb's right hand curl only a bit, and his facial muscles tense, drawing the corners of his thin lips down. He couldn't see the left revolver. It was blocked out by the neck of the young man's horse. That was the weapon he was concerned with. McNabb could get a jump on him if he was left-handed, but he'd still have to get it above the horse's neck to shoot him.

"Hell," the man on the end spit and said in disgust, "who does he think he is. He ain't but one man."

That's your cue, Tandy, Callum thought.

Tandy, as if reading Callum's mind, stepped out from inside the barn, his Winchester rested lightly in the crook of his left arm, his big right hand ready to whip it into action. "You boys best listen to him. That's Callum Logan. He was drilled right through the center of his chest with a .50-caliber ball, and he's still here. The Shoshone believe he can't be killed." Tandy gave a short laugh. "Course you could try him, like the others have."

With the addition of the second man, the riders started getting nervous. The rider next to McNabb leaned over to him and said, "This ain't all of 'em. I was with Langston when we stopped 'em. I recognized Bart Porter, and he ain't in sight. Neither is that wooly old man. He looked like one of them old mountain men, and if he's lived this long, he's a man with the bark on. I bet he's the one who put that bullet between Jack's feet back at the ranch. He could be lyin' out somewhere. I ain't likin' this at all."

"All right, boys. I said no more warnings. I don't want to have to kill you." Callum was looking at the young fella when he spoke.

The left side of McNabb's lip rose in a sneer, and he leaned slightly toward Callum. "I don't run from no man."

Callum Logan saw the man's left arm twitch down, and he began his draw. His eyes were locked on McNabb, but, with his peripheral vision, he was watching the other riders. The man next to McNabb threw his hands up, as did two others, but four of the men were drawing. Callum stepped to his left, his right hand flashing down for the Colt resting in his holster. He saw the kid's left hand rising to bring his weapon up and over his horse's neck. Callum's movement to his left meant the kid had to bring his weapon farther around to get it pointing toward Callum. He knew it would be close. He had always been fast, but knew there was someone out there faster. But it wouldn't be today.

A split second before he registered the boom of the Sharps, one of the riders who had been drawing his six-gun toppled from his horse, and at the same instant Callum fired. A blossom of red appeared over Quick Jim's heart, rapidly spreading on the light green material. The yard turned to confusion. From behind him, inside the house, Callum heard the crack of a Henry at the same time Tandy fired from the barn.

Horses reared in panic. The front legs of one came down across the back of a riderless animal, and both horses and man fell in a scrambling heap. The man next to the kid yelled, "I warned you about that old man!"

The three remaining men quickly brought their animals under control while ensuring their hands were well clear of their guns. "Strip those gun belts!" Callum ordered. The three remaining riders dropped their gun belts to the ground while making sure everyone could see their hands were clear of the revolvers.

"Now take those rifles out of the scabbards and toss them to the ground. Do it nice and easy. I wouldn't want to have to empty another saddle."

Three rifles hit the ground hard.

Tandy moved closer to the house, his rifle in a ready position, and Armando stepped outside, his also ready. Callum walked over to the kid. Quick Jim McNabb was on his back, gray eyes glazed and staring at nothing Callum could see.

He looked up at the rider who had been next to McNabb. "How old is he?"

The man was staring down at the boy. "He said he was twenty-five. Said he's killed seven men. Seen him kill two. He was fast."

Tandy, still watching the riders, those on the ground and in the saddle, said, "Not fast enough."

Callum looked at the four men on the ground. Two were moving, and two were still. One had half his neck blown away from where the bullet from the .52-caliber Sharps had hit him. "All right, get down off those horses and pick up your friends. Get them in the saddle, and get 'em out of here."

Ana started out to help the wounded men, and Callum held his arm in front of her, halting her progress. He shook his head. One of the wounded, his voice tight with pain, said, "Mister, I'm hurt bad. I need help."

Callum said, voice cold and hard, "You planned on giving pain to this family when you rode in here. You even threatened the little girls. You chew on your own pain and think about it on the ride back with your compadres." The unwounded men remained on their horses.

Callum turned to Tandy. "Anybody you see not climbing off their horses, knock them out of the saddle."

Liking neither choice of being shot or physically knocked from their saddle, the stunned men quickly dismounted and started loading the two wounded men on their mounts.

When Callum saw they weren't bothering with the dead ones, he said, "Don't forget the dead bodies. You rode in with them, now ride out of here with them."

During all the action, Floyd remained hidden, watching and waiting.

Once they were all loaded, Callum said, "Tell Davies this is just a start. We don't take kindly to thieves and killers. As far as you boys are concerned, if you're smart, you'll collect your money and find another job a long way from here. Now, git."

Bluster and threats gone, the men quietly turned their horses and walked them slowly from the yard, careful of the chickens and pigs.

Several large bloodstains remained in the dirt of the yard. A rake leaned against the front wall. Tandy handed his rifle to Armando, picked up the rake, and scraped each blood spot in the hard Texas ground, raking it until there was no longer any sign of blood. As soon as he was finished, Armando called the children outside. They walked hesitantly through the open door, eyes big as they looked around the yard. Alexa, her long, black hair shining in the sunlight, turned wide, innocent eyes up to Armando and said in a small voice, "Papi, did you hurt any of those men?"

He knelt down beside her and hugged her little body to him. "Yes, my little one, I did. They came to hurt our family."

"Oh," she said, looking around at the empty yard. She gave her papi a big hug, then pushed out of his arms and ran to the back of the house where they had been playing, the other children following.

"Hard country, but kids adjust," Callum said to no one in particular. He watched the riders' dust slowly fade until they were out of sight.

Armando moved forward beside Callum. "Thank you, señor. I hate to think what might have happened if you and Tandy and Señor Floyd had not been here. Those are very bad men."

"Yes, they are, but you find those kind all over the world. Out here, on the frontier, its necessary to protect yourself and your family. You did a mighty fine job today, and I'm obliged. That fella you shot was drawing down on me when you fired."

Floyd walked up carrying his Sharps in one hand and Spencer in the other. "They were *all* drawin' down on you, boy, 'ceptin' the one I shot. He hadn't gotten that smoke pole outta his holster 'fore that big hunk of lead ended his ambition. He come out of that saddle like he'd been roped." Floyd shook his head. "Why'd you give them so many chances? That kinda vermin needs killin'."

"I agree," Callum said, "but we had the kids here. I was hoping they'd leave without a ruckus."

"I been 'round long enough to know that kind came to kill, and they weren't gonna be satisfied until they added another death to their count. Alls they know is killing. Best kill 'em and get on with it."

Callum knew his uncle could be a hard man. He had matured in an unforgiving school, allowing no man to take advantage of another. Floyd Logan had little patience with men on the wrong side of the law and had sent several to meet their maker.

Turning to Armando, Callum said, "It's over for now, but they'll be back with many more men, and soon. They'll be coming in with blood in their eye. It's time for you and your family to leave."

Armando was shaking his head. "No, señor. I have told you I will not be driven from my land, and look how we stopped them."

Callum too shook his head. "You can't stay, Armando. We know what we're talking about. We've dealt with these kinds of people. Davies will hire more men, and the next time they show up, they'll come in with so many people we won't be able to stop them. What you've got to realize is this will all be destroyed." He swept his arm across the house, barn, and corrals. They'll burn it to the ground. You killed one of them, and they know it. They'll be looking for you. They'll destroy not only you, but all of your family, if they catch them."

Callum could see the desperation on the man's face. Everything he had worked so hard for all these years, gone in a moment. He placed his hand on Armando's shoulder. "Armando, things can be replaced. If we win this fight, we'll help you rebuild your house, your corral, and your buildings. It'll be better than it is now. But you don't want to have to try to rebuild a family."

Ana, who had been listening to the conversation, came up to her husband. Tenderly placing a hand on each side of his face, she said, "*Mi amore*, we built this once, and we can do it again. Señor Callum says they will help. Let's load up the wagon, take the animals we can, and leave. We can go to your brother's place just across the river in Mexico. We will all be safe there."

Callum watched the man. He could see pride battling with love for his family. Armando wanted to fight, but fighting could mean sacrificing his family. Callum said softly, "My friend, we *have* to go, and we have to go now."

With a sigh, Armando looked into his wife's eyes and said, "Yes. We will go."

"Good," Floyd said. "Get all your family, gear, and animals ready. We'll head out today. How long a ride is it, Armando?"

"Señor, it will take us a week, seven days. For your return, probably five."

"Then we best get moving. We don't know how long it's gonna take Will to get back here."

While Armando and Tandy went off with Ana to tell the kids and begin the work of loading and gathering, Callum walked Floyd away from the house. They found a large mesquite, cleaned the thorns from a couple of spots, and settled to the ground.

Still a limber man for his age, Floyd crossed his legs, as he had done so many times before, pulled a stem of bunchgrass, and sticking it in his mouth, started chewing. After watching the bustle around the house, he said, "What's on your mind?"

Callum said, "Uncle, we could be in big trouble. Those gents we shot today are for sure crooks, but a judge in a court of law ruled that the Double R is Davies's, and a sheriff delivered the eviction. You understand what I'm saying?"

"Of course I do, boy. I ain't stupid. You're thinking we just elected to go up against the law. We'll just tell the law those killers rode into Armando's yard, on Armando's land, and tried to take his wife and daughters. We stopped 'em."

Callum watched a red-tailed hawk sail silently into the mesquite tree and light on a limb above them. Both men fell silent, watching the hawk eye them. The majestic brown and cinnamon-colored bird turned its head sideways so that it could stare at them with its golden brown eye. Soon deciding there were better, less populated trees around, it spread its wide wings. With hearty thumps, the impressive bird lifted itself out of the mesquite, giving them a perfect view of the near white underside of its wings and brown-speckled belly. They watched it climb from the tree, find a lifting current, and stretch its wings wide, gliding higher and higher.

Floyd, silent, watched the hawk until it was out of sight, then turned wistful eyes to Callum. "Son, that was my official welcome to the Rockies. After travelin' for days, I come across that snow-covered ridge and seen Jeb Campbell standing out in front of his cabin. Right then, a big golden eagle sailed over those mountain peaks straight for me. When he got there, he just circled and circled above, welcoming me. It was then I knew I was home." He shook his head. "Hard to believe, that was nigh on forty years ago, and I'll tell you something else. I'd sure like to have some of that snow right now."

Floyd turned his head to the side, removed the grass stem,

and spit. "Pshaw. Would you listen to this old man rambling about them mountains, and here I sit in this Godforsaken country called Texas. I swear, I *know* He must've give this land to the devil, 'cause it's too blamed hot for anyone else. Now, what was we talking about?"

Callum smiled at his uncle. From the time he was a toddler, he had heard wild stories about his uncle Floyd, and he knew they were all true. After clearing his throat, he said, "What are we going to do after leaving Armando and his family in Mexico?"

"Dang, boy, you brought me out here just for that? We're gonna leave these fine folks in Mexico, then we're gonna come back here and get the Double R back. Those other boys'll be joinin' us soon. We'll figure it out as we go. The main thing is gettin' these folks outta here." Floyd looked back at the house, where they were already loading the wagon. "Speaking of going, let's get back over there and help. The sooner they're loaded, the sooner we're on our way."

12

Will and Bart crossed the Nueces around noon of the second morning. Low, the river had been easy to cross, no more than two feet deep at the deepest point. They had stopped in the river bottom and allowed the horses to drink. From the bottom, all they could see, above the high banks, were the thick trunks of pecan trees. This was a perfect spot for an ambush by renegades, so they didn't stay long.

"Let's go, Smoky," Will said and gave the horse a quick squeeze with his knees. The big grulla blew into the water, shook his head in protest and began walking toward the bank. Though Bart bumped his little mustang bay twice, it still took one last drink before moving. The two horsemen, first Will, then Bart, leaned forward over their mounts, the animals scrambling up the steep deer trail that slanted up and over the worn, six-foot bank into a stand of old-growth pecan trees.

The tall, dark green trees covered the banks of the river. During the fall, the ground would be carpeted with a thick blanket of pecans. This time of year, few pecans remained, having been harvested by mice, hogs, crows, and, of course, squirrels, including the noisy little fox squirrel that sat on a long, low limb hanging over the river and barked incessantly at them.

Will rode on, shaking his head. Everyone and everything within earshot of that squirrel knew they were here.

Bart said softly behind him, "If we didn't need to be quiet, I'd blast that little rascal clean off his limb. He'd be mighty tasty in a stew tonight."

Will said, "It's tempting, but I think the sound of your .44 just might carry a little farther than his barking. We don't want the wrong people knowing our location."

Bart nodded, saying nothing.

Renegade Apaches still raid from across the border, Will thought. *Plus the Mexicans, who do the same thing as many local ranchers. They cross the Rio Grande and rustle stock. Most lawmen on both sides look the other way.*

He rode out of the tall pecan trees into the shorter, more deadly mesquite. It was just like Armando said. Though the mesquite and prickly pear were bad, it was thinner hereabouts than farther up the Nueces. Here, it was easier for a rider to get a horse through the thorny plants without injury. He passed one patch of pear that was twenty feet wide and at least seven feet tall. Nearing the opposite side of the patch, a covey of bobwhite quail exploded from under cover of the big leaves. Thankfully, both horses remained calm, only rolling their eyes and doing a short side step. He had seen men thrown because of the sudden explosion caused by those little birds. It wouldn't do to be thrown in this mesquite- and prickly-pear-infested countryside.

After riding for over a hundred yards, the pale green of the mesquite began to thin, and they rode up a low, rocky hill. Halting before topping out, Will removed his hat and eased Smoky forward only far enough to lift his eyes above the top of the hill. From that vantage point he was able to scan the broken countryside, examining every place that provided the possibility of cover to a hostile.

With his body hidden behind a wall of mesquite, a large whitetail buck stared at the intruder. As still as a statue, the majestic animal's eyes were glued on Will. His velvet-covered antlers were already wide, and he presented an excellent opportunity for a neck shot. Will waved Bart up beside him, and the two sat watching the animal.

"Mighty pretty sight."

After a few more moments, Will clucked to Smoky and moved out ahead, Bart following. At their movement, the buck, followed by three more, bounded through the mesquite, quickly disappearing from sight. Once they were on top of the hill, they turned north, paralleling the river. *It won't be long now,* Will thought, *if they're still here.*

They had ridden a little more than two miles when they crossed a trail more used than the others they had crossed. Will nodded at the trail, Bart acknowledged the signal, and the two turned toward the creek. After clearing the mesquite, and upon entering the pecan grove, the sound of a hammer going to full cock was accompanied by a voice calling from deep within the trees.

"I'm thinking it's a wrong turn you laddies made. If having those healthy bodies ventilated by a .44 leaves you a bit squeamish, I'm saying you should be heading in a different direction."

Will said, loud enough to ensure he was heard clearly, "Danged if I don't think that voice must belong to a good-for-nothing Scotsman I know."

MacGregor stepped out from a massive pecan tree and waved. Bart and Will rode forward. Nearing him, Will watched Mac mount and urged his horse toward them. "It's happy I am to be seeing you laddies." He reached over and grabbed first Will's and then Bart's hands in a powerful shake.

Will examined his friend. More white hair peeked out from under his hat than when they had parted in Abilene. The hazel eyes still held their mischievousness, but they were also showing the wrinkles of time and worry. He had always been a barrel-chested man, and still was, but he had slimmed down, and not in a good way. He looked older and tired.

"It's good to see you, Mac," Will said. "Where's Darcy?"

The Scotsman leaned back in the saddle. "'Tis a long story, my friend. Follow me to our fine castle, and I'll be telling you."

They rode silently through the tall pecans, the only sounds coming from the horses' hooves and the creaking leather of the saddles. Even the normal sounds of the mockingbird and cardinal singing, or the scratching bark from the sharp, grasping nails of the squirrels as they raced through the trees were miss-ing. It was as if a funeral procession were passing through their domain, and the animals were paying homage.

They rode around a thicket of tangled briars, and in front of them appeared a small cabin with a lean-to barn off the east side. *From the looks of it,* Will thought, *it might just be large enough to squeeze in six animals if needed.*

Dismounting, Bart took the reins from his friends. "I'll water the horses. Back in a minute."

"That's a lovely deed you do," Mac said, and led Will into the cabin. "I'd offer you some coffee, but it's no cooking during the day. Though the trees should spread the smoke, we're not desiring of anyone finding us."

Will looked around the inside of the small cabin. It was mostly bunk beds, with a fireplace in the middle against the back wall. There were enough beds to sleep eight, but it looked as if only Mac was currently occupying the space. Several chairs sat against the sturdy, windowless log walls, leaving barely enough room for a small table that would seat four. "Not the Remington Ranch home," Will said.

"No, laddie, the mighty have certainly fallen. Grab a chair, and we'll sit outside. 'Tis cooler in the out-of-doors."

Will grabbed one chair, and Mac grabbed two. They set them

near the front wall, close enough where they could lean back against it if the whim hit them.

After sitting down, Mac took out his pipe, knife, and a plug of tobacco. He offered it to Will, who declined, and started shaving tobacco into his pipe. "Aye, I suppose you're still not a drinking man either."

"What's happened around here, Mac? How could this Englishman just ride in here and take over your ranch?"

"It's yours too, laddie. We never took your name off the deed. It's yours, mine, Darcy's and Wade's, god rest his soul. As to how it happened, that is something I'm still asking meself."

Once he had shaved enough into his pipe, he carefully rewrapped the tobacco and slipped it back into his vest pocket. Taking the butt of his knife, he gently tapped the shavings, packing it into the bowl, slipped his knife back into the leather scabbard, pressed lightly on the tobacco around the edge of the pipe bowl, placed it in his mouth, and gave a tentative draw. Holding the pipe between his teeth, he took a match from a container in his other vest pocket, lit the match by jerking it across his pistol holster, and carefully lit the tobacco, drawing at the same time. After several puffs, he nodded again, shook out the match, smashed it in his fingers to make sure it was out, and dropped it in a bucket that sat next to him.

Will, though impatient to hear what had happened, knew there was no rushing his friend when he was going through his pipe-lighting ritual. It was the very same every time.

He watched Mac drop the match into the bucket and take a long draw from his pipe, holding it for a moment, then slowly exhaling with an audible sigh.

"Now, you ask what happened. One day this fancy-dressed Englishman shows up at the ranch, and let me tell you right out, Will my lad, you cannot trust an Englishman. That is why I left my sweet land of Scotland. It was my life's goal to get away from

Englishmen, and here they've followed me across the sea and this fine country to my little piece of heaven."

Will watched his friend grow more agitated as he talked, his pipe puffing like a coal-fired train engine.

"I swear," Mac continued, "the devils will follow me all the way to hell!"

The Scotsman paused, removed his pipe, and took a deep breath of the clean fragrant air of the pecan grove. "Sorry. The hard feelings between Scotland and England go back a long way. But I was saying, this blasted Englishman, all duded up in his fancy clothes, shows up with his man Langston, a cold killer."

He had made the killer remark just as Bart returned with the horses. Bart stopped and looked cooly at Mac. "Did I miss something?"

The Scotsman shook his head. "No, no, nothing about you, lad. I was talking about Langston."

Will and Mac walked over to Bart. "Here," Will said, "let us help."

Looking at Will, Bart asked, "Have you told him yet?"

"No, he's been talking, and I wanted to find out what happened to Darcy."

A quizzical expression on his face, Mac said, "Told me what?"

"I've been wanting to find out about Darcy," Will said, "but I might as well go ahead and tell you. My memory returned."

"What? Your memory has come back? Is it everything you can remember? You remember the battle? How is it you're feeling?"

"Slow down, Mac. Yes, it has returned, and I can remember the battle, everything. Course there's a blank from the time I was shot to when I woke up, but other than that, I remember it all, and I feel fine."

Mac stepped up and grabbed Will's arms high on the biceps. "Laddie, it's a happy man I am for you. So, tell me, what's your name?"

"My name is William Wallace Logan. I go by Will, and I found my family in Colorado."

"Colorado," Mac said, "isn't that interesting. Here we thought they were back east."

Will grinned at the puzzled man. "They were, but that's a long story. There's also a second part to this." Will paused as he looked at Mac, his grin growing wider. "I'm married."

"No, I'm not believing it. You married? I thought your mind was all involved with that nurse back in Washington?" He tapped his left temple. "I must think. What was her name?" Suddenly looking up, he said, "Deborah Coleman, that was it. What about her?"

Now Will laughed outright and then said, "That's who I married."

"No. You wouldn't kid an old Scotsman, now would you?"

"Honest truth. We married last month, just before I left for Texas and the ranch."

"I'm not believing it." Suddenly he thrust out his big right hand. "Congratulations." He paused before continuing, then said, "Will. I'll be having to get used to that, Will Logan. You are a lucky man."

"Yes, I sure am. Now let's hear about Darcy while we take care of these horses."

Each man took his horse into the makeshift barn. After unsaddling them, they removed bridles and blankets and hung them on the rails and dowels Mac and Darcy had made for tack. Then they began rubbing down the horses. While they worked, Mac talked.

"Let me tell you what happened. Davies shows up waving a piece of paper and saying he owns the Double R. I tell him to take his English rear off my ranch or I'll throw him off. Langston, sitting there cool as an Englishwoman's heart, he is, calmly moves his hand near his holster and says, 'You might want to rethink that idea.'

"My fine Darcy comes to my rescue. I'm knowing I don't have a snowball's chance of beating Langston, but when that gunman's hand moves near his gun, Darcy steps out of the barn with a couple of hands, and all three ear back the hammers on their Henrys. 'Tis a wonderful chorus the sound of those hammers was to my ears. It didn't faze Langston. He just moved that hand back to his saddle horn and said cooly, 'Another time, then.'"

Mac stopped brushing his horse and looked over its back at Will and Bart. "I'll tell you, that Langston is a cold customer. It's thinking, I am, that he is as deadly as one of those little coral snakes."

Bart continued rubbing his horse, but said quietly, "Maybe, but he bleeds like everyone else. No matter how bad they are, or how bad they think they are, there's always someone badder and faster." He looked at Will.

Will had been bent over brushing Smoky's side. He rose. "So did you see the paper? Is that when you left?"

"Oh, no. It was then we ran them off the ranch. But Davies waved that paper like it was a royal decree and said the land and all the cattle were his, and he would be back. We were concerned, but not much, because we had all of our purchase documents. There really was nothing to worry about, or so we thought.

"A couple of weeks later, Davies and Langston, along with ten or so more riders, show up with the sheriff. The sheriff hands me a copy of the deed and an order of eviction and said to gather up our personal things and get out. Of course we argued. We showed the sheriff our papers, but it was of no use. Unfortunately, the Englishman had bought himself a judge in San Antonio, and he stole our ranch." Mac stood there shaking his shaggy head.

"So that's it? You have no legal way to regain your ranch?" Will asked.

The men finished with the horses, put some feed in the small trough, and for a moment, watched them eat.

"Let's move back out front," Will said and led the way to the chairs.

When they were seated, Will said to Mac, "You still haven't told me what you've done with Darcy."

"Patience, lad, patience." Mac looked at the bowl of his pipe. It was out.

He stared at it, started for the tobacco in his pocket, then stopped, just shook his head, thumped out the ashes in the bucket, put the pipe in his vest, and leaned back against the wall. "We left. We had to. We paid off the boys, fortunately we had enough left, and extra, from the cattle drive to Abilene, but there wasn't enough to keep them employed. We had to turn them loose. Several are waiting in Dog Town to see what is going to happen. It's sorry I am I can't pay them, but they're good men, they'll find work."

"So where is Darcy?" Will asked.

"He left in the middle of April for Austin."

"Austin," Bart asked, "what's in Austin?"

"Not what, laddie. Who," Mac said. "Senator Joseph Barlow is the name. Darcy knew of him from a lawman he had known years ago. The lawman was his son and said that his pa was one of the few honest and fearless lawyers he knew. That's why he headed to Austin."

"Seems like a long time to be gone," Will said. "From here to Austin, taking it easy would probably be about a twelve-day to two-week ride. If a man was pushing and had a couple of horses, I guess maybe seven to nine days. So say it takes a month, round trip, that still leaves him way more than a month for the lawyer to get this figured out. We'll be looking at July in just a couple more days. He should be back by now, if for no other reason than to let you know what's going on."

"Aye, seems like it to me too, but I'm not knowing how long these legal fights are a-taking, so here I am." At this point, Mac stopped, stared at the ground, and shook his head before turning to look at Will. "All I know is fighting, but I won't fight the law, so I sit and wait for Darcy."

"So when he left," Bart asked, "he didn't know for sure how long it might take him?"

"Naw, laddie, neither of us did. We built this little cabin far out of the way from everything, stocked it up with plenty of supplies, and then he took off. I'm about to go out of my mind, sitting and waiting. You're having no idea how happy I am to be seeing you here."

Will removed his black Stetson, set it on a knee, untied the red bandanna Deborah had given him, wiped his forehead, then the sweatband, and repositioned the hat on his head. As he was tying the bandanna back in place, he said, "I'm glad we found you, but we're not going to sit around. It's time something was done. You showed me the purchase agreement, the deed, everything. It was all legal. I'm heading for Austin to find Darcy. Mac, you can wait here in case Darcy returns, or you can leave him a note, and we'll all go."

Mac clapped his hands on his knees. "Aye, it's finding out I'm after. A note it is. When do we leave?"

Will turned to Bart. "What do you think? Spend the night here, give the horses a little rest, and leave in the morning?"

"Sounds good to me, boss. It sure won't hurt 'em to rest up a bit. Shoot, it won't hurt me either."

"Guess that settles it," Will said. "We'll leave in the morning."

13

Callum brought up the rear with Tandy, driving the small mixed herd. Horses, cattle, pigs, piglets, and several burros meandered along behind the wagon. They had just crossed the Nueces River, en route to Eagle Pass on the border of Texas and Mexico.

Callum guided Shoshone over to Tandy, who had his bandanna pulled up and over his nose to combat the dust. They had been traveling for four days. So far, it had been an uneventful trip other than the dust. The taller grass had given way to a parched land sprinkled with bunchgrass, greasewood, and mesquite.

He watched the wagon sway, sometimes perilously close to tipping. The ground, though appearing level to the distant eye, was rough, strew with broken rock, shallow trenches caused by heavy runoff during sudden, explosive thunderstorms, and deep arroyos. Plus, with the children and all the items Ana had insisted on crowding into the limited space, the wagon was overloaded. *Good thing we're not traveling far,* Callum thought, watching the four-horse team labor with the load. They had been rotating horses three times a day, and the animals were getting worn out.

Nearing Tandy, he nodded his head toward the near left edge of the stock, where the dust was lighter. Tandy nodded and followed Callum's lead. Once the two men reached their new position, they pulled the bandannas to their necks, and Callum picked up his canteen, enjoying the heavy weight of it. Crossing the Nueces, they had filled all of their barrels, water bags, and canteens, which would provide plenty of water for the remainder of the trip. He tossed it over to Tandy.

"Much obliged," Tandy said, pulled the stopper, turned the canteen up, and took a short swig.

Callum watched as the young man swished the water around in his mouth before swallowing. He had known Tandy only since last year, when Will had shown up with him and Bart at their ranch in Colorado. He knew him as a hard worker, a man who was devoted to his brother. Will had never told the whole story about their relationship, but Callum surmised there was definitely a story.

Tandy tossed the canteen back. "Thanks. A little dry."

"Yeah," Callum said, "and a *little* dusty."

They both laughed at that. The two men were comical looking. Between their hat brims and the bridge of their noses, their faces were brown and blotched with caked dust. Both had blue eyes, Callum's a light, almost cold, blue, and Tandy's a deep blue that often still showed the mischievous quick humor of youth. But today, both men's eyes looked like white and blue marbles floating in a sea of mud.

"You should see your face," Tandy said, and laughed again.

"Imagine it looks a lot like yours, boy." Callum grinned back at him. Then he looked down at his clothes. Everything was coated with the same layer of dust. Where the sleeves of his shirt wrinkled, the wrinkles were like brown canyons, which exploded when he shook his arm.

"How many more days, you reckon?" Tandy asked.

"From what Armando says, should be no more than three,

maybe two. He's got enough horses to change out on the wagon, so he's thinking we might see Eagle Pass sooner than later."

"I been there before," Tandy said.

"Oh, yeah? Much to see?"

"Like any border town. Rough around the edges. There's folks there who'd just as soon shoot you or knife you as look at you."

"Sounds nice."

"Not too bad. Food's good, if you like your food spicy." He grinned again at Callum.

"I'll tell you," Callum said, "we've been eating mighty fine with Ana cooking. It'd have to go some to beat her."

Tandy glanced back in the direction of the country they'd passed. "Think they're following us?"

"I'm surprised they haven't caught up. I was sure they'd have returned almighty quick, maybe the next day, so yeah, I think they're following us. I just don't know if they'll catch us before we cross the Rio Grande." He turned around to check behind them once more. He had been keeping an eye on their back trail for the entire trip, and each time he was relieved to see no dust.

Callum looked across the small herd to see a couple of bunch quitters they had been having trouble with since leaving the Ruiz home. The two cows were drifting away from the herd and angling around, back to the ranch and their home range. "Gotta go," he said, pulled his bandanna back up over his nose, turned Shoshone toward the two longhorns, and trotted toward them. When the cows saw him, they broke into a run. He nudged Shoshone, and the big appaloosa leaped forward, rapidly narrowing the short distance. Rounding the two, Callum slowed his horse, pushed the two back to the herd and settled down to a dusty, uncomfortable ride.

Far ahead of the wagon, Callum saw Floyd rise in the saddle, stare, turn and trot back to the wagon. Callum motioned for Tandy to cover the drag, and nudged his horse into a trot toward the wagon.

"Well, ain't you a sight," Floyd said as they came together.

"Be glad to trade," Callum replied, pulling the bandanna down.

"No, I'm fine." Turning serious, the old mountain man said, "We got company. Two, maybe three miles ahead, coming our way." He turned to Armando, who was driving the wagon. "Best get the kids inside and keep 'em quiet. Don't know if these fellers are friendly or not. Keep your rifle handy, just in case. Don't think it's Apaches. From what I know about them fellers, you don't see them until it's too late. We'll just have to wait and see. May be army. The dust cloud's awfully tight, but the way they're coming, it won't be long."

Callum looked around where they had pulled the wagon to a stop. It was a slight depression, fairly open for thirty or forty yards, with only a few greasewood and mesquite around. Not a bad place to make a stand, if needed. He looked over to the wagon. Even while Floyd was talking, Armando had gathered the kids into the wagon. The older ones, with their mother, had been walking alongside, primarily to lighten the load, but the parents also knew everyone would sleep better if the children were tired when they went to bed. Ana had climbed into the wagon next to her husband, and Callum saw she had a shotgun leaning against her leg.

He looked over at her. "You good with that weapon, ma'am?"

"Why, yes, Señor Callum, I think I am."

Armando nodded his head earnestly. "*Si*, Callum. She is very good. She can knock a chachalaca right out of the air."

Callum gave a short nod. "That's good, ma'am. You just might need to be."

The dust was being kicked up by a small group of riders. Floyd was the first to say, "Soldiers, everybody relax." He took the time to kick one leg out of the stirrup, slide his hat to the back of his head, and cross his leg over the saddle.

As they neared, Callum could make out it was a troop of six

riders. A lieutenant was in the lead, alongside a sergeant, with four additional troopers. The animals had been at a trot, but the lieutenant held up his hand, the sergeant gave an order, and they slowed their horses to a walk, finally bringing them to a stop at the wagon.

"Howdy, Lieutenant," Floyd said.

"Good afternoon, sir," the young second lieutenant responded. "I am Lieutenant Osborn, and this is Sergeant Sneed." Osborn saw Ana in the wagon and touched his hat brim. "Morning, ma'am, sir." He nodded to Armando.

Floyd said, "That's Señor Ruiz and his wife and kids." Heads were sticking out from behind Armando and Ana. "This here is my nephew Callum Logan, and that feller back in the dust is Tandy Jacobs."

Greetings completed, Floyd continued, "What's got you out here on this almighty hot day, Lieutenant?"

"Patrol. We're looking for Apaches. There's been a dustup near the river. We had a report of several crossing the river into the US. We're out showing the colors."

"You got a guide?"

"No, sir. The major ordered another patrol out ahead of us, heading to the northeast. Our only guide rode with them."

"Then you boys best keep yore eyes peeled," Floyd said. "Them Apaches can come right up out of the ground. They'll be on you before you know it."

Sergeant Sneed looked at his officer. "That's what I've been saying, Lieutenant Osborn. The men need their sidearms and rifles at the ready."

"Sergeant Sneed." The lieutenant turned in his saddle to face the sergeant. "You may order the men to make their revolvers ready, but they don't need to ride around this country handling those hot rifles. I don't want any of my men reporting to sick call with blistered hands."

The sergeant immediately ordered the men to unfasten the

revolver flap that covered their weapons and bend it back inside their belts. This way, if they needed the weapon, they could reach it quickly.

Osborn turned back to Floyd. "Have you seen any sign of Apaches?"

"Nope, I ain't. But I'm here to tell you, when you don't see 'em, you need to be doubly alert. I fought 'em some in Colorado, and they're the slickest Injuns I've ever seen at hiding."

"Thank you for your information, Mr. Logan. What are you folks doing out in this country?"

"We're taking the Ruiz family to Piedras Negras, then we'll be coming back."

"Where are you from?"

"Well, we're from Colorado, down to help some friends. Once that's taken care of, we'll be headin' back." He wiped his brow. "Goin' back can't come soon enough."

The young lieutenant nodded. "Yes, sir, I understand. It does get hot down here." He nodded to Armando and Ana. "We must be moving on. Good luck to you.

"Sergeant, move them men out."

The sergeant waved his arm, and the patrol moved forward. The sergeant rolled his eyes at Floyd as he rode by. In a short time the patrol had traveled out of sight, marked only by their plume of hanging dust.

Callum said, "A second lieutenant leading a patrol with hostiles around, and it doesn't sound like he's listening to his sergeant." He shook his head. "I guess we can pray they don't run into those Apaches."

"Don't waste yore prayers on them boys, Callum. Send 'em up on our behalf. Those Injuns could have spotted us and figured we'd be a lot easier pickings."

"Uncle, I've been praying ever since we left. I don't want that Davies bunch to catch up with us either. Now, hopefully, they'll run into the patrol instead of jumping us."

"Nephew, I'm proud you're on speaking terms with the Man upstairs. Hopefully he'll smooth the path for us."

Callum turned to Armando, who had been watching the two men. "Let's move it out, Armando, and since we've been told Apaches might be around, reckon you might keep the kids in the wagon."

Armando flicked the reins to the four horses, the trace chains clanked with tension, and the wagon jerked forward.

ANA WAS DRIVING the wagon when they sighted Eagle Pass. Other than running into the army patrol, the trip had been quiet. Armando had ridden with Floyd into Eagle Pass and across to Piedras Negras to let his brother know they were on their way.

The dust at drag was still just as heavy, and the heat was searing to any exposed skin. Callum, along with everyone else, wore leather gloves extending well past his wrists to cover his gray and green checked shirt. It was hard to tell any color because of the dust.

The sight of the green trees along the Rio Grande, and in the two towns, was a welcome sight. He was looking forward to grabbing a bath and a good night's sleep, with no standing watch, before heading back. The last couple of days, after meeting the soldiers, had been a little tense. Apaches were a factor that no one wanted to add to their concern.

The children had been cooped up inside the wagon for the last two days. Nearing the streets of Eagle Pass, they were clamoring to get out, to see. Ana spoke sharply, and everyone settled down just as a group of riders appeared out of the river bottom and raced toward them. Clamoring, and clapping this time, broke out again as the older children recognized their papi and uncle in the lead of the vaqueros. Well back of the riders and from a far street, a carriage came into view as their uncle drew up next to the stopped wagon.

From drag, Callum watched with interest, wondering what the brother of Armando might be like.

Mounted on a beautiful golden palomino, Armando's brother was an impressive sight. Taller, heavier, and older than Armando, he was dressed in a rich brown suit with a short jacket and tight pants, which flared open around the boots. It was all trimmed in silver. His shirt was brilliant white, sporting a brown leather string tie. A large turquoise stone, cradled in silver, held the strings of the tie together. His thick white hair, cut just below his ears, set off a firm but friendly face, darkened even more by the southern sun. It was softened somewhat with age, but still showed the strength required to survive and flourish in this country.

With a dramatic and gallant gesture, he removed the large dark brown and silver embroidered sombrero from his head and, sweeping it low, bowed to his sister-in-law. In Spanish, he said, "My lovely sister Ana, you are still as beautiful as when I first met you. Welcome. My home is your home. It is wonderful to see you."

Ana smiled to her brother-in-law, replying in Spanish, "Antonio, you are still as handsome and full of flattery as ever. Thank you."

Now a frown replaced his smile as he slipped the sombrero back on his head. He gazed at the children's faces staring out at him from around their mother. "Who are these strange children? I do not know them. They are much too old." Then his face lit up with a big smile exposing shiny white teeth. "Wait, could these strong-looking men be Felipe and Pablo, and the beautiful young women, Isabella and Alexa? No, it cannot be."

Felipe and Isabella grinned, maintaining the dignity befitting their age, while Pablo and Alexa jumped up and down in the wagon, yelling, "Yes, Uncle, yes. It's us."

"Why, I believe it is. Welcome, my beauties." Then Antonio studied young Marco, who was sitting on the wagon seat next to his mother. "Who is this fine young man? I do not think I am familiar with him."

Ana placed one arm around Marco and said, "This is our little Marco." She looked down at her tiny son. "Marco, say hello to your uncle. This is Don Antonio Fernando Ruiz Bautista, but you may call him Uncle Antonio."

Antonio moved his palomino close to the wagon and held out his arms. "Marco, would you like to ride with your uncle?"

The little boy thrust out his chubby arms, and his uncle leaned over and scooped him into his, hugging him close. Marco laughed with glee.

The carriage that had been following behind the vaqueros pulled up, waiting. Antonio waved it forward. "It is not fitting for my family to drive this wagon when there is more appropriate transport available. Handing Marco to Armando, Antonio stepped from the sparkling saddle, inlaid with silver, and reached up for Ana. "Let me help you. One of my vaqueros will drive your wagon. Come, children." He turned to one of his men. "Raul, the wagon."

"*Si, jefe*," the man said as he handed his reins to a companion and leaped from his horse. He moved briskly to the wagon and helped the children down, smiling, when Felipe waved him away and jumped down. The vaquero stepped up into the wagon and picked up the ribbons.

Antonio helped Ana and then the children, hugging each one except for Felipe and Pablo, whom he solemnly shook hands with. Once everyone was in the carriage, he rode back to Callum and Tandy, who had lowered their bandannas.

Callum watched the older man ride up, looking very dignified and regal on the palomino.

Reaching them, he said, in fluent English, "I am Antonio Ruiz. Welcome to my humble home. I thank you for protecting my brother's family. These vaqueros will take care of the stock. Please ride with us."

"Howdy," Callum said. "I'm Callum Logan, and this is Tandy Jacobs. We thank you, but we've got to find our uncle, and we both need a bath before we meet any civilized folks. We'll just grab a hotel room, and once we're cleaned up, we'll head on over."

Armando had ridden up with his brother. Both men shook their heads. Antonio said, "No, Señor Callum. Come with us. Your uncle is at my home. I suspect he has already bathed and is enjoying a little relaxation."

Callum said, "Thank you, Don Antonio, we are grateful. I would ask that your vaqueros be especially careful of the little pigs. They are favorites of that young fella you have with you."

"Please, it is only Antonio. I will tell my men, and Callum, mine is a working ranch, we too know about the dirt." He spoke quickly to two of the vaqueros, who nodded and responded with, "*Si, jefe.*"

The carriage had already started for town. Antonio and Armando led the way, at first trotting, then walking their horses once they had reached the carriage. Callum and Tandy were next, and then the remaining vaqueros. Callum grinned when he heard a vaquero say to one of those remaining to drive the stock, "*Adios, pastor de cerdos,*" herder of pigs.

Now that everyone was safe, Callum's mind shifted to his brother. *I wonder if he's having any luck finding his friends. I know he wanted to stay with Deborah, but he felt like he owed his friends. Guess that might be the Logan curse, always bent on helping others.* He yanked his bandanna off for the umpteenth time and wiped his sweaty, dirty face. *I agree with Uncle Floyd. I'm ready to be back in the mountains.*

14

W ill led the way onto the rickety pontoon bridge that spanned the Colorado River. The hollow clunk of the horses' hooves combined with the bridge's swaying from the river current to give him a skittish ride on Smoky.

Mac, bringing up the rear, said, "I'll say to any who'll listen, those ferries are looking much more inviting than this contraption."

Will said nothing. He was busy watching Smoky as the horse, usually sure-footed and calm, lifted his feet high, almost prancing along the cross-planked platform. With no railing, the current from the river caused rhythmic undulating. With the constant vibration from the steps of other travelers, horses, and wagons, he was ready to be across the long, unstable span.

The shore, growing closer with each of Smoky's high, nervous steps, supported a deep cut road rising from the river surface up the steep bank to Brazos Street in Austin. Bustle assailed their ears even before reaching the Colorado River. The sound was a low-pitched, garbled blend of trace chains rattling, men yelling commands, women talking, and the constant rattling and bump of wagons. After the quiet peace of the range, broken only by an occasional cow lowing, crow calling, or coyote howling, the approaching noise of a busy city was almost painful to their ears.

Will felt a last nervous quiver run through the grulla's body as they cleared the last cross-plank of the bridge and stepped onto solid ground. "I know, boy. I'm as glad to be across as you are." He turned in the saddle to Mac. "You know where this lawyer's office is located?"

"I have not the slightest idea. But the lad Darcy said it is called the Barlow Law and Land office."

Bart spoke up. "We can ask at the stable. I know a good one. Name's Platt's Livery. He's been around a long time. He saved my bacon a while back. Let me have a horse when I was broke and needed one mighty bad."

"Lead the way," Will said.

Will recognized the smell as they slanted up the road. It was near the same smell found in all of the other cities he had known. Smoke from fires for cooking or heating of metals in blacksmith's shops or just heating, in the winter, combined with the smell of animals and humans. The outhouses, small pastures, and corrals gave off their own perfumes. The blending of them all infused a person's senses until those smells became familiar and no longer offensive.

Bart led the trio north on Brazos. Reaching Pine, he turned right, rode for one block, and turned left on San Jacinto. The three rode along a corral to their right till reaching the front of the large stable. Across the upper portion of the two-story stable was written, in wide, red, block letters, Platt's Livery. On the south side of the stable was a long watering trough, lengthy enough for six horses to drink side by side.

The three dismounted, and, Smoky leading, the horses pushed forward to the trough. Heads dipped, and they began drinking the cool water.

Will ran his fingers through the black mane, flipping it to the other side of the gray neck, then gave the horse a couple of solid pats. "Been a long trip for you, hasn't it, boy?"

Bart snorted, placed both hands to his sides, and leaned as far back as he could, then tilted from side to side, trying to stretch stiff muscles. "Don't know if it's been a long trip for him, but it sure as shootin' has been a long one for me. My backside feels like it's ridden over half of Texas, and, come to think of it, it has."

Will eyed his friend. "It looks and smells like you're carrying most of it on you."

"Aye," Mac said, "a hot bath would be welcome to this old body."

"Not a bad idea," Will replied. "Let's see this lawyer, then we'll get cleaned up and grab some city grub."

"Howdy, gents. Hot day for riding."

The three looked to the entrance of the stable to see a man, his face covered with sweat and soot, wiping his hands on the end of the long blacksmith's apron he wore.

Bart stepped forward, extending his hand. "Howdy, Mr. Platt. Don't know if you remember me. I'm Bart Porter."

"Why, sure I do. I also remember you sending me the money for that horse, much obliged." He grinned and examined the younger man. "Glad to see you're still alive and kickin'. There was a rumor you got shot up a while back."

"Only a little," Bart said. He waved his arm at his companions. "These are friends of mine, Will Logan and Mac MacGregor."

Will and Mac stepped forward and shook Platt's hand.

"You fellers call me Frank." Platt scanned Will from boots to hat. "Looks like yore mama did right by you."

"That she did," Will said, "and we'd be obliged if you could do right by our horses."

"Yep, that I can," Platt said. "Looks like they've seen some miles. I'll take real good care of 'em. They'll think they're in one of them mas-sage parlors. A bait of oats and corn, add in some rest, and these boys will be brand new."

"Thanks, Frank," Bart said. "Could you tell us where we can find the Barlow Law and Land office?"

"Why, I sure can, and let me tell you, you won't find no better than Senator Barlow." Frank leaned in, speakin' in a low confidential tone. "Normally you ain't gonna hear me say nothin' good 'bout no lawyer, but he's near the best of the breed. He'll do you square."

"And where's his office?" Will asked.

"Up thataway," Frank said, "take a right at Pine, then one block to San Jacinto and take a left. It'll be on the corner of Pecan and San Jacinto, on the northwest side. You cain't miss it." Using his hands, he outlined a big square. "Got a big glass front window that says Barlow Law and Land.

"By the by, fellers, how long you planning on staying?"

"Don't know yet," Will replied. "At least overnight." He reached into his vest pocket to dig out money to pay Frank for a night's stay of the horses.

Frank waved a hand. "No. I wasn't hinting at that. It ain't necessary to pay now. I was just curious. Gets me in trouble sometimes. You can pay me when you leave. I charge two bits a day for stablin' a horse or mule. That gets 'em a good rubdown along with corn or oats or both. Yours'll be gettin' both, like I said. Looks like they could use a good meal."

"Thanks, Frank," Will said. "After we stop by Mr. Barlow's office, we'll have a better idea how long we'll be, so we'll stop by, tell you, and pick up our gear."

Frank waved, gathered the reins of the three horses, and led them into the stable.

Following Frank's directions, the men went up Brazos, turned right on Pine, took a left on San Jacinto, walked a block, crossed Pecan, and stood at the large front window of Barlow Law and

Land. Inside, they could see a man hunched over a desk, absorbed in his work.

Will opened the door and led the men into the office. Inside and to the left of the entry door was a desk. At the desk sat the young man they had seen from the outside, busily working, a stack of papers next to him. At their entry, he looked up and said, "May I help you, gentlemen?"

Will nodded. "We're looking for the lawyer who might have talked to our partner, Darcy Smith."

The man stood. "Yes, sir, that would be Senator Barlow. He isn't in right now, but I expect him back any moment. You're welcome to have a seat." He motioned to four comfortable-looking, plush wingback chairs sitting on the opposite side of the room, in front of two walls filled from floor to ceiling with books.

Will shook his head. "Thanks, but we just came in off the trail, and we're mighty dirty. We'll stand till the Senator gets back. Anyway, we've been sitting in the saddle for quite a few days. Standing feels mighty good."

The young man smiled. "I understand, but the Senator says those chairs are for his clients, and believe me, sir, he wouldn't mind you sitting in them at all."

Will shook his head again. "Much obliged. We'll stand."

The young man shrugged, said, "Suit yourself," and returned to his papers.

Will walked over to the bookcase and began examining the books. He had never been the reader his brother Josh was, but he still enjoyed reading. He pulled several of them from the shelves, turned pages in each, enjoying the respite, and slid the books back in place.

"You able to read them words?" Bart asked.

"Mostly. Many are over my head. We used to have a library when I was a boy. Nothing so grand as this. Ma read to us all the time."

Bart shook his head. "Weren't neither one of my folks able to read or write. Ma could sign her name, and she taught me how to sign mine, but when it comes to reading or writing anything, I'm out of luck."

The three men turned at the sound of the door opening. A tall, white-haired man walked in, closed the door, and removed his black Stetson, very similar to Will's, and hung it on the hat rack. Will liked the honest face immediately.

"Senator Barlow," the young man said, looking up from his papers, "these gentlemen are here to see you. They are partners with Darcy Smith."

"Gentlemen," the senator said, his deep, rich voice filling the room, "welcome to Austin. I am Joseph Barlow. Let me guess, Hank Remington would be the tall one."

"Correct, Senator," Will said, shaking his hand. "And this is Liam MacGregor."

Mac shook the senator's hand, saying, "It's pleased I am to meet you, Senator."

"You also," Senator Barlow said.

Bart stepped forward, and Will introduced him. "This is Bart Porter."

"Howdy, Senator Barlow," Bart said.

Shaking Bart's hand, the senator said, "I've heard the name."

"Probably nothing good," Bart said.

"No, on the contrary, Mr. Porter. I heard it from a sheriff who said you had defended yourself in an honorable manner, and there was nothing to the complaint that had been sworn out against you. He said the complaint was instigated by those in search of vengeance."

"That's true, Senator. I ain't never shot a man what didn't deserve it."

"Good." Senator Barlow turned to Will. "And you are Henry Remington?"

"Senator, I am and I'm not. There's some explaining needs to be done."

"Please, gentlemen, come into my office." The senator turned to his clerk. "David, would you get another chair for our guests?"

David jumped from his desk, picked up a chair, and hurried it into the office. He placed it in front of the big desk, and as he was pulling the office door shut behind him, the senator said, "David, I don't want to be disturbed."

"Yes, sir," David said, and started to close the door, but Bart caught the latch.

"Sorry, I'm not a partner. I don't belong here."

"Nonsense," Will said. "You're welcome to stay."

"Aye, laddie," Mac chimed in, "you may not own part of the ranch, but you're welcome to hear anything we have to say."

"I appreciate it, but the less I know about it, the happier I am. I'll head down and grab our gear, then get us some rooms." He turned to the senator. "The City Hotel still good, Senator?"

"It is. In fact, I would recommend it, and you can tell whoever greets you, Senator Barlow sent you over."

"Thanks," Bart said, and pulled the door closed. His boots and spurs could be heard crossing the outer room. The front door opened, then closed, and he was gone.

"Have a seat, gentlemen," the senator said, moving behind his massive oak desk. He seated himself, and, ignoring the passing wagon visible through his window that looked onto San Jacinto Street, looking at Will, said, "All right, you have my attention. You say you are, but you aren't Hank Remington. Would you care to explain?"

"It's kind of a long story, but I'll make it as short as possible." Will spent the next few minutes telling the abbreviated story of how he had ended up with two names. "And that brings us to our situation today. Since you met Darcy Smith, and you've been working on our situation, hopefully you can tell us what's happening."

"Indeed I have, gentlemen." He turned to Mac. "Mr. MacGregor, I am both pleased and sorry to tell you that I believe you have fallen victim to a charlatan. This Sir Wilford Pemberton Davies III is a very elusive individual. Sir Davies was indeed in the army and knighted for bravery. But the information I have received indicates he died in the city of New York last year. His butler, who had been with him for only a few years, disappeared at the same time. Coincidental with the butler's disappearance, a sizeable sum of money and valuables also was, and is still, missing. As yet, there is no proof that Sir Davies's man stole his possessions, but the authorities in New York City would like to have the opportunity to talk to him."

Will looked at Mac, then said, "So this Davies at our ranch is an imposter?"

Senator Barlow raised his hands, palms forward. "It appears so. I have some good friends in the city, and I hope to have a telegraph message from them as soon as they have more information."

"Senator," Will said, "if this man is, in fact, the butler of Sir Davies, who died in New York City, then his documents are fake."

Senator Barlow reached into a drawer of his desk and pulled out a copy of the deed to the Double R ranch and the bill of sale. He quickly scanned them and laid the papers on his desk, smoothing them out with his hands. "Gentlemen, these are copies, certified, I had made from your documents. I can attest that these are true and correct, registered, stamped, and filed correctly. I am truly sorry you gave up your ranch, for in this country, the saying 'possession is nine-tenths of the law' is very true."

Mac's face turned red. "Senator, I'm asking you kindly, is it explaining you could do as to what response I should have had when the sheriff rides in with Davies and eleven other men and says the imposter's papers are true and we've got to get off our own land?"

The senator shook his head. "I did not mean to offend you, Mr. MacGregor. There is nothing you could have done but leave. However, I'm telling you that you own your ranch free and clear. This man Davies, imposter or not, does not have any right to be there, no matter what kind of papers he has. I personally rode to San Antonio and visited with Judge Pearson, who happens to be a good friend. He says he has no memory of, nor is there any record of Davies ever having a case before his court."

Mac sank in his chair. "I let this thief of a man, this Englishman, ride onto our land and steal it with a piece of paper?"

"He didn't just fool you, Mac," Will said, "he fooled the sheriff. This is simple. We'll ride back down to Dog Town, tell the sheriff, and throw them off."

"That's exactly what I told Darcy," Senator Barlow said. "He left here with a copy of the necessary documents, along with the deed and bill of sale he possessed, and was going straight to the sheriff of McMullen County."

Will looked at Mac. "I guess we must have missed him. By the time we get back down there, it could be over. Shoot, he's probably sitting on the porch . . ." He stopped at the worried look on the senator's face.

Senator Barlow, his brow wrinkled in concern, said, "Gentlemen, it did take some time for us to proceed with the investigation. However, I returned from speaking with Judge Pearson at the end of April. At that point, it only took two days to get all of the legal documents drawn up for Darcy to prove this Davies a fraud. He was returning to you, and then, Mr. MacGregor, the two of you would take it to the McMullen County sheriff."

He paused and called, "David, could you come in?"

Moments later the door opened, and David said, "Yes, Senator?"

"Do you remember what day Darcy Smith left on his trip back to Dog Town?"

"No, sir. Give me just a moment."

The young man turned and disappeared. Will could hear him turning pages. In only a few moments, he returned.

"He left our office for the last time on the twenty-seventh day of April."

"Thank you, David," the senator said.

David pulled the door closed, and his steps could be heard returning to his desk.

"This is the eleventh of July. He would have had over two months to reach you. I'm very sorry, but I fear something might have happened to him."

"Senator," Will said, "he had all of our papers with him. Everything that would prove the ranch belongs to Mac and Darcy rode with him. If something happened to Darcy, Mac has nothing to prove ownership."

"It's Darcy," Mac exclaimed, "who is concerning me now, Will, not the blasted land or cattle."

Senator Barlow said, "I can relieve you of one worry. Any papers that pass through this office have certified copies made of them. It takes a little extra time, but quite often can prove well worth it. So we have copies of all of your necessary documents. You needn't worry about the papers."

Will was on his feet. "Good. Senator, if you could give us the copies, we'll be on our way. We must do our best to find Darcy."

"Please sit," Senator Barlow said, holding up one hand. "It's not quite that simple. We only made one copy. Therefore we need to make a new copy of all the papers and have them certified by our local judge. That will take two days."

Will felt the need to be on their way. They had to find Darcy. Wade had already been killed. If something happened to Darcy, that would leave Mac with both of his good friends gone. "Can it be done any faster, Senator? We really need to be on our way. He could be out there with a broken leg. We've got to be on our way."

Senator Barlow gave a solemn nod of his head. "I know you're worried, but you know this country. Two months? If he's fine, you'll find him. But hurt, he'd be dead by now. And gentlemen, I am sorry, but we have to have that time to draw up these documents correctly. Getting them done in two days is already a rush. Both David and I will be working into the night, but we will have them for you the day after tomorrow. Let's say ten o'clock in the morning. David should be able to get them back from the judge by then. That will be Wednesday, July thirteenth."

Will and Mac started to stand.

"Just a moment, Will, you said you had documents proving your name change?"

"Sure, Senator," Will said, and patted his vest. "I've got them right here in case I run into an army problem."

"If you will allow me to take them, I will include an additional document ensuring there will be no problem with your name change."

"Senator, I don't mind giving them to you, but I'd like for you to no longer show me as a partner in the ranch. It rightfully belongs to Mac and Darcy—"

Mac grabbed Will's forearm in an iron grip. "Listen, laddie, and listen close. You have a rightful share in this ranch. You always have, and you always will. I want to hear no more about this—ever."

Will looked into the sad, hazel eyes of his friend and said, "Alright, Mac. This is the last. I will never mention it again."

Mac relaxed his grip on Will's forearm and lifted his hand. Will slipped his hand inside his vest, pulled the papers out, held them for a moment, and then handed them to the senator.

Senator Barlow saw the hesitation and smiled. "Don't worry, Mr. Logan, I will take good care of these papers. I'm sure you have no desire to repeat your last experience with the army."

Solemnly, Will shook his head. "No, sir. I sure don't."

"I think that will take care of it, gentlemen." The senator rose, extended his hand, and shook the hand of Mac and then Will as they both stood. "I am truly sorry to be the bearer of such bad news, but hopefully you will find him recuperating at some ranch along the way."

"Thank you, Senator," Will said.

Senator Barlow ushered them to the front door, and as they were leaving, Mac said, "It is here we'll be, sharp at ten, day after tomorrow, and a good day to you."

15

Callum heard the shot, followed by the crash of several more. The day was much the same, hot enough to melt metal, but the first shot took his mind completely off the heat. He reached for his Spencer as Floyd and Tandy were reaching for their rifles. All three were riding with their pistol thongs loose, for the threat of Apaches was still hovering over the border country.

Reaching back, he drew his binoculars from the saddlebags. Scanning the distant country, he caught a hint of dust. Pointing, he handed the glasses to Floyd.

His uncle watched for only a moment and passed them back. "I'm guessing that's the army patrol, and they finally found those Injuns."

Callum nodded, took back the glasses, and handed them to Tandy, who said, "See a little dust, but that's all."

Another shot carried across the prairie.

"I hate to ride in there blind," Callum said, "but that's about the only thing we can do. Those boys are in trouble. If we sit around here thinking about it, they could end up feeding the buzzards."

"Let's go, boys," Floyd said. He kicked his horse in the flanks. The animal leaped forward, Shoshone and Tandy's horse alongside. The three men, grasping their rifles in one hand and their reins in the other, raced toward the fight.

Callum charged over a low rise covered with greasewood and bunchgrass. An Apache leaped to his feet no more than fifteen yards to Callum's front. The Indian's rifle was centered on Callum's chest. A shot from the army patrol rang out, and the man slammed facedown on the hot, rocky ground, blood spreading quickly between his shoulders. A blossom of smoke rose from the wide arroyo to their left. The tops of several horses' ears could be seen sticking up above the bank. Floyd, to the left of Callum, turned toward the arroyo. Callum yelled at Tandy, and they both followed Floyd.

Callum saw his uncle pass a short greasewood bush, and behind him, first the dirt moved, and then from the ground sprang an Apache warrior, bow fully drawn. With no time to aim, Callum whipped the Spencer up like a handgun. His strong arm and wrist steadied it for just a second, and he pulled the trigger. The bullet hit the man as he was about to release the arrow. He took one step, tried to steady the bow, and released. Callum, his heart in his throat, saw the arrow fly straight for his uncle's back.

The Apache was tough. Even with the .52-caliber hunk of lead slamming into his body, he still managed to aim and fire, and he was close. The arrow caught up with Floyd just as he dropped into the arroyo, cutting through the deer-hide jacket and slicing a shallow groove in the top of his shoulder before passing through and burying itself in the opposite bank.

Callum breathed a sigh of relief, seeing the arrow continuing its flight. He leaped into the arroyo behind Floyd and wheeled Shoshone out of the way just as Tandy charged over the broken bank. The men leaped from their horses and dashed to the bank's edge, alongside the soldiers. Inside the banks of the arroyo, the remaining troopers were cautiously peering over the edges.

Three, one the sergeant they had met earlier, faced the direction Callum and his group came from, and two were against the opposite bank behind them. Callum looked around for the lieutenant. He thought the young man was missing until he spotted a covered body stretched full length under a blanket.

"How many?" he asked.

The sergeant replied, "I'm guessing we evened up the numbers. As close as I can tell, when we found them, or more likely they found us, there were ten. We got one before you arrived, plus those two. Means there's at least seven, and with the loss of three men, there'll be a lot of upset wives when they get back. Maybe this'll make 'em take off."

"Apache ain't much on giving up," Floyd said, "least not those I've known. But you never know. They can be mighty notional." He looked around at the two mules. "How much water you carrying?"

"We're in pretty good shape. Even as hot as it is, we've got three days' worth."

Floyd shook his head. "Considering you're still a couple of days out from the fort, it depends on how long they hold you here."

The sergeant nodded.

"I guess that's the lieutenant," Callum said.

"Yes, sir," the sergeant replied. "One of 'em got him as he was trying to unlimber his Spencer." The sergeant shook his head. "I tried to tell him we needed to have those rifles in hand, but he wouldn't listen. He was a fine young fellow. Straight out of West Point and still green, but fair with the men. I liked him."

Floyd nodded. "I saw you tryin', Sergeant. It ain't your fault. Life can just be like that. We do our best and enjoy our time."

The sergeant, still dejected, looked back at the covered body. "Yes, sir. You're sure right, but it would have been nice if he'd had a little more time. He has a girl back east. I guess the major'll be writing another letter."

Everyone, silent, maintained their vigil, watching for any movement or indication of something out of place.

The heat waves rose, distorting the distance, making it dance and sway. Dust devils crisscrossed the prairie in erratic patterns, as if they were in a hurry to arrive, to an ever-changing destination. Callum examined each greasewood, each patch of grass, and every rock. He would start on one side of the patch, greasewood, or rock, scan around the edges for anything out of place, anything unnatural, and move to the next. He knew the Apache were capable of blending in with any landscape.

An hour had passed since they'd dashed into the draw. During that time, there had been no firing of either arrows or bullets. It remained deathly still. Sweat ran down Callum's forehead, filled his thick eyebrows until there was no more room, then dripped into his eyes and continued down his nose. He wiped the sweat, but maintained his lookout. He had gone over one greasewood, no more than twenty yards in front of him, several times. He had examined every limb, thoroughly looked over the base, and gazed to the side, allowing his peripheral vision to keep it in sight, possibly catching something direct examination had missed, but up to now, nothing.

He was passing over it again when he noticed a small mound just behind the greasewood's base. *Has that mound been there?* he asked himself. *I don't remember it.* He leaned over to Floyd. "See the greasewood almost straight in front of us, about twenty yards?"

"Sure do."

"Good. Get ready. There's a small mound of dirt out there. I swear it wasn't there the last time I scanned that bush. I'm gonna put a ball into it, and we'll just see what happens. Let me know when you're ready."

Immediately Floyd said, "Ready."

Callum's Spencer roared, and a surprised brave leaped up from behind the greasewood, blood streaming from his left shoulder. Before the crash of Callum's Spencer could fade, Floyd fired. The bullet struck the Apache over his heart, driving the hunk of lead through the vital organ. The Indian collapsed to the ground. Silence returned.

Another hour passed, then another. The sun drifted lower in the western sky. Floyd had been stretched out next to his nephew. He turned, checking first up the arroyo, then in the opposite direction. Nothing.

"I'm going to give those two a hand," Floyd said as he left Callum and joined Tandy and a trooper on the opposite bank.

Callum continued his watch next to the sergeant. Leaning over, the man said, "Think they're gone?"

Callum shook his head. "I wouldn't want to stand up and find out. I'm thinking if your count's right, they should be down to six. I figure they're trying to make a stay-or-leave decision. They've lost near half their men. They want scalps and booty, but they don't want to take any more losses back to their wickiups. So my answer, Sergeant, is I have no idea."

The sergeant, evidently in a talkative mood, said, "Where you from?" to Callum.

"Depends on how far you go back," Callum said, eyes continuing to scan the prairie. "Originally, we're from Tennessee. We moved to Colorado after the war and started a ranch up there."

The sergeant tossed a thumb behind him toward Floyd. "I'm guessin' he's a dyed-in-the-wool mountain man."

Callum nodded. "Yep. My uncle Floyd's been in those Rocky Mountains for close to forty years." A touch of pride slipped into his voice. "He trapped with the likes of Jim Bridger and Kit Carson, fought and killed a grizzly hand to hand, and seen more than most men ever read about."

The sergeant turned his head to look at Floyd, whose back was facing him. "I'm betting he fought himself a pile of Indians in all those years."

"That he did, but he lived with them too. He's a man who has great respect for those folks. Took him an Indian wife, a beautiful woman, to hear his friends tell it. Had a son, too. He loves those mountains."

The sergeant shook his head. When he spoke, his voice was filled with awe. "Why, reckon I've never seen a real live mountain man. I guess there aren't many left." He turned to Callum. "He ought to write a book. I bet it'd sell like hotcakes. I'd read it."

Callum chuckled. "My ma and pa and all my kin have said the same thing. He always gives us the same answer." Callum deepened his voice to imitate Floyd and said, "I'm livin' life. I ain't got time to be writin' about it."

"All right," Floyd said, facing the prairie from the bank behind them, "I'm not so old I'm deaf. You young fellers can stop flappin' your lips about me, and keep your eyes sharp for those Apaches."

Growing serious, Floyd continued, "You were wondering if they would leave or attack. I'm thinking they'll give it one last try. Probably at dusk. I reckon they're waiting for shadows to cover up their approach. Shoot, that one brave made it all the way to that greasewood not twenty yards away, in broad daylight, without being seen until Callum spotted something out of place. All they need are a few shadows, and they'll be able to crawl right into our laps."

Sergeant Sneed said, "Stay alert, troopers. I know you're tired, but go to sleep now, and you might sleep forever."

Time clicked by. There was no visible movement on either side of the dry gully. Out of sight in the distant sky, a hawk cried. Somewhere far away, a coyote tuned up for an evening serenade, but near the arroyo where the troopers, Logans, and Tandy lay, there was no sound, not even the mournful call of a dove, only silence.

Shadows began to stretch as the sun drifted lower. A trooper pulled out a pipe and started packing it with tobacco.

Callum saw it and said, "Suck on it or chew it, but don't light it."

The trooper frowned at Callum. "They know we're here. Won't make any difference."

"You're right. They know *we're* here. They don't know *you're* here. They look for weak chinks to knock out. They know no one smart would draw attention to himself, and anyone who did would be careless. A careless person is a better target than an alert person."

The trooper snorted. "That don't make no sense. They know we're here." He put the pipe in his mouth and reached for a match.

The sergeant gave a sigh and said, "Nolan, put the match up."

Grumbling around the unlit pipe in his mouth, Nolan palmed the match. The shadows grew longer.

Floyd pulled his knife, sticking it in the bank next to him. "I just heard buckskin scrape on a limb. Get ready." Callum copied his uncle. He laid down his rifle and drew his Colt with his right hand and the big bowie knife with the other.

There was no shot, no loud Indian yell, only the soft whisper of buckskin on rock and sand. Suddenly Apaches appeared all around. They were like ghosts. One moment nothing, and then rising out of the ground, running, leaping, diving into the arroyo.

They were brutally quick. A knife blade flashed for Callum's throat, but he parried it with the barrel of the Colt. He felt the man's hot breath, and in the fading light, he could see the hate and determination in the man's eyes. He had only an instant to respond. He knocked the man's knife away with the barrel of his revolver, but the man's weight and his leap from the bank above carried them both onto the rocky floor of the arroyo. Callum felt the strength of the smaller man as, with his left hand, he clamped a viselike grip on Callum's gun hand and tried to twist, in hopes of wrenching the gun from his hand.

While the Apache was twisting his right wrist, he whipped his knife back around for a low ripping slash into Callum's lower belly. But though surprised by the suddenness of the attack, he had been alerted by Floyd's warning. Slamming into the ground, he held on to his knife, and his long left arm went under the Apache's arm. The point of his bowie knife found soft tissue between the Indian's ribs on his right side. Callum drove the point through the right lung and all the way to its hilt, reaching the man's heart. Hot blood gushed from the wound, covering his hand and arm. Yanking the knife out, he threw the struggling body into the gulley, leaped to his feet, and spun around, searching for his next opponent.

A confusion of tangled, writhing bodies filled the arroyo. He turned in time to see his uncle throw an Indian from the bank to the ground and fire as the man leaped up. The sergeant stood over another Apache, smoke rising from the barrel of his revolver. Tandy had knocked an attacker's knife away and wrenched the man's shoulder so hard, it was pulled from the socket. He now held the Indian on the ground while the man stared up at him, showing no emotion, no pain. A trooper leaned against the embankment, choking and gasping for air, blood pouring from his throat.

Callum saw several shadows vanish over the bank, and moments later, they heard the sound of hoofbeats rapidly retreating. The fight was over. The Apaches were gone, leaving three dead and one captured. The desperate attack had lasted no more than a couple of minutes. Again, silence reigned over the evening.

The sergeant and two of the others hurried to help the injured trooper. Callum looked at Floyd, who nodded, and the two of them, still alert for another attack, though they didn't expect it, moved to Tandy and his captive.

"Who you got, boy?" Floyd said, looking down at the cold, solemn eyes staring back at him.

Before he could answer, Nolan, face contorted with hate,

swung his revolver toward the prone Indian, said, "Dirty redskin," and pulled the trigger.

Callum, near the trooper, had seen the gun start to swing and knocked it up as the man pulled the trigger. He wrenched the revolver from the man's hand and brought his own to bear on Nolan's chest. "Calm down, trooper. There'll be no murdering here."

At the shot, the sergeant jerked around, immediately realizing what was happening. "Nolan!" he shouted. "Get over by the embankment and keep watch. As of now, you're on report. If you try to do harm to that man, I'll see you hanged."

Insolently, Nolan said, "Nobody's gonna hang me for killin' no Injun."

Sergeant Sneed turned to face the trooper. "You may be right, but mess with me, and I'll leave you out here in this desert for the rest of the Apaches to take care of. Now shut up, and get over there."

Nolan turned and walked the short distance to the embankment, his back to everyone. Callum handed the man's revolver to Sergeant Sneed. "How's your wounded man?"

The sergeant shook his head. "He's dying. His throat's been cut. There's no way we can stop the bleeding."

Callum nodded. "Sorry. What do you plan to do with *him*?" He motioned toward the Apache, who had sat up and was looking around the arroyo.

"We'll tie him up and take him back to the fort. They'll keep him in jail for a few days and then release him back across the river. He'll be back. It never stops."

In the arroyo filled with death and gore, the sergeant grinned in resignation. "Guess it keeps my paycheck coming."

"I guess it does," Callum said.

Within minutes the trooper struggling to breathe gave a final, shuddering gasp and died. Will glanced at the Apache. The man showed no emotion. He sat staring down the arroyo. His dislocated shoulder joint showed awkwardly through the skin.

Tandy looked at Callum. "I can fix it. It'll hurt like crazy when I do it, but I've done several. It's pretty easy for me. I've got the weight for it."

"Let's do it," Callum said. He motioned to Floyd. "How about telling him what we're about to do."

Floyd stepped toward the Indian and began talking to him in sign language. He stopped and turned to the sergeant. "Sergeant, he said yes. He would need the arm in the afterlife, for as soon as we leave, the pony soldiers will kill him."

Sergeant Sneed had been wrapping the dead trooper in a blanket. He looked up at Floyd. "Mr. Logan, you can tell him that just ain't so. We're taking him back to the fort, where they'll probably release him."

The Apache stared at the sergeant, then said, "Humph."

"Tell him it's going to hurt mighty bad," Callum said, "and ask him if he's ready."

Floyd spoke quickly with him, his hands flying.

The Apache gave Callum a disdainful look and answered.

Floyd said, "He said to do it. Pain doesn't scare him."

Callum stepped to the Indian's side and grasped his good arm while Tandy took the bad one in his hand. He moved it around until he had it in the right position and yanked hard. The jerk almost pulled Callum from his feet, but he managed to hang on and keep the Apache in place. With the jerk, there was an audible pop as the shoulder joint slipped back in place. The only indication of any discomfort by the man was a momentary narrowing of eyelids. Otherwise, by his outward appearance, no one would have ever suspected he felt anything.

Once the prisoner's arm was back in place, Sergeant Sneed told two of his remaining men to tie up his feet and hands, hands behind his back. They did as they were told, and then dragged the man where he could lean against the bank or stretch out to sleep.

"Will you be heading back east?" Sergeant Sneed asked Callum.

"Yep. In the morning. We'll be on our way early, while it's cooler."

"Yeah," the sergeant said, "we'll pull out for Eagle Pass and the fort then, too. Thanks for your help. We would've been dead men if you three hadn't come along."

"It worked out," Callum said. He turned to his uncle. "How about some sleep?"

"Good idea," Floyd said. "Who takes the first watch?"

"We'll follow the sergeant's orders."

Sergeant Sneed said, "You men get some sleep. We'll split it up into three-hour shifts to make it easy."

Floyd had already spread his bedroll, and Tandy wasn't far behind.

Callum said, "Don't mind if we do. Thanks." He spread his bedroll, and before he drifted off, he heard his uncle snoring.

16

W
ill walked down the stairs of the City Hotel, and except for the dark thoughts of Darcy, he felt good. It was nearing the end of their second day in Austin. There had been time for him to replace his worn-out clothes, get a haircut, a shave, and a couple of hot baths. The first night, he had slept until daylight, which he hadn't done in weeks. The only other downside, besides Darcy, was the distance to Deborah. She was hundreds of miles away. His heart pulled with the desire to be with her, and he wondered how much longer it would be before they could be together again.

Descending the stairs, he spotted Mac sitting in a heavily cushioned Victorian armchair, reading a newspaper. Nearing his friend, he asked, "What's the paper?"

"The *Weekly State Gazette*. It was left here." He indicated the side table next to his chair. "I imagine whoever read it was as disgusted as I am."

"Mac, you're old enough to know the only news you get from a newspaper is bad news."

"Humph. You're sure right on this one. Seems our illustrious Governor Davis wants the legislature to give him the power to declare martial law any time he feels like it." He folded the paper and, disgusted, tossed it on the side table to join a worn *Scribner's Monthly*. "I know the man fought for the union, but he's sure made a pathetic governor. My hopes are folks will vote him out and never let him near a public office again."

Movement on the stairs caught both men's attention. Bart, hair trimmed and shaved, looked like any other cowhand with new clothes, boots, and hat, except for the cold, appraising, green eyes. The gun on his right hip rested comfortably, as if it was part of him. But the hard face broke into a grin upon seeing Mac and Will. "You two clean up mighty well. Hope you're hungry. I swear my stomach thinks my throat's cut and pulled my backbone in as a witness."

Will laughed. "Seems like you've done nothing but eat for the last two days.

Bart replied, "My mama always said a man's got to feed an appetite so it don't devour him. Never figgered what it meant, exceptin' when a man's hungry, he oughta eat."

"The restaurant in the hotel is fine," Mac said.

"Reckon it is," Bart said, "but there's a place just down the street that has the best steaks you've ever slapped a lip over, and they're not as pricey as here."

Will slapped him on the back and said, "If it's alright with Mac, then it's fine with me. Whatever we do, let's make it quick before I drop from hunger."

The three men laughed again, and Mac said, "Aye, makes no difference to me as long as we sit down to a table quick, fast, and in a hurry."

Feeling good, they left the hotel and, with Bart's directing, were soon at a sizeable restaurant labeled Austin Steakhouse, and just under the name, it read, "Steaks big as Texas and just as good!"

They marched up to the door, and Will reached for the latch. Before he could open it, the door flew open, and three husky men stumbled out into Will and Mac, knocking them off the board-walk. They both kept their feet, which was more than could be said for the three cowboys, who fell, in a tangle, in the dusty street. Will stepped to the nearest, extended a hand, and said, "No harm done, boys. Let me help you up."

The cowhand he had extended his hand to slapped it away, cursed, and said, "Keep your help to yourself." He and his companion struggled to their feet and, unsteady, stood glaring at Will and his friends. Finally, the biggest of the three sizeable men said, "Somebody oughta teach you a lesson."

Will had never run from a fight, but he didn't mind sidestep-ping one occasionally if nothing could be gained by it. Tonight he felt generous. He had just enjoyed a good bath, he was covered with new clothes, and his hair was cut. He had no desire to roll in the dirt, especially in the manure-laden main street of Austin, and besides, these three men were drunk. The last thing he wanted to do was hurt a bunch of drunken cowboys. "Look, boys," he said, "you didn't see us, and we didn't see you. Let's just call it even and go our separate ways."

The June evening had cooled appreciably. The town board-walks were crowded with families and couples enjoying the cooler breeze. Will noticed several had stopped, while others were slowing, and still others were gathering their children and rushing them away from a possible fight. The sun had set, and the shadows were lengthening.

"Hear that, Rinso?" the smallest man said. "He wants us to go away. I guess he doesn't want us to hurt him, big fine fella like him."

"I heared him, but I don't have much of a hankerin' to be on my way. Least not before I whup up on him."

Mac had spotted two Texas State Police walking up the street toward them. He waved them over. When they approached, the older policeman said, "What's going on here?"

The three drunken cowboys stumbled around and assessed

the new arrivals while Will said, "Officers, we need your help. We were just going into the steakhouse as these gentlemen were coming out. We ran into each other, and they stumbled into the street. It seems they want satisfaction, but all we want to do is go into the restaurant and have a steak."

The officer said, "Looks like no harm's been done. Why don't all of you move along."

Rinso couldn't take his eyes off Will. Even in the shadows of coming night, the threat on his face was clear.

"Aye, 'tis agreeable with us, Mr. Policeman. You have a fine evening."

The three of them turned to enter the restaurant. Several people who had stopped and were watching blocked the entrance. Bart said, "Excuse me," and stepped forward. The interest of the people was broken, as was that of all the others who had stopped to watch what was certainly about to turn into a fight. They stepped out of the way of Bart, and everyone resumed their movement. Bart opened the door and entered, followed by Mac and then Will.

They found an open table, sat, and relaxed. "Well," Mac said, "it's for sure that little incident turned out better than I expected."

"I agree," Will said. "It looked like we were in for a fight. Not that it would have been much of one, as drunk as those boys were."

"There lies the problem with drinking," Will said. "Men do stupid things they'd never do if they were sober."

"Too true, lad, too true."

The waitress, a young blonde about Bart's age, hurried towards their table. Will and Mac watched Bart watch her as she made her way through the maze of tables, hips swinging to miss the patrons, apron tied tight around her tiny waist, and a constant smile on her face. Her hair was pulled back and gathered in a large bun at the back of her head, and her smiling lips exposed shiny white teeth.

When she reached the table, she smiled at both Mac and Will, but her smile widened when her eyes fell on Bart. Her green eyes gazed directly into his green eyes as she said in a breathy voice, "I am so glad you are all right. I was sure those three troublemakers would start a fight. Every time they drink, they start something, but usually they're not in this part of town. I've warned Sam over and over, one day he's going to meet a man who will really hurt him, but he just laughs at me and calls me a girl."

Bart's smile dropped, replaced by a look of resigned disappointment. "You know them?" Bart asked.

She sighed. "Unfortunately, I do. The big one is my brother, Sam. He runs with the other two. Jingles, he's the small one, if you can say any of them are small, and is the troublemaker, always stirring the pot, as mama used to say."

She paused, turned green eyes on Mac and Will, and said, almost as a second thought, "I'm so sorry, you men look hungry, and I'm talking way too much."

Before either of them could say anything, Bart said, "Oh, that's all right. They don't mind at all. What did you say your name was?"

Turning back, her smile for Bart only, she said, "I didn't, but for you, it's Susie, Susie Capps."

Will cleared his throat and said, "Thanks for asking, Susie. I'll take a steak with all the trimmings. The same for my partner, here. You'll have to ask the doe-eyed fellow what he wants."

Bart turned red and gave Will a hard look, but when he looked back at Susie, he was smiling. "That would be just fine with me too, Susie."

"Then I'll make sure yours are next." She spun around and, hips swinging, pranced into the kitchen, Bart's eyes following her every step.

Once she was gone, he turned his attention to Will, his smile gone. "What'd you mean by that crack?"

Will, his face the picture of innocence, turned to Mac. "Do you have any idea what he's talking about?"

"Nary a one. I swear it's probable he doesn't either. I fear our young friend has been smitten by a little blonde beauty. He may never be the same."

"Alright, that's enough," Bart growled. "I'd hate to have to do what those drunks couldn't do and whip the both of you."

Will smiled innocently at his friend and looked around the sizable room. *Functional,* he thought. *Nothing fancy, like the hotel restaurant, but functional. Big, with every inch of spaced used.* Circular, square, and rectangular tables filled the wide area. Along the walls were small tables able to seat only two, but all of the tables, no matter the size or shape, were occupied. Ten minutes hadn't passed before Susie returned, balancing a tray with three huge plates, the edges of each plate extending over the side of the tray, in her right hand above her head. In her left she carried a large pitcher of water. Glasses tinkled in her apron pocket.

Bart leaped up as she reached the table and took the tray, holding it for her as she placed each of the huge plates in front of Will and Mac and at Bart's place. When the tray was empty, she removed the three glasses from her pocket, setting a glass by each plate, and poured water into each. All this time, Bart stood there, eyes glued on the pretty girl's face.

Finally, she set the pitcher on the table, turned to Bart, took the tray, her smile beaming at the stricken gunfighter, and said, "Why, thank you, kind sir." Then more businesslike, she said to all of them, "I'll be back with your pie when you're finished." She gave Bart a quick smile, spun around, her skirt rustling, and quickly disappeared toward the kitchen. Bart stood, eyes wide, watching her retreat.

"Steak's getting cold, laddie," Mac said around a big piece of steak.

"What?" Realizing he was gawking at the empty kitchen doorway, Bart, red again, dropped into his chair.

Will shook his head and, between bites, said, "Mac, looks like our boy has lost his appetite. Maybe we ought to split his steak."

Mac, having definitely not lost his appetite, thrust another piece of steak into his mouth, moved it into a cheek, and out of a full mouth, said, "Aye, 'tis a sad thing when a man falls under the spell of a woman. It'll not be only his appetite he loses." At the same time he reached across for Bart's plate.

Bart slapped the wide hand away and growled toward his two companions, "Leave my plate be. And no, I ain't lost my appetite." Scowling, he cut a hunk of the steak and thrust it into his mouth.

Will, enthralled with the salty, juicy flavor of the tender steak, chased it with a heavy forkful of mashed potatoes. He was feeling good and wasn't through with his friend. "Mac, would you look at the size of that hunk of meat on Bart's plate? Why, that must be half a cow, and look at ours. They're not even a fraction of the size of his."

In truth, Bart's steak was a bit larger, but all three steaks left little room for the potatoes and red beans. They were piled over the edge of the meat.

"Aye, 'tis sad to see such blatant preference in a fine restaurant. I'm thinking this tiny piece of meat won't even begin to relieve my starvation."

Bart started to scowl, then a big grin covered his usually hard face. "Yeah, you boys are so right, and I'll tell you why. It's my good looks, and the two of you are so blasted ugly."

The three of them burst out in laughter. The people at the near tables who had heard the conversation were also smiling and laughing, while those out of earshot only stared. They continued eating, and all that could be heard, besides the clinking of knives and forks on the plates, was an occasional belch and the other sounds satisfied men make as they eat.

Finally, the three leaned back at the same time and shoved their cleaned plates away. Will said, "Bart, I'd say you guided us to the right place. That was a fine meal."

"Aye, it was music to my belly, for sure."

They had no sooner pushed their plates away than Susie was on her way to their table with three large pieces of steaming pie and a pitcher of thick cream. She set them on the table, flashed Bart another smile, and picked up the empty plates. While dropping off the pie and clearing the table, she said, "This is cookie's delicious peach pie. Folks come from as far as San Antonio, when the peaches are fresh, just to eat his pie. I'm sure you'll like it. With a little cream over it, it is heaven." Her last sentence was solely for Bart. Turning back for the kitchen, she tossed her head and said, "Coffee's on the way."

She quickly returned with the coffee, but by the time she arrived, the men had devoured half of their cream-covered peach pie.

Will said, "Susie, this is mighty good. You tell your cook if he's not married, I'm proposing, and I'll trade these two rannys for him right now, no questions asked."

She grinned at Will. "I'll tell him, but he's already married."

Bart pointed at Will. "So's he, but the food was mighty good, Susie. And so was the company. I hate to be forward, but if a man don't take chances, he don't get ahead. Would you mind if I walked you home tonight?"

It was Susie's turn to blush. She smiled at Bart. "That would be really nice, but I don't even know your name."

Bart jumped to his feet. "The name's Bart, ma'am, and I'm mighty pleased to meet you."

"I'm pleased to meet you too, Bart. I get off at eight o'clock. If you could be here then, that would be nice. It's not too late, is it?"

Before Bart could answer, a man's voice, low but clear, said, "That's Bart Porter, the gunfighter. He's killed seven men."

Bart's head jerked around to locate the speaker. Hard green eyes searched the face of every man sitting in the direction the whisper had come from. Some men met his eyes, while others stared at their plates, but it was impossible to tell who had spoken those harsh and deadly words.

Will watched his friend turn back to Susie. Bart's live, excited green eyes that had so danced at the unknown possibilities of the future only moments before were now hard and sad.

Concern showed on Susie's face. "Is it true, Bart? Are you Bart Porter the gunfighter?"

He nodded and with a stern, lifeless voice said, "It's true, but I never killed a man who wasn't trying to kill me."

Again the whisper came from across the room. "Liar!"

This time Bart whirled and stared in the general direction of the voice. No one stared back in defiance. No one stood to take responsibility for the words. Everyone remained quiet.

Bart spoke in the direction of the whispers. "Why don't you stand and face me? I'll take my gun off. I say it again. I have never shot a man who wasn't trying to kill me."

The sounds were gone from the restaurant. Plates clanking, pots clanging, and glasses tinkling, only seconds earlier, were gone, and a charged silence fell over the room.

Bart's head turned slowly as he looked at each man in the direction of the whisper. "I don't know who you are, and I don't know why you said what you did. But I tell you here and now, you are a coward. A low, crawling on your belly coward."

Will and Mac stood. Will said, "Come on, Bart. We'd better go."

Bart shook his head. "Not yet."

He turned back to Susie, but Will could see the light was also gone from the girl's eyes. Her face was filled with dismay and horror. He watched as Bart recognized the new expression.

"We'd best forget tonight. How much do we owe you?" Bart said.

Woodenly, the petite green-eyed blonde said, "Fifty cents a meal."

Each man pulled out six bits and dropped them on the table.

"Wait." The call came from just inside the kitchen. Will and the others turned as a middle-aged man walked into the dining room. Purposefully, he marched straight up to Bart and extended his hand. "I'm Louie Franklin. This is my establishment." While many of his customers gaped at him, he shook hands with Will and Mac. "I saw what you fellows did out front. You could have created a fracas out there, but you elected to prevent it. I heard what the no-account said about you, young fellow, and it wasn't right." His voice rose. "I'd say that qualifies as a most cowardly act. If I knew who it was, I'd throw him out, but you boys are always welcome here. Come back any time." He bent over and picked up the three fifty-cent pieces from the table and handed one back to each man. "I figure the three quarters are for Susie, but as far as the meals, they're on the house."

Bart said, "That's mighty fine of you, Mr. Franklin. I sure didn't mean to cause a disturbance here. Howsomever, I gotta tell you that food made my taster celebrate. Those steaks were probably the tenderest I've ever eaten, and the pie, oh my goodness, that pie was fine. Thanks for the free supper, and next time we're in town, we'll be back."

"As long as I own this place, and I plan on owning it until they put me in the ground, you'll be welcome. You boys ride safe."

The restaurant had returned to its low hum of conversation and clicking knives and forks against porcelain as they stepped outside. Travel on the streets had thinned. There were only a couple of people on the boardwalks. A lone horseman rode up the dark street.

Will turned to Bart. "You alright? That was pretty rough in there, specially Susie."

"Yeah, I'm fine. It ain't the first time I've been called a killer, and it probably won't be the last."

"People just like to gossip, laddie," Mac said. "It's a bad thing, but believe you me, where you find people, you'll find gossips.

Don't let it be a bother to you, and if the girl wasn't willing to give you the benefit of the doubt, then that's her loss."

Will stepped off the boardwalk into the street. Mac and Bart followed. It was dark now, and the men concentrated on the dusty street, especially Will, with his newly shined boots. None of them wanted to step in a pile of horse apples.

They were following Congress to the hotel and had moved to the east side of the street.

Will said, "I'm surprised those drunks were satisfied with leaving. That one looked dead set on getting a piece of me."

Before either of his friends could reply, three men moved out of the next alley, blocking their way to the hotel.

"Reckon you spoke too soon," Bart said.

"I was hoping to keep these clothes clean for a while. Guess a while is up."

"Hold up," the biggest of the three said.

Will and his friends walked up to the three drunks and halted. "So you boys just couldn't leave well enough alone?" Will said. "The smartest thing you could have done was go home and sleep it off. You've still got the chance, just let us by." Will could barely make the men out in the darkness. He picked out the biggest. "According to Susie, you must be Sam Capps."

"You talked to my sister?" Capps demanded.

"We did. She was much nicer than you. Come to think of it, she was a lot prettier too. Course, in the dark you don't look near as ugly as you did earlier."

"I'll show you ugly," Sam said. He took one step toward Will and swung.

17

The three riders crossed the Nueces and halted in a stand of trees. A small herd of longhorns fed where the treeline joined the prairie. The men had gotten an early start, and past the trees, the sun rose in their eyes. Each man pulled the brim of their hat lower. Callum watched a herd of whitetail deer feed alongside the longhorns. Occasionally a head would pop up, gaze around, looking for possible trouble, then drop back to the ground. Four doves sailed through the trees, their wings making a rhythmic whish-whish-whish sound as they passed. Only a mile or two remained to the Ruiz home.

"You think their home's all right?" Tandy asked. Both men shook their heads, and Callum answered, "Can't say. We'll see before long."

"Yessir," Floyd said. "We know they chased us. We found their tracks, but I reckon they weren't enthusiastic enough about finding us. Their kind don't hanker to being shot at by folks who know what they're doing." He bumped his horse in the flanks, starting the gelding forward. "Now let's be moving. There ain't but one way to find out."

Callum clucked at Shoshone and followed Floyd, with Tandy alongside.

Since the Indian fight, they had been allowed to sweat in peace. Hot as it was, they had no more trouble. The prairie was bone dry. West of the Nueces, they ran into cowhands pushing a herd of about a thousand cattle. They were headed north for Abilene. Making a late start, the drovers were concerned about the cattle making it with no rain. Grass would be dried out, though still nutritious, it was more susceptible to fire, and most of the waterholes would be dry, providing nothing for the thirsty cattle. But the owner was desperate and needed to sell the herd for more than he could get in the Texas markets, which couldn't have been much above five dollars. Going or staying, either way was a big gamble.

Armando and Ana's home was on a little creek that ran into the Nueces farther south. As they rode, Callum hoped their home and buildings would be intact, but feared the worst. Davies gained nothing by burning them, but the men who rode for him didn't care. Burning the family out would be sport for many of them.

He thought of Armando's protests. The husband and father had wanted to return with them to fight for his property. Don Antonio had even been willing to bring his vaqueros over the border to fight the *bandido* Davies, but he and Floyd had been able to reason with the men. Don Antonio and his men would have caused an international incident and might have gotten everyone chased and killed by the army. Certainly, the army would have supported Davies over a force from Mexico.

Still, Callum understood the desire of a man to protect his property and deal with interlopers. He had dealt with them in years past, and harshly. Fortunately, Armando had remained with his family, where he belonged until this was settled.

Nearing Armando's place, they saw several small bunches of Double R cattle that had drifted well west of the ranch. In them,

Callum saw only a few altered brands. It was just like he figured. Those men were hired killers. There was nothing in them that leaned to hard work. Above the patch of oaks, far in the distance, he thought he saw faint movement. They continued forward, the oaks growing closer and the movement clearer. Smoke. Not much of it, but enough to bode ill for the Ruiz home.

Instead of riding around the patch of oaks, they elected to thread their way through the thicket, staying under cover as much as possible. Reaching the eastern edge of the trees, they pulled up and examined what little was left of the house and barn. Both buildings were still smoldering, casting a thin veil of smoke. The riders must have waited to burn the buildings, in hopes the family would return. Though no flames remained, Callum could feel a burning deep in his being. This had been uncalled for. No good, honest man would foster, much less allow this to happen. With all of his education and titles, Davies was just as much a monster as the men he hired.

The three of them sat in the trees, watching the smoldering embers, imagining what it must have looked like going up in flames. The adobe walls didn't burn, but the roof, furniture, and personal items in the house and barn were nothing but embers.

"Don't make any difference if they're in the mountains or in Texas, animals are animals," Floyd said. "This has gotten out of hand. We need to straighten those fellers out, and soon." They sat their horses a while longer, waiting and watching. Deciding it was clear, Callum clucked Shoshone forward, and the three of them walked their horses into the yard. The first place Callum went was the corner of the house nearest the well. He and Floyd had left a sign, a large flat rock lay on the ground with two smaller ones side by side on top of it. It was a sign used by the Logan clan, meaning we'll be back in two weeks. It hadn't been touched. Here it was, nearing the middle of June, and Will still wasn't back.

"Why don't you take a rock off," Floyd said. "We'll check back every week or so. No tellin' how long that boy might be."

Callum removed one of the smaller rocks, knowing Will would read the sign.

Tandy had walked to the well. After looking in, he began to curse, something the young man never did.

Both Callum and Floyd joined him at the well. Looking into it, they could see a pig floating in the water. All three men stared down at the bloated animal. "It took us weeks to dig this well," Tandy said. "The ground is hard as a rock. We'd have to use the pick to break up a couple of inches, then shovel it out. It seemed like it took forever to get far enough down to just reach softer ground." He looked at Floyd. "Water's precious in this country. Why would any man poison a well?"

Floyd shook his head. He placed a hand on the boy's shoulder. "It ain't for us to know what drives evil men. The only thing we can do is make sure they don't harm other folks."

Tandy maneuvered a rope around the dead pig's leg. After several tries, he managed to cinch it tight. By putting rocks in the well bucket, they were able to sink it below the pig, and using the leg rope and the bucket, they slowly pulled the animal near the top of the well. Once close enough, Floyd grabbed the hind legs, and the three of them hefted the porker out and onto the ground. They examined the animal and found no penetrating wounds.

Floyd looked down on the dead pig. "They threw that pig in there alive. I've killed my share of animals. I've killed 'em to sell their hides, to wear their hides, and to eat. But when I see men, whether they be white man or Indian, torture innocent people or creatures, it makes my blood boil. They could've at least killed that pig before throwing him in that well."

Callum stood shaking his head. "This gives us an indication of the type of men we're up against. We can thank them for doing this."

Tandy's head snapped toward Callum. "Thank them? Why would we thank them?"

"Because, Tandy, this gives us a little more insight into the type of men we're dealing with." He grabbed one of the feet of the pig. "Grab a foot. Let's drag him off a ways, so at least the coyotes and buzzards can have a meal."

Tandy took hold of a foot, and the two men dragged the animal away from the burned-out house.

The men returned to find Floyd walking through the skeleton of the home. His face was grim, set in determination. Callum had seen the same look not only on his uncle, but also his pa, and knew a reckoning was coming.

Floyd shook his head. "Nothing left here. Best we can do is mosey on over to Dog Town. I'm interested to hear what the sheriff of this county has to say about a constituent having his home burned out."

Dog Town was a dusty little town at the mouth of Leoncita Creek on the Frio river. The last thing it could be called was bustling. Made up of a ramshackle hotel, a closed saloon, with the faded sign hanging loose from one end and unreadable, the town did not roll out a red carpet to the weary traveler. The sheriff's office sat alongside the Bolton General Store & Saloon, which appeared to be one of the few buildings maintained. Just down the street, another building, a home, painted and well maintained, had a horse tied to the front hitching rail, and an elderly man sat in a rocker on the elevated porch. At the end of the street was the livery.

"Not booming," Floyd said.

"Never has been," Tandy replied. "I spent some time here during the war. There could be some folks here who aren't real happy to see me."

Callum gave Tandy a searching look. "Anything we should know about?"

Tandy grinned. "Nothin' that'll get us shot. Just might be a few hard feelings." He pointed at the house where the man was sitting. "That's Molly Flynn's place. She keeps a boardinghouse. It's a lot cleaner than the hotel, no bedbugs, and the food's a ton better. The old feller on the porch is Doc Jemson. He ain't no real doctor. Don't know how he got the handle. He's just been called that for as long as I've been around."

Callum asked Floyd, "It's about supper time. You want to eat or see the sheriff first?"

Floyd nodded toward the sheriff's office. "We'd better catch him before he heads for supper."

Turning the horses toward the sheriff's office, Tandy said, "This might be one of the more unpleasant moments. Sheriff Pepper probably doesn't remember me too fondly. I whipped his son pretty bad, laid him up for a couple of days. He ain't a bad sort, just doesn't think much of me."

Floyd grinned around Callum at the young man. "Anybody in this town like you?" Before Tandy could answer, he chuckled and then said to Callum, "Maybe we oughta just leave him under one of them oak trees on the outskirts of town with some jerky. Might keep *us* out of trouble."

Callum grinned and glanced over at Tandy, who had heard the remark, but not the chuckle, and looked worried.

"Naw," Callum said, "we can't keep this growing boy from his food bag. It might stunt his growth."

Tandy looked at Callum and then Floyd, realizing they were joshing him, and said, "Molly likes me, and she's the finest person in this town." Nearing the hitching rail, he lowered his voice and said, "I think she's sweet on Bart, and he likes her, too."

Floyd and Callum looked at each other as they guided their horses to the hitching rail in front of the sheriff's office.

"Well," Floyd said to Tandy, "ain't you just a fountain of valuable information. Shoot, we didn't need to come into town. We could've just asked you."

Tandy grinned back at the older man. "Growing up, I lived nearby."

Floyd was shaking his head as they dismounted, looped their reins over the rail, and walked into the sheriff's office, with Callum in the lead. Like the town, it wasn't much of an office. An old, blackened potbellied stove stood on dirty clawfoot legs, doubling as heater during the wintertime and coffee warmer year-round. Behind and in the wall to the left of the door was a window so dirty the dried and splintered wall of the closed saloon, across the narrow alley, could barely be seen through the glass. A spider had been at work for a long time, for the upper edge of the window had a solid covering of sticky web.

Callum stepped farther into the small space. To the right of the door, and no more than the length of a tall man, sat the sheriff behind his cluttered desk, his feet propped up on a stack of wanted circulars, sipping a cup of coffee. He laid his newspaper down and, boots still pointed at them, said, "Help you?"

Will looked around before speaking. The wall to his right gave way to a large window, allowing the sheriff a clear view of the street, or it would have had it been clean. This window, much like the one looking onto the alley, was in need of a good scrubbing. On the opposite side of the sheriff was the jail. The vertical bars, from floor to ceiling, formed half of the wall, ending just before reaching the potbellied stove. There were two cell doors, each opening into a space no larger than eight feet long and six feet wide. A bunk with two beds, one on top of the other, was in each cell. There were no windows in either cell.

Callum thought, *Wonder when the sheriff last picked up a broom?* Cigar butts littered the floor near the full trash can alongside the desk. Old newspapers were stacked in front of the gun cabinet behind the sheriff.

He examined the man. Average height, thinning gray hair that, like the office, hadn't seen a cleaning in far too long. A feeble attempt at a mustache, gray and sparse, graced his upper lip. In

186 DONALD L. ROBERTSON

addition, he had a pair of thick, wire-rimmed glasses, hooks barely visible over his protruding ears. His face was round and full to match his belly, with red cheeks and a nose streaked by blue veins from years of drinking.

Tandy stepped forward. "You're not the sheriff. Where's Sheriff Pepper?"

The fat man slowly removed his feet from the desk, scanned the three men, ending on Tandy, whom he looked up and down. "I'm Sheriff Chadwick." With a pudgy right hand, he pulled the spectacles from his face and, using them as a pointer, aimed them at Tandy. "You might watch your tone when you address an officer of the law, young man."

He turned back to Callum. "I asked, what can I do for you?"

Not liking the man's appearance or the man himself, Callum said, "You know the Ruiz family who lives west of here?"

The man nodded, his jowls shaking as if they were full of jelly, and said nothing.

"Señora Ruiz was first insulted by Davies's hired help, and then those same men attacked the family, shooting up their home with their children inside."

The sheriff's chair groaned as he leaned back and crossed his arms above his ample belly, allowing his forearms to rest on the mass. "And what's your name?"

"I'm Callum Logan, this is Floyd Logan, and this large fella is Tandy Jacobs."

The sheriff nodded while he was thinking. He leaned forward again, chair once more protesting, and shuffled through the mass of papers on his desk while talking to himself. "Logan, I've seen something with Logan on it somewhere." He continued to shuffle for a few moments longer. Finally he pulled out a circular, looked at it, looked back at Callum, and looked at the paper again. "You say your names are *Callum* and *Floyd* Logan?"

"That's right," Callum replied, his tone brusque.

"You any kin to a William Wallace Logan?"

"Yes," Callum said. "What's the problem?"

"Well," the sheriff said, pausing as he looked over Callum and Floyd, "this here circular is a wanted poster for the arrest of Mr. William Wallace Logan, for the desertion from the Yankee Army." He paused again, then added, greed showing in his little eyes, "There's a hundred-dollar reward. You wouldn't happen to know the whereabouts of this deserter, now would you?"

Floyd spoke up. "Number one, Sheriff, he isn't a deserter, and he has the papers to prove it. Number two, he is not with us, and we do not know where he is."

Chadwick gave them a sideways stare. "You sure you boys don't know?"

Callum felt his ire rising. He moved closer to the edge of Chadwick's desk. "You calling us liars, Sheriff?"

The sheriff's watery gray eyes blinked a couple of times. *Looks like an owl at noontime,* Callum thought.

Then the sheriff's face started turning red. "Don't you git testy with me, boy. I'll throw you in this here slammer and lose the key."

Callum stepped closer, eyes locked on the sheriff. He came up short, stopped by the man's desk and Floyd's firm grip on his arm.

Floyd, using a sweet voice, unusual for him, said, "Why, Sheriff Chadwick, we ain't testy at all. We just want you to know Will sure ain't no deserter. Now could we get back to our original question? What about that Davies bunch firing on the Ruiz family?"

The sheriff, somewhat appeased, again leaned back in the complaining chair. "Mr. Logan, I'm sure you must be mistaken about who it was. Sir Davies is a fine man and is doing his best to build up this town. He's even offered opportunity for the town folks. You must be mistaken. Maybe I should talk to the Ruizes."

Callum, his temper threatening to slip from his grasp, said, "That'd be kinda hard—"

He was cut off by the squeeze of Floyd's hand.

Floyd said, "Maybe you should, Sheriff. That'd probably be a good idea. You oughta ride on out there and talk to Señor Ruiz." He reached up and touched his hat. "We'd best be going, now, if we want to eat supper at Miss Molly's place. Sorry to bother you, and we'll bring William by as soon as he gets here, so he can clear up this little misunderstanding."

The sheriff's face had lost its flame-red appearance and returned to the normal ruddy complexion he had been sporting when they came in. "*You* stop by anytime, Mr. Logan, anytime at all, and bring your relative by. I'll be glad to straighten out any confusion."

Callum's anger was boiling as they walked out of the office and mounted their horses. He looked at his uncle, who gave a short shake of his head, and they rode silently toward Molly Flynn's boardinghouse.

18

As big as the man was, he was quick and surprised Will with his speed. The blow caught Will just below his ear and staggered him. He took a half-step back to regain his balance, and the heel of his boot caught the edge of the boardwalk. Now completely unbalanced, he fell, turning slightly, and struck the end of a hitching rail with the middle of his back. He felt a sharp pain in his spine, and his legs collapsed.

"You knocked the daylights out of that big ole boy, Sam. Stomp him. Stomp him now!" Jingles Smith shrieked.

Will's back burned like fire, and his legs were tingling, but feeling was returning quickly. He waited in place, wiggling his toes as Capps jumped toward him, intent on stomping his face into the ground. When he fell, he had fallen next to a pile of drying horse apples. He grabbed a handful, and when Capps raised his big boot to stomp him, he tossed it all into the man's face.

Horse manure burns like fire if it gets into a man's eyes, and the minute it hit Capps in the face, all intentions of stomping Will left him. Anyone watching could see his only desire was to free his eyes from the intense burning.

While Capps rubbed his inflamed eyes, Will grabbed the offending hitching rail and pulled himself erect. Standing tall, but still wobbly, he watched Capps rub his eyes and moan.

Rinso started to move forward, and Mac coldcocked him with a short right jab that landed on his left temple. Jingles, seeing himself as the only one left in action, shoved his hand toward the revolver he carried behind his waistband. The metallic click of a cocking hammer carried through the quiet night and froze him in place.

"You might want to rethink that decision, mister," Bart said, the .36-caliber Navy Colt having suddenly appeared in his right hand.

Standing only a few feet away, Jingles Smith could see, in the escaping light from the adjacent building, the gaping hole of the muzzle steady on his chest. Sobering quickly, he slowly eased his hand from the butt of his pistol and extended it out to his side. "I weren't going to draw, mister. I was just a-wantin' to make sure it was there. You know, in case I need it."

In a flat tone, devoid of emotion, Bart said, "You won't need it, Smith. You'd best just leave it be." He glanced over at Will and the bent-over Capps. "You all right? I seen yore back hit that rail."

"I'm fine. Lost the feeling in my legs for a minute, but it's coming back. I seem to be much better than Mr. Capps, here."

Capps was still rubbing his eyes. "You blinded me," he said and cursed.

"You've got a mouth as bad as those horse apples. Come over here." Will grabbed the man by the back of his shirt and walked him to a nearby horse trough. "There's a horse trough right in front of you. Wash your eyes out, and they'll be fine."

Will watched him bend over and hesitantly start washing his eyes. "Capps," Will said, "you've got a solid punch, and you made me see stars for a second, but don't make the mistake of thinking you whipped me. I eat your kind for breakfast. If you're smart, there won't be a next time." He looked over at

Mac and Bart. "You two had enough excitement for one evening?"

"More than enough for me," Bart said. He stepped over to Smith and yanked his revolver from his waistband.

Smith just stood there, in the darkness, arms spread.

"See the desk clerk at the City Hotel. He'll have your weapon. Be careful who you try to draw it on. The next man might not be as patient as me. He might kill you."

They walked around the fallen Rinso, the man still out cold.

Will looked down at him and said, "What'd you hit him with, Mac?"

MacGregor held up a massive fist and said, "Only this, and I didn't hit him hard."

Will shook his head, gave a short laugh, and, back still throbbing and legs tingling, placed one hand on his Scottish friend's shoulder for support. The three of them, with Will setting a slow, halting pace, walked toward the City Hotel.

LEADING an extra horse apiece and one additional packhorse, the men rode up to the Barlow Law and Land office at precisely ten o'clock Wednesday morning. They dismounted, tied their mounts, and entered the office.

David, Senator Barlow's clerk, was still engaged behind a mass of papers. He looked up from his desk and said, "Good morning, gentlemen. The senator is in his office and is expecting you."

"Thanks, David," Will said and led the procession through the open door. Senator Barlow sat behind his desk, several documents spread in front of him.

"Good morning, gentlemen."

Will noticed the senator's watchful gaze as he limped carefully toward the chair and took a seat.

"Morning, Senator," Will said as he cautiously lowered himself to the chair. Mac and Bart also greeted the senator and took seats. Will looked across the desk at the documents. "You have quite a few papers there."

"Yes, these all belong to you." He indicated both Will and Mac. Then he looked back to Will. "Are you able to ride?"

"Oh yeah," Will said, "fully capable. A little sore, but I'll get over it. In a few days I'll be like new." He said it with more confidence than he felt. Sleeping had been tough. It was difficult to find a position to relieve the sharp pain that extended down his left leg. It was the same leg that had been broken from a gunshot wound at the battle where he had lost his memory. He adjusted himself in the chair to relieve some of the pressure against his back.

"I'm glad to hear it," the senator said. He looked at Mac and then to Will, handing Mac a pen. "I need you to sign these papers, and we will be finished with your paperwork."

Both Mac and Will signed the documents.

Waiting for the signatures to dry, the senator explained, "While the certified copies were being made, I had an extra set made so each of you will be able to carry one with you. Will, there is also an additional document to go along with the one you received from the army, affirming the validity of your name. As you can see, in addition to your signature, there is that of the judge, and my signature as former senator of the state of Texas, and David's as a witness."

Will shook his head. "Never thought losing my memory and changing my name would be the cause of so much paperwork."

The senator chuckled and said, "Yes, it does seem silly, but I think you would rather carry these papers than have to repeat what you recently experienced with your army."

"I reckon I would, Senator. Your point makes these papers feel a lot less troublesome."

"I hope you men find Darcy," the senator said as he deftly

folded the papers, slipping them inside three different, heavy envelopes. He folded over the flaps, tied them, and handed two to Will and one to Mac.

The three men stood. "Aye," Mac said, "it is our hope we will find the young man resting at a ranch house along the way."

The senator had also risen. "I also received some information on the butler for Sir Davies. Before becoming a butler, it seems he was a less than successful actor in London, with the stage name of Erasmus Lockwood. Unless there is another Sir Wilford Pemberton Davies the Third, which I sincerely doubt, the man is Lockwood and has used the wealth he stole from Davies to forge the appropriate documents and pay for his gang."

Will said, "Thank you, Senator. After finding Darcy, we will first contact the sheriff. I'm hoping the law will move Lockwood and his gang off our ranch. But if he does nothing, we'll take care of it.

"What do we owe you, Senator?"

"Twenty-five dollars. You can pay David on the way out, and good luck to you all."

"We're much obliged," Will said.

The three friends shook hands with the senator and left his office. At David's desk, Will pulled a sack from his vest pocket, took out a double eagle and a half eagle. "Senator said it was twenty-five bucks."

David held out his hand, and Will dropped the gold coins into the waiting palm. David said, "Thank you, gentlemen. Have a good day." He took the money, dropped it into a side drawer, and was hard at work before they reached the door.

Will pulled the door open and stepped into the morning heat, followed by Mac and Bart. The three untied their horses and swung up on their mounts. Turning south on San Jacinto, they rode in silence until reaching Live Oak Street, and turned right.

Bart, riding his bay and leading his spare horse and the pack-horse, said, "We agreed we ain't takin' the bridge, right?"

Will turned in his saddle and grinned at his friend through the pain in his back, which jolted down his left leg with each step Smoky made. "What's the problem, Bart? You not hankering to lead those animals across that sturdy bridge?"

"No siree, I sure ain't."

"Aye, laddie, that's making two of us. That Mr. Platt said there was a fine crossing all the way down at the end of Live Oak street."

"Good," Bart said. "I've crossed there several times, and this time of year, the water won't get near these horses' knees. It'll be a lot more solid, too, than that blamed rickety bridge. I swear, the next time the Colorado floods, and it does every year, they'll find those pontoons down in the Gulf of Mexico."

The three men held up at Congress Avenue and waited for a hole to open up in the constant traffic. Their holdup was primarily freighters, both arriving and departing from the capital. Many had traveled from as distant as the port of Galveston. Finally an opportunity presented itself. They raced between the big freighters, once across slowed to a walk, and continued down Live Oak, crossing four additional streets until reaching Nueces. Once across Nueces, and just before Live Oak stopped at the edge of a thicket, a side road took off to the left. It led them down the steep bank and to the river's edge.

As Bart had said, the flowing water barely reached the horses' knees. Once across, they followed the road to where it intercepted the main road between Austin and San Antonio. Turning south, the trio rode in silence, each wrapped in his own thoughts.

Will was thinking about Deborah. *What's she doing right now? Did Ma talk her into going back to the ranch, or is she helping her uncle, Dr. James? She likes her work. My bet is she's in Pueblo with her uncle and aunt. I'm a lucky man. She supported me, totally, when I needed to come south to help. It'll be a fine day when I can get back to her.*

"So, are you thinking about where our Darcy lad might be?" Mac asked.

"I hate to say it, Mac," Will replied, "but I think he's dead. There's so many ways for a lone man to die in this country."

"You're right," Bart chimed in. "There's still Indians, mostly renegades, but still here. Snakes, a man can get bit by a snake anytime. You boys remember Potsy. His brother was kilt by a snake when he squatted to do his business. Why, a man can whack himself with an axe and either bleed to death or git an infection, not to mention gettin' kicked in the head by a horse, or drownin' in a creek, or even breakin' a leg by missteppin' off a log." Bart shook his head. "Mighty dangerous to travel alone."

Will nodded his agreement. "There's one thing you haven't mentioned, Bart. This Sir Davies or Lockwood, or whatever his name is, could have sent men out to waylay Darcy. If that happened, they may have found the papers on him, and Lockwood could be aware of the investigation. If they killed Darcy, Lockwood could think he's home free."

They rode on in silence, the distance slowly falling behind them. The fastest route between Austin and San Antonio was the road they were traveling. Though it was heavily traveled, a single rider, even leading an extra horse, could weave through and around the traffic, leave the road if necessary, and still make better time than trying to cut across the rough country.

They asked travelers, stopped in at ranches along the way and inquired of them, but no one remembered seeing Darcy. No one, that is, until one of the last ranches before reaching San Antonio. They rode into the ranch yard, and since no one was in sight, they dismounted at the watering trough in front of the barn and corral, allowing their horses to slake their thirst. As the animals drank, a cowhand strolled out of the barn. "Howdy," he said.

"Howdy," Will replied. "We didn't see anyone around to ask, so we decided you folks wouldn't mind if we gave our horses some water."

"Not at all, name's Wally Siefort. Help yoreself."

"Thanks," Will said. "I'm Will, this is Mac, and he's Bart. We're looking for a friend of ours. We're from the Double R, down by Dog Town, and we're up here looking for a partner of ours, Darcy Smith."

At the name, the man nodded vigorously. "Heck yeah, before I left home, l lived in Corpus and rode with Darcy in my first ridin' job. He's a fine feller."

"So it's Darcy *Smith* you know?" Mac asked.

"That's sure as shootin' what I'm sayin', and I can go you one better. I was mighty pleased to see him a couple of months back. He stopped over and spent the night with us 'fore headin' on south." Here the cowboy stopped, rolled the large cud of tobacco in his mouth, and spit a stream toward the corral. "He told me about the problem you folks are having with that danged Englishman. He said he had the goods on him, and that feller would be hittin' the road pretty soon."

"When was this you saw him?" Will asked.

The cowhand scratched the stubble of his beard and gazed at the big mesquite tree shading the entrance to the ranch house. "Let me see. We'd been gatherin' cattle . . . It must have been right at the last of April. Yes, sir, I remember now. The boss pays us on the last day of the month, and that was the day Darcy rode in. I'd just been paid."

"Wally," Will asked, "did he leave the same day?"

"No, sir, he did not. He stayed the night with us and left right after breakfast the next day. That'd be the first of May."

The horses had finished drinking and were cropping at the grass growing around the trough.

Will glanced at his friends. "If you boys are about ready, we'd best be on our way."

They stepped to their horses. Once up on Smoky, Will said, "Wally, much obliged for the water. You ever head down Dog Town way, drop in at the Double R. You'll always be welcome."

Wally touched a finger to the brim of his beat-up hat. "Yore mighty welcome. Winters get a little cool up here. One day I might just get an itch to head south and look you up."

The three riders turned their horses for the road and trotted out of the yard. The dust kicked up by the hooves drifted across the trail in the light breeze, which offered no cooling. Heat waves rose from the distant hills, distorting the brown and green hillsides. Will held on to his hope that they would find Darcy. His three friends had survived the war. Wade was dead from a point-blank rifle shot by a rustler, and now Darcy could be dead. After this was over, and he left to go back to Deborah, Mac would be alone, all of his friends dead or gone. *Life can be hard,* he thought. He watched an armadillo work diligently hunting for bugs and ants next to the trail. The little animal ignored them as they passed no more than ten feet from him.

Yes, it can be hard, he thought, *but it's the only life we have, so we'd better make the best of it.* His somber face brightened as he thought of his wife. Mac and Bart had pulled ahead of him and were turning on the San Antonio Road. He bumped Smoky and, with his spare horse on lead, trotted after his two friends.

19

Callum, Floyd, and Tandy rode in silence until well clear of any eavesdropping ears. Floyd surveyed the town. There was no one outside. Even the old man in Molly's rocker was gone. Turning his head, he said softly, "Callum, I stopped you because that sheriff is on Davies's payroll. There's something fishy going on here. You notice he never answered Tandy's question about Sheriff Pepper. Maybe we'll be able to find out what's going on from Tandy's friend Molly."

Callum, understanding, cooled quickly and nodded at the livery. "Why don't we ride on down to the stables, get the horses taken care of, and come back. That way they can get fed and watered, and if we decide to stay, they'll be done."

Floyd nodded, but Tandy looked longingly at the boarding-house as the men rode by. Callum saw the look. "Tandy, you know her. Why don't you and Floyd get off here and let her know she'll have three more eating and staying with her."

They pulled up, and Tandy said, "You sure? I don't mind helping. In fact, I'll be glad to take 'em to the livery myself, and you can go on in."

"Nope, you go ahead."

"Don't have to ask these old bones twice. Thank you, nephew," Floyd said.

Callum watched as his uncle slowly unwound from the back of his horse. *I hate to see it,* he thought, *but age is catching up with him. All this time in the saddle, from Colorado here, then to the border and back, why, it's wearing on me. He must be near stove up.* The two men pulled their rifles from the scabbards, removed their saddlebags and bedrolls, and walked toward the boardinghouse steps. He waited until they walked up the steps of the boardinghouse before continuing his short ride to the livery.

He had just stepped down from Shoshone when the liveryman stepped out of the stables. "Howdy, neighbor. Been doing some travelin', I see."

Callum leaned back, hearing and feeling his joints pop. "Too far. Got room for some horse flesh?"

"Always do. Name's Bing Dingham. Say, you don't look to be from these parts," he said as he gathered the horses' reins. "Let me see." He thought for a moment. "Why, I'm guessin' you're from Tennessee. Am I right?"

"By way of Colorado," Callum replied, "where it's a dang sight cooler."

Bing shook his head. "Yessir, it's been mighty hot the last few weeks. Reckon we're probably in for a mighty big storm, as hot as it's been. Right now, though, I'd take a storm of just about any kind if it could break this heat."

Callum nodded and, thinking he might get a little information from the talkative man, asked, "I see the sheriff is Chadwick. Didn't there used to be a Sheriff Pepper around here?"

"Shore was. Been here up 'til just a short time ago. He was dry-gulched." The man removed his hat and shook his head. "Awful shame. He was a good man. Didn't get along well with the new owner of the Double R ranch, though. Sheriff seemed to always regret throwing the old owners off. Why, he told me he didn't trust that uppity new British character who claimed he owned the ranch. Said the man had all the papers, so he had to enforce the law, but for some reason he couldn't or wouldn't explain, he didn't trust him at all."

"That's a real shame. Our friend indicated that the sheriff might not be too happy to see him, so he was really surprised to learn Sheriff Pepper was no longer the sheriff."

"Who's yore friend?"

"Big fella," Callum said, "by the name of Tandy Jacobs."

Bing let out a low whoop and broke into laughter. When he finally got himself under control, he said, "I reckon not. Tandy was always gettin' into trouble. Then he whipped the sheriff's son to a fare-thee-well. The boy made some comment to Tandy about his ma. Don't know what it was"—he chuckled again—"but it sure didn't set right with Tandy. That Pepper boy, names Brooks, but everyone started calling him Blaze 'cause he fired up Tandy so. Funny thing, it took, and now that's what he goes by, Blaze Pepper." He laughed again, "Get it? Blaze Pepper. Like hot? Pretty catchy, ain't it?"

Callum, caught up in the story, couldn't help but laugh. "Yep. Pretty catchy. So is Blaze Pepper still around?"

"You know, that's a funny thing. He never held no grudge against Tandy, though he spent several days in bed. I talked to him about it years later. He said he had it coming. Never should have talked about Tandy's ma like that. Turned out to be a fine feller. He's got him a little place south of here."

Callum was tiring of the talk, and besides, he was hungry and didn't want to miss supper. Wanting to bring the conversation to an end, but still needing to know what had happened to Sheriff Pepper, he reluctantly asked, "So the sheriff was dry-gulched?"

"Oh yeah, terrible thing. Supposedly he had ridden out to the Double R. By the way, it was named after those boys' friend, Hank Remington. A heck of a man. I met him several times before they headed out to Abilene. Anyway, I still call the ranch the Double R, can't get used to the new name, Circle something."

"The sheriff?" Callum prompted.

"Oh yeah. Coming back, he was ambushed. Whoever did it must have had a right smart hate for the man. They emptied their Henry into him. He was shot up so bad he wouldn't have held water, holes everywhere, legs, arms, body, head. You almost couldn't recognize him. Must've sounded like the next war. Why—"

Callum cut him off. "Did they ever find out who did it?"

"Nary a bit. Suspicions are one of the men he sent to prison. He sent many a man to Huntsville. He was a hard sheriff, but good."

"All right," Callum said, trying to bring the conversation to a close. "Think you can take care of our horses? May be only a night, or it may be a couple of weeks."

"Sure can. They'll be mighty happy, too. Give 'em a good rubdown, a little corn, maybe some oats. These horses'll be happier than a pig in slop. It'll be two bits a horse a day, or a buck fifty a week."

Callum said, "Thanks. I've got to get going before I'm too late for Miss Molly's cooking." He pulled his Spencer from the scabbard and untied his bedroll and saddlebags, throwing the saddlebags over his left shoulder.

"Well, lands-sake, feller, you shouldn't of stood around jawin' so long. What'd you say yore name was?"

"Callum Logan," Callum said, turning away and stepping out as quickly as he could.

To his retreating back, Bing called, "Hurry up, now. She shore don't like for people to be late."

Before entering the home, Callum removed his chaps, laying them across the banister, dusted his pants with his hat, and rubbed his boots on the back of his trousers.

Walking in, just to his left was a dining room through open double doors. In the room sat several men, including Tandy and Floyd, gathered around a long table capable of seating at least ten, two more if the diners were crowded together. An attractive woman and a younger woman were picking up plates as he walked in.

The older of the two pointed toward the chair next to Floyd and said, "Well, sit it down, cowboy, you only barely made it. I think I might be able to scare something up. The calf tongue and brains are finished," she said, picking up the empty calf's head from the table. "How about a slab of beef, biscuits, and beans?"

"That sounds fine to me, ma'am," Callum said.

"Don't ma'am me. The name's Molly, and I expect you to use it. What's yours?"

Callum, having sat where he had been told, looked at the woman carrying the heavy calf's head, and said, "My name's Callum, Molly, and I expect *you* to use it. You need some help with that head?"

"Goodness," she said, "fresh and polite. What a combination. No, *Callum*, my daughters, Fran and Jackie, are all the help I need. Make yourself comfortable, and you'll be eating before you know it." She addressed the others. "Folks, your fresh pie will be right out."

One of the drummers across the table said, "Molly, you wouldn't have any of that fresh, thick cream to go with it, now would you?"

"Why, Hiram," she said, flashing a smile at the portly man, "you know I always have plenty of cream when I know you're coming."

"We waited on you, boy," Floyd said as Fran lifted his cleaned plate from in front of him.

"I can see. So how were the brains?"

"Mighty good, but not near as good as the tongue," Floyd said. "The brains had a different color and taste to it, but it was real flavorful."

Jackie, Molly's youngest daughter, set two large pitchers of fresh cream on the table and said, "That's the fresh red fish we got from Corpus. We occasionally get fresh saltwater fish from there. Later in the year, when the oysters are ready, we'll mix in oysters. It's really good then."

The other drummer spoke up. "I can attest to that. We"—he indicated the drummer next to him—"stay here quite often, traveling our route, and the oyster mixed with the calf brains is absolutely delicious."

Callum could feel his hunger growing by the second. He watched Fran and Jackie bring out large pieces of blackberry pie. He could see the steam rising from the pie, and looked longingly at the piece Fran set down in front of Floyd.

"Wait your turn," Floyd, seeing him looking, said, then grinned. "It'll be worth it."

A few minutes later, Molly came out with a thick, smoking hot steak. On the side were mashed potatoes and, he was thrilled to see, fresh green beans. When she had mentioned beans, he figured her to mean red beans, the kind trail hands ate all the time.

She recognized the look of pleasure on his face when he saw the beans. "Grown in my garden out back. You'll like them."

"Molly," Callum said, "I haven't had fresh green beans in a long time. I can't wait."

She set the plate in front of him, looked at the younger men, both cowhands, and asked, "How are you boys doing?"

With mouths full of blackberry pie covered with fresh cream, they could only nod and go, "Mmmm."

"Good, I'm glad you like it." She eyed the cowhand at the end. "How's the ranching business, Blaze?"

Callum, enjoying his first taste of green beans, had just slipped a piece of steak into his mouth. At the mention of the name, he looked at the young man. He was a pleasant-looking fellow, who had, at one time, had his nose realigned by someone's fist, but other than that, if he was in fact the man he'd heard about today, he looked none the worse for wear.

"Going pretty good, Molly. Here lately I've been missing a few cattle. Haven't yet figured out exactly why."

Tandy, who had been busy making the blackberry pie disappear, finished his, belched, and said, "Pardon, Molly. That was a mighty good meal."

"No pardon's necessary, Tandy. I'm so glad to see you're alive."

Tandy looked around Floyd and said, "Callum, this feller losing the cattle is Brooks Pepper. We used to know each other. He's Sheriff Pepper's son. Goes by Blaze now."

Blaze nodded. "Howdy, Callum. Pleased to know you. Tandy speaks highly of you folks, specially yore brother Hank." The man paused and shook his head. "Sorry, Will. Ever'body around here thinks of him as Hank." He tossed a thumb at the young cowhand sitting next to him. "This here is Farley Cooper. He works for me."

Farley, still working on the blackberry pie, dipped his head and mumbled, "Howdy," through a full mouth.

Callum looked over the two men. Blaze, other than the slightly sideways nose, looked like any cowhand you'd run into on the range. His brown hair hung close to the collar of his gray homespun shirt. A green and black bandanna, tied close, hid a short thick neck that carried a square, honest, windburned face already showing the lines of hard work, worry, and sun.

Farley, too, was cut from the same cloth. Thick eyebrows did their best to hide deep-set blue eyes, but had difficulty concealing the humor that appeared ready to break loose.

Blaze said, "You may have heard of me. My reputation around Dog Town is the feller Tandy beat the daylights out of." He reached up to his nose, feeling the rough bridge, where it made a slight turn to the left. "It galls me to admit it, but I had it coming. Feller ought not say what I did."

Floyd said, "We all make our mistakes and take our lickings. That's what you call life, boy. Says a lot for you that you can man up to it."

Blaze grinned, giving Tandy a long look. "I'm just glad it happened when we was boys. Now he's growed into a giant. I wouldn't fancy gettin' slammed by one of those widow-makers." He indicated Tandy's hands, which were nearly twice as wide as every man's at the table besides Callum and Floyd.

Callum laughed and then said, "I know I sure wouldn't want to collide with one of those fists, but Blaze, you mentioned you're missing some cattle?"

"Yessiree. I sure am. Kinda puzzling, too."

"How long has it been going on?"

Blaze took a minute to calculate, then looked at Farley, who had finally finished his pie. "What would you say, Farley? Four, five months?"

"'Bout that, boss." Farley had a slow drawl, the words coming out like molasses in the wintertime.

Callum said to Blaze, "Sorry to hear about your pa. When did that happen?"

Blaze's brown eyes tightened with anger. "Six months ago, and I wish I could find the yellow belly who dry-gulched him. I found the spot where the shooter hid. He left a bunch of cigarette butts there, you know, roll your own. He waited for a while. He's patient, and I reckon he knew Pa was coming." His jaw muscles worked with anger. "Shot was no more than fifty yards at the most, probably closer to forty. He didn't have to be good. He just let him get close and opened up."

"I'm real sorry, Blaze," Tandy said. "He was a good man. Reckon me and my bunch made his life miserable for a while. I'd sure like to change that."

Blaze shook his head. "There was a war goin' on, Tandy. Ever'-body did some things they regret. Anyway, he shot Pa full of holes. Way more than he needed to kill him. There were bullets in both knees, elbows, wrists, hands, not to mention the ones in his body and head. I never before seen the like."

Molly came in carrying two plates, a piece of pie on each one.

Jackie, her youngest, came in with her and removed Callum's empty plate. Molly put one piece of pie in front of Callum and set one piece at the end of the table, next to him. After pulling out a chair, she sat and said to Jackie as she was leaving the room, "Jackie, just put those last dishes on to soak. We'll wash them later. You and Fran get a piece of pie and come out and join us."

"Yes, Mama," Jackie called as she continued out of the room.

Turning to Floyd and Callum, Molly said, "After the meals, if there's time, the girls and I like to join the guests for dessert."

"That's mighty nice," Floyd said. "Makes it almost like home, doesn't it, Callum?"

"Sure does," he answered, facing Molly. "Hope you don't mind my getting to the point. Do you know anything about Davies?"

"My," she said, "you do get right to the point. I don't know much. I know he blew into town with a bunch of men and took over the Remington Ranch. Ran your brother's partners off the ranch. In all fairness, he used the law, but Sheriff Pepper was not happy enforcing it. In fact, he was trying to find out more about Davies and his eviction notice when he was killed."

Callum nodded. "What about this Sheriff Chadwick? Do you know anything about him?"

The girls joined them with their pie, Fran sitting next to Blaze. Callum noticed Molly keeping an eye on her fourteen-year-old daughter.

She waited a few seconds, then slowly turned her head to face him. "He is a sorry excuse for a sheriff. He worked as a swamper in the saloon that shut down. He's been here for several years. Short-tempered man. Takes offense very easily. Shouldn't be in charge of cleaning an outhouse, much less being sheriff."

"A swamper in a saloon? How did he go from there to sheriff?" Callum asked.

"I can tell you," Blaze said. "When the old saloon shut down because the owner wasn't making enough here in Dog Town, he moved to Corpus and opened one there. Pa felt sorry for Tim and hired him to keep the jail clean. That was about two weeks before Pa was killed. He was thinking about letting Tim go. All Tim did was sleep in a cell and sweep out occasionally. If Pa wanted the place cleaned, he still had to do it himself."

"All right," Callum said, "but how did this guy get appointed sheriff?"

"It doesn't make sense," Molly said, "but when Sheriff Pepper was killed, nobody wanted the job, so the mayor appointed Tim, since he'd been working in the sheriff's office as interim sheriff until we could elect one."

"How long's that been?" Callum asked.

Molly thought for a moment. "Four or five months. Davies hadn't been here long. Isn't that right, Blaze?"

"Yep. Little over four months."

"Why," Callum followed up, "is Chadwick such a believer in Davies? To hear him tell it, Davies is a gift to Dog Town."

"Yes," Molly said, "you'll find that opinion from several of our good citizens. It seems Mr. Davies has proposed a means for the townspeople to potentially make some very big money."

Puzzled, Callum asked, "How could he make money for the townspeople, other than indirectly?"

Molly, having finished her pie, placed her fork on the plate, slid the plate out of the way, and, placing her elbows where her plate had been, leaned toward Callum. "I'll tell you how."

20

Callum leaned toward his host.

"Davies talked to the mayor and asked him to call a meeting of the town leadership and business owners. When everyone was gathered, he proposed, as he put it, 'An investment opportunity,' a business opportunity."

Frowning, Callum said, "Business opportunity?"

"Yes," Molly said, "let me explain. He had the financial books on the ranch and the two cattle drives."

"How did he get those?" Callum asked.

"I do not know, but he had them. And he talked about the exorbitant amount they made on the two cattle drives. He showed everyone the books, where each drive netted close to ninety thousand dollars."

Callum nodded. "Sure, you can make some big money, but there are big risks. The cows can be run off. They can be lost to Indians, rustlers, in fires, stampedes. I mean, the list goes on and on. It's a big gamble."

"He mentioned that, but," Molly said, "there's a lot of money to be made. He kept emphasizing that point, and he's quite a talker. He had a lot of people excited. He said that his goal was to make a home here, and he would like to provide anyone who liked to invest in his herd the opportunity to make some real money."

Floyd shook his head. "This is crazy. Regular people could lose their life savings. Ranchers do what they do because they have to. That's all they know, and you've got to drive to Kansas to get to a decent market. A few hit it big, but many lose everything they have, and end their lives working on someone else's cow herd. It's not something to put your savings into, not unless you have enough extra you'd still have money if the herd is lost."

Molly nodded at Blaze. "He tried to explain it to them, and some of the folks got really mad that he had never offered them the same opportunity. Mr. Bolton also tried to reason with those who were there, but was shouted down. The sheriff and quite a number of other people liked the idea. Some were going home to get their money, others to the bank. It was crazy."

Callum was still puzzling over the idea. "But he can't start a drive now. It's already too late in the year. They'd never make it. As dry as it is, the cattle would starve or go mad with thirst. When's he planning on doing it?"

"He said he'd be startin' right away," Blaze said, "and with all the money they were gonna make, this would be the best Christmas they ever had. I tried to tell 'em, but they flat wouldn't listen. So I told 'em they was all crazy, and washed my hands of the whole deal. I left before it ended up with me having to shoot someone to protect myself."

Callum couldn't believe what he was hearing. "So these folks freely gave the money they worked and sweated for to Davies?"

Molly nodded, and Blaze said, "Yep."

Callum shook his head. He looked to see Floyd and Tandy doing the same. To Molly he said, "Did you?"

She looked at him like he had gone crazy. "I've worked too hard to build this place. The last thing I want to do is lose it on some wild gamble. There is no way I'd do something like that.

Anyway, I don't like or trust that Englishman and his foreman, Langston."

"Did the sheriff?"

Blaze answered him. "No way. If he's making what Pa was, he's bringing in fifty dollars a month, and knowing him, he spends that on liquor at Bolton's. He ain't got any money to invest."

Callum leaned back, stretched, and yawned. "Sorry. I hate to break this up, but it's been a long day. If you've got room for us, I'd better be hitting the bed before I fall out of this chair."

Molly stood, and so did the men. The drummers had been quiet through the discussion, now excused themselves, and headed up to bed. After telling them goodnight, Molly said, "Callum, your room is the first door to the right, at the top of the stairs, and Floyd, you're right next door to Callum. Tandy, your old room is available downstairs if you'd like that one."

"That'd be real nice, Molly."

Blaze and Farley had put their hats on and now extended their hands. "Mighty nice to meet y'all," Farley said. "Tandy, good to see you. We've got to be gettin' back to the ranch. Just came in for some supplies, and I figured a meal cooked by someone other than Farley would be real welcome."

Farley grinned and said, "Goodnight, y'all."

"Good to see you, Blaze," Tandy said. "I mean it, and I'm right sorry about your pa."

"Thanks, Tandy."

The rancher and cowhand disappeared out the door. Fran watched Blaze leave, and Molly watched Fran, until she clapped her hands once, and said, "Let's go, girls. We need to get the dishes done and the kitchen straightened for in the morning."

The girls dashed off for the kitchen, and Callum led the tired procession upstairs.

∼

STARS COULD STILL BE SEEN through the window when Callum threw the covers back and dropped his feet to the plank floor. He had cleaned up as best he could, with the water in the pitcher, before going to bed last night. The clean clothes from his saddlebags were waiting where he had laid them just before settling into a deep sleep.

He first pulled his socks on, then his dark brown pants. Then picking up each boot, he shook it out by beating it on the end of the metal bed frame. He watched closely, in case a scorpion had decided to make a home of his boots last night. When nothing fell out, he slipped them on. Then he pulled the clean red and brown checked shirt over his head, tucked it in quickly, put his hat on, and swung his gun belt around his waist. He adjusted the holster until it felt right, shoved his hat back, and noted the washbasin was empty and clean. He picked up the pitcher, full. Callum thought, *Wonder when they cleaned out the basin and brought in fresh water. I don't remember a thing.* Concern wrinkled his brow. *Sleeping that hard could get a man killed, but it sure felt good.*

Leaving his gear, he opened his door just as Floyd stepped out of his room. "Well, good morning, sleeping beauty," Floyd said.

Callum frowned. "What's that mean?"

"It means you were sleeping so sound a whole passel of Indians could've come into your room without you knowing anything about it."

"How do you know how I was sleeping?"

"Young Miss Fran tapped on my door this morning with a clean basin and a pitcher of fresh water. She had one for you, but she said she didn't knock because she could hear you snoring. I told her to give it to me, and I'd put it in there. So we just rightly switched out your water while you sawed away." Floyd shook his head. "If I slept like that in them mountains, my hair'd be hanging somewhere other than my head."

Callum headed down the stairs. "Stop your picking and come on."

Callum heard his uncle grumbling as he made his way down the stairs. Tandy was sitting at the table, putting peach jam on a buttered biscuit.

"Boy," Callum said to Tandy, "the last time I saw you, food was getting stuffed into your mouth, and it still is. Did you eat all night?"

Tandy waved to him, ignoring the remark, and stuffed half the biscuit into his mouth. Callum shook his head and took a seat next to him.

After greeting Molly and the girls, the three men worked through breakfast quickly. The sun was up but still low. Its orange light reflected in the windows across the street. Callum stood just as five riders pulled up in front of Molly's boarding-house. "Looks like trouble," Callum said. "Keep it out of the house if we can." He called to the kitchen, "Molly, you and the girls stay back there. Trouble just pulled up in front." He removed the thong from his revolver and checked his Bowie knife. Hopefully neither of the two would be needed, but they'd better be ready.

The first rider was through the door, calling, "Hey, Molly, get some of those biscuits out here." He started to say something else when he turned toward the dining room and saw Callum, Floyd, and Tandy standing facing him. He froze.

Someone shoved him farther, stumbling into the house, and a raised voice from outside shouted, "Don't block the door, Nash. You got some hungry men out here."

The men behind him piled into the room, slid to a stop, and followed the gaze of Nash, turning to look at the three men facing them. The loudmouth said, "Well, look what we've got here, boys. We must be about the luckiest fellers in the country." He looked at Callum and moved his glare to Floyd. "I been looking for you, old man. You made a big mistake."

Floyd stood relaxed, watchin' the big gunman. "You seem a little loud, sonny. Somebody forget to change your diaper?"

The big man reddened and went into an exaggerated crouch, his right arm held in an arch toward his gun. Floyd remained in his relaxed position, a cold smile on his face.

"Boys," Callum said, "here isn't the place for this. Molly provides a nice clean eating establishment. We wouldn't want to mess it up. We'll be glad to accommodate any of your needs, but let's do it outside."

Molly came around the corner of the kitchen, a double-barrel ten gauge leveled at the five men. As she stepped into the room, she moved to the side of Callum's group to allow for a clear shot. "You men, take it outside. You want to kill yourselves, it's fine with me, but I'll not have you shooting up my place. The first man who goes for a gun gets a full load of buckshot from this ten gauge. Now get out."

The crouching man held his position. "This old man killed a friend of mine, and I aim to see him dead."

Molly stood solid with the shotgun, the barrel trained on the man's belly. "You go for that gun, and you'll never see anything else. I'm not joshing you, Abe, and I'm not afraid to use this."

"Listen to her, Roydon," the man who had met them on the trail and at Armando's home said. "Let's take it outside, but I'm telling you, you don't want any part of him."

Slowly Roydon straightened. "I want you, old man. I'll be waiting in the street."

"I'm not big on short guns, boy, but I've been known to use 'em. I've already had a fine breakfast here at Miss Molly's. You're gonna miss your chance to taste one of those fine biscuits if you keep this up."

The other man said, "Roydon, I'm tellin' you. Don't mess with him. He's pure poison. I've seen his kind. Even if you beat him and put a bullet or two into him, he'll kill you. There just ain't no stop in them mountain men."

Roydon slammed his revolver back into his holster and shoved a dirty index finger at Floyd. "Outside, old man. Five minutes."

Floyd nodded. "Alright, sonny. Today's just as good as any other for you to join your dead friend."

The five riders cautiously, eyes staying on Callum, Floyd, and Tandy, backed out the front door. Callum watched through the windows as they trooped toward the general store and saloon. "Looks like they're after a glass of liquid breakfast."

"Good," Floyd replied. "Nothing like a few drinks to settle your nerves and slow your reactions."

Molly lowered the hammers on the ten gauge and, with concern in her voice, said, "Floyd, you don't have to do this. That Abe Roydon is nothing more than a killer. He's no more a cowhand than I am, and he's got plenty of money, a lot more than any cowpuncher makes. He and that bunch are in here almost every morning for breakfast. They've run off most of my regular customers with their loud talk and threatening looks."

Floyd smiled at the attractive woman. "That's mighty nice of you, Miss Molly, but you and I both know that meeting that loud-mouth is exactly what I have to do."

The drummers had been caught halfway down the stairway, on their way to breakfast, when the gunmen had burst into the house. They continued down, and Hiram, the portly one, said, "Mr. Logan, we travel a good portion of this country." He indicated his companion. "Stanley and I have both seen this Roydon in action. He's a bad one. He has a bad temper, and he's mean. We saw him shoot a man down in the streets of Saint Gall, and the man had done nothing more than bump into him."

"I thank you, sir," Floyd replied, "but there's some things a man has to do, and this is one of them."

Stanley spoke up. "Yes, sir, we saw him in action. He carries those two guns and acts like he favors his right, but we saw him draw his left pistol in Saint Gall, surprised everyone, especially the man he was drawing against."

Floyd nodded his head to Stanley. "I sincerely thank you, sir. That is good information. I'll watch for that little move." He turned to Callum. "Nephew, I'd best be getting out there. If something should go wrong, you boys hightail it out of here. They'll be coming for you."

"We'll be ready, Uncle. Don't you worry about us. You've got some work to do." He turned to Tandy. "Would you go get our rifles?"

"Sure thing, Callum," Tandy replied, around the biscuit in his mouth. He stuffed in the remaining portion as he jogged up the stairs.

Floyd shook his head. "I swear that boy eats more than three cowhands."

Molly smiled at Floyd. "He always has, but look at him. There's a lot there to feed. He's as big as three cowhands."

"That he is, ma'am, that he is. I thank you for your hospitality and fine cooking. You can tell your girls I'll be back for more."

She had leaned the shotgun in the corner next to the hat rack by the front door. She moved up to Floyd, stood on her tiptoes, and after placing her hands on his shoulders, gave him a light kiss on his cheek. "I do hope you are, Floyd Logan. You are a fine man."

He grinned at her, the scar on his left cheek turning a little red at the edges. "Molly, I don't know about that, but I thank you for your sentiments." His face turned serious. He removed the Colt from its resting place in his holster, checked the cylinders, and dropped it back, making sure it slid smoothly in and out of the holster. Next he pulled the second one from his waist. This holster was in the front, at an angle, the muzzle slightly down, and the butt facing his right hand. After checking it, he slid it back in place, looked at Callum, and said, "It's time."

Tandy had returned with the rifles and handed Callum his

Spencer. Callum took it, looked at Molly's shotgun, and said, "Molly, could you spare me a few more cartridges for your ten gauge? I think I'd prefer to carry it this morning."

Molly turned to the kitchen and called, "Fran, would you bring me the box of shotgun shells, please."

Moments later, Fran arrived. Molly motioned to Callum, and she held the box out to him. It was open. He reached in and pulled out a handful of the heavy brass cartridges, dropping three in each of his vest pockets. "Thank you, Fran."

The girl's face was white with fear. "Please be careful."

"We'll sure do that, honey," Floyd said. "Now don't you worry."

Fran stepped back beside her mother and grasped her arm.

Callum, leaning his Spencer next to the shotgun, picked up the ten gauge and broke it open to confirm it was loaded. The two brass cartridges, tranquil and threatening, lay ready in the chambers. He snapped it closed, looked at Floyd and nodded.

"All right," Floyd said and stepped out the front door.

Callum followed and stepped to his uncle's right. He scanned the town, eyes missing nothing. Another hot day was on the way. The sky was clear except for an occasional white, puffy cloud floating by, pushed by a southeast breeze much stronger where the cloud was than here on the ground, where the wind was still. A pair of mockingbirds battled for singing dominance, first one then the other trilling a new tune. Near the other side of the street two large dogs, sun seekers, one brown the other mottled gray, lay in the dust where the first sun was striking the street. They eyed a lone cat trotting across the wide street, its tail whisking back and forth as its eyes tracked the possible threats. A normal morning in the little South Texas town.

Tandy stepped to Floyd's left, and Callum eared the hammers of the shotgun to full cock, the threatening, metallic clicks joined by that of Tandy cocking his Winchester's hammer. Up the street, near the general store, Roydon stood, waiting. The other four were nowhere in sight.

"I don't like the looks of this," Callum said. "It looks like a setup."

"I reckon," Floyd said, his voice cold and distant. "You just keep 'em off my back."

Callum knew his uncle's mind was focused on Roydon. The older man had survived too long in those high mountains to solely concentrate on the gunman. His senses would be constantly searching for other threats, but would be centered on the man waiting for him.

Floyd stepped into the middle of the street, turned toward the gunman, and his voice booming in the silent street, said, "You waiting for me, sonny?"

21

D ust devils danced across the undulating prairie. Lizards lay in the shade of mesquite and prickly pear, their mouths open as they panted to at least maintain a livable body temperature. Even the occasional fly buzzed around the riders with little enthusiasm. Most of the cattle they'd seen were standing in the shallow ponds formed in the low spots of rivers and creeks. Those creeks still running flowed only a trickle of water, the narrow stream racing from pond to pond as if in fear of evaporating. Overhead, a random buzzard glided in wide continuous circles, never flapping his wings as he rode the rising heat from the parched ground.

Will pulled the pinto to a stop. Smoky, on lead, took a couple of tentative steps forward as if he considered stopping next to Will, changed his mind and stopped. Both horses stood with their heads drooping. Will removed his Stetson and bandanna, wiped the Stetson's sweat band dry and the sweat streaming into his eyes. He immediately regretted not stopping under a mesquite tree to mitigate the blazing, unrelenting sun. Through his hair, and especially along the scar along his head, his scalp felt like it was going to melt. Moving quickly, he slapped the hat back in place and continued to search the parched land for some hint of Darcy.

They had been crisscrossing the country for the last four weeks, working their way slowly to Double R country. Rain hadn't fallen since before they left for Austin, and now, the parched land was reflecting it. The prickly pear and mesquite, great survivors in droughts, were even looking wilted and thirsty.

Will bumped Smoky in the flanks to get him started and slowly continued to search the brush country. Occasionally he would catch a glimpse of Mac or Bart, the trio spread wide, searching the thirsty land for some sign of Darcy. He dropped down into a creek bottom, finding a deep hole that hadn't, as yet, surrendered to the sun and heat. Dismounting, he allowed the pinto and Smoky to drink their fill.

Moving a little distance from the horses, he kneeled, keeping his gun hand free, and scooped water up with his left. The water was wet and good, but warm. It slaked his thirst but offered little cooling. He knew how to fix that. Removing his hat, he dipped and filled it in the pond, held the hat high, and slowly poured it over his head and shoulders. Leaning forward, he shook his head, throwing streaks of water into the air from his long hair. *That's cooler,* he thought.

Dipping another hatful of water, he poured it over Smoky's head and then another hatful over the pinto's. Both horses whipped their heads, throwing water all over Will. He laughed at them, momentarily refreshed, and climbed back into the saddle. The sun was lower, and he needed to keep looking.

Riding up and out of the creek, he spotted several buzzards circling far ahead. *It's worth investigating,* he thought and bumped the pinto in the flanks. The horse started walking in the direction of the black harbingers of death.

Probably a dead calf. Maybe even a deer or horse. As he rode closer, he was able to make out more buzzards. It had to be something large. A rabbit, even a jackrabbit, or other small game wouldn't warrant this many buzzards. Nearing, he could see the lowest ones sailing down to the ground. *Funny about buzzards,* he thought. *Sometimes they're almost polite. They sail around in the air, in layers. The lowest layer lands, and the next lowest moves down, each layer moving lower. Then a few of them on the ground take off, and the next layer lands. They just keep that up as long as there's enough to eat. Course, when they're on the ground, they'll fight each other for a piece of meat.* He shook his head. *Funny birds.*

He continued to ride, growing closer to the circling birds. Nearing, he could see they were landing on a steep, rocky knoll. It was thick with brush and prickly pear. A quick thought ran through his head. *Lord, I'd take it as a favor if this isn't Darcy.* He dismounted, flipped the lead and the reins around a bush, and reached for his Spencer. The metal was almost searing to the touch. Thinking better of his choice, he elected to continue with only his holstered Remington revolver, though he did slip the leather thong from the hammer.

He eased around a mass of prickly pear pads with three-inch thorns waiting to stab an unsuspecting arm or cheek. Once around the pads, he was into scrubby catclaw and blackbrush so thick there was no way to push through it. He squeezed into a narrow space between the prickly pear and the brush, occasionally getting a glimpse through the thicket. He could make out a shallow, rocky depression inside the screening brush that circled the top of the knoll. It was here the buzzards were landing.

"Yo, Will, you up there?" He heard from where he had left the horses.

"Yeah, Mac. Don't try to come up. I've already stabbed myself on this blasted prickly pear. It's a good thing I'm wearing chaps, or my legs would be pincushions. So far, I can see where the buzzards are landing, but I can't see what they're after. Have you seen Bart?"

"Aye," Mac called from below. "I can see him working his way over to us. I'm thinking he spotted the mess of buzzards. I'd say it'd be hard for any man to miss that many of the vile creatures."

Will moved sideways, feeling the prick of an occasional thorn in his back and behind his legs. Slowly, he worked his way around the edge of the wall of brush. Eventually, almost rubbing the prickly pear pads, he found a tiny opening through the brush in front of him. It was low and tight. The only way for him to get past it was to get on his belly and crawl through, not a pleasant thought.

He pondered his choices for a moment, took a deep breath, and kneeled down. His gloves would protect his hands from most of the things with sharp points, and his chaps and boots would give him protection from his waist down. But his chest and belly might be in trouble. He tied his vest closed as tight as he could get it. Finally, he removed his hat, for there was no way it would make it through the opening. Rising, he gripped the hat by the brim and sailed it over the prickly pear and down the hill toward Mac.

"Get my hat, Mac."

"Aye, laddie, I see it. I'll take care of it."

Will kneeled and started sweeping in front of him, clearing the ground of as many of the thorns and stickers as possible. When it was sufficiently clean, he lay down and slipped his head and shoulders through the narrow opening. He felt his back scrape on the lower edges of the thick brush, but fortunately felt no stabbing thorns. Working his way slowly, he cleared, crawled, cleared and crawled. Sweat rolled down into his face. The salt and dirt carried with it burned and scratched his squinting brown eyes. He blinked to try to keep it out, for that was his only defense. The brush was too tight to extend his elbow far enough to bring a hand back for a wipe.

He could see the brush, half a body length ahead, widening. His only thought was for Darcy. *The buzzards are after a deer. It has to be a deer.* Finally, he extended his left arm and cleared the last bit of trash, thorns, and goatheads, tiny, barbed multi-thorned pieces of hell, and pulled himself forward into the opening.

He gave a sigh of relief, stood, and the stench of dead, rotting flesh struck him harder than a charging two-thousand-pound longhorn steer. What little breeze there was couldn't reach behind the wall of brush and thorns, so the smell was held inside the circle of brush. Buzzards were clustered together behind a circular rock parapet.

It's no animal, Will thought. *That wall was built by a man.* The buzzards on the edge of the wall had been watching Will as he crawled through the brush. When he straightened, they leaped into the air, heavy wings beating against the hot air, trying to find enough lift to drag their bodies out of the windless pocket of brush. Several dragged over the brush tops, barely getting airborne.

When the outer ring flew, more red heads popped up from behind the parapet. Will stepped toward them, and a few followed their disappearing companions into the air.

The smell brought to Will's mind that of a battlefield, a memory he wanted to keep forgotten. Reluctantly, he walked forward. The first things he saw, beyond the remaining buzzards still feeding voraciously, were the boots. His heart fell. He bent over and picked up several rocks, hurling them at the buzzards. With only a squawk or two, the last few leaped into the air, leaving behind one huge buzzard that only now stopped tearing at the flesh. It turned to Will, spread its wings, and glared, defending its find.

Picking up a bigger rock, Will tossed it at the bird and shouted, "Get out of here before I shoot you." The buzzard squawked, hopped to one side, and finally heavily beat its wings to lift its gorged body from the knoll.

Will forgot the buzzards. He had a good look at the knoll. To one side, saddlebags had been tossed. He could see how the rocks had been gathered to form a wall against bullets, for no man who made it in here need fear a charge from any side. The pear and brush were too thick. But they didn't stop bullets. That was what the wall was for. Inside the wall was a depression deep enough to give a man plenty of protection from firing below. Inside the hole was covered with empty Henry casings. Both of Darcy's revolvers and his Henry lay against the wall. There must have been quite a battle here.

No longer able to put it off, he examined the body. As hardened as he was to death, the sight made his stomach turn. It was Darcy. Always laughing, pulling practical jokes, Darcy. Even after Wade, his best friend, was killed, he'd snapped back and before long was his old self. Now his body lay blackened, swollen, and torn by the buzzards.

Will looked away and tried to picture what had happened. He could see the dry water bag next to the torn body, along with the two canteens. He picked up the canteens and shook each one. Both empty. It was obvious. Darcy had died of thirst, alone, except for his enemies, allowing him to die in this heat. Several cans were open and empty along with his bag of jerky. Darcy's bag of Arbuckle was the only container with anything remaining. *He loved his coffee. It must have killed him to have to stop drinking it to preserve the water.*

At one end of the hole was a shallow firepit. Blackened by days of use. The rocks balanced a beat-up coffee pot and a small iron skillet.

Remembering his friends waiting anxiously below, Will yelled over the brush, "It's Darcy. He's dead. Looks like he died of thirst."

Bart called from below, "I can see why. I've ridden around the hill. The ground is cut to pieces with horse tracks, and there's empty Henry cases all over the place. Doesn't look like it was that long ago."

"No sense you boys trying to get up here. Plenty of rocks around. I'll bury him, but it'll take a while."

"Reckon we can camp here tonight," Bart called. "I'll take care of the horses."

Will turned to his gruesome task. He moved the sun-heated weapons outside the hole, along with the saddlebags. Darcy had his bedroll with him. Will shook his head in wonder. How could Darcy have gotten all these things through the brush? Did he already know about this place? It was a terrible choice for a last stand, a small hill out in the open with no water. There was no spot, no draw near to hide his horse. Why would he choose this hill to make a stand, unless he was pushed, and if he was pushed, how could he get so much equipment through the brush and up here in such a short time?

He shook his head and took one more look at the body. He hadn't noticed before, but Darcy's right leg looked unnaturally twisted. He grasped the leg to straighten it, and it separated below the knee. The trouser had been torn through by the buzzards, and Will was standing there with Darcy's leg in his hands. Instantly his stomach turned. He could feel the gorge pushing up and into his mouth. He swallowed quickly. Once more, and again. Finally his stomach settled, and, almost reverently, he pulled the remaining portion of the trouser leg down so that he could see the bone, jagged. The leg had been broken.

His mind was churning with questions. Darcy's supplies, his rifle, the wall, how could he have handled all of those things *and* with a broken leg. How? Slowly his mind calmed. He needed to take care of his friend. He would figure the questions out later. He gently laid the leg at the end of Darcy's knee and stepped back.

Sorry it came to this, Darcy, Will thought. *I wish I'd been here for you.* He felt a moment of guilt wash over him. If he'd come back with them after selling the herd in Abilene, maybe he could have prevented this from happening. *But if I'd come here, there would have been no Deborah.* He shook his head, straightened what was left of his friend's body, and spread his blanket over him. It was hard to believe these remains had once been Darcy. Carefully he began laying the rocks in place. It was as if Darcy had gathered his own rocks for his grave.

Once started, the work went quickly. Will removed his vest, but even without it, his checked shirt was quickly soaked in sweat. His gloves were old, and now they were tearing, exposing callused fingers and hands to the hot rocks. He'd switch them for his new ones when he returned to the horses. Setting the last rock firmly in place, Will stood next to the tall mound. Neither buzzard, coyote, nor wolf would get to what remained of his friend's body. Will examined his handiwork and bowed his head. After a moment of silence, he contemplated his trip back through the tangle of brush and prickly pear. He could shove both revolvers in the back of his waistband. With his vest pulled down over the pistol butts, they shouldn't catch in the brush. He looked at the Henry and the saddlebags. They presented a problem.

"Gettin' dark soon," Bart called from below.

Surprised, Will looked around. He had been so intent on taking care of Darcy, he hadn't noticed the darkening sky. He could actually see a couple of stars beginning to glow. *I'd best get moving. I'll drag the saddlebags with a foot and push the Henry ahead of me. Hopefully I won't get hung up.* He took one last look at the rock pile that would forever mark his friend's grave, dropped to his knees, and carefully crawled forward. It was cooling under the brush. The ground was still hot, but he could feel a noticeable change in temperature. He started forward. It was awkward, but at least on his trip in, he had cleared most of the thorns and goat-heads from his path. He shoved the Henry forward, pulled the saddlebags up with a boot toe, and, with the drawn-up leg, pushed forward to the Henry.

The crawl wasn't long, but it was strenuous. Will, big and strong as he was, had ridden all day, pushed through the pear and brush, crawled into the mound, and finally buried his friend, all while his sore back complained. He was whipped, but he had only a little bit farther. Nearing the end of his crawl, the darkness chasing what little light he had, relief flooded his tired body. *Almost there,* he thought. *Just one more push and I'll be able to stand.*

He drew the saddlebags up with his foot. For the last time he drew his knee as close as the thick brush would allow, shoved the Henry forward, and using the drawn leg, pushed hard, driving the Henry and his body forward and into the opening. He wasn't past the prickly pear yet, but at least he was out of the brush and could stand. Will pulled the saddlebags closer with his foot, braced himself with the rifle hand, and stretched back for the bags.

Besides Will's heavy breathing, from the heat and exertion his body had been through, there was no other sound in the brush. Pilgrims, who depend on their knowledge from material written by armchair naturalists, would swear to it as a fact. A rattlesnake always rattles before it strikes. They would be wrong. From inside the dark brush, the five-foot rattler struck Will's arm just below the top of his right glove. Had they been new, the gauntlet-like gloves might or might not have kept the fangs from piercing his flesh, but these were old and worn thin. The fangs sliced through as if they were going through fresh-churned butter.

Will felt the sting of the bite and then the burning pain as the snake pumped its venom into the wound. Reacting nearly as fast as the snake's strike, Will's right hand lashed out and grasped his attacker just behind its head and yanked, ripping the fangs from his arm.

With his wounded left arm, he whipped one of Darcy's revolvers from behind his back, eared the hammer to full cock, and, with the muzzle of the weapon almost against the snake's head, pulled the trigger. The head exploded, blowing blood, skin, and flesh all over Will. But now, the only thing that mattered was time. He had to get out of this prickly pear patch fast and get to water.

He threw the headless, writhing body to the ground, shoved Darcy's pistol behind his waistband, picked up the Henry and saddlebags, and pushed around the outer perimeter of the brush until he came to the narrow opening in the prickly pear.

Almost with the roar of the shot, Mac called, "Are you all right, lad?"

"Not even a little bit," Will shouted. "Rattler got me! Get Smoky saddled. I need to get back to the creek we passed a couple of miles back."

He slowly started through the prickly pear, forcing himself to be slow and methodical. He could hear camp being broken and horses saddled. Even as he carefully moved the thorns, he could feel his arm swelling, and his body, which had been hot all day, was growing hotter as the day cooled. He had to get out and down the hill to Smoky. He could make a dash for the creek. He needed water to rinse the wound and cool his poisoned body. He'd seen men snakebit, and it wasn't pretty. If there was anything good about this, it was the fact that it was a rattlesnake and not a coral snake that bit him. With the rattler, he had a chance, but if it had been a coral snake, he'd already be dying. *Who knows,* he thought, *I may be dying now. Only time will tell.*

22

Callum, his eyes roving over the few buildings in the one-horse town, paused to watch his uncle step into the street.

Roydon, a confident smirk on his face, called, "I'm gonna kill you, old man. You waited too long before curling up in front of yore fire like those two cur dogs. It'll be too late for you now."

Floyd turned toward Roydon. "Sonny, you sure talk a good fight. I imagine your friend I drilled with that big fifty Sharps was about as good at fightin' with his mouth as you are."

Callum could see the gunfighter's smirk disappear, and the man's face, beneath the darkness burned into his skin by the Texas sun, reddened in anger. *Good*, Callum thought. *Get good and angry.* He knew the cool thinking of his uncle. He had seen him in action. His only concern was that age might have slowed him down enough to allow the gunman to beat him. But he also knew speed wasn't everything. Callum knew Roydon was a dead man. Just like the gunfighter in Molly's had said, there was no quit in the old mountain man. He be shooting as long as there was a moment's life left in him.

He said to Tandy, "Stay on this side of the street, and keep your eyes open. Roydon's friends are hiding and waiting for their opportunity. I'm sure their plan is to ambush Floyd and us just as soon as Roydon draws, so be ready. See you when it's over. I'm crossing to the other side of the street."

He stepped out behind Floyd and strode quickly to the opposite side. Now he could watch the windows above Tandy. He knew the big man was doing the same thing.

Floyd stepped forward, walking nice and easy, as if he were out for a spring stroll in a park. His long legs closed the distance quickly.

"That's far enough," Roydon said.

Floyd kept walking. "I'm an old man, sonny. I've got to get close enough to be sure of my shot. But you're not gonna find out what it is to get old."

I know what you're doing, Callum thought. *If that gunman doesn't draw soon, it'll be too late. It'll be so close, both men will die. Put pressure on him, Uncle.*

Sure enough, the gunman made his move, and just like the drummer said, though his right arm was bowed out and hovering over the revolver, he drew with his left hand.

When his hand shot down to his weapon, a window broke on a second story above Tandy, showering him with glass. A man stepped into the opening and thrust a rifle barrel out the window.

Callum could see the barrel was pointed at his uncle, but even as he saw the man, and just before the glass broke, his reflexes were firing. Smoothly, the butt of the ten-gauge shotgun flew to his shoulder, just like following a flushing quail. He fired as the butt pressed tight against him, and the front bead settled on the chest of the man in the window. The eighteen single-aught buckshot spread as they flew across the street toward the upper window. By the time the shot reached the shooter, they had spread to the point that nine would completely miss. But the remaining nine, each equivalent to a .32-caliber pistol bullet, arrived on target, to strike him or his rifle a split second before the man squeezed the trigger. The first one struck the side of the Henry's barrel, knocking it to the right and up. It was instantly joined by a companion that first struck the man's right pointer finger in the knuckle, where he was holding the rifle forward of the receiver, and took the finger with it. Two more struck the receiver before their companion buckshot drilled into his face, arms, and body. His face disappeared in a flash of blood, flesh, and bone, while his chest and abdomen sprouted blossoms of red. He was dead before he hit the floor.

Callum had missed the report of Tandy's rifle in the roar of the shotgun. He heard glass shattering above him, and a body fell, rolled along the short distance of the front roof, and plummeted to the ground, dust boiling in the street where he landed.

From the corner of his eye, Callum captured the gun battle between Floyd and Roydon. Floyd was still fast. It was hard to believe a man his age could get a Colt into action that quick, but he wasn't fast enough.

Roydon had a tense smile, almost a grimace, on his face as his revolver came up only slightly ahead of Floyd's. It was impossible to tell whether Floyd's talk had affected the gunfighter, the rifle blasts, the shotgun, or he just threw his first shot, but the bullet struck the ground between Floyd's feet. The man's smile disappeared as his six-gun barrel recoiled up, bringing the hammer nearer his thumb. His hand clawed for the hammer, jerked it back, and tried to level it at Floyd. But time had run out for Roydon. He had shot many a man and left them to die in the dirt, but he had never run into a situation like this. Where he might be the one in the dirt.

Floyd brought the barrel of the Colt level as Roydon clawed for the hammer. Centering the barrel on the third button, just like he had been taught, and passed on to every man he had taught, he pulled the trigger. The .44-caliber bullet raced for its destination, slamming into Roydon and driving him back. Momentarily he was stunned, overcome with surprise, but from where Callum stood, he could see the man's expression turn from surprise to determination.

He watched as Roydon stopped his backward stagger and spread his legs wide, as if trying to find a balance point. His gun was coming level again. But before it could reach level, Floyd fired his second shot, this one striking the gunman in his right shoulder. His right arm dropped to his side, and he again slowly began to bring the revolver in his left hand up. Floyd shot for the third time. The bullet struck him in the chest, but he still stood. Every time he was hit, his revolver sagged off target, but each time he labored to bring it back in line, Floyd shot him again.

With his fourth shot, Floyd dropped the weapon into its holster and drew from his crossdraw. Roydon still hadn't gone down. It looked as if he would finally get the weapon up high enough to fire at his opponent. Floyd took a dueler's stance, carefully aimed, and squeezed the trigger. This time the .44 slug did its duty. Striking the gunman at the bridge of his nose, it crashed into the brain pan and ended the life of a deadly killer. The man's legs, no longer receiving commands from his brain, collapsed, and he fell in a heap.

Callum's ears rang from the gunshots. His eyes traveled to windows, doorways, and alleys, but there was no more firing or suspicious movement. He stepped farther into the street. Reaching his uncle, he said, "You all right?"

"Right as rain, boy. Nary a scratch."

"I thought he had you there at first," Callum said, his eyes constantly moving.

"Well, you sure ain't by your lonesome. I knew he had me beat when the muzzle cleared his holster. There was no way I could get mine up that quick, but he sure left the gate open on that one. Would you believe it hit right between my feet?"

Tandy had joined them, and the three men faced in different directions, watching and waiting, just in case. "Good thing it didn't go any higher," he said with a grin.

"I'll second that," Floyd said. He left the two of them and walked over to Roydon. Kneeling down beside the dead man, he straightened him out and placed the man's hat over his bloody face.

Callum could hear Floyd's knees pop as he slowly stood. People were coming out of the buildings and onto the street, walking over to the dead man. Several stood around staring at the man prone on the ground. Callum said, "You two ready to head back to Molly's?"

Floyd pulled his watch from his vest pocket, pressed the catch to allow the top to spring open, and said, "Never fails. It always seems longer. All this took only three minutes from the time we walked out of Molly's."

Tandy, in disbelief, stared at Floyd. "That cain't be right, Floyd. You sure your watch ain't stopped."

Floyd held it up to his ear, listened, and said, "No, youngster, running smooth as a dollar."

He held it over so Tandy could listen. The boy held his ear to the watch, and his eyes opened wide. "Well, I ain't never thought of that. Time can really slow down when you're busy."

Callum grinned at Floyd. "You're right there, or sometimes it can speed up. Time can be as fickle as a trollop's heart. Why don't we get back to Molly's, pick up our things, and mosey on out of here? I had hoped to be able to stay a while, but after this . . ."

"Yeah," Floyd said, "I think Davies might send his men after us. Let's get a move on."

"Hold on," a harsh voice said from behind them.

They turned to see acting Sheriff Chadwick.

Callum said, "You just get back into town, Sheriff? Too bad you missed all the action."

"Don't smart-mouth me, mister. What's going on here?"

"It's more like who's going, Sheriff. We're leaving town before Davies's crew comes riding in here for a necktie party."

"There's three men dead here," the sheriff said. "You've got a heap of explainin' to do before you go anywhere."

Floyd looked at Callum and nodded toward the sheriff.

Callum rolled his eyes in acceptance and turned to the sheriff. "Didn't you see any of this, Sheriff?"

"I wouldn't be askin' if I'd seen it."

Callum pointed to Roydon. "He said he was going to kill Floyd. He drew first. I'm sure there are plenty of witnesses to that fact. Floyd killed him. Those other two characters tried to ambush us, and we shot 'em. That's it, Sheriff. Have a good day." Callum turned to walk away.

"Wait a minute, you need to write it down and sign it."

Callum turned around again. "Sheriff, what we need is to get out of here. We're leaving now. First we're going to Molly's to get our gear. Then we're going to the stables to get our horses. If you want to write it down and bring it to us at the livery, I'll sign it. Otherwise, we're gone."

A man who looked like a prosperous rancher said, "It's just like he said, Sheriff. I seen it all. These fellers were defendin' themselves. Those dead ones were tryin' to kill 'em. I'll sign that statement for you."

"Alright, Mr. Mason." Speaking to no one in particular, the sheriff said, "Get the dentist. Tell him to put on his undertaker hat and get over here to pick up these bodies. I want 'em off the street. As hot as it is, they'll swell up like balloons in no time."

Callum nodded his thanks to Mason and joined Floyd and Tandy, who were well on their way to Molly's. Catching up, he said, "We need to get a few supplies before we leave. No telling how long it'll be before Will gets back."

Both men nodded, but said nothing. They continued their long strides to Molly's.

They were greeted by Molly, her two daughters, and the two drummers. Everyone was full of praise and gratitude they were unharmed.

Callum broke open the ten gauge and started to unload it.

"No, don't do that," Molly said. "I leave it loaded. The girls, thanks to their papa, know to treat all guns as if they are loaded."

"That's the way to do it, ma'am," Floyd said.

Molly stepped up to grasp one of Floyd's hands. "Mr. Logan, I'm so glad you are safe. We were very concerned."

"Why, I'm genuinely grateful. Thank you."

Fran came forward and threw her arms around Floyd's neck. "I'm so glad you weren't hurt, Mr. Logan."

Floyd patted the girl on the back. "That's right nice of you, Fran."

Fran and Molly stepped back, and Jackie, standing with them, said, "I'm glad you're safe."

"Why, thank you, Jackie," Floyd said. "It means a lot coming from you."

Callum snapped the breech closed on the shotgun, drawing attention away from his embarrassed uncle. He handed the weapon to Molly, removed the five extra shells from his pockets, and passed them to Jackie. "We're going to be pulling out."

"But you must stay," Molly said. She gave the shotgun to her oldest daughter, who left the room to put away the weapon.

"No, Molly, we have to go," Callum said. "When Davies gets wind of this, he'll be after us. I know his type. He won't let this kind of affront go unpunished. The farther away from here we can get, the better off we are, and you. He strikes me as the type who holds a mean grudge. Now if you'll excuse us, we've got to get our things and be on our way."

Before she could say anything, he and Floyd headed upstairs, and Tandy went to his downstairs room. Callum had packed all of his gear before breakfast, so he only needed to pick up his bedroll and saddlebags. He was out the door and down the stairs when he heard his uncle coming down the stairs behind him. Jackie came back into the parlor with Tandy.

She was asking, "When do you think you'll be back, Tandy?"

"No telling, Jackie, but we'll stop by if we can. Here you go, girl, give me a hug." She wrapped her little arms around his neck, and with one free arm he lifted her from the floor and gave her a big hug. Placing her gently on the floor, he said, "You keep growin' like you've growed since last I saw you, and you'll be plumb grown when I see you next."

"Oh, Tandy, don't be that long," she said.

Molly laughed. "Tandy has always been good with the girls. When Jackie was little, he used to take her around with him. She just adores him."

Molly stretched on tiptoe and threw her arms around Tandy. He hugged her tight for a moment, then released her. "You have grown so big and strong," she said, feeling his huge biceps. "And you've become a really good man." She gave him a steely look that dissolved into a smile. "You had me worried for a while. I'm so glad you got that job with the Double R."

"Yes, ma'am, I am too. It made all the difference. If it hadn't been for Will, I might be riding with the likes of Langston. That scares the daylights out of me."

She smiled again. "But you're not."

Fran came out of the kitchen with a full tow sack and handed it to Callum.

"What's this?" Callum asked.

Molly smiled. "Just a few things the girls and I put together. It will stave off hunger for a while."

"We thank you, Molly," Callum said. He held up the bag. "How much we owe you?"

"Not a thing. Just enjoy it, and if you should see Bart, tell him to stop by."

"I'll do that."

The three men touched their hats and were out the door.

"Let's get the horses, and then we'll swing by the store," Callum said.

They covered the short distance quickly and walked into the

livery. Bing Dingham was pulling the cinch tight on Shoshone. The other horses were saddled and ready.

Surprised, Callum said, "Morning, Bing. What are you up to?"

Bing looked around, looked back and finished with the cinch, and said, "Figured you boys would be anxious to visit somewhere else pronto, so I just thought I'd help."

They slid their rifles into the scabbards and began tying on gear. Callum patted Shoshone on the hip. "How are you doing, boy? Did you get plenty to eat?" He said to Bing, "Thanks for your help. That is mighty neighborly of you." Pulling out six bits, he dropped them in the man's hand.

Bing dropped them in his dirty apron's pocket and said, "Think nothin' of it. You just rid this country of three belly-crawlin' snakes who'd strike at anything or anyone. That Davies is just as bad. He's got people thinkin' they can get rich on a trail herd. Most of these folks know better, but there's a few who are seeing easy money. Those folks are giving that Englishman every dime they have. To my notion, they might as well toss it in the Frio and watch it float downstream to the gulf."

He stopped, watching the three men mount. When they'd settled in their saddles, he continued, "If Davies were doing this in the spring, maybe, but not now. It's way too late."

Callum said, "You're right, Bing. When we came down from Colorado, it was already dry. By now . . ." He shook his head. "I wouldn't care for a grasshopper's chance in that country.

"We'll be seeing you."

The three rode out. Taking a right turn, they saw the girls waving from the front window, lifted a hand, passed, and pulled up in front of the general store.

"Let's make this quick," Callum said. "I want to find where Davies is holding this herd he's putting together. To do that, I figure we've got a lot of riding to do."

23

One last turn and Will was in the open. Only scattered brush lay between him and the horses. When Mac and Bart saw him, they both came running.

Voice slurred, Will said, "I'm fine." His knees buckled, but they caught him, and with the help of his friends, he made it to Smoky.

Mac said, "You're no fit to ride, lad. Let me lay you down here, and we'll fetch water from yonder creek."

Will shook his head. "Get me on Smoky . . . Got to get to the river."

They helped him on his horse, and he heard Mac tell Bart, "You bring the other horses. I'll get him to the river. Make it quick."

For a moment he faded, only feeling the jolting of the running horse through his sore back and leg. Then Mac was at his side.

"Come on down, laddie. We're here. I'll get you to the water."

"Here . . . Already?"

"You passed out. It was in the saddle I had to hold you. Now come on, be a good lad and slide that leg over."

The next thing Will remembered, he was lying in the water. His arm was in a vise so tight it was causing him excruciating pain. He opened his eyes. A fire was burning on the rocky creek bottom. Mac gripped his arm in both of his big hands while Bart cut an X over the bites.

Bart was saying, "Mac, I don't know if this is going to do any good. It's a long time since the snake bit him."

"Aye, you're right, but we can only do our best."

Will's eyes were only slits when he opened them. He grinned, through the pain, at his friends. "Thanks, fellas. Sorry to be such a bother."

He heard nothing, for he passed out again.

Through the following days he remembered little. The fire. The gunpowder poured into the cuts where the snake bit him. Bart lighting it. And the pain, constant pain. He heard cursing. He didn't hold with it. His arm felt as if it would break off, and his head felt near exploding. It seemed to go on and on.

His eyes opened into the bright afternoon sunshine and the intense heat, but it felt good. He looked at his arm. It was still swollen, but nothing approaching what it had been. He thought he remembered waking and asking Bart to cut it off, but he wasn't sure.

Bart had the fire going, and to one side sat a coffee pot.

His throat felt dry and rough. When he spoke, his voice was more like a frog's croak than a human voice. "Anything left in that pot?"

Bart, his hat pushed to the back of his head, looked around. Surprise and relief showed in the circles under his eyes and the tired lines of his young face. "Well, if it ain't sleeping beauty come back to this world. Welcome back." He poured a little coffee in a cup, stood, and walked it over to Will. "How you feelin'?"

Will made an act of looking around. "Where's the longhorn that stomped me?"

Bart grinned, then his face grew serious as he squatted to the ground next to Will. "Good to hear a sane voice come out of you. You've had a pretty tough time, pardner. Mac and I thought we were gonna lose you a time or two."

Will looked around. "Where's Mac?"

"Somebody's gotta keep a lookout so that crooked outfit don't surprise us. We've been switching watches every few hours."

Will took a sip of the coffee and grimaced. "I just thought I wanted this." He handed the cup back to Bart and said, "Could I talk you out of some water?"

The cowhand laughed. "Boss, you can have whatever you want, as long as it's water or coffee." He got up, tossed the coffee to the ground, walked to the edge of the creek, dipped up some water with the cup, and brought it back.

Will took the cup and turned it up. He brought it from his lips empty. "I'll tell you, Bart, that tastes near as good as if it were out of one of those snow-fed streams on the Colorado ranch." He handed the cup back to his friend. "Another?"

On the third trip, Bart detoured to the stack of supplies and picked up a canteen. He brought it back and set it next to Will and said, "In case you want any more."

Will grinned up at his friend. "Thanks."

Bart sat on a log that, some time during the last few days, had been pulled up near Will. "How you feelin'?"

"Much better than I was yesterday." Puzzled, he asked Bart, "How long have I been out?"

"Five days. Like I said a minute ago. It was a couple of times you looked done for. Your arm swole up more than twice its size. I was thinkin' the skin might even split, but it didn't, and, through all that time, you had an almighty bad fever. We tried to keep a blanket on you, but you kept throwing it off. You was in bad shape."

"I remember waking up a couple of times. Both times Mac had those big mitts on my hand and arm, holding it while once you were cutting, and the other time you were burning my arm where you cut."

"Right on both counts," Bart said. "First time I had to cut it to get the poison out, and the second time Mac said we ought to cauterize it. I poured powder into the cuts and lit it. Both times you yelled something fierce and called us everything but a gentleman."

Will shook his head. "I just remember the pain. Sorry about the language. Guess my ma would have used up her soap supply washing my mouth out if she'd heard me."

"No cause for an apology. A man ain't responsible for what he says when he's out like you was, and believe me, you were long gone."

Will reached for the canteen and took a long swig. "When's Mac supposed to be back?"

"Any time, why?"

"We need to get moving. Every day we're here is another day Davies or Lockwood or whatever his name is can continue to dig in. We've wasted too much time already."

Bart shook his head. "Will, we ain't gonna be going anywhere for a few more days. You're not up to it."

Determined, Will rolled over on his side, drew his legs up. Just sitting up made him feel dizzy and unsteady, but he continued his attempt. He began pushing himself erect with his right arm, but once the arm was extended, carrying all of his upper body weight, he teetered back and forth, hung balanced, and collapsed back on his bedroll. He lay there panting like the lizard he had seen on the hot ground a few days before.

"Guess I'm not as strong as I thought I was."

Bart shook his head. "I've seen folks snakebit before. Some died, others were mighty sick for days, like you, and others were feeble for a long time. You just gotta relax and let yore strength come back. A big strong feller like you, in your prime, I reckon you'll be fine. It'll just take a while."

Will chuckled. "I'm sure not feeling very strong right now."

"You're alive, ain't you? Just give it time. You feel up to eatin'? Mac fixed up some stew in case you woke up."

At the mention of food, Will felt hunger pangs. His stomach growled, and Bart stood up. "Guess that's the answer. Give me a minute, and I'll have some over here."

While Bart was heating the stew, Will examined his arm. Most of the swelling had gone down. The arm was still sensitive to the touch, but it was looking better. The X Bart had cut was healing nicely, but it was a grayish-blue color from the powder that had been burned in it.

Guess I've got me a permanent tattoo, Will thought. He held the arm up so he could see the wrist from different angles in the light. Examining it closer, he could see the snake's bite marks, where the sharp fangs had cut into his flesh, centered and on each side of the X. He shook his head. *That snake must have been mighty upset. The second trip near his home was just too much for him. I guess that's a good example of biting off more than you can chew.* He chuckled to himself at the thought. *There's got to be a lesson in there somewhere, but it's too deep for me. Wonder what Deborah will think of my new tattoo.*

He stared at the mark a little longer. *Why, if you ran a line between the two bites, it would cross the center of the X. That just might make a good brand. We could call it the X Bar or the Bar X. You may have given me an idea, Mr. Snake.*

Will had a grin on his face when Bart came back with the stew. The man examined him curiously for only a moment, then handed him the plate and sat down on the log.

Will put a spoonful of the stew in his mouth. It was heavenly. Beans, onions, and some kind of meat, he had never tasted anything more delicious. He shoveled several spoonfuls into his mouth before Bart said, "Might want to take it easy. You ain't had much to eat over these last few days."

Will paused, took a breath, swallowed, and said, "You have no idea how good this tastes. I swear this is the best stuff that's passed my lips in my life."

Bart rolled his eyes. "I tend to credit that opinion to the fact you ain't had anything to eat in five days. That's a pretty good possum stew, but it ain't that good. I've tasted some of yore ma's cookin'.'"

Will watched Mac ride in while Bart was talking. "I didn't see you turning your nose up to it, laddie."

Bart shook his head. "I ain't sayin' it ain't good. I'm just sayin' it ain't the best thing I ever tasted. Howsomever, had I not eaten anything in five days, I might feel the same way." He looked over at Mac. "You see anything out there?"

"Nary a thing, and since you're so interested, I've not seen a cloud in the sky."

"Good. I've never liked making a camp down in these creek bottoms. A man could get himself dead doing such a thing. If'n it should rain up the creek, a flash flood could catch us down here, and we'd be goners."

"Aye, right you are, laddie. But it's been kind of important to be down here near the water."

Will spoke up. "Howdy, Mac. It's good to see you. I agree with both of you. I think now would be a good time to move the camp out of this bottom and up under some of those big trees."

Will had finished his plate of stew and the two corn dodgers Bart had put on it. Bart took the plate, moved to the water's edge, and washed it off. "You feel up to some more, Will?"

"You bet I do. I get another plate of that stew in me, and I'll be able to leap on top of that bank from right here."

Bart rolled his eyes again and dipped another plate of stew, dropping two more corn dodgers on the edge of the plate. He brought it back and, handing it to Will, said, "I'll start breakin' camp. It'll be quick, since we'll just be moving out of the bottom."

"I'll give you a hand," Mac said, then turned to Will. "It's happy I am a-seeing you looking better. You gave us a tremendous fright. We thought you were done for."

"Thanks, Mac. That's what Bart said. I owe you two my life."

Mac said, "I could save your life ten times and never be even. You're owing me nothing." He turned to Bart and, while Will continued to eat, helped him move the camp.

BREAKING dawn caught Will and his friends loading up camp. He had rested for an additional two days and, though still weak, felt up to riding. The seven days of recovery from the snakebite had been good for him in one way. His back and left leg were feeling much better. When he walked, he no longer had any sharp pains down the leg, and there was no ache in his back.

The swelling around the snakebite had returned to near normal. His wrist was still sore, and the skin of his lower arm was sensitive to the touch. Other than a permanent blue Bar X tattooed on his left wrist, he felt good.

For the last two days they had discussed, rehashed, and discussed some more their next move. Will had decided, the others finally going along with him, to head to Armando and Ana's place first. Mac had wanted to go to the sheriff, and after the death of Darcy, Bart was ready to ride into the Circle BB with guns blazing. But Will had carried the decision, reasoning they had been gone for a long time, and his brother, Floyd, and Tandy would be worried.

"What about the dust we saw southwest of here?" Bart said. "It could be those killers. We might run into 'em."

Will, catching Bart's tone, turned from cinching Smoky. "Bart, it sounds like that's what you're hoping for."

Bart, relaxing his tense jaw muscles, said, "I'll tell you, Will, it sure wouldn't break my heart. Those no-goods need their comeuppance, and I'm itchin' to give it to 'em.

"You seen only a few of them horse tracks. While you was up that hill with Darcy, I circled it. It was cut to pieces with tracks, and there was a big fire where they camped—for a long time." The gunman viciously yanked the piggin' string tight around his bedroll. "They had them a real fine campout while Darcy lay up there, his leg broken and short on water."

"I know," Will said, "it riles me too."

"Aye," Mac chimed in as he swung into the saddle, "the poor lad died of thirst and in terrible pain from his broken leg. That was almighty cruel, and them breaking it too."

Will and Bart mounted, and leading their mounts, the three moved out of the trees along the creek, scanned the prairie, and eased their horses forward into the lightening day. The sun was slipping above the trees behind them, and they could already feel the heat on their backs. The blue night sky had changed to a light, copper-tinged blue, forecasting another blazing day, and there was not a cloud in the sky.

They rode in silence for several miles until Will spoke up. "We don't know for sure they broke his leg."

"That's the only way it could've happened," Bart said. "We finally figured out, the only way he was able to get all that gear up there was to throw it over the brush. For sure, he didn't throw his rifle, but the coffee pot and skillet, his bedroll and saddlebags? That's the only way he could've gotten anything up there, and if he could throw stuff up, so could they." With the three of them riding alongside each other, Bart turned so he could look directly at his friend. "Will, you know it. You know those big rocks up there you talked about weren't all there to start with. They was throwing rocks as big as they could handle up at him."

"Dang it!" Bart slammed his fist down against his saddle horn, causing his horse to jerk. He patted him on the neck. "Sorry, boy. It's all right."

Will waited. He had heard Bart go over his idea on Darcy's broken leg several times. It made sense, and it made him angry, too. If Darcy was protected by the brush and slope of the hill, so were those gunmen, he couldn't shoot through the brush and down at his assailants. *So they got to him the only way they could, with rocks, and then they just let him die.*

Bart went on. "I know that's how they done broke Darcy's leg. They tossed one of them big boulders, maybe it took two of 'em to toss it up there, and it crashed down on his leg." He emphatically nodded his head. "Yes, sir. That's exactly how it happened. They couldn't git to him any other way, so they just threw that rock, listened to him in pain while they ate and drank and let him die. I know that kind. They're worse than rattlers." He stopped for a second and looked at his friend. "Sorry, Will."

Will stared back. "No problem here."

"Good," Bart said. "Like I was sayin', worse than rattlers, and the only way you can deal with a rattler is the way you done yours. So yeah, I'm hopin' we run into 'em. I'm just itchin' to." Bart lapsed into silence, and the three rode on across the undulating prairie broken only by scrub oak, mesquite, and prickly pear. Not a breeze stirred.

Later, they switched horses and continued to ride, never seeing another human being. They were on Remington Ranch range now. The cattle they saw were wild, but of those they were able to get close to, most still carried the RR brand. Occasionally they would see a Circle BB, but there were very few. Davies, Lockwood, or whatever name he was going by, had hired gunmen not cowhands. Men who shied away from honest work. Men who rode to kill. They had no interest in building anything other than their reputations. Men whose guns and loyalty, such as it was, were for hire to the highest bidder.

Will had been feeling the Logan anger building. He fought to contain it, for he didn't like the man he became when it was loosed, and now it was growing, and if it broke free—he had to control Bart, but he also had to control himself. He remembered Darcy's body, and he knew the cruel, protracted death his young friend had endured. Payment would be extracted. The time was near. First they would go to Armando's to get Callum, Floyd, and Tandy. Then the sheriff would be next. Allow the law to administer justice, but if it failed its duty, the Logans would see justice done.

24

Will walked Smoky through the trees toward Armando's. The only sound was the horses' hooves crunching the leaves with each step. He glanced first left, then right. The men had spread out. Mac weaved his way through the oak thicket to Will's left, Bart to his right. For the first time in weeks there were high thin clouds overhead, helping to contain the blazing heat of the sun.

He felt a strange anticipation, maybe even apprehension approaching Armando's home. By now, he should be able to hear the children playing or the chickens or pigs, the normal sounds of a busy farm, but he heard nothing. The oaks, which had been too thick to see through, began to thin as they neared the edge. He slowed Smoky, catching the first glimpse of the home. Nearing the edge, he pulled up. From his position, he could see the yard, the house, and the barn, or he should have been able to see them. Now all he saw were darkened adobe walls, a few remaining stubs of burned boards, and ashes. No children were playing, no chickens clucking, no farm sounds, only the sound of the South Texas prairie.

Mac and Bart guided their mounts near enough to speak. The

three sat in silence for long moments, staring at the destruction of the once happy home.

After scanning the countryside and ensuring there were no threats, Will eased Smoky from the trees. Mac and Bart rode alongside. Will guided the horse to the front yard, dismounted, and walked to the exposed remains of the home. He walked through it, stepping carefully around the burned and fallen timbers.

Finally he said, "What I don't see pleases me."

Bart spoke up. "No graves."

"Aye," Mac said, "and no bodies."

Will nodded toward the well. "Look at that."

On each side of the well was a black X, and the flat rock cover for the well was over the opening with another black X on it. "Somebody left us a message. I'd say the well has been poisoned."

Bart spoke into the stillness. "I think Armando got his family out of here. I remember them talking about having folks across the river in Mexico. I'm hoping that's what happened."

"Aye, laddie, and they must have taken everything with them. There is nothing around, no chickens, pigs, mules." He made a quick look around again. "There is also no wagon. Even if the wagon was burned, the metal tires would remain. Gone, it is. It's right you are. They managed, somehow, to get away. Maybe Callum and Floyd and Tandy, they went with them, for protection, you know."

"You're right, Mac," Will said, walking to the corner of the house by the well. He saw the flat rock against the wall and knelt. A smile broke across his stern face.

"Well, will you looky here. Either Callum or Floyd left us a message. It's good to know at least one of them is still alive."

Bart and Mac dismounted, ground hitched their horses alongside Smoky, and walked over to Will to see what had gotten his attention. On the ground was a flat rock, with a single stone sitting on top of it.

"What's that mean?" Bart asked.

"The flat rock means they've been here, and this smaller stone on top means they'll be back within a week. So all we have to do is wait here until they return. Odds are, it'll be less than a week."

"Then what, laddie?"

"Like we decided, Mac, we'll go to the sheriff. He can't help but believe the documents we have with us. Why, Mr. MacGregor, you'll soon be sitting in your own easy chair, in your own ranch house."

"Aye," Mac said, "but both the boys are gone, and you'll be heading to the north country for your bride. It's a lonely place it will be, I fear, and me knowing little of the cattle business."

Will, too, feeling the loss of his two friends, felt for Mac in his loneliness. For all the complaining Mac did of the old country, he had friends and family there. Here, his best friends were dead, and the others would be leaving as soon as the battle was won. "Mac," he said, "don't you be worrying about being alone. We'll figure something out." But he had no idea what that something would be, for he had to leave to get back to Deborah. He missed her and wanted her with him.

Bart kicked a burned stub and said, "I'm not sure I can sit around here for a week. There's some scores need settling, and I aim to do it."

"*We* aim to do it," Will corrected. "But first, we all need to get together. If everyone's alive, that will double our numbers. Also, if we can find some of the hands, we will have even more. You know Lockwood, I refuse to call him Davies, if he still has money, will hire more gunmen. We can use any of the men who rode with us before."

Bart nodded. "I know you're right, but it's hard to wait. After finding Darcy like he was, I'm the bill collector, and I'm ready to collect."

Will stood. "Bart, I agree with you, but we can't rush into this. That would be suicide. The goal is to win without anyone getting hurt. Wouldn't you agree?"

Bart finally relented and, with a touch of grim humor, said, "Will, there are several I want to hurt mighty bad."

"I'm with you on that, but for now, let's find a good spot for a fire and get a camp set up."

THREE DAYS HAD PASSED, and even Will had to admit he was ready for some action. Each day they had ridden out scouting the country, but they never saw another rider. Cattle were beginning to gather near the rivers and the few creeks that still held water. The ground was cracking. Every plant and animal longed for water.

Bart rode in from the creek. "It's shapin' up to be a mighty hard winter. The grass is burning to the roots, and there ain't much nourishment there. If we don't get rain around here soon, come spring there won't be any cattle to drive, 'cause they'll all be dead."

Moments later a voice spoke softly from the oak thicket. "If I were a hostile, you'd all be dead."

Will shook his head, stood, and turned toward the treeline. Within seconds, three familiar horses appeared. "Howdy, boys," Callum said as they rode up.

They dismounted, and hearty handshakes were joined all around as Mac was introduced to Callum and Floyd. He held Tandy at arm's length. "My goodness, boy. It's only a year that has passed, and you've become a giant of a man. It is pleased I am to see you."

Tandy gripped Mac's hand. "I'm mighty glad to see you too, Mr. MacGregor."

Mac laughed and said, "Mr. MacGregor it is now. Call me Mac, boy. You've earned it."

"Yes, sir, thank you," Tandy said, grinning down at the Scotsman.

Floyd said to Will, "We were starting to wonder if you'd ever show up. My goodness, you've been gone for months."

"We have," Will said, "but know a lot more now than when we left. Coffee's brewing for them that drinks it. Pull up a log and have a seat."

The talking went on for hours. The men had unsaddled their horses, and Tandy led them all to the creek for a drink.

Late into the night they continued to share what had happened to each group. If it was possible, faces became grimmer with Will's telling of finding Darcy's body. Bart told of the snakebite, and everyone had to see Will's wrist, which, by now, had completely healed. Will and his group were relieved to hear about Armando's family safely moving to Piedras Negras. Callum shared their Dog Town trip and Floyd's gunfight. At the mention of Molly, Bart perked up.

"How's she doing?" he asked.

Callum grinned at the cowhand. "She said to tell you hello, and to stop by the next time you were in the country. You might want to do that, or not, depending on what your feelings are."

Will said, "If I remember correctly, she was sweet on you, and it looked like you might've felt the same way."

Bart eyed Will. "I'll have to admit, she's a nice lady, and her two girls are special. I've never seen two kids so willing to help folks. It'd be nice to see 'em."

Floyd looked over at Callum. "Did you tell Will about the paper the sheriff has on him?"

"I forgot that." He turned to his brother. "Sheriff Chadwick has an old wanted poster on you. It shows a reward of one hundred bucks."

Tandy popped up. "Yeah, boss, we thought about turnin' you in and collectin' it, but figured Deborah might be upset with us."

"I guess she would," Will said, trying to hold a hard expression as he glared at Tandy. "But not near as upset as I'd be."

Tandy shot back, "We didn't figger that'd be a problem." Though it was obvious the young man was trying to maintain a straight face, he broke into a big grin.

Callum shook his head. "Remind me to play poker with you, boy. I could walk away a rich man."

Floyd slapped Tandy on his broad shoulder. "Don't feel bad, son. A man who can't keep a straight face is a man you can trust, and I reckon everyone around here would trust you with their life."

"Well . . ." Will said.

"That's enough funning," Floyd said. "How are we gonna do this? There's some of us who'd like to mosey up north to those mountains sooner rather than later."

Will nodded. "First thing we need to do is go to the sheriff. From the sound of his reaction to Davies, I don't expect much, but we should at least make it our first stop. Then we'll put out word that we're looking for our old hands. Maybe some of them will show up. I'm thinking we'll need as many men as we can get."

Mac spoke up. "Sorry I am, Will, but there is no money. Davies attached everything, including the remaining money we had in the bank from the cattle drives. The paper said something about the gain being from his land, therefore the money was his."

"Don't worry about the money, Mac," Will said. "I still have the funds you three insisted on paying me for my share of the last drive. It'll be enough to pay cowhands and get the ranch going again."

It was Mac's turn to shake his head. "It's bailing us out again, you are. I'll be thanking you, but I'll not be turning it down. Like we said in Abilene, you were a partner in this ranch, and whether you're here or not, you'll always be."

Bart stood. "I'm tired of talking. If that's the plan, what are we waiting on?"

Callum nodded. "The man's got a point, and we're burning daylight. We'll need more supplies, especially ammunition, and Bart will have a chance to see Molly."

Will stood. "Let's ride. It's time we take on Mr. Davies-Lockwood, Langston, and his whole gang. I'm with you, Bart. I'm tired of waiting."

∾

THE DUST CHASED the riders as they rode into Dog Town. They swung their horses toward the worn hitching rail in front of the sheriff's office. Almost in unison, they swung from the saddle, and spurs jingled as they trooped into the sheriff's tiny domain.

The man was in his normal position, feet on the desk, chair leaned back, and reading the newspaper. Surprised, he dropped his newspaper to his lap, looked at the men who filled his office, and lowered his boots to the floor.

His perpetually flushed face lost a little of its glow with his recognition of Mac. "What are you doing here, MacGregor?"

"Good morning to you, Sheriff Chadwick. It's some business we have with you, now. Would this be a good time for you?"

Before the sheriff could respond, Mac continued, "Good. You may remember Mr. William Wallace Logan by a different name. Do you remember him, now, as Hank Remington?"

The sheriff, starting to collect himself, growled, "I do, and I also remember I've got some paper on him." He started shuffling through the scattered stack of wanted circulars and old newspapers.

"You'll not be needing the wanted poster, laddie. We have some documents here that will clear up, once and for all, the misfortunate false claims of my good friend Will being a traitor." He nodded to Will. "If you'd be so kind as to show the sheriff the documents."

Will stepped forward with papers in his hand. The first one

he put in the pudgy hand of the sheriff was the one declaring his true and legal name. "You'll see there, Sheriff, when I was Hank Remington, I had amnesia caused by a head wound. This certifies that years after my recovery, I remembered my correct name. Not only is it signed by a judge I'm sure you're familiar with, but there are several witness signatures."

The sheriff looked it over, then looked up at Will, having to crane his head back to look the tall man in the face. "Alright, I see this. It says you remembered yore name, but it don't say nothing about this poster." He had found the wanted circular in the pile on his desk and waved it at Will.

Will handed him another document.

The sheriff looked it over. His disappointment was apparent as he let the one-hundred-dollar reward poster slip from his fingers, returning to the pile of refuse on his desk. "Alright, I guess you're who you say you are, and there ain't no reason to hold you, so you and yore friends can go."

No one moved. He looked up at Will and then over at Mac, obviously confused that the men were still in his office.

"There's one other thing, Sheriff," Will said.

The sheriff watched Will fold the papers up neatly and slip them into an envelope before thrusting the envelope into an inside pocket of his vest. After they were stowed and safe, he reached into the other pocket, pulling out another envelope.

"We're requesting your assistance with this." Will opened the envelope, removed the document, and again handed it to Sheriff Chadwick. The paper stated the property currently occupied by a Sir Wilford Pemberton Davies III, in fact, was owned by Liam MacGregor, Darcy Smith, and William Logan. Any and all law enforcement representatives were authorized and requested to ensure the ownership of the Remington Ranch and all materials, equipment, and accounts were returned to the rightful owners.

Sheriff Chadwick's lips moved as he read through the document. When he reached the section addressing the new owners, he stopped, his eyes grew wide, and he looked up at first Will and then Mac. Neither of the men said anything. The sheriff looked down and began to read. He read the document several times, his disbelief obvious in his wide-eyed expression. Finally, he licked his lips, cleared his throat, and looked up.

"Uh, well, what do you want me to do about this?"

"As you can see, Sheriff," Will said, "you are authorized and requested to evict *Sir* Davies from our property and accounts. That means that all funds in the bank belong to us. With this documentation, I don't think we'll need your assistance with the banks, but we would like for you, as Sheriff Pepper did, to make up a posse and evict anyone currently on our ranch."

Will watched the sheriff work through his problem. From what Callum and Floyd had told him, it appeared the sheriff was on Lockwood's payroll. If that was the case, the man had to be in a terrible quandary.

The sheriff still did not reply.

Will gently retrieved the paper from the sheriff's hand and held forth another. "You'll find this document at least as interesting as the first."

The second document was an order to arrest and detain the man known as Sir Wilford Pemberton Davies III. It stated that the real Sir Davies had been found dead in New York City and was being impersonated by an Erasmus Lockwood, Davies's butler, who prior to becoming the man's butler had been a British actor.

The sheriff looked up at Will, watery eyes wide, and mouth open. He finally closed his mouth, licked his lips, and wiped them with the back of his sleeve. "He's a fake?"

Will nodded. "An actor. From what we found out in Austin, he was never very successful, unless you count his latest acting episode. I understand he has persuaded several people to invest in his upcoming cattle drive."

"Uh, yeah," the sheriff replied, "he, uh." The sheriff stopped.

His round face had lost all of its normally flushed color, and he was sickly pale. "Oh my, there's a bunch of people who've invested with him. Some of 'em gave him their very last dime in hopes of striking it rich." He looked at Mac. "Davies, or Lockwood, he told 'em how much you fellers made, and they couldn't wait to give him their money. They was almost beggin' him to take it. Ain't no tellin' how much he took in."

"Then," Will said, "I think it's your duty to ride out there and arrest him."

The sheriff looked first at Will, then his eyes traveled to Mac. He shook his head, opened a drawer, and pulled out a bottle. He stuck the cork sealing the bottle into his mouth, bit down on it, yanked it from the bottle, spit the cork across the room, and turned the half-empty bottle up. After several swallows, he lowered the bottle and said, "Who-wee, I needed that." He stood, his legs quivering, pulled the star from his vest, and dropped it on the desk. Looking at Will through watery, gray eyes, he said, "I quit, fellers. I was a lot better swamper than I was a sheriff. Now, that Sheriff Pepper, he was a fine man. He gave me a job when I needed it after the saloon shut down. When he was gettin' suspicious of Davies"—he shook a finger at Mac—"and he was. He said something smelled about that whole deal. He was bushwhacked. Davies came by to talk to the sheriff, and I heard him and Langston talkin' after they seen the sheriff weren't here, about how Davies wanted the sheriff gone. I never heard nothin' else, but I heard that."

Will looked down on the man as he pushed past him, heading for the door. He felt disgust, but he couldn't help but wonder what had happened that would bring Chadwick so low.

"Nothin' but a swamper," Chadwick mumbled, already beginning to stumble. Heading out the door, he could be heard saying, over and over, "All I'm good for is swamping. Ain't never been good for nothin' else." He turned toward Bolton's store and saloon and was gone.

25

W ill watched the ex-sheriff stagger from the office. He was prepared for several reactions from the near useless lawman, but this was not one of them.

"Mac," Will said, "why don't you take these documents to the bank and see if we can recover any of your money. I feel sure Lockwood has drained the account, but we can at least try." He handed the Scotsman the papers. "Callum, why don't you and Floyd try to round up as many of the folks who invested in the fake drive as you can. They'll make a good posse. When you get them together, we'll ride out and take care of Lockwood."

Callum shook his head. "No, Will, we need to get a sheriff appointed by the mayor." He turned to Mac. "This place is so small, does it even have a bank or a mayor?"

"Aye, laddie, it has both. The mayor is Edward Bolton. He owns the store and saloon."

Will watched his brother. *What is Callum thinking? We've disagreed before, brothers do that, but now we need to stop Lockwood. We need to pull together.* "Hold up, Callum. We don't have time to have an election. We need to shut down Lockwood and Langston."

"Look, Will," Callum said. "Mac's going to be stuck with a history, a reputation here, no matter how he gets the ranch back. It'll either be for good or bad. Don't you think it would be better if he gets the ranch back using the law?"

Will was getting frustrated. He could feel his temper rising. He jabbed his left index finger toward the door. "What I think is that we need to get out that door, on our horses, and after Lockwood. We need to put a stop to him, and we need to do it now!"

"I'm with Will," Bart said, moving next to his friend. "We need to get on our horses, round up whoever is with us, and give Lockwood and Langston and all their gang a little frontier justice."

Callum turned to Mac. "Why don't you get to the bank and take care of the money situation. We'll walk as far as Bolton's store with you and talk to the mayor. Hopefully it won't take long to appoint a new sheriff."

Will could feel himself starting to steam. Somewhere, deep inside, he knew his brother was right, but Lockwood had to be stopped, and he had to be stopped now. He headed for the door. "Come on, Bart. Tandy, are you coming with us? Uncle?"

Tandy shook his head. "Boss, you're wrong. Callum's got the right idea. You remember when you beat some sense into my head? It worked. Now it's your turn to listen. Callum's on the right track. There's law in this country, and we need to use it."

"Your brother's right, Will," Floyd joined in. "As much as one side of me wants to ride out of here and blow Lockwood and Langston to kingdom come, it just isn't the right thing to do. As long as we've got the law, let it work. That's what we planned to do in the first place. Let's at least talk to the mayor. You know it won't take long."

Bart stood beside Will, facing the other four, eyes and voice drawn tight with anger. "What's wrong with all of you? Don't you want to punish the killers of Darcy? Those snakes could be trying to escape right now. We need to stop this talking and replace it with some good ole Texas justice."

The brothers faced off. Each, in his own way, tough and determined. Will hadn't fought Callum since they were young, but he could feel the urge rising. They had always respected each other. He knew his brother wasn't a coward, but he also knew he didn't feel like giving in to him.

"Come on, Will," Callum pleaded. "Let's at least do like Floyd said, let's talk to the mayor. This is a small town. It's only a short walk to Bolton's store."

Will felt the thoughts burn through him like a smoking brand, *Only a short walk. Only a couple of minutes. What if those minutes allow Lockwood and Langston the time they need to disappear? I won't allow it! They've got to be stopped.*

"Let's go," Bart said and started for the door. Will made a step to follow him. Callum let Bart pass, but stepped between Will and the door.

Will's pupils had shrunk to almost pin size, and he could feel the urge to strike. His brother was two inches shorter and didn't have the reach Will did, but he knew Callum was a fighter. He would be a dangerous opponent, but right now his anger was taking control. He could feel it. This rage needed an outlet, and Callum was preventing him from pursuing Lockwood. Callum hadn't seen Darcy's body. He hadn't seen the cruelty of Langston and his gang.

"I don't want to fight you, Will. We're only talking about a few minutes. If the mayor delays appointing a sheriff, I'll ride with you, but you can't do this. It's not you."

Will could feel the sweat flowing from every pore in his body. He was ready. He could strike right now and be on his way with Bart. He felt his muscles tensing.

Floyd said softly, "What about Deborah?"

Without realizing it, he had begun to crouch, arms bowing away from his body in anticipation of the first blow. He saw Bart standing in the door, waiting, as tense as him. Somewhere in the recesses of his mind, a whisper repeated, *What about Deborah?*

What would she think? What would she think of him fighting a brother who was only trying to get him to stop, think, and follow the law? What would she think of him chasing a man explicitly to kill him? Would she be able to forgive him? Would he be able to forgive himself?

Floyd's words startled him. Slowly, his muscles began to relax. He straightened from the crouch, and his arms dropped to his sides. He saw his brother standing in front of him, willing to do whatever was necessary, to even sacrifice himself to prevent him from going outside the law. He took a deep breath. Filling his lungs was almost painful, but hot and dusty though it was, the air smelled good, refreshing to his body. The tension flowed from his muscles.

He looked first at his brother, then his uncle and Tandy, and said, "Thanks. Why don't we go see the mayor."

"That's a good idea," Callum said. "I'm glad you thought of that."

A burst of relieved laughter sounded from the four of them. Bart stood, watching. Will looked at his friend, who stood just outside the open door. "We're going to be a few minutes with the mayor. Why don't you go down and say hello to Molly."

Will could see Bart was filled with rage, ready and craving action, violence. He walked outside and put his arm around the man's shoulders. "We'll get 'em, Bart. Just a little bit longer."

Bart gave a stiff nod and said, "It may be too late." He did not look at the others when they came out of the sheriff's office. Shrugging Will's arm from his shoulder, he strode well ahead of them to Bolton's store, stopped, and stood by the entrance.

Floyd said quietly, "Keep an eye on Bart. He's deep-down mad, and he strikes me as a man who carries a grudge."

Callum, followed by Floyd and Tandy, stepped past Bart into Bolton's store and saloon. Bart said to Will, "I'll wait here."

Will replied, "What about Molly?"

Bart stared into the street and gave a stiff, sullen answer. "Ain't the time."

Will started to reply, thought better of it, and followed Floyd through the door.

Inside, the sales goods were separated from the saloon by a wall that ran the full length of the store. A wide, double door, normally open, allowed access between the two sections. Bolton was in the saloon portion, trying to persuade Chadwick he'd had enough. So far he'd been unsuccessful. Will motioned him for him to come into the store side.

He explained quickly what had happened. "You should consider appointing a sheriff immediately. Otherwise, folks are going to ride out to the Double R and either get themselves killed or be a party to a lynching. That's not something you want your town to be known for."

Bolton shook his head. "Of course not. I tried to explain to those people the risk they were taking by giving Lockwood their life savings. But they were so focused on the money, they were past reasoning. There will be town citizens who will lose everything if they don't get their money back. When they hear about this, there'll be a lynching party, and it'll happen quick."

"It'll turn into a bloodbath," Floyd said. "Those men with Langston know which end the bullet comes out of. They'll blow your folks out of the saddle, without a decent leader."

Bolton looked around the store.

Will thought with surprise, *Looks like he's hoping to find a person to appoint to the sheriff's office right here in his store.*

The storekeeper's gaze stopped when it reached a man in the back. Only his hat could be seen above the tall shelves. Motioning Will to follow, the mayor started toward the hat. When they reached the cowhand, Bolton said, "Blaze, this here is Will, Floyd, and Callum Logan. I think you know Tandy."

Blaze nodded and said, "Howdy, met Callum at Molly's."

Each of the men said, "Howdy," and shook Blaze's hand.

"Yep," Callum replied.

Blaze looked around the group, his gaze finally settling on the mayor.

The mayor looked to Will to pop the question, but Will shook his head and then snapped it toward Blaze. The mayor took a deep breath. "I guess you noticed Chadwick in the saloon."

"Did. Looks like he's tyin' one on."

"He's quit."

Now Blaze eyed Bolton with a wary look, saying nothing.

Bolton shifted his weight from one foot to the other. "We need a new sheriff."

"I reckon you do," Blaze said.

"I'd like to hire you. The pay is seventy a month, room and board."

Blaze, with a forefinger, pushed his hat back an inch while looking Bolton straight in the eyes. "I know what the pay is, and it ain't that. Besides, I've got a ranch to run."

Bolton, following suit, slid the green plastic visor to the back of his head, pulled a handkerchief from his pocket, and wiped his sweaty forehead. "Your pa was with us a long time. It takes time to get up to what he was making."

Will watched the exchange, knowing Blaze had the upper hand from the beginning. He said, "Mayor, we don't have time to bargain."

Bolton shot an irritated look at Will, not intimidated by his size.

"Also," Blaze said, exaggerating his slow drawl, "what does the city council say?"

"Dang it, Blaze," Bolton replied, yanking the visor back in position, "I tell the council what to think. One hundred dollars with room and board provided at Molly's when you're in town."

"And when I'm out?"

Frustrated, the mayor said, "Yes, yes, we'll pay for your expenses. Now will you take the job?"

"A couple of things. I can still work my ranch when I need to. You can hire me, and you can fire me, but you cain't tell me what to do. Am I clear?"

Bolton gave a sigh of relief and thrust his hand out to Blaze. "Clear."

Blaze took the outstretched hand. "You got you a new sheriff, Mr. Mayor. All I need is the badge to go with it."

Will had picked up the badge from where Chadwick had dropped it on the desk. He handed it to Blaze.

The man took it, looked at it, and said, "Reckon I oughta be sworn in."

"Yes, of course," Bolton said, and strode to the front of the store with Blaze and everyone else following him. He pulled a Bible out from under the counter, spun around, and thrust it in front of Blaze. "Place your left hand on the Bible and raise your right hand."

Blaze did as he was told, and Bolton said, "Do you swear to do your best to uphold the law of McMullen County and perform the duties of acting sheriff of said county?"

"Yep, I sure do," Blaze said.

"Then, as mayor of Dog Town, and representing the county of McMullen, I hereby appoint you, until the next proper election, acting sheriff. That does it."

Blaze slipped the badge on the right side of his vest. "Pa always said this danged badge made a fine target for his enemies." He looked around the group. "So what's going on?"

Will, after sending Tandy with the mayor to buy supplies, primarily ammunition, showed Blaze the documents and briefed him on the situation. After listening to Will's account and examining the documents, the sheriff went into the saloon and questioned the now drunk Chadwick at length. By the time he had finished, supplies had been purchased, and the men were ready.

Mac walked in as they were about to leave. To Will he said,

"Money's gone, lad. There's less than fifty dollars in the bank account. He's cleaned us out."

Will clapped his friend on the shoulder. "Don't worry. With what I've got, there's plenty. Let's worry about important things, like catching Lockwood and Langston."

"I'm with you," Mac said, looking at the badge on Blaze's chest, a frown on his face. "It was a Pepper who threw us off our ranch."

"Pa was following the law," Blaze replied, "though he was suspicious. I've seen the proof of your ownership. It'll be a Pepper who puts you back on your ranch. I need to round up several good men, and we'll be on our way."

Bart eyed the new sheriff as he came out the front door of the general store. Pepper nodded at him and went on his way. As the others came out, Will and Tandy walked up to him. Tandy handed him a bag with powder, shot, and .44 Henry ammunition.

"You might need this," Will said. "As soon as the new sheriff rounds up his posse, we'll be on our way."

Bart took the ammunition from Tandy and turned a cold eye on Will. "Lockwood's a fox. We'll be lucky if we catch him, and he's the reason for all of this. If we'd left when I wanted, we might have caught him, but I'm tellin' you, he'll be long gone." He turned from Will and Tandy and marched toward the horses.

Tandy shook his head. "He's mad, Will, plenty mad. I ain't never seen him like this."

Will watched the back of his friend stride away from him. "You're right, Tandy. I just hope he can get over it. I'd hate for this to cause a rift between us."

Floyd and Callum joined them, overhearing what Will had just said, and they all watched their friend walk away. "Afraid it already has, Will. Like I already told you, that boy holds a grudge. No matter what happens today, he won't ever forget the day you chose us over him."

"But I didn't," Will said. "Thanks to the three of you, I chose right over wrong. We've got law in this county, and we at least need to try to use it. If it can't step up, then we provide the justice, but law first."

"Instead of arguing with a hardhead like you," Callum said, "I wish I'd gone down to Molly's and gotten something to eat. Now it's too late." He pointed toward the livery. Eight horsemen came riding, the sheriff in the lead.

The posse stopped in front of them. "You men going with us?"

"Wouldn't miss it," Will said.

The four of them walked quickly to their horses. Bart was in the saddle. They swung up and turned their horses to the sheriff, who was waiting with the others.

"What's the plan?" Will asked.

"The plan is—"

The sheriff was cut short by the sound of approaching horses coming at a run. Riders burst into view, whipping their animals as they raced toward town.

Bart, the first to recognize the leader, yelled, "It's Langston and his gang."

There was only time enough to draw rifles or flip thongs from their six-guns before the men were upon them. The approaching riders yanked their horses to a stop only feet from the posse.

"What's this?" Langston said. His burning eyes darted from Will to Callum to the posse, and finally to the badge on Blaze's chest.

The gang's horses, unsettled with the sudden stop and the marked tension in the air, milled, nervous with muscles quivering.

Blaze said, loud enough for everyone to hear, "Quint Langston, you and your gang are under arrest for the murder of Darcy Smith and the theft of the Double R ranch."

Langston, without a word, yanked his revolver from his holster and put a .44-caliber slug in Sheriff Pepper's leg. With his move, hands flashed to holstered weapons or whipped up long guns. Will had been watching Langston closely, and as soon as his hand moved for his weapon, he drew and fired. The bullet would have struck Langston in the heart, except for the milling horses. One of Langston's men, on a fine-looking but agitated pinto, tried to stop the animal in its lunge forward, moving the rider in direct line with Will's muzzle. He took the slug high, through his left side, and collapsed, falling from the saddle.

26

The street exploded. Over the mass of rearing, screaming horses, entangled with yelling men, falling on both sides, the roar of a shotgun could be heard amid the bark of handguns and rifles. Through it all, Langston managed to turn his horse and, riding over one of his fallen gang, dashed back the way he had come. Two of the gang were down, but most followed their leader out of town. One of the men, hit hard, barely managed to stay in the saddle. He gripped the horn with one hand, the reins with the other, his horse racing to get away from the frightening noise.

Bart, six-gun blazing, took off after them.

"Bart!" Will called, but either he hadn't heard or ignored Will.

The fight ended as fast as it began. Several of the posse were down, including the sheriff, but miraculously, all of the Double R crew were still in the saddle. Callum had blood on his arm, and Tandy's left hip was red, but everyone else seemed fine.

"You two alright?" Will called.

"Just winged me," Callum replied.

"Ain't my blood," said Tandy.

Will looked down at the sheriff.

"I'll make it," Blaze said. "Take whoever you can, and get after 'em."

Will spun Smoky around, called, "After Langston," and galloped out of town. He was followed by Callum, Floyd, Mac, and Tandy, plus two other men. Bart had already disappeared behind the trees, only dust remaining.

They raced down the street, made the first turn, and dropped down a slight slope behind a patch of mesquite. In the distance, at the point of a small plume of dust, rode Bart. Will urged Smoky forward. If Bart caught up with the gang before they arrived, he'd be shot to pieces.

Will could tell they were slowly gaining. He looked around him. He registered the two posse men who joined them. Evidently the gunfire had cooled a number of tempers, because there had been at least seven other men riding with the sheriff, and only two were down. Over Smoky's extended, pumping neck, Will shrugged. It took special men to ride into a gunfight knowing what was coming.

Bart looked back, saw them, and slowed his horse to a walk. Catching him, Will said, "How far ahead?"

"Not far. There's a river bottom another mile or two. I'm thinkin' they pulled up and plan on thinning our numbers."

"Let's bet on that." He held up his hand, bringing the men to a stop. Once halted, he said, "Men, we think Langston and his bunch stopped ahead in the dry riverbed. There's a good chance they're waiting to ambush us. I'll take two men and swing to the south. Maybe we can turn the tables."

"I'm goin'," Bart said.

"I'll ride along, to keep you two out of trouble, nephew," Floyd added.

"Good. Callum, why don't you take charge of this bunch and wait here. When you hear shooting, come a-running. By the way, did anyone see Lockwood with Langston?"

Several shook their heads. Floyd said, "He wasn't there. I was looking for him, but no luck. He either sent those boys into town, or he may have outfoxed them, too."

Will thought about it for a moment. "Could be, but we'll worry about him after we take care of this bunch." He swung Smoky around and turned south, paralleling the direction of the river, still out of sight. Floyd and Bart swung in with him.

They rode south for a couple of miles, until reaching an area where Bart was sure they could turn, unseen, toward the river. From here, the distance and the trees along the river would screen them from the dry-gulchers. They turned back west, keeping the horses at a walk to prevent dust from rising.

Across the flat prairie, the distant treeline beckoned. Their eyes traveled across the trees and brush, trying to spot anything out of place, a glint, a movement, anything. Nothing indicated a human presence. They kept advancing.

Approaching within gunshot, Will felt himself slipping back in time. He could almost swear he was back in the war, expecting the trees, at any moment, to erupt in withering smoke and fire. It sent a chill down his spine. *Will I ever move past the war?* He had known some men who went mad from only thinking about the battles. Forcing the panic-filled thoughts from his mind, he rode forward, eyes searching.

They entered the woods, separating to ride through the thick brambles along the river. At some places, deer and cattle trails were the only way they could continue to the edge of the river's high bank. Those same trails led them to sloping descents where the horses could scramble down into the river bottom. They dismounted and pulled their rifles from the scabbards. Callum led Smoky along the steep, slanting trail, stopping halfway to the bottom. He examined first up the river, to the north, and then its southern extremity and along the visible portion of the opposite bank. It was clear.

Bart and Tandy followed him into the rocky bottom. Each

shrinking at the clink of their horses' shoes over the rocks, many rubbed smooth from the inevitable flow of water, dry now and exposed. A deep hole of the life-sustaining liquid beckoned in the river bottom. Will motioned to it, and they led the horses to where, after their run, they drank greedily.

Before the animals were ready, the riders pulled them away, not wanting them to overdo it, and led them to the opposite bank. Once up the other side and into the trees, Will gave a quiet sigh of relief. Before mounting, he said softly, "Rather than trying to slip up on them in the trees, with all of these leaves and debris, let's move to the outer edge. I'm thinking they'll be concentrating on their back trail. We'll take it easy and see what happens."

The two men nodded, and they mounted, walked their horses to the outer edge of the trees, and turned north, up the river. They had ridden half the distance when Floyd held up his hand. Will and Bart guided their horses next to the older man and pulled them to a stop.

"Boys," Floyd said, "this here is my bailiwick. Why don't we pull up, and I'll go on ahead. I can make better time than these horses, see more, and be quieter. I'll be back shortly."

Will knew his uncle's ability. He looked at Bart and nodded. The three men dismounted again. Floyd slipped off his chaps and tossed them over his saddle. Next he pulled a heavy pair of Shoshone boot-high moccasins from his saddlebags and switched them with his boots. He unlimbered his Spencer, nodded, and took off at a ground-eating trot.

Bart shook his head. "Look at that old feller go. If I ever make it to that age, I sure hope I can move like he does."

Will nodded, thinking of the stories he had heard about his uncle running for hours. He watched him disappear around a tall oak. Within thirty minutes Floyd returned, stepped from the tree-line behind them, and whispered, "Hey."

Both Bart and Will jumped. Neither had heard a sound.

Floyd quickly switched boots, slid his Spencer back into the scabbard, and tied on his chaps. "They're up there. Looks to be seven or eight. Couple of 'em are wounded, one hard. They're all ganged up on the east bank, waitin' for the posse. I'd say we'd best get on up there. They're startin' to get a bit antsy."

The men mounted, and Floyd led the way. Twenty minutes later, he held up his hand and dismounted. Bart and Will joined him. Whispering, he pointed diagonally up the creek and said, "Right up there. Will, how do you want to handle it?"

Will leaned forward so both Floyd and Bart could hear his whisper. "We slip up to the bank behind them. We'll have the drop on 'em, so we'll give 'em the chance to surrender."

Bart shook his head. "Those men are killers. You saw what they did to Darcy. They've killed other men and thought nothing of it. They don't deserve a chance. I say we slip up behind them and kill as many as we can. That'll save the county time and money."

Will stared at his friend. He didn't recognize this side of him. This was killer talk. "No. We give them a chance." He leaned toward his friend so the black, dusty brim of his Stetson was almost touching the brown, bent brim of Bart's. "If you can't do that, then you stay with the horses. Floyd and I will take care of this."

Bart's face was white under his sun-baked skin. His jaw muscles worked continuously, and his hands played with the butt of his .36-caliber Navy Colt. He glared at Will, but finally said, "All right, I'll do it your way." Spinning around, he drew his additional Navy Colt resting in his saddle holster and slid it behind his belt.

When he turned away, Floyd, with raised eyebrows, shot Will a look.

Will said, still softly, "Uncle, you stay on my left, and Bart, you'll be to the right. Don't shoot unless they make the first move."

Will and Floyd, carrying their Spencers, moved out with Bart armed only with his short guns. They slipped slowly through the trees, voices carrying to them from the riverbed.

"I think we oughta pull out," someone said, answered by, "We're staying. They've got to come this way. If they haven't showed up by dark, then we'll go, but not before."

The three men crawled the last few feet to the edge of the elevated cutbank. Lying behind thick brush, Will cautiously eyed a stream of large red ants working diligently at the edge of the embankment. Tearing his eyes away from the tireless laborers, he studied the riverbed eight feet below them. There were three lookouts watching the east approach, where they expected the posse, while the others gathered around a fire, drinking coffee.

The man who had been hard hit lay to one side, the lower portion of his shirt covered with dark blood that had flowed down, soaking his trousers red. He lay on the rocks, moaning. One of the men drinking coffee said, "I wish he'd shut up. All that groaning's gettin' on my nerves."

Across the fire, another man bridled at the comment. "Slade, you'd be cryin' like a baby were you hard hit as he is. Now shut yore trap, or I'll shut it for you."

The man called Slade lifted angry eyes at his accuser. "If we weren't busy right now, I'd shut yours permanently."

Another man spoke up. "Langston'll take care of both of you if you blow this. He'll be on his way back anytime now, so's you'd best calm it down."

The first man's grumbling was barely audible to Will. "He oughta be back by now."

Will took that as his cue. Rising, he could see Floyd and Bart from the corners of his eyes, each about ten feet to his left and right and following his example. Standing on the bank, above the men. Will's clear voice rang across the river floor, freezing the men in position. "You boys unfasten those gun belts and lay your rifles down. The piper's arrived, and it's time you pay up."

Will took in the whole scene. It was like he was an observer watching the action from afar. He smelled the aroma of the coffee the men had brewed and were drinking, and could hear the clink from spurs striking rocks. He watched, waited. The faint taste of iron in his mouth reminiscent of past battles caused him to move his head to the side and spit.

Bart growled, "You heard the man, girls. Drop your weapons or die."

Something about Bart's voice, maybe the low tone, possibly the threat, or simply recognition, but one of the men yelled, "That's Bart Porter!"

These were all fighting men. Some had, at one time in their lives, been on the right side of the law, but for whatever reason, today they found themselves with the prospect of at least prison or, at the worst, the wrong end of a rope. At the yell, almost in unison, they went for their guns.

Will, holding his Spencer like a pistol, fired into one of the farthest men. He was one of the lookouts, and he was wearing a dark brown vest over a red shirt. In the left vest pocket, a bag of Killickinick Smoking Tobacco extended from the top. As he pulled the trigger, Will could see a portion of the blue government tax stamp and the word Hunting in red. The bullet plowed dead center through the vest pocket, blowing tobacco and shredded paper over the falling man.

In a three-beat motion, Will tossed the Spencer to his left hand and drew the Remington from his holster. Floyd and Bart had fired in unison with him. He settled the .44-caliber revolver on the nearest standing man, for now there were three on the riverbed. The man, his gun smoking, was pulling down on Floyd. Will fired, the explosion of his weapon lost in the cacophony of battle. This time the bullet struck the man in his right leg, turning him. He fell, dropping his weapon and grabbing his leg. Two other men threw their weapons to the rocks and stretched their arms high above their heads, as if trying to reach nonexistent clouds.

Will's and Floyd's guns were silent, firing had stopped, when Bart fired again. One of the men with his hands up had extended his arm at Will, and in it was a hideout gun. Fortunately for Will, Bart saw it in time. His bullet caught the man in the forehead, just above his left eye, turning him as he collapsed. The gun fell unfired. "Thanks, Bart, goo—" He turned to his friend to see him lying facedown on the ground, his right arm extended, holding the smoking Colt.

Rushing to him, Will knelt even as Bart struggled to get up. He gently pushed his friend onto his back and, over his shoulder, said to Floyd, "Keep an eye on them."

Floyd said, "My pleasure. How bad is he?"

Will opened Bart's vest to see blood spreading along his right side. "Not good."

Bart laid his head back, his hat brim becoming a pillow in the brush. "Pardner, I ain't feelin' too fine." His eyes rolled to the back of his head, and he passed out.

Will removed his razor-sharp Bowie and slit the shirt to the shoulder, opened it, and took a look at the wound. The entry hole, low on the right side, was bleeding, but it wasn't pumping in squirts, but was a slow steady flow, which was a good sign, at least no artery had been hit. He rolled Bart over enough to see his back. There was no exit wound, so the bullet was still inside. It would have to come out.

He heard his uncle slowly making his way over to him while the moaning of the wounded men in the riverbed grew louder. "How are you?"

"Why, nephew, I'm right as rain, but it looks like you ain't noticed, but you've got a little blood on your sleeve."

He hadn't noticed until Floyd mentioned it. Now he felt the sharp, burning pain in his right bicep.

Floyd, keeping an eye on the wounded and the one man still

standing, said, "You boys stand easy down there. We'll take care of you mighty quick." He looked down at Will. "I know you got some experience with that kind of thing, but I think I've probably fixed more bullet wounds than anyone around, includin' the doctors. You want me to have a look?"

Will picked up his Spencer and stood, keeping watch over the remainder of Langston's gang. "Help yourself. He'll be better off with you than me."

Floyd laid his Spencer carefully on the ground and knelt beside Bart. He began examining the wound.

Will heard the posse before he saw them. Callum and Tandy were at the head, immediately followed by Mac, and then the two men from the original posse. Callum pulled up and called, "Everybody all right?"

Will yelled back, "Bart's been hit. Doesn't look good. Tandy, can you get one of those men to help you, and come up here? We need to get Bart down to the water. He needs to get this bullet out."

One of the posse members jumped from his horse. "I'll help."

Tandy and the other man found a trail up the bank and were standing over Floyd and Bart in minutes.

"Floyd will tell you what he wants. I'll get the horses and bring them around by the road. Floyd, I've got your Spencer." His uncle, busy with Bart, only nodded. Will picked up the rifle and with both in hand headed back for the horses.

It only took him seconds to stow both rifles. He pulled an extra bandanna from his saddlebags and tied it around the wound on his arm. Finished with the bandanna, he untied the horses from the brush, mounted, and led them to the road and down into the creek. But as quick as he was, Bart was already stretched out on a blanket near the waterhole and fire. He took the animals to water. Tandy walked over.

"Will, I'll take care of these boys. Why don't you go check with Floyd. He wants to talk to you."

"Thanks," he said, handing him the reins. On his way to Floyd and Bart, he looked around the scene. There were two men unscathed in the fierce, but short, gunfight. Those men were tied and sitting against the opposite bank. The remaining man in the posse stood guard on them and three others who were wounded.

He gave them a cursory glance and continued to Floyd's side. From where he stood, he had a good look at Bart. His friend was looking pale and drawn. The site around the wound, once the blood had been wiped off, was red, already looking inflamed. He laid his hand on his uncle's shoulder. "He doesn't look good."

"No," Floyd said, "he doesn't. That bullet's got to come out, and there's no tellin' how much leather and cloth from his vest and shirt it took with it. That trash needs to be removed and the wound cleaned. We can get the bullet out, but if we leave the other in, he could still die."

"What do you suggest?"

"They've already got a fire going. I've got some instruments I picked up from a horse doctor suddenly had no need for them, years ago. Those boys"—he indicated Langston's gang—"have plenty of fire-water. I can use it to clean out this wound. If you'll dig those things out of my saddlebags and get me a bottle or two of their liquor, I'll get busy."

When Floyd first mentioned the instruments, Callum had headed to the saddlebags. He held up a package wrapped in soft deerskin.

Floyd saw him and said, "That's them."

Returning, he picked up two bottles near the fire and brought them with him, placing them on a flat rock next to Floyd.

"Much obliged," Floyd said. Opening the packet, he laid it next to him, on the rocks, exposing the unusual instruments. "Now, if this boy can stay passed out until I'm done, it'll be the better for him."

Mac had moved up next to Floyd. "Aye, I saw much of this in the wars. He'll be having no fun should he awaken."

On cue, Bart's eyes flew open. The first person he saw was Tandy leaning over Floyd's back, watching. He smiled up at him. "Hi ya, Tandy, boy, you got here fast." He looked at Mac and Callum. "Mac, it's good to see you. You too, Callum."

Floyd picked up one of the bottles. "Here, son, you'd better take a couple of long swigs of this. You're gonna need it. I've got to go diggin' in your side for that bullet. It ain't gonna be a picnic for you."

Realization struck him along with a wave of pain. He clinched his teeth and lay silent, his body rigid.

Floyd picked up the bottle and, when his eyes opened, gave it to him. "Best take some more of this. Don't worry about it running out, there's plenty. These fine fellers don't mind you drinkin' all of it."

Bart took the bottle and turned it up. After several swallows, he looked at Will. "Don't wait around here for me. You need to get after Langston. If he and Lockwood get away, it's all a waste."

Will eased up next to his friend. "You saved my life. I never saw the hideout gun. If it weren't for you, I could be stretched out next to you or dead."

Bart gritted his teeth with another wave of pain. When it passed, he said, "Then thank me by getting those two." He reached out and gripped Will's forearm. "Do it now, Will. Don't wait."

"I'm going with you," Callum said.

"Me too," Mac and Tandy said at the same time.

Will shook his head. "Sorry, Tandy. You'll be needed to get these folks back to town. In fact, I'd recommend you send someone back and bring a couple of wagons. It'll make it a lot easier."

Tandy shook his head. "I hate not going with you, Will. I oughta be there."

Will gripped the big man's shoulder. "You've been there many a time. Now you need to help Floyd and Bart, here. Will you do that for me?"

Tandy nodded. "Yep, but you three be careful."

Will nodded. He mounted Smoky. His brother and Mac mounted, and the three of them galloped toward the Double R.

27

G alloping toward the Double R, Will's mind churned with thoughts of Bart. The man had been so angry at him, yet still saved his life. Back in the sheriff's office, he had been angry at Callum, but the anger toward Callum was gone, replaced with the burning desire to catch Langston and Lockwood. He would see those two brought to justice, and soon. Hopefully, Bart would be on the mend when he returned.

Finally, it was time. Time to end Lockwood's reign and finish Langston once and for all. Only a few more miles lay between him and his quarry, and time. Time never ceasing, always ticking. Had they taken too long? Did the minutes spent in Dog Town provide the opportunity the crooks needed to disappear? He hoped not. He would have a hard time explaining their escape to Bart.

The horses were in a lather when they pulled up beneath the crest of the low hill near the entrance to the Double R. All three men reached into their saddlebags, removing their binoculars. As one, they dismounted and tied their horses to the scrubby grease-wood bushes. Stooping first and then crawling to the rim of the low ridge, they glassed the house, bunkhouse, and barn. One horse was tied in front of the house, and two in front of the bunkhouse.

Will came to a quick decision. "Callum, take Mac, and you two check the bunkhouse. It looks like Langston went straight for the house. Lockwood didn't strike me as the kind of welcoming person who would allow anyone else to live in the house but himself. I'm betting Lockwood is either dead or gone, and Langston is trying to find the stash, or whatever he imagines is there."

"I think you're right," Callum said. "Let's do it."

"Aye, lads, I agree."

The three men backed off the ridge, mounted, and rode around to where they would approach from the offside of the barn, allowing the large structure to block the sight of their approach from the house and bunkhouse. They rode through the back door of the barn and dismounted. Will took a couple of loops with the reins around the post at the end of a stall. Callum and Mac did the same. The three of them left the barn through the front door, with Callum and Mac turning left toward the bunkhouse, and Will heading straight across the yard to the main house.

Instead of entering through the front door of the house, he eased along the side of the tall porch until he reached the door at the corner that entered into the kitchen. The familiar smells of cooking he had enjoyed in this kitchen were gone. Skeeter's perpetual pot of coffee, always on the stove, was still there, but empty. The house seemed a ghost of memories. His hand dropped to the long kitchen table and swiped along the side. He could see the streaks his fingers left in the dust. Skeeter would never allow his kitchen to get into this shape. All because of one man. He heard shuffling from the office and the crash of something dropped and broken.

With his Remington in hand, he eased past the double doors connecting the kitchen and sitting room. On the other side of the sitting room, adjacent to the fireplace, the office door stood partially open. From inside the office came a curse and another crash, a drawer slamming to the floor. Will, wishing he had taken the time to slip on his moccasins, eased across the wooden floor in his hard leather-soled boots. Striving diligently to keep from stepping on a creaking joint, he slipped past the cowhide-covered couch that would seat five people, and was approaching the office door when it was yanked open. Langston stepped into the sitting room, head down, staring at papers he held in his hand. Sensing he wasn't alone, he raised his head. Will smiled at him. Not a friendly good-to-see-you, but a cold, scornful smile.

"We finally meet again, Quint. Where's your boss?"

The killer's eyes darted from left to right. "You alone?"

Will's smile, almost wolfish, grew wider. "I'm looking for your boss, Quint. The show is over for you and your gang. Several are lying dead in the riverbed. The others are on their way back to Dog Town to stand trial for the murder of Darcy Smith and whatever else they're wanted for. What are you wanted for, Quint?"

Will watched the gunman take a deep breath and relax. *He thinks I'm alone,* Will thought.

"You overplayed your hand, Logan. You may have taken out some of my men this time, but you won't live to enjoy that small success. You might as well hand that gun over, because if you don't, my boys are gonna fill you so full of lead, you'll sink like a rock."

"Where's Lockwood, Quint?"

The gunman's forehead creased with wrinkles, and his dark eyebrows pulled together. "Who?"

"Lockwood. Don't you know?"

Langston continued to frown. "Logan, I don't know no Lockwood. Don't play games with me."

Will's face broke into a wide grin. "So he conned you too."

Langston was getting mad. "Nobody's conned me. Now tell me what you mean."

"Where's Sir Davies?"

Langston's face turned from anger to bewilderment. "Danged if I know. He left yesterday morning to go to Dog Town. Said he was meeting with some investors from Corpus. That's the last I've seen of him. We was ridin' into town to see if he might be havin' a problem with the townsfolk, when we ran into the posse and that new sheriff, Pepper. Said we was under arrest for theft? We ain't stole nothing. Sir Davies has all the legal papers, all signed and righteous. Some of 'em even signed by a big Texas judge."

Will shook his head. He dropped the Remington back into the holster, reached inside his vest, and pulled out an envelope. Before tossing it to Langston, he said, "Can you read?"

Indignant, Langston said, "Humph, course I can read."

Will tossed the envelope over to the gunman. "Then read it and weep, Mr. Gunman. The great Quint Langston has now officially been conned. They'll be laughing from Galveston to El Paso."

Langston carefully opened the envelope, pulled one of the papers out, and started reading. His eyes snapped up to Will in disbelief, then back down to the document. He opened the second one. After reading it, he went back to the first. When he had finished, he started cursing. Long and loud vile curses spewed from his lips. He cursed Davies. He cursed Lockwood. He cursed New York City, and he even cursed himself for being so stupid. Stopping finally, he looked up at Will. "I can't believe it. I knew he was one of those dyed-in-the-wool knights from England, Sir Wilford Pemberton Davies the Third." He shook his head, still in shock. "I knew this time we was gonna be rich. He even showed us how. It was a cinch. He mapped it out to where we could understand what he was saying."

The killer was almost beyond himself. His forehead wrinkled in a deep frown, alternated with a twist of his head in bewilderment, then a hard grin of sardonic humor. Looking down at the papers again, he shook his head and said, softly, almost to himself, "He even took our money. Not just the money he was going to pay us, but whatever extra we had. He *allowed* us to invest in his upcoming cattle drive. It was gonna be the cattle drive of all time. It was gonna be a record breaker that would go down in history."

Suddenly, the calm of the late afternoon was shattered by a burst of gunshots, muted by the walls of the house and the bunkhouse.

Langston's arm shot down to the butt of his revolver, but silence returned abruptly before his hand touched the weapon. He stared at Will. "Reckon you ain't by yourself."

"Nope, I'm not." Will stood relaxed, his right arm hanging loose, near his Colt. "I'd say somebody won."

"Yeah, the question is who?"

The gunman's eyes darted toward the front door and back at Will. "I'm leavin' now."

Will held his smile. "No, Langston, you're going nowhere except maybe a pine box or jail. It's up to you."

The gunman's hand was inches from the butt of his revolver. Will's papers were strewn on the floor in front of him. A calmness settled over him, his hand relaxed, and he straightened. "Logan, I'm pretty sure my men won. Otherwise yours would already be in here. You're a gutsy feller. I'd bet you want to keep on breathing, so you just keep standing right there while I walk out of here. I promise you I won't draw on you. I just want to catch Lockwood and get my money back." A tiny tic at the corner of his left eye activated. It ticked only once.

"Last warning, Langston," Will said.

The gunman took a step toward the door, and his right hand flashed with the speed of a striking rattler. Will watched the gunman's fingers close around the revolver butt and start lifting. He could see Langston's thumb pulling the hammer back even as the weapon rose. The muzzle cleared the front of the gunman's holster and started its rotation upward.

But it never made it to the horizontal. For his brain had registered Langston's draw with the tic of the man's left eye. Langston was fast. Faster than almost everyone Will had seen before, but he wasn't fast enough.

Will knew both Callum and Josh had always been faster than him, but he had never been a slouch. Fast? He had never considered himself fast, but reckoned he could hold his own.

The first blast of his New Army Colt .44 caught Langston a little low, in the center of his belt buckle, deforming the lead ball, flattening one edge to knife sharpness. It cut through the shirt and sliced into the gunman's belly.

Will knew he had fired too quickly, but even as his weapon fired, his brain was sending signals to his hand as his eyes fed information for recalculating the next shot. It was almost like he was a spectator. He watched Langston's revolver pause in its upward arc, the killer's body taking the impact of his shot. The man's trunk bowed back only slightly, his face showing surprise, and he jerked the trigger. The bullet flew true to where it was pointed, ripping a chunk from the edge of Will's left boot. The recoil threw the man's handgun up and to the right, bringing it more in line with Will's body. Langston labored to work the hammer and stabilize the muzzle, but stability would not come, for Will's second shot struck, this time more on target. The lead ball, traveling at seven hundred feet per second, smashed through his shirt, the right side of his breastbone, and deep into his body.

Will, weapon ready for a third shot, watched Langston strain to bring his revolver to bear. Momentarily veins stood out on his forehead, even as the man's strength was leaving him. His legs gave way, and still clutching the Colt, he collapsed on his left side. Blood pumped from Langston's body, threatening to flow over the papers he had been holding. Will kicked the gun from his hand, bent over, his weapon still covering the fallen gunman, and quickly gathered the papers. Then he knelt by the dying man.

"This should be you," Langston said with a groan. "Nobody's ever beat me."

Will said, "Always someone faster. This time it was me. Next time, who knows? Now tell me, where was Lockwood headed?"

The man's face had turned as gray as dried cedar, and before his eyelids closed, his eyes rolled up and back.

Will holstered his weapon and with his right hand grabbed the gunman's shoulder and shook him hard. "Quint, stay with me. Lockwood duped you. You can't let him get away with it. Where did he go?"

The man heaved himself back to consciousness. His pale gray eyes searched the room before finding and focusing on Will. He gasped, "Don't know for sure . . . He talked about South America . . . A ship . . . Taking a ship . . . Galveston." His empty right hand suddenly grabbed Will's sleeve and pulled him closer. Will leaned over to hear the man's dying whisper. "Kill him. Promise me you'll kill him. Nobody can con Quint Lang . . ." His breath slowly left him in a long sigh. His hand lost its grip on Will's shirt and fell loosely to the floor.

Will looked at the crumpled gunman. He didn't look mean or dangerous now. *Did he have a mother whose heart he had broken? I wonder,* Will thought. He rose as Mac and Callum burst in through the front door. The two of them slid to a stop.

Callum said, "You all right?"

Will, still looking down at the dead man, nodded. He looked at the papers in his hand, surprised they were there, then checked and folded them before sliding the two documents into their envelope. He turned to his friend and brother. "Lockwood fooled them, too. He must be a lot better actor than those English critics gave him credit for. He even had them giving him *their* money to invest in his pie-in-the-sky cattle herd. Can you believe it? Langston and his gang worked for free and gave him their own money. Langston was convinced they'd be rich and famous for the huge cattle herd they drove to Kansas." Will stood shaking his head. Finally he looked up.

"Lockwood has to be stopped. He swindled half of Dog Town, and he's carrying their life savings with him. Langston said he's headed for Galveston. He also said Lockwood mentioned South America. He'll go to Galveston, and if he makes it in time, he'll be out of our reach. I've got to get there before he leaves." He paused, looked at the dead man, and then handed Mac the envelope with the documents proving he owned the Double R. "Mac, I hate to do this to you, but I've got to go. I'll stop in Dog Town and send some boys out to help. You were in Austin. You know these papers prove you own this ranch. Build it back like it was before." He looked at his brother. "Callum, I'm asking you to stay with Mac and help him until this place is back together. There's a lot of work that needs to be done around here, but I've got to catch Lockwood. Time's running out."

Callum stepped forward and slapped a hand on his brother's shoulder. "Don't worry about us. You do what you have to do. Now get out of here, brother. Take care of yourself, and don't get on any ships." The last he said with a little grin.

Mac nodded. "Aye, laddie, ships are not good for your health, and there's a lassie waiting for you. Take care of your wee self."

It was Will who grinned, now. "Boys, you won't catch me on a ship. Calm your minds." Raising his hand in salute, he headed for the door.

Stepping outside, he took a deep breath, smelling the hot, sweet Texas air. It was good to be alive. Then he saw Smoky standing, head low, waiting. His horse was thinner, tired. *I can't take him on this trip to Galveston*, Will thought. *It'll be way too hard. He needs a long rest and good food. I'll leave him in Dog Town. He's earned it.* Will took only a moment to pat the horse on the neck and give him a scratch behind his ear. Smoky's ear twitched. "It's been a hard run since Colorado, boy, but you'll have plenty of time to fatten up in Dog Town."

Swinging into the saddle, he turned his tired but willing companion toward the road, and they started for town.

WILL WAS WHIPPED. He had pushed hard since leaving. Smoky was now living the life with Bing Dingham at the stables in Dog Town. He missed his horse, but Will wanted him fat and sassy for the long trip north to Deborah. When he had time to think, which he'd had plenty of on this ride, his heart ached. Once back in Dog Town, they'd be on their way.

Looking back on his departure from Dog Town brought a grin to his grimy, unshaven face. For a while, it looked like he'd have to fight both Floyd and Tandy once he had told them he was going alone. Neither of them, especially Floyd, liked the thought of staying behind while he raced to Galveston. However, reason won. Both men, especially his uncle, knew one man traveled faster than three or even two. Floyd was the first to give in and then Tandy. Though they had eventually accepted Will's decision, neither had been happy about it.

What was even more interesting was that Tandy had a new job, but he had made it clear he was ready to quit to go with Will. Blaze had appointed him deputy sheriff. Will's grin grew wider. After hearing all the stories about Tandy, he felt sure some of the folks around the town looked askance at their new deputy.

He slowed Red, a chestnut he'd swapped for at the livery in Brazoria, to a walk. A couple of hours of sleep, caught in the straw of the livery in Victoria, about halfway to Galveston, was all he had had since before leaving Dog Town. Eyes grew heavy, and his mind drifted to a gurgling stream, darkness, moonlight, and a Latin beauty sitting by his side. *Angelita,* he thought, *how is your life?* The lovely face turned up to him, and he saw the tear, but she turned away quickly.

The crash of surf to his right jerked him awake. He yanked his head up and shook it violently, almost dislodging his hat. With his right hand, he slapped himself hard on both cheeks. "Stay awake! We're almost there." The chestnut plodded on. Again his head began to drift lower toward his chest, and his eyes, though he fought to keep them open, slowly closed.

Bart had looked bad. The doctor wasn't optimistic, and Molly was beside herself. She had insisted Bart and Blaze be brought to her boardinghouse and put in separate rooms. She and her girls, besides running the boardinghouse and serving meals, were taking care of the wounded men. Blaze, however, was recovering quickly. The bullet had not broken his leg, and, though it had been a deep, nasty wound, it was healing well. Molly, having great difficulty restricting the sheriff's movement, tried to comply with the doctor's orders to keep him immobile.

Will's head jerked up again, the crashing of the surf insistent in his foggy brain. He was near the end of his journey. He had crossed from San Luis Island to Galveston Island on Follett's Ferry, the weather holding calm and clear. The crossing had been easy, with only the early morning cloud cover and mild gulf breezes to contend with. His chase had been long, but he would soon know whether or not he had wasted all of this time, energy, and horseflesh in vain. Changing horses in Beeville, Goliad, Victoria, and Brazoria had worked out well. The two stretches from Beeville to Goliad and Victoria to Brazoria had been long, but because he was using two mounts and alternating, the animals made it, tired but uninjured.

He laughed to himself. They weren't near as tired as he was. Besides the two-hour stretch in Victoria, all the sleep he had managed was what he had snatched in the saddle. The rising sun brought warmth to his face, chasing away the chill he felt from the cool, damp southeast wind off the gulf.

To his left was West Bay. Between him and the bay, the island's salt grass swayed in the wind. Thousands of marsh birds, plying their early morning trade, whether fishing, as the blue heron did, or chasing insects, like the vocal red-winged blackbird, created a cacophony of sound. The brackish ponds teemed with wildlife. To his right, on the other side of the massive sand dunes, the waves rolled onto the sandy shore. Occasionally, a larger one, possibly traveling all the way from Cuba, crashed onto the coastline, pulling him out of his trancelike sleep.

But he was awake now. Another hour, and he would be riding into the active port city of Galveston. His making the turn south to San Luis Island and taking the ferry had saved an extra day of travel. *Did Lockwood take this same route,* Will thought, *or did he take the more traveled route, the safer route?* A gap in the tall sand dunes showed him the blue gulf, covered by scattered low clouds scurrying above the surface, reflecting the golden light of the early morning sun. In the distance a tall ship, white sails glistening, cut through the waves on a southerly heading. *Is it Lockwood's ship? Am I too late?*

28

Tired, but with adrenaline pumping, he was wide awake. He trotted Red past the first houses on the east end of Galveston. At eight in the morning, the city was awake. People hurried along the boardwalks.

Galveston brought back good memories of the livery owners Les and Nellie. In fact, that was where he had gotten Buck, one of his favorite horses, although Smoky had proven himself over the past few months.

He passed Wilson Mercantile, turning toward the Mason Brothers' Shipping office. In front of the office he pulled up. Slowly, he swung his right leg over the saddle and eased his weight onto it. He was stiff and thankful his long, hard ride was over. After tying his two animals to the hitching rail, he entered the office.

It was as if he had flashed back two years. The office looked exactly the same, Rockland Mace was behind the counter, sitting at his desk, bent over manifests and bills of lading. He didn't look like he had aged a day. Hearing the door, he looked up from his paperwork and, seeing Will, said, "Good morning, sir, is there something I can help you with?"

Will walked to the counter and removed his hat. "Good to see you, Rocky. How've you been?"

It took only a moment for recognition to flood the man's face. He broke into a wide smile, thrust his hand across the counter, and said, "Hank Remington, by golly, sir, it is good to see you."

Will grasped the man's hand. "It's good to see you, too, Rocky, only it is no longer Hank Remington. My memory returned. My name's William Logan. Folks call me Will."

Rocky's smile grew larger. "William Logan, a good name." He gave Will an inquiring look. "It appears you've traveled a ways. Might I be of assistance?"

"I'm hoping." He went into a brief explanation of his mission and a description of Lockwood.

Rocky nodded. "Yes, we have a passenger who fits your description. His name is Wilford Davies. He boarded the *Swift* yesterday morning. The destination is Cuba. I understand he plans to sail to South America." He looked up at Will when he said, "You might remember the *Swift*."

Ignoring Rocky's remark about his familiarity with the *Swift*, he asked, "When did it sail?"

Rocky shook his head. "Oh, it hasn't sailed yet. It was scheduled to sail on the afternoon tide, but a large portion of the freight had not yet arrived. Normally we won't hold a ship, but this was a very large load of cotton. It's supposed to be sailing as soon as it is loaded." He came out from behind the counter and moved across the room so he could look northeast out his front window that looked onto the Strand. The office was located where the wharves, ships, and bay were visible from the front window. Taking only a moment, he spun around, grabbing his coat from the rack at the end of the counter. "Come on," he shouted and headed for the door. "We may still be able to make it. Looks like he's just now starting to add sail."

The two men were almost run over by a heavily laden cotton wagon when they dashed across the street in front of it. The driver, yanking the horses to a halt, shook his fist and cursed them. Ignoring him, they continued their run. Closing the distance, Will recognized the vessel. It was the same one he, Mac, Darcy, and Wade had taken from Baltimore. It had been only four years ago, but seemed an age.

Rocky was fast, and tired as he was, Will had to work to keep up with him. They slid to a stop at the water's edge as the gangway was being stowed by several hefty longshoremen.

Will had been looking over the people at the railing of the ship as he ran. Since the *Swift* was a freighter, it had only a few berths for passengers. Will had a personal knowledge of the tight quarters available and felt sure everyone would be on deck. His eyes traveled across each passenger, most waving to loved ones or friends on the wharf. He spotted a man turn and hurry below. Lockwood. He had only seen him once before, through his binoculars, but he would never forget the man's chiseled face. He yelled at Rocky, "He's on board. We've got to stop the ship." The clipper had begun to move forward slowly on the slackening tide.

The master stood on the bridge, watching the commotion. Rocky yelled to him, "Stop! You need to stop."

Immediately, the master called orders, they were passed on, and the minimal sails the ship carried grew slack and began to flutter. But the tide and momentum of the ship continued to carry it forward, away from the wharf. The longshoremen watched as the ship, with sails down, lost headway. It had almost cleared its position at the wharf, with only the stern remaining abeam. A line shot out from the ship. It was picked up by a longshoreman, who was joined by the rest of his crew. Pulling, they drew the line and then the heavier hawser attached to the line and began pulling the ship back in place. The men wore no shirts, and their thick muscles stood out like ropes as they strained. Against the tide it was a battle though the force from the sails had stopped. Very slowly, they drew the laden clipper ship back toward its moorings.

Will held a bridle on his impatience. He knew these men were experienced at their work. He knew it was now impossible for Lockwood to escape. But apprehension still lurked in the back of his mind. Slowly the ship returned to its position. The captain, concerned about losing the tide, wasted no time expressing his displeasure to Rockland Mace for halting his ship.

The gangway finally slid back in place, and Rocky, followed by Will, raced on board. Will, knowing the master's authority, held his peace while Rocky explained. At appropriate points in the conversation, Will removed each document from the envelope and handed it to the man. Finally, the master turned to the first mate and said, "Bring me Mr. Davies."

"Aye, sir," replied the mate. He turned, relayed no orders, but personally strode to the cabin area. Moments later, he returned without the Davies impersonator. Unbelieving, Will stared as the man approached.

"He's nowhere to be found, sir. The cabin is empty except for his baggage."

"Master," Will said, "I think he figured out who I was and left the ship. If you wouldn't mind removing his baggage and making a thorough search of the ship, I'd be much obliged."

While he was talking, Will was busy scanning the shoreline as far as he could see. There were other ships tied to the wharf behind the *Swift*, so much of his vision was blocked alongside the wharf.

The master nodded and gave the orders. Will turned to Rocky. "I'm going to have a look down the wharf. He's either hiding on board the ship, or he took to the water. If you'll have his baggage taken to the office, I'll meet you there. He's got to be around here somewhere."

Will turned and in four long leaps was off the *Swift*. He ran west, along the line of docked ships. He had passed three when he saw a paunchy, white-haired man step from behind a load of freight and begin to run, weaving through and around the piles of stacked cargo. Seeing his quarry, Will increased his pace.

Quickly, Will caught the older man and gave him a shove, causing him to sprawl onto the rough timbers of the wharf. "Easy, man, easy," Lockwood yelled, the accent totally gone.

"Finally," Will said. He reached down, grabbed the man by the back of his expensive coat, and yanked him to his feet. Blood stained his knees and hands where they had scraped across the rough wharf. Will turned him around and felt shock stab through him. It wasn't Lockwood. "Who are you?"

The man, indignant from the rough handling, said, "I'm Jeremy Stills. Got a farm north of here. Just in town to drop off some cotton."

Bewildered, Will looked around, almost expecting Lockwood to spring into sight. Seeing nothing unusual, he said, "Why did you run?" He looked the man over. "And how did you get wet?"

"Well, sir, you ain't gonna believe this. Just a few minutes before you come into view, a feller climbed up out of the bay. He looked around, spotted me, and walked, all proud and tall, though he was streaming water, over to me. He had a funny accent, but he asked me if I'd put on his jacket, jump into the water, then run if a big man came running down the wharf looking as if he was searching for somebody. Said he'd give me two double eagles."

"Get on with it, fella," Will said, looking around, trying to spot Lockwood. "I don't have all day. Which way did he go?"

"Well, you gotta understand. My cotton ain't done too well this year. No rain, don't you know. Make's it mighty hard, what with tryin' to feed the wife and six kids whilst I take care of the farm. Naturally, I said sure I'd do it. Why, I'd darned near do anything to make forty bucks. That's a good month's wage."

"Naturally. Which way did he go?"

"Now that there is another funny thing. He said you was a friend of his, and he was just going to stand back behind us and watch. Get a good laugh, you know? I thought, don't you know, forty dollars is an awful lot of money for a laugh? Course I ain't said anything. I need that money. But when you knocked me to the ground like you did." The man stopped and gave Will a sorrowful look. "I knowed you for sure weren't no friend of his." The man looked at the blood on his hands and knees. "But this ain't bad. I been hurt worse than this pickin' cotton. You know how them blasted plants eat you near alive. But looky here." The man looked admiringly at the coat Lockwood had given him. "Shoot, I got a nice coat out of it, too. It's my lucky day."

He was on the other side of that stack of freight, Will thought. *I ran right by him, within an arm's length.* He turned, looking for anyone who might look suspicious. Whipping back around to the man, he said, "Did he say anything else to you?"

"No, sir. He ain't said nary a word."

Will watched the *Swift* pull away from the wharf. It moved slowly until the first sail was unfurled. Catching the breeze, the bow swung smoothly away from the wharf as it sailed east before turning around the east end of the island into the gulf. His mind raced through scenarios. *Did Lockwood manage to find a hiding place on the* Swift? *If he is on shore, where would he go? Would he try to get away and simply save himself? No. He could carry some of the money, but he couldn't carry all he had swindled. The man had worked too hard at his thieving. He'd try to get to whatever piece of baggage housed his dishonest gains. Where is the baggage?*

Will left the wet, bewildered farmer and raced back to Rocky, who was standing on the wharf, watching him. "Rocky, where's the baggage?"

Rocky pointed to the wagon making its way between the cargo stacks to the street.

"Come on," Will said, "we've got to get to it." Without further explanation, he dashed toward the wagon. Having passed the cargo stacks, it had picked up speed. Turning onto Strand, the back end skidded around the corner as the wagon headed west.

Behind one of the cargo stacks, Will almost ran into the driver of the wagon. He stood watching his wagon making its way down the street. As soon as Will came into sight, the man pointed to his wagon. "That feller pulled a gun on me. He was hiding behind here." He pointed to the stack he had come from.

Will was breathing hard. Normally, he ran easily, but he was near exhaustion, and his body was beginning to revolt. He jogged across the street, darting between carriages and wagons, and reached Red just as Rocky came running up.

He swung into the saddle and said to Rocky, "Get the law, and send them after me."

Rocky waved as Will maneuvered the tired chestnut into the traffic.

The wagon was out of sight, but Will watched for openings between oncoming traffic, and when the opportunity was presented, he passed several wagons. Nearing the outskirts of town, the congestion began to thin. Seeing the end of Strand, he turned left up to Main and made a right to continue west and out of town. In the distance, he could see a wagon racing along the road, throwing up a cloud of fine sand carried into the salt grass by the wind.

Will patted the red horse on the neck and said, "Just a little longer, Red. We're almost done." While the distance widened to the wagon ahead, Will kept Red at a steady lope. It wouldn't be long before the single horse, pulling the wagon at such an extreme pace, would be exhausted.

He followed for a couple of miles. The wagon had never gotten so far away it was out of sight. Now Will was closing on it. He could see Lockwood leaning over, whipping the tired animal. Every few moments, he would turn and stare back at Will, then face forward and whip the horse again. When Will had closed to within a couple of hundred yards, Lockwood suddenly stopped the wagon, stood up, looked first at the salt grass and brackish pond water lining the bay side of the road, and then at the sand dunes between the road and the gulf. Finally making up his mind, he leaped from the wagon seat to the ground. He fell, lifted himself erect, and clambered up and over the sand dune, disappearing from sight.

Will continued to the wagon. The dapple gray gelding stood head down, blood from the bloody stripes on its back combining with the thick lather dripping from his heaving body and making small pink puddles on the ground. "Sorry, fella," Will said to the gray. He swung from Red's back and grabbed his canteen, pouring water into his Stetson as he walked to the horse. He filled the Stetson only a third full and held it while the big animal first smelled, then thrust his nose deep into the hat. The water disappeared quickly. Will patted him on the cheek. "No more for now. Folks'll be along to take care of you, and don't you worry, I'll be taking care of the fella who whipped you."

The big horse turned his head to watch him as he walked back to Red and climbed aboard. He wasn't worried about Lockwood getting away, but he was anxious to close this chapter of his life. He had a lovely wife, a long way off, to get back to, but now, there was a score to settle.

Lockwood was the cause of Darcy's death. He was the reason Bart was lying in a room, maybe dying. He had taken something Mac and Darcy and Wade had built and almost destroyed it. It was time for justice. He leaned over and yanked the whip from its stand in the wagon. Guiding Red toward the dune, he turned him, found a cut through the dunes, and rode to the beach side. The surf rolled in rhythmic waves pushing up the wide beach before rushing back to the sea as if in a hurry to leave the land. He looked east, nothing. Turning his head to the west, he could see Lockwood struggling in the sand. The soft sand along the dunes pulled at his feet, causing him to sink with each step. Will watched and, at a walk, steered his horse toward the fugitive.

Overtaking the thief, he felt his anger continue to boil. Will had known the bite of a whip, and he hated the thought of any man whipping either man or animal. Lockwood had slipped lower, if that was possible, in Will's estimation.

When within reach of the whip, he flicked the tip at the man's rear. Lockwood jerked forward and screamed, "Don't hurt me. Please don't hurt me."

Thanks to his quick movement, he fell in the sand again. Quickly turning over, one hand rubbing where the whip had bitten him, the other extended palm forward and up at Will, he said, "Please, Mr. Logan, don't hurt me anymore. If you want, I'll give your friends their money back, but don't hurt me."

Will felt his stomach turn and his anger dissolve into disgust. This actor might have played a part as a strong leader, but he was neither a leader nor strong. All Will wanted to do was turn this poor excuse for a human being over to the law.

Lockwood, still out of breath, labored to his feet and looked Will over. He continued to rub the whip burn, but now, after getting a good look at his pursuer, he appeared to Will to believe there was a good chance he wouldn't be whipped or shot. A conniving glint filled his eyes. He leaned forward and said, "Mr. Logan, if you'll let me go, I'll split the money with you. There's more than enough for two."

Will felt dirty just being around Lockwood. He listened for horses, hoping the law would get here pronto to take him into custody. He was tired of this sleazy little man. Home called to him, with Deborah.

A horsefly buzzed around his head and tried to light in the stubble of his cheek. With a swat of his hand, he knocked it away, but in the process his eyes were shifted from his captive. Will had been holding the whip in his right hand. The last thing he expected was for Lockwood, the conman, to draw on him. When he looked back, he was staring down the barrel of a .36-caliber Colt Model 1862 Police with a three-and-a-half-inch barrel. In that instant, the man had changed from the sniveling coward who was begging for his life to a haughty killer.

29

"My, my, how the worm has turned," Lockwood said. His mouth spread in an emotionless grin, showing perfect teeth, while blue eyes glared with hate. "I shall enjoy great pleasure in blowing you out of that monstrosity you Texans call a saddle, and I'll do it with this little pistol. Oh"— Lockwood glanced down at the Colt with mock concern—"and please don't worry, *Mr.* Logan, this was not my pistol, so it did not get wet when I took my little swim. This pistol belonged to the driver of the wagon. He was quite kind enough to leave it for me in a holster next to the seat. Wasn't that nice? He was so afraid my tiny, soaked derringer was going to kill him. Why, he didn't even try to draw this handy little revolver."

How stupid can I get? Will thought. He watched Lockwood enjoying his moment, and a thrill of hope flashed through him. The hammer had not yet been pulled back. A smile lit his face. He had a chance, not a big one, but a chance. "You're really going to kill me, Lockwood?"

"You are a most brazen man, Mr. Logan. You sit there smiling while I hold the gun. You western men do puzzle me. But enough talking. Yes, I am going to kill you, and it suits me to do it right now."

Will's smile widened. "In that case, Lockwood, you might want to pull the hammer back first."

The actor's eyes grew large. He turned the revolver sideways and stared at it. At the same time, Will threw the whip at the Englishman's face and flung himself off the opposite side of Red. Lockwood jerked up his arm to deflect the whip, cocked the Colt, and fired where Will had been. Hitting the ground rolling, Will yanked his Remington from the holster, waited just a second for his roll to clear Red, and shot the actor in the chest.

Lockwood dropped his gun, grabbing the wound with both hands. Tears ran down his cheeks, his lips moving, opening and closing before he said, "You've killed me."

"I reckon so," replied Will, watching the life flow from the evil man. Staring down, he wondered, *Why would this man rob Davies and assume his identity? Would anyone ever know how Lockwood chose the Double R, or what prompted his decisions in New York, bringing him so far west to the Texas frontier? There are so many unanswered questions.* Will shook his head as the sound of racing horses intruded on his thoughts.

Before he looked up, a raindrop struck Lockwood in the middle of his forehead, followed by another. Will removed his hat and looked into the gray sky. Clouds had rolled in, and as far as he could see in every direction, the sky was covered with clouds. Clouds that were releasing rain. He let the cooling drops run through his hair and over his face, put his hat back on, and turned to meet the posse.

The sheriff and Rocky, both with guns drawn, were in the lead. They pulled up as Will was holstering his revolver. "You alright?" Rocky asked.

"Fine. Lockwood's a little under the weather."

The sheriff looked at the sky, got down from his horse, and bent over the dead man. By now the rain was steady. He straightened, held out a cupped hand, caught a few drops, and wiped them over his face. Smiling, he said, "Mighty welcome stuff. I'm Sheriff Jackson, and I'll be needing your statement."

"Glad to give it, Sheriff. First, I need to check a couple of things." He bent, pulled the man's shirt up, and unfastened a belt beneath the shirt. With one hard yank, he pulled it out from under the dead man's body and opened one of the pouches— folding money. Will nodded and handed the belt to the sheriff. "I'm bettin' you'll find more of this and probably gold and silver in his bags. He stole it from the man whose name he took, a Wilford Pemberton Davies, the Double R ranch, and the folks of Dog Town."

The sheriff shook his head. "Looks like a lot of money here. How'd he steal it from the ranch and those Dog Town people?"

Will stretched his long arms and took a deep breath of the salt air. The rain had picked up. It wasn't heavy, but steady. "Sheriff Jackson, as much as I'm glad to see this rain, I'd just as soon explain everything in your nice dry office?"

"Good idea," the sheriff said. He turned to the posse. "You boys load the body in the wagon and follow us in. Keep an eye on them bags, and bring 'em to me as soon as you get to town."

WILL PULLED up at the watering trough in front of Bing's Livery in Dog Town. He let the horses drink, then rode them into the stable. It felt good to be out of the rain. The return trip had taken almost two weeks. It had been two weeks of continuous rain. Getting across the rivers had been a big problem. Many of the ferries weren't running because of the swollen rivers, and it didn't take a genius to figure out those rivers were going to get a lot worse before they got better, since the rain hadn't stopped. Eventually, he had managed to persuade, threaten, or cajole the ferry operators to take him across. But he was here, at last. He swung down from his horse and loosened the cinch. Bing came out of his office, which was really his tack room with space for a small desk and chair. "Well, I'll be doggies if it ain't Will. Boy, you look like the biggest drowned rat I've ever seen. Welcome back. How do you like our rain? It's been doin' this for nigh on to two weeks, and I don't see any sign of it lettin' up."

Will took off his slicker, shook it, tossed it on a hook, and knocked his hat against a stall to get most of the water off. His first words to Bing were, "How's Bart doing?"

"Mighty fine, but he's got Molly beside herself. He's turned into a worse patient than Blaze."

"I've got to stop by the bank," Will said, "but then I'll go see for myself." He was untying his saddlebags when Bing walked up. Pulling the tie loose, he said, "That imposter persuade you to invest any of your money?"

Bing shook his head. "No, sir, not a thin dime. I recognized Davies, or Lockwood, whatever you want to call him, as a charlatan when we first met. No, sir, he got no money from me."

Will nodded. "Anybody who did might want to talk to the mayor." He patted his saddlebags. "I've got every bit of their money right here, and after the bank, I'm headed to the store to pass it over to the mayor. Reckon he, or anyone he designates, will be handing it out."

Bing halted what he was doing and stared at Will. "You foolin' me? You got all their money back?"

"I got it all. Seems Lockwood was saving every nickel he stole so he could live the high life in South America. He even had the money he stole from the real Davies. Lockwood had big plans."

Wiping down the other horse, Bing shook his head. "Now ain't that something. Who would've thought you could get all that money back."

"We got lucky," Will said. He looked outside the open barn door. The rain continued to fall. He shook his head and looked at the slicker he had just pulled off, reached for it, and slipped it back on. He pulled the saddlebags and Spencer from his saddle. "Thanks for the horses, Bing. I'll settle up with you when I leave."

With each step he took across the water-swept street, he sank. When he'd left almost a month ago, dust had covered everything. The continuous rain had collected all of the dust and converted it to mud, clinging, boot-sucking mud. For, as each step drove at least ankle deep into the quagmire, it took balance and strength to break the clinging suction for the next step. Add to the mud a five-foot-wide river coursing past the front of the bank. Once a man's boot sank into the mud, it meant the almost calf-high water neared the top of his boot. Any precarious step or wobbling loss of balance trying to extract a foot from the mud would be rewarded with a waterfall over the top of the boot.

Will plodded on through the mud, head down, allowing his wide-brimmed Stetson to protect his face from the steady rain, and with each measured step, worked his way across the street to the bank. He paused at the edge of the rushing water, sighed, pulled his hat tighter, and began to cross.

He had almost made it when he heard a woman's scream. She had been hurrying through the mud, with her baby, when, in his judgment, one of her feet must've gone deeper into the mud. In her effort to extract her foot, she lost her balance, and in falling, her small daughter's wet hand slipped from hers.

Will looked up to see a tiny little girl tumbling in the surging current. One moment her head was above the muddy water, the next, beneath it. In his left hand, he held his rifle. The right gripped the saddlebags. Leading up to the door of the bank were two wooden steps that opened onto a small porch, over which was a cedar awning. The saddlebags weighed close to forty pounds, and the porch was at least ten feet away and built at least three feet off the ground. With no time to think, he swung the saddlebags behind him and then on the forward swing, thrust them up and ahead with every ounce of power he could summon.

The instant he released the bags, he grabbed for the little girl. She had been wrapped in a small blanket, and his big hand closed over the outside edge of the blanket as she passed, but she started rolling, unwrapping the blanket like a string unwrapping from a top, and continued by him. His only chance was his left hand. The hand holding his Spencer.

He dropped the Spencer and lunged for the little girl. His hand found her hair, and she screamed when the force of the water pulled it tight. That was all he needed. Instantly his right hand wrapped around an arm, and easing the tension on her hair, he lifted her enough to get his right arm around her body. The force of the water carried the blanket down the small but turbulent river.

While he held and comforted her, he watched the blanket follow the little river. The street turned, but the running water continued straight, through a pasture and into the Frio River. When the blanket hit the river, it disappeared under a broken limb speeding down the roiling brown river.

"My baby, my baby," the woman called from the other side of the temporary yet deadly current.

"Hold on, ma'am."

Will, with the little girl solidly held in the crook of his right arm, knelt, felt the rush of water over his boot top, and grasped his Spencer in the mud. He lifted it, barely hearing the sucking sound when the mud released it, and slowly made his way across the current.

Reaching the other side, the little girl's arms shot out for her ma. Will held her out, and the woman snatched her from his grasp. "Oh, thank you, thank you. Did you see her blanket go into the river?"

"Yes, ma'am, I did."

"It was awful. I shouldn't have brought her out. It's all my fault. If you hadn't been there. Oh ..."

"Ma'am," Will said, "I'm just glad I was here, but you need to get her home and dried off."

"Yes, I do, don't I. Oh, I don't know how I can thank you."

Will was conscious of the pouring rain and his rifle covered in mud. *At least it'll get cleaned off,* he thought. "Ma'am, take care of your daughter, and be careful going back."

"Yes, thank you, I will." She turned and, holding her daughter to her tightly, started away.

Will watched her make her way back up the street, finally disappearing around a corner. He looked at the porch to see his saddlebags lying on the planks. *Thank goodness,* he thought, *I'd hate to think after all the work spent recovering it, the money washed down the Frio.* Glancing to the left of the entrance, at the bank window, he saw faces staring out. He made his way up the two steps, stood his Spencer where it would continue to get rained on, picked up the saddlebags and went inside.

THE RAIN QUIT the evening he arrived in Dog Town, but he had to stay another four days. All of the creeks between the town and the Double R were out of their banks, and it would be impossible for him to get to the ranch. Even after they receded, a couple of them had made it hard crossing, but Smoky was up to the job.

Will sat silently looking the ranch over, with his binoculars, from his vantage point on the hillside. The Double R was busy. Several cowhands were working around the corral and barn. He watched as Callum and Floyd walked out onto the porch from inside the house. They looked up toward the hillside. He saw his uncle say something, and they both waved. He waved back, put away the binoculars, and started down the hill.

Mac and Tandy had joined them by the time Will reached the hitching rail in front of the house. Floyd was the first to speak. "It's about time you got back, boy. You've been gone long enough to chase that feller all the way to New York City. Get down off that horse and say hello to your old uncle."

Will grinned and swung down. "I feel like I've ridden all the way to New York and back. What's going on around here? I see you've got some new hands."

"Aye," Mac said, "not all new. Word got around pretty quick. Most of the old crew are back with us, and we've hired a couple of new ones for a while until we get the place back in shape and rebrand what we need to. Come on in and tell us what happened. You hungry?"

"Mac," Will said, "I'm so hungry, I could eat the south end of a northbound Rocky Mountain Canary."

"Good, then it's a surprise you'll be having."

They walked into the house, and Will glanced at the floor where Langston had died. It had been scrubbed, but the blood-stain was permanent, a reminder of harder days. They walked into the kitchen, and Will was shocked to see a big pan of dough-nuts on the table, and standing on the other side was Skeeter O'Riley, their old cook.

"How'd they find you, Skeeter?" Will asked.

Skeeter was a man of few words, but a genius in the kitchen. "Didn't. Came back and went to work."

"He ain't kidding," Tandy said. "We got up one morning, and he was in here cookin' breakfast. He's been here ever since."

"Aye, lads, and he'll be here as long as I'm having a say."

They sat around the table, and everyone grabbed a doughnut. "They call that bear sign in the mountains," Floyd said. "Mighty tasty." He turned to Will. "So don't hold out on us, boy. What happened?"

"You first," Will said. "What about Armando and Ana?"

Callum spoke up. "They're back at home. We've got some men over there rebuilding. I think they're mighty happy about their new place."

"You didn't tell 'em everything, Callum," Tandy said.

Callum grinned. "I guess I didn't. Looks like Armando and Ana made good use of their time in Mexico. They've got another Ruiz on the way."

All the men laughed, and Will said, "That is mighty good. I'm glad to hear it." He turned to Tandy. "Bart was telling me you decided to hang up your badge. I figured you'd found a home."

Tandy grinned. "I didn't much care for the job. I had to throw some of my friends in jail, and it wasn't no fun. Besides, I had a better offer."

Will's eyebrows rose. "Oh really? Sounded like Blaze had them paying you pretty well."

"You heard him, laddie. He had a better offer. Now this is dependent on it being all right with you, since you're still a partner, but I offered both Tandy and Bart a piece of the ranch. Darcy had no living relatives, and Wade's folks, well, you're already a-knowing their feelings toward that fine boy, and Will, I suspect you'll be leaving. They've been good friends, and I just figured . . . Floyd said he thought it was a dandy of an idea. What is it now, you're thinking about the matter?"

Will could see Tandy watching him closely. "Is that what you want, Tandy?"

"Will, I can't even imagine being so lucky. I'll work hard to make this a go. You'll be proud of me."

Will looked across the table at the huge young man. He had changed so much from the disrespectful, even mean youth he had met so many years ago. He had turned into exactly what Molly had said, "a good man." "Tandy, I'm already proud of you. With Mac to guide you, I think the three of you, Mac, you, and Bart, can make this ranch something to be proud of. I'm all for it."

Tandy looked down at the table and said softly, "Thanks, Will."

Floyd slammed his hand down on the table. The crash made the pan of doughnuts jump, along with everyone else in the kitchen. "Enough! It's your turn. Tell us what happened with Lockwood."

Callum leaned back in his chair, another doughnut in his hand, and said, "Start talking, brother. We're dying of curiosity."

"Well, it was like this . . ."

They talked late into the evening. Will found out what he suspected was really happening with Bart and Molly. They were getting serious, and both girls were happy about it.

Finally, Will yawned and said, "I'm going out on the porch."

He stood, stretched, and strode to the front porch. Standing there, he gazed across the moonlit prairie. Coyotes barked at the moon while something snuffled at the east edge of the porch. A light breeze drifted across the clear sky.

Deborah, Will thought, *are you looking at this same moon right now? I miss you, and I promise you I'm coming home.*

He heard steps come up behind him. Steps he recognized as Callum and Floyd. Callum moved to his left and Floyd to his right. The three men stood together so alike and so different, yet each comfortable enough with the others to stand silently and enjoy the night and sounds.

After a while, Floyd spoke. "I'm thinkin' you've made up your mind, boy. Is tomorrow the day?"

Will smiled at the thought of Deborah waiting for him at the end of the long ride home. "Yes, Uncle, I reckon it's time."

AUTHOR'S NOTE

I hope you've enjoyed reading *Troubled Season,* the fifth book in the Logan Family Series.

Here's a piece of historical information you might find interesting. You may have thought Dog Town was a product of my imagination. It was not. There was a Texas town with that name. Located on the Frio River a little over an hour from San Antonio, Dog Town is now Tilden, in McMullen County. Originally settled around 1858, it was first given the name of Rio Frio. Supposedly, it received the name of Dog Town due to a bunch of drunken cowboys, who decided to decrease the dog population in Rio Frio. Later, the name changed to Colfax, and then to Tilden, in honor of Samuel J. Tilden, who came in second in the 1876 presidential election.

If you have any comments, what you like or what you don't, please let me know. You can email me at: Don@DonaldLRobertson.com, or you can fill in the contact form on my website.

www.DonaldLRobertson.com

I'm looking forward to hearing from you.

BOOKS
Logan Mountain Man Series
(Prequel to Logan Family Series)

SOUL OF A MOUNTAIN MAN
TRIALS OF A MOUNTAIN MAN
METTLE OF A MOUNTAIN MAN

Logan Family Series

LOGAN'S WORD
THE SAVAGE VALLEY
CALLUM'S MISSION
FORGOTTEN SEASON
TROUBLED SEASON

Clay Barlow - Texas Ranger Justice Series

FORTY-FOUR CALIBER JUSTICE
LAW AND JUSTICE
LONESOME JUSTICE

NOVELLAS AND SHORT STORIES

RUSTLERS IN THE SAGE
BECAUSE OF A DOG
THE OLD RANGER

Made in United States
North Haven, CT
14 June 2022